FULL CIRCLE

The Next Generation
Volume V

A Novel by

Kathleen Rigdon Highley

ISBN 978-1-956001-23-5 (paperback)
ISBN 978-1-956001-24-2 (eBook)

Printed in the United States of America

*With love and respect for ALL the children
who have been a part of my life:
I have learned and loved and lived a full life through each one of you!
May you be the generation that will reach the world for
Jesus Christ, guide your own children toward our heavenly
Father, and walk as a light in this dark world.*

Contents

CHAPTER ONE

*And hope does not put us to shame, because God's love has
been poured out into our hearts through the Holy Spirit,
who has been given to us* (Romans 5:5 NIV).

Annie Jo Parker slammed out the back door, squinting against the sun, struggling to catch a full breath. Frustration scooted through her veins like hot butter on corn. So many emotions crowded her mind. It had been years since she'd enjoyed a comfortable relationship with Austin Anderson. As children, they'd been inseparable, growing up on neighboring ranches. They'd spent hours and hours in each other's barns—whether to welcome in a new litter of pups or to gaze in wonder as a new colt wrestled its way into the world. The best of friends.

Shaking off the memories, she skipped down the back steps, needing to get far away from Austin's dad. It didn't matter what he said or what excuse he made for his son. Austin had crossed a line he couldn't uncross.

And she hadn't told a soul.

No wonder her parents were confused about her attitude. Not to mention her brothers. But she would deal with all of that later.

Jake Anderson had been blaming his son's despicable behavior on the loss of Mrs. Anderson for over a year.

But Annie wasn't buying that. She knew Austin, all too well. Had learned stuff about him the hard way. Stuff his father didn't know. A rush of unwelcome advances washed over her, making her shudder, despite the warm rays that kissed her face.

Why couldn't Austin accept the fact that her father's ranch was off limits? He'd been acting like a stubborn jerk. Like he could force her to change her mind and take whatever he dished out. But no matter how much he bullied her, Austin Anderson would *never own* her.

Nothing between them could be the same again. Not ever. They'd been close growing up. Just kids, being kids. They played chase, raced horses, learned their trade in the rodeo arena. As pals.

Then Austin started winning big and got greedy, pushy—demanding and angry.

Annie blew the bangs off her forehead and stuffed a wad of hair beneath the navy-blue scarf her mother had knitted with loving hands, forever mindful of its value. Settling her cowgirl hat low on her forehead she strode toward the barn, calming as her nostrils filled with the unique scent of horseflesh, hay, and the moldy leaves of autumn. The scent of home. The scent of the world as she'd known it, since birth. A scent that could calm her in an instant. Drawing in a deep breath, she began to absorb the change, as her nerves settled.

Annie Jo Parker had reached national champion status as a barrel racer. But she didn't feel much like a celebrity today—more like a rose left too long without water.

All because of a boy who refused to let her be and leave their ancient relationship in the past. *Relationship* might be too strong a word. Annie didn't care for Austin beyond friendship. Never had. She had tried, but he didn't affect her that way. She loved him as a friend. And she'd spent years trying to convince him of the fact. But somehow, he'd gotten it into his head that they should get married, join their families' ranches, combine their winnings, and get wealthy in the process. He'd become obsessed.

The bruises she had suffered at his hand and his onslaught of cruel words that she couldn't get out of her head were all that remained of that unhealthy affiliation. Stepping back into the fray was out of the question.

Annie frowned and pushed aside the disturbing images. Zipping her jacket, she picked up speed, thankful her father hadn't built the barn a mile away from the house. The familiar crunch of gravel under her boots helped ground her. She could use a long ride to shake the entire Anderson family from her head.

Annie hurried into the barn, a sanctuary in and of itself. Her spirit soothed further as she made her way to each bay, speaking softly to the first five horses—each exchange helping her focus on her blessings. She had grown up seeking solace among these beauties. A cocoon of safety when life went awry.

But as she reached Glory's stall, goosebumps formed on her flesh. The spooky kind. Something was wrong. Her treasured companion didn't stand tall in greeting; but lay still in the hay, wheezing, her eyes closed. What was going on? She'd been fine the last time they'd raced the practice barrels a few weeks ago. She was old—almost as old as her owner's twenty-seven years—but she hadn't been sick or frail. Her father would have said something.

She yanked open the stall door and fell to her knees. Tears streamed down her face and soaked the neck of the first horse she'd raced barrels with at age eight. Cinnamon, with a blonde mane and tail, she'd been amazing in the arena. Glory, the only name that fit. Annie stroked her damp hide and pleaded, "Don't leave me, girl. I'm not ready to let you go."

She settled close by and fumbled to get her phone out. Finally, with some effort, she managed to make the call. "Doc Andrews? It's Annie Jo. Glory is in distress." Struck with the reality of the words and what they meant, her composure failed. She sputtered, choked, tried again. "Can you get out here, like right away?" She concentrated. *Focus.* "She isn't breathing well, won't stand up or even open her eyes." Her hand trembled as she reached out to touch the heaving side of her friend.

"On my way," said Doc. "I'm just up the road a bit."

"Thank you."

Annie collapsed against the wall behind her—waiting, weeping, praying, for close to half an hour. She couldn't bring herself to think about burying her best friend, yet the probability slammed into her heart with a force that sent a shock through her whole body.

"Annie?"

"Back here, Doc." Praise God, he made it. Hopefully in time to save Glory.

Annie forced herself to stand and wipe the tears off her face. She met the vet outside Glory's stall. "I'll give you a minute with her while I call Dad." She could only hope her fingers would work, that she could see through watery eyes.

"Thank you," said Doc Andrews, with a light touch to her shoulder. "Sam was walking Jake out to his truck when I got here. I told him you'd called, so he should be here any minute."

A few seconds later, her parents came running into the barn. Rivers raced down her cheeks as she made eye contact with her father. The strongest and bravest man she had ever known. He'd been her rock, her mentor…her *daddy*.

His eyes got big, and he picked up his pace. "What's going on?"

She managed to squeak out, "Where are Josh and Mack?" They would want to be here.

"I called them right after I talked to Doc," he said.

"Thank you."

Swallowing the bile that worked its way up into her throat, she answered his question. The only answer she could give, at the moment. "I don't know," she said with a shrug. Chewing on her lower lip, she ran her hands up and down her arms, as if she were cold. She wasn't. She was terrified. "Doc is looking at her now."

Annie stutter-stepped forward and fell into her father's arms. He held her and let her cry, just like she knew he would. They shared an unspoken language, a knowing that sometimes baffled her brothers. They claimed it stemmed from her being the baby and the only girl. Maybe, but she didn't care. She closed her eyes and leaned into him.

How blessed she'd been to have a strong father, a close-knit family. She hugged her dad tightly for a few more seconds, then stepped out of his embrace, determined to face the truth. Deal with it. Just like she'd been raised to do.

Another five minutes passed before Josh and Mack joined them. At least the family would be together to say goodbye. Because Annie had a feeling that's exactly what they would be called upon to do. Today.

The stall door looked far away but Annie needed to get to it. Get back to Glory. With slow, heavy steps she shuffled through the hay strewn at her feet then braced herself as she stared down at her friend. Doc Andrews caught her eye, and with a slight shake of his head solidified her greatest fear. The sorrow in his eyes made her stomach heave. Glory's once-labored breathing had turned shallow, barely discernable. The flutter of eyelids had stilled.

The day dragged on, until late that afternoon Glory breathed her last. Annie, her parents, and her brothers stood by in silence, hands clasped, like a human paper chain, as Doc Andrews stood, brushed the hay from his jeans, and joined them.

"I did everything I knew to do. She was ready to go, so we have no choice but to let her. I'm so sorry for your loss, Miss Annie. I know how much Glory meant to you."

"Yes, sir. Thank you for coming." Stunned, the words sounded robotic, as a flood of tears washed her face. She didn't know if she would ever stop crying.

"Glory and I go back to her birth," Doc continued. "I'm glad I could be here…for the end."

His trembling voice soothed her some. He really did care about the animals God placed in his care. Her family had relied on his expertise for as long as she could remember. He had been there when they'd lost more than one calf, and for many difficult births along the way. He had camped out half the night with them when Glory was born.

Never once had he let them down. And not today. Annie knew in her heart that if Doc Andrews could have saved Glory, she would be standing next to the rail right now, nudging Annie's shoulder and encouraging her to get the saddle so they could get going.

Dad spoke. "We appreciate you coming on such short notice."

"Your family has always been special to me, Sam. Is there anything else I can do?"

"No, we'll take it from here, Doc."

Silence filled the barn for a long, stretched-out minute after Doc Andrews left.

"I'm sure gonna miss her," said Annie, staring down at her beloved companion with whom she had shared every secret through the years. Their relationship had been more fulfilling than screaming through the pages of a diary and more healing than traditional therapy could ever be.

"We will all miss her, sweetie," said Mom, as she rested a hand on Annie's forearm.

Another stretch of quiet reverence passed, before Dad continued, "Okay, boys, we have a big chore ahead of us."

His words jarred Annie back to reality. He was right. But she recognized when he was trying to protect her.

"I'm helping," she said, her voice firm and sure. She pulled away from her mother, straightened her shoulders and dried her eyes with the sleeve of her flannel shirt. "And don't try to talk me out of it. I need to do this. You know I do." Annie paused for a silent prayer for strength and mercy, before finishing her thought. "I need to help load her into the wagon and be there when she is lowered into the ground. It will make me face the reality that I've lost her."

In three long strides she reached her father's side. Dropping her head back, she looked into his eyes, trying to make him understand. If she didn't do something, she would go crazy. "Please," she pleaded. "Let me help."

His arms went around her, and she absorbed his powerful presence. She stayed there, cradled in his warmth, until the tears dried, and determination temporarily replaced desperation.

The time had come to put to rest a family member they could never replace.

***

Glory had passed away on Saturday. Blessedly, Annie Jo hadn't heard from Austin since then; and his father had stayed on his own turf. For two whole days. And she wanted it to stay that way. She hadn't expected Austin to throw a fit when she told him that the mare, he'd had his eye on in the spring, was no longer for sale.

She would never do business with him again. She would never let him close enough to touch her, to belittle her, or slap her. Never, ever again.

Annie didn't want to give Austin even one excuse to set foot on Parker land. So far, she had managed to convince her dad that she needed some space between her and Austin, without a blow-by-blow description to showcase the decline of their friendship.

It had taken practiced skill to keep her father's suspicions at bay.

She probably should have told her father that Austin had turned into a bully. That wrestling the reins on the backs of bulls had inflated his ego so much, he thought he'd become entitled—that she owed him her loyalty, her love, her very life. Not gonna happen.

A fresh surge of anger threatened to overtake her—but she pushed it back down.

Telling Dad the truth would stir up trouble and cause a rift between him and his lifelong best friend, who still staggered in the grip of grief.

She just couldn't bring herself to do it.

She didn't want to hurt her father; but disappointing the man who had demeaned, humiliated, and hurt her didn't cause the slightest ripple in her clear conscience.

She had been praying that Jake and Austin would stay calm, distant even. She had no desire to see either one of them, to hear their names, the sound of their voices, or any report regarding them. She wanted to be left alone.

She shoved both men out of her head, tugged on her favorite "go-to-town" boots, and slipped into the burgundy western top she'd worn at the final performance of the final rodeo, the season before. She thought the memory of that huge win would further help lift her spirits. White piping and pearl snap enclosures made perfect accents to its rich color. She felt… well, pretty, for lack of a better word. And she hadn't felt pretty in a really long time.

She shrugged on her latest purchase—a butter soft leather jacket, in black. It was early September, but the temperatures had been unseasonably cold, of late, for which she was grateful. A cool autumn, even a nippy one, beat the sweltering effects of an Indian summer.

She turned her focus to the errand she needed to run in town. A simple return of merchandise that had been delivered broken. She'd been disappointed, because the gift was for her parents' wedding anniversary, now a mere week away.

The aggravation of having to replace what she had considered the perfect gift temporarily overshadowed her frustration with Jake and Austin.

She'd been putting off making the trip; but decided it would serve as a perfect distraction today.

Anyone or anything else vying for her attention would just have to wait.

CHAPTER TWO

May the God of hope fill you with all joy and peace as you trust in him, so that you may overflow with hope by the power of the Holy Spirit (Romans 15:13 NIV).

James Baldwin left the office early and found himself downtown, frowning and kicking rocks out of his path, the only comfort for his soul, the pounding of his boots against the sidewalk. He had pulled into a parking lot on 82nd Street to look up the address on GPS, yet again. He had only been back in town for two weeks, had never driven in Lubbock, before today, and kept losing his way. Frustrated couldn't begin to describe his angst.

It shouldn't be this difficult. But his mind kept drifting, getting him off-course with each new troubled thought. His heart still sped up when he thought about the pressure he'd been under to move back. He still didn't understand why he had caved. Coming to terms with the fact that his family had convinced him to leave Nashville and return to Lubbock, Texas, where he'd been born, wasn't going to be easy.

Pushing aside the nightmare that had driven his family out of this city after his father passed away all those years ago, himself a young boy of ten, he forced himself to focus. Man up. Deal with his current reality.

He was here now and needed to find a way to be content. He glanced around, making himself appreciate the fact that the Lubbock City Planner had the presence of mind to place trees in strategic places along the boulevard to break up the monotony of concrete. A row of live oaks and silver leaf maples stood majestic along the outer border of the shopping center, closest to the wide street. It was early in the season, but the leaves had already begun to change, as if they knew something the rest of them didn't. He appreciated the boldness that painted a colorful picture against a cloudless sky. But it seemed nothing could block the wind in this flat country. He picked up speed then ducked into a corner, frustrated with his current state, his brothers, with God himself, if he would admit it. How had it come to this? He had protected his heart, lo these many years, and still his family would not let him live in peace. He didn't need a girlfriend, a soul mate. A wife, of all things. He didn't need anyone, really. A self-made man, or so he told himself on a regular basis, for the past two decades.

His cell phone buzzed in his pocket. He fished it out, and as though he had conjured up one of them, in his mind, he read his brother's name on the screen. *Matt. Great. What did he want?*

"Hey, bro," said James, keeping his voice light, but wary, nonetheless. "What's up?" James listened for about three seconds before the tiresome aggravation surfaced. "I don't care what her name is, Matt. I just had this conversation with Paul. Not happening. No way. Rule number one when I agreed to move back to Texas: no blind dates. I can't believe you're even suggesting it."

James didn't even try being diplomatic. His brother would forgive him, eventually. How many times did they have to have this same discussion? It was beginning to wear on him.

Raised voices from inside a small novelty shop to his right pulled James up short. He mechanically said goodbye to his brother, ended the call, and moved closer to the building. The altercation tugged at his inclination to dissect things, take them apart, and figure out how to put them together again. To right wrongs and protect others. It's what his techno security company was all about.

He felt compelled to find out if the woman needed help. Which did not mean he needed a woman, no matter what his brothers thought. So many senseless blind dates. He was done with all that. Done.

James entered the front door, aware of the tiny tinkling of a bell above his head.

"I understand what I'm saying, Mr. Wong," said the woman. "Do you?"

When Mr. Wong didn't answer, the lady swung A long strand of wavy, dark auburn hair over one shoulder and said, "No, I don't think you do." She let out a sigh of frustration, which compelled James forward.

"May I be of assistance?" he said.

The lady with the captivating hair turned to face him. He stopped dead still, and gazed into the largest, greenest eyes he had ever seen. His mouth went dry in an instant and his brain pressed pause. No words came to mind. Suddenly he knew the meaning of dumbstruck. A foreign experience for the accomplished, stalwart, independent man he had forced himself to become.

"Do you hold a management role in this establishment?" Her voice hurt as much as her eyes. Velvet, but firm, and just as intoxicating. As was her hair. Her build. Her cowboy boots. Intoxicating.

"No, ma'am, but I speak a little Chinese?" He managed to get the words out and set aside the mesmerizing beauty before him. Somehow. He formed the statement as a question, to see if it might make a difference. If she needed his help to communicate with the confused young man behind the counter, he'd be happy to accommodate her. Otherwise, he wanted to run out the door and forget he'd ever encountered those eyes. Eyes that could trap a man into a forever relationship. *God help me, if you're listening. If you're paying attention to my life in the least bit.* Good grief, he sounded ridiculous. He knew God loved him. But James had stepped away for a season and was just finding his way back. He could do this, no problem.

"Well, it couldn't hurt. I'm certainly not getting anywhere."

"What seems to be the problem?" said James, stepping closer to her. Big mistake. She smelled like vanilla bean ice cream; he'd swear it. Would she punch him if he slipped his arm around her waist and inhaled? Of course, she would. What was wrong with him? Women didn't usually have this effect on him. He was cautious and guarded. Usually.

He tried hard to listen, to focus, to concentrate. She wasn't making it easy. Did she know the hypnotizing effect she had on men? Did she care? Was she even aware of her great beauty?

"So, what do you think?" she said.

Uh-oh, he was in trouble. He hadn't listened to a word she'd said. How could he get around this one? And what was wrong with his muddled brain? He had met many glamorous women in his day who had wormed their way into his brothers' good graces to get a date with him. Women who wanted to snag him for his money then trick him into wedded bliss. But he'd rejected or avoided them all. At the tender age of ten he had decided not to go down that path. The news of his father's death had crippled him, and he'd determined he would not be the reason a widow and her children had to live in grief, to struggle without a provider.

But no woman had ever made shivers run down his spine, tied his tongue into a knot, or stalled his mind. Not until today.

What to do?

A lightbulb went off and James turned toward the store clerk. He rattled off a paragraph in Chinese and listened to the guy's response, with no interruption in the connection of synapses, no hiccup in concentration, and not a drop of sweat on his brow. Good, he hadn't completely lost touch with himself. He still had full control of his faculties—if he kept his eyes straight ahead and his thinking on topic.

He chuckled at something the clerk said then froze when the lovely lady's hand rested on his forearm. The zing that raced up to his elbow seemed to paralyze him. But only for a moment. He managed to turn his gaze toward her then gulped. What was happening to him? Had the Lord, who created and governed the universe, sent him in here to meet this lady? The draw seemed that powerful, like he'd had no choice in the matter. Why? James had made himself perfectly clear when it came to women. God should know that by now.

He shook off the thoughts and swallowed hard. The princess smiled at him, which only made things worse.

"Are you chuckling at my expense?" she said, a hint of humor amongst the frustration. She raised one exquisite brow and waited. Oh, right, she was waiting on him.

"No, ma'am," he said, pulling himself together. "Mr. Wong was just telling a joke."

"Not a good time," she said, her arms crossed in front of her and one finger tapping out her displeasure on the opposite arm. Her upper body was encased in a shimmering, deep burgundy, western style top, with pearl snaps down the front and up wide cuffs at her delicate wrists. "I have a long list of chores to get done while I'm in town today," she continued. "And I'd like to get on with it. You know, check this one off and move on?"

Her voice broke into his thoughts and, by yet another miracle, he managed to engage her in conversation. "Yes, ma'am," he said, swallowing a lump that had worked its way up into his throat. "I apologize." He could appreciate a list maker; he was a list maker himself. He had acquired the information she desired but feared that if he shared it with her, she would leave, and he would never see her again. *Never see her again? No, I must see her again.*

So what if she leaves? She is nothing to you and you are nothing to her.

But I could be, he argued with himself.

Another shake of his head and James smiled at the stranger, suddenly full of curiosity. What was her name? Where did she live? Was she married, engaged, going steady? A woman of such magnificence would have to be, right? *Not necessarily.*

"Ahem," she said, a bit of irritation seeping into her tone.

"Oh, sorry. Yes, the manager will be happy to replace the item that arrived broken. Just pick anything in the store of equal value."

"Well, that wasn't so difficult, now, was it? Maybe you should suggest they hire an interpreter, full-time."

"Yes, ma'am, I'll tell him." *If you'll tell me all about yourself and let me follow you around for the rest of the day.*

"Well, if you'll excuse me," said the enchantress, in that smooth-as-silk voice that captured his entire being. He could listen to her talk all day. Every day. "I'd best get started. I'm meeting my roommate for coffee at ten and it's already past nine."

A sliver of hope filled James's dark thoughts. A roommate meant she wasn't married. A glance at her left hand revealed no engagement ring, so maybe no fiancé either. A steady beau, on the other hand, was quite feasible. Did he dare ask?

She stepped away toward a hutch filled with exquisite China. He stood very still and stared as she walked past him. Watched her tight-fitting jeans carry slender legs gracefully across the floor. Watched her thick wavy hair swing gently from side to side as it scraped her waistline.

The temperature in the room shot up. James took a determined step toward the door. *Keep it together, Baldwin. She's way out of your league. You're not even in the market, remember?*

He turned away from the vision of loveliness and said farewell to the clerk in Chinese. Even more than the high-level meetings he had attended for JB Enterprises, this moment in time made him grateful for the hours and hours he had spent learning the foreign language that had brought him good fortune in this quaint little shop.

He took another step toward the door. But he stalled there, the pull of the intoxicating woman more than he could resist. What could it hurt to ask her name? No one ever died from asking a siren her name. No, wait, they did. Right?

Regardless, and with no thought for his own life, James changed direction, moved across the room and stood next to her, his gaze intent on the glassware in front of him, as though he'd never seen such a splendid display of art. A full minute dragged out before he heard her giggle at his side. A grin snaked across his face. Giggling was a good sign. Wasn't it?

"Something funny?" James moved his eyes to look at her, but not his head. This could be fun.

The woman turned to face him—even stepped one boot length closer to him. One side of her lip curved up. She didn't move or say another word. James let the moment stretch out. He discretely inhaled the scent of her, again. Hopefully, she wouldn't notice.

"It's vanilla essential oil. Would you like me to get you a bottle for Christmas?"

Sheesh. She had noticed.

James shrugged. "Sorry, I've never smelled it before. It's rather intoxicating."

"Oh really? No one has ever mentioned that to me."

"Someone doesn't know what he's missing."

She laughed then. A delicate laugh that challenged the tinkling bell above the shop door. Made James want to soak her up like a sponge. To know every detail of her life. To take her shopping or horseback riding or maybe to Paris. Would a cowgirl feel at home in Paris? In a matter of minutes, she had changed his life forever. And he didn't even know her name.

"Are you always this smooth, this witty?"

It was his turn to laugh. "Never been accused of either one, ma'am."

She looked surprised, like she didn't quite believe him. If she only knew how truthful he'd been, she might turn and bolt. He couldn't be sure, of course, since he'd never asked. Had any woman ever discerned anything about his personality, his quirks, the things that made him laugh, the things that mattered? No, he felt certain. No one had ever looked deeper than his bank account. Wow.

She must not know who he was, he reasoned. Perhaps she didn't subscribe to *Techno Today*. Or read the society column in the *Avalanche Journal*. How refreshing to meet a woman who seemed not to assume that he could be the answer to all her financial woes and provide a measure of security for her far into the future. A woman unfamiliar with his dashing debonair self.

The air between them grew thick with a degree of expectation James had yet to experience. He really wanted to get to know this person. This magician who held his heart in the palm of her hand.

"Might I ask your name, ma'am?" he said, angling himself to face her. He held his breath, his hands firmly at his side. Would she be willing to give him a chance to get to know her? A chance to discover the secret that had broken down his walls, within minutes. Walls he had spent years designing, erecting, perfecting, reinforcing. Walls that now trembled with the threat of collapse.

She smiled again and his knees about buckled.

"I guess it couldn't hurt. You did come to my rescue, after all."

"Yes, ma'am." He grinned at her, and she returned his smile. The most dazzling, intoxicating smile he had ever encountered. He hadn't realized women of this caliber even existed. *My word.*

"My name is Annie Jo Parker," she cooed, her hand extended toward him. "Thanks for saving me."

"Ha. Very funny."

"And your name, sir?"

"James Baldwin, at your service."

His hand met hers and she gripped his hand with a surprising amount of strength. She was petite, appeared delicate, but had a handshake that rivaled most of the men he'd met in board-room settings. A woman this put-together, confident and charming just might hold his interest long enough for it to matter. His ears filled with that glorious laugh, and he wanted to run away with her to some enchanted, deserted island. "Nice to meet you, James Baldwin."

"The pleasure is all mine."

He prolonged the grasp of her hand until she began to pull away. "Sorry," he said. "I'm just so blown away by you. I've literally never met anyone who could make me trip over my own tongue."

She glanced at the grandfather clock in the corner and gasped. "Oh dear. I'm already late. Guess I'd better get. Thanks again. Maybe I'll see you around."

Annie Jo Parker didn't pick out a dish to replace the broken one or linger near the hutch to continue their conversation. Just shrugged at him, offered one more adorable grin then raced toward the front door.

James followed her with his eyes, unable to make himself chase her down. If she'd wanted to see him again, she would have said something. If she wanted him to have her number, she would have offered it. His heart ached with the thought.

Hey, Baldwin, did you give her your number or ask to see her again? No, I didn't think so.

"Oh."

James straightened to his full height of five foot ten inches, plus what little the heel on his cowboy boots provided. His height usually made him self-conscious. The shortest Baldwin brother, and all that. But oddly enough he didn't feel that way today. Annie Jo Parker was a tiny thing, the top of her head barely reaching his chin, including the heel of her red Lucchese Juliette boots. He had made her laugh and feel rescued.

"I'll just have to find her again," he mumbled, as he slowly made his way out the door, the tinkling bell bidding him farewell.

He'd set out on a mission that morning, and now he couldn't for the life of him remember what it was.

CHAPTER THREE

Be joyful in hope, patient in affliction, faithful
in prayer (Romans 12:12 NIV).

Annie held herself together until she stepped out on the sidewalk. Her insides squirmed like a bed of worms. A giggle bubbled up into her throat. She tamped it down, practically holding her breath, then raced to her pickup truck. She climbed behind the wheel then relaxed and let joy burst out of her. She'd been mesmerized by a man. A man who made her laugh. A man with chocolate brown eyes and a confidence that spoke to her soul. A gentleman.

She pressed her back against the seat and closed her eyes. Yes, she was going to be late, but Bethany would wait patiently. Her roommate knew Annie Jo better than anyone and wouldn't be surprised by her tardiness.

Regardless, Annie needed a little time to absorb the past fifteen minutes. A picture of Austin rushed to her mind, but she dismissed him without a second thought. He acted like he owned her. He cheated on her but did not want to set her free. Too bad. She had cut him loose over a year ago, before his mother had shown any signs of deterioration. Before he could play on her sympathies and manipulate her.

Then the sight of Austin with the nation's second-best barrel racer slammed through her head. A roll in the hay. Literally.

The boy she had shared her childhood with had grown up to be a complete jerk. A punk who had begun a drunken, possessive attitude in high school that had only gotten worse. Sad, considering their long-time family connections.

Again, she shoved the brute out of her head. She had no patience for him or his antics. Suddenly, a handsome, intelligent, witty man had replaced Austin's frowning countenance. A well-dressed man who sported a western cut sport coat, just-right jeans and a pair of boots that impressed her. A man who spoke Chinese and just happened to be passing by the gift shop at the precise moment she needed a translator. A message dropped from heaven? She had to wonder.

The handsome stranger had her name. Would he try to find her? Or was he simply playing her with his wit and charm and language skills?

She would wait and see. She absolutely would. Maybe even pray about it. God cared about the little things of her life, she believed that. But this didn't feel like a little thing. Something big was happening here. A tremor shook her hand as she reached for the shifter. She would meet Bethany as planned. Go about her day as planned, and struggle to keep her mind on task. So, she'd met a hunk with rich brown eyes and a deep voice. She didn't need to act like a crazy person. If she wasn't careful, she'd lose her head and race back in there—and make a fool of herself.

Annie shook the thoughts out of her head and pulled into traffic and headed toward Quaker Avenue. One quick stop at United then she would head for Starbucks. With any luck she'd be there by half past ten.

Annie told her pickup to call Bethany.

"Hey, girl, where are you?"

"Sorry. I'm running a few minutes behind." She had met James Baldwin fifteen minutes ago and still sounded breathless. She could hear it in her own voice.

"Something exciting?"

"What makes you say that?" She tried to steady her voice. It wasn't working.

"Annie, how long have I known you?"

"You're right."

A laugh burst its way to the surface. She would not be able to keep a secret from Bethany. She never could. They had been best friends since kindergarten, for Pete's sake. What could come of her meeting with James Baldwin, anyway?

"I hope it's a man," said Bethany, with an uncharacteristic giggle. Bethany had been described as demure by more than one person. Only at special moments did she laugh with abandon and act like the junior-high version of herself.

"Bethany," said Annie, caution in her voice. "I'm hanging up now. I'll see you in a few."

Annie disconnected the call with Bethany laughing in the background. Bethany, her best friend. Bethany, tall and thin and supportive. They shared a house—now that construction on Annie Jo's ranch house had been completed. A compromise with Annie's father. *Of course, I want you to have your own place, Sugar, but I'm not comfortable with you living alone. It's a ranch, Annie Jo. Anything could happen. Although the rest of us will be available, we're not close enough in event of an emergency. Humor me, won't you?* She could hear her father's voice in her head. He wasn't about to back down.

So, she had given in to her father's request and asked Bethany to live with her. And things had worked out, well enough.

Quaker Avenue took Annie across town to 19th Street, and she arrived at Starbucks precisely at ten-thirty. A big smile spread across her face when she spotted Bethany seated outside, across from an extra tall, black-haired man Annie thought she recognized as Samuel Gerard. She had seen Bethany's pictures of the man. *Good for you, girl.*

So much for girl time. But it didn't matter. Annie needed to chew on the latest development in her life before she revealed her interest in James Baldwin. To anyone. Even Bethany.

Interest in James Baldwin? What was she thinking? She had only just met the man and had no idea if she would ever see him again. Oh, but she wanted to. Somehow. Maybe she would Google him and see if anything interesting showed up. Something good and wonderful that would substantiate her delicious suspicions about the man. She wanted to know everything about him. What did he do with his time? Where did he live? Not a cowboy, obviously, his boots were too clean. His sport coat had definitely been tailor made. His hair was perfect, a little longer in the back, hanging in delicious curls over his collar. And those eyes. Yeah, she wanted to know all there was to know about the intriguing James Baldwin.

***

Back at his office, James gawked at the picture that came up on the computer screen. He thought he'd seen the enchanting side of Annie Jo (AJ) Parker in the shop on 82^(nd). But the articles he'd been reading made even that unforgettable memory pale.

AJ Parker, National Champion Barrel Racer, Wins Again. The headline topped page one of her personal website. Annie Jo Parker had not been difficult to find online. James had ordered lunch delivered in and spent the full hour watching videos of AJ Parker in all her glory. The question of whether she might be interested in horseback riding had been answered. Big time. She must have been riding her entire life. The group of pictures on her website depicted the humor and fire he had witnessed at the store; but they also showed determination and dedication.

"How do I find her?" he asked himself. "Think."

He scrolled through more articles regarding her career then slammed on the brakes when he read the name of her father's ranch in the middle of one of the interviews. Parker ranch, Idalou, Texas. Simple enough.

James pressed the intercom button. "Terri, please get me a number for the Parker ranch. Thank you." He didn't wait for her response, just released the call button and went back to Annie Jo's website. Fifteen minutes passed before Terri buzzed him. "I have that number you asked for, Mr. Baldwin."

The final conference call of the day ended at six that evening, the day after James Baldwin had met Annie Jo Parker. Much to his surprise, the impact of meeting the intoxicating woman had not dimmed in the slightest, as the hours wore on. Maybe if he hadn't absorbed so many videos, branded his mind with numerous photos, been captivated by every word he read about her career.

Maybe if she hadn't smiled at him or had refused to give him her name. Maybe if he'd never heard her voice or seen those intoxicating green eyes. Maybe then he could have pushed their meeting aside and gone on with his life.

But he had absorbed miles of footage, read article after article, and gazed into those hypnotic green eyes—in person. He had heard her voice and encountered that intoxicating smile. Felt the thrill of her hand in his

Taking in a deep breath he reached for his phone. It only took a few seconds to dial the number Terri had provided.

It rang twice before someone picked up.

"Hello," said a woman, who was *not* Annie Jo. Of that much he was certain.

Suddenly self-conscious, James ran a hand through his hair and said, "Hello." It came out squeaky, like a kid in junior high school whose voice had begun to change. So, he cleared his throat and started again. Ignoring the sweat that gathered in his palms and the fear that raced up his spine, he said, managing to control the tremor that threatened to destroy his confidence. "My name is James Baldwin. I met Annie Jo yesterday but failed to get her number." He swallowed the phlegm that crawled up his throat and continued, "Anyway, I was hoping you might be able to help me get in touch with her."

"One moment, please," said the woman.

James checked the second hand on the antique clock above the fireplace in his office. Sixty full seconds ticked by, before he heard another voice on the line.

"Hello. This is Annie. How may I help you?"

James closed his eyes. It was Annie, alright. The sound of her voice brought to mind the vanilla scent that had floated toward him yesterday. The scent that still made his nose hairs quiver with delight.

"Annie, this is James Baldwin," he managed to say. "I hope I haven't called at a bad time."

"I'm helping Mama with supper. Would you like to join us?"

Whoa. Meet her family the day after he met the girl? Wasn't that a little quick?

"Uh," he said, with an awkwardness he had never experienced. Not ever, in all the meetings he had attended and all the business risks he had taken. And never with a girl. He had managed not to put himself in awkward positions with girls. *What am I doing? What is wrong with me? Have I lost my mind?*

Just when he had convinced himself to make some excuse and hang up, Annie laughed. A melodious sound that made him forget his own name.

"I'm kidding, James," she said. "Really. Don't be scared. Although you will need to meet everyone at some point, don't you think?"

"Uh," he said again. It seemed to be the only sound he could utter. His ego was taking a beating here.

"Wow, you really are scared, aren't you? I'm sorry. I had no idea you would be so sensitive. Really, I apologize. So, would you like to tell me why you called my parents' house?"

Sweat trickled down the center of his back. Annie Jo Parker was quick on her feet, and he sounded like an idiot. A total idiot with no education or training. No couth.

"Maybe you remember. We met yesterday in a little shop on 82nd," he began again, determined to redeem himself for sabotaging himself and messing up this conversation with the only woman he'd ever met who could tie his tongue in knots and give him brain freeze.

He then said 'hello' again, in Chinese, followed by a chuckle. It seemed to be the only logical way to get this conversation headed in the right direction.

Boy, did she remember. Her whole body relaxed. Not Austin, by any stretch of the imagination.

"Of course, how are you?" There, that sounded normal. Right? She would gladly give this adorable man, who seemed suddenly shy, a fresh start. She shouldn't have teased him. If only she had considered that he might be nervous. He had, however, seemed totally put together, just the day before.

"I wanted to follow you around like a puppy," he admitted, bringing her mind back to the present moment. "And I've never been so happy that I could speak Chinese."

There, he sounded more like the man who had captured her heart in a matter of minutes.

They'd met by accident. A tender look through chocolate brown eyes had made her feel special, in an unassuming way. The timbre of his voice had wrapped itself around her and warmed her to the core.

James Baldwin. He stood six inches above her in height and wore a brand-new Stetson and thousand-dollar boots, with ease. A real gentleman who made her feel like a lady. She had wanted to run her hands through his dark brown waves and find out how it would feel to kiss his full lips. Five minutes after they met.

"How did you get this number?" she said, not commenting on the puppy reference, although it warmed her heart to know he felt that way.

Regardless, no way would her mother give out their unlisted number to a total stranger. He was sure to pick up on the doubt that coated the question. Was the handsome man she remembered a total liar? A wolf dressed in perfectly fitted, professionally creased dark jeans, a tailored jacket that fit his broad shoulders, just right, over a white button-down shirt that hugged a well-developed chest. Could she trust him? Love him? Be with him?

Whoa. Slow down there, girl. You're getting carried away with yourself. Listen to his words, without jumping to conclusions or indulging in a fantasy that has no real substance. You just met him yesterday. A meeting she would not soon forget. If ever. But still, she didn't even know the man.

James chuckled again and her day improved by leaps and bounds. "That's the best part. Apparently, your mother knows my assistant, Terri Sanders. Terri gave your mom a glowing review, and here we are."

"Nothing sneaky about you, is there?" she said, beginning to relax. Annie Jo knew Terri, as well. Terri had raised her children in Oakwood United Methodist Church. And if Annie Jo's mama trusted Terri's assessment of the gorgeous cowboy, she could too.

Besides, it just felt right. Something cosmic and other-worldly drew her to him. He seemed like a brilliant ray of sunshine, sent to penetrate the gloom that had shadowed her existence, far too long.

James Baldwin was more than a distraction. He was a hot, right-out-of-the-oven cinnamon roll, with lots of gooey icing. Just the way she liked them.

Annie Jo closed her eyes and sent up a silent prayer. Short and sweet, but heartfelt and sincere. Then decided to take a chance as peace engulfed her spirit.

"No, ma'am," he said, with a smile in his voice, which further calmed her even though she had to concentrate to remember what she had asked him. "Straight forward as they come. I was hoping for the honor of seeing you again. And like the idiot I am, I failed to get your number yesterday. If you're interested, I'd love to make reservations for us at Cattle Baron on Friday evening. *This* Friday evening."

He paused a moment and prayed while he waited for her answer. He could scarcely believe he had managed to get out an entire paragraph. This woman unnerved him. In a pleasant way. But unnerved him, still.

Please, Lord, help me know what to do and say when it comes to Annie Jo Parker. I already like her a lot and would love the chance to get to know her.

"I'd like that," said Annie in that silky voice he'd follow anywhere.

James just about shouted Hallelujah! But he managed to keep his cool and evened out his breathing before he responded. "I'm glad you're available," he said. "May I pick you up at six-thirty?"

Annie's voice became a mumble. She must have covered the handset. He could just make out the words. "Yes, ma'am. Okay, no problem. I'll tell him."

"Six-thirty will work," said Annie. "But Mom says you need to come out to meet the family before then."

Meet the family. What was she, fifteen?

Meet the family. The idea rattled around in his head, making his tummy quiver with nerves.

Meet the family. Not the day after he met the girl, but in the same week. Could he do it? Could he make himself *not* do it?

"Uh, that would be nice." Why did he keep saying 'uh'? "I'll check my schedule and see what I can work out."

He sucked in a quick breath and said, "Okay, then, if you'll send me your address and personal cell number, I'll pick you up Friday at six-thirty. Thank you, Annie. I look forward to an enchanted evening."

Ugh, he sounded like a doofus. Which, of course, had already been established. The sweet tinkling of Annie's laugh pushed the tension out of his limbs. Mostly.

"What?" he said.

"You sound like the words to a song. Relax, James. Everything will be all right. I'll text my address and cell number, just in case you get lost. Bye, now. I'll see you later."

She chuckled again before the line went dead. James whooshed out a breath and dropped his head onto the desktop. He hadn't been this pumped or scared since the last science fair of his senior year in high school or this nervous since he made his first presentation before a roomful of high-dollar investors, who might help launch his company—if he said the right things and did the right things.

Lord, help me do the right things and say the right things with Annie Jo. I really want to find out how she might fit into my life. He sensed he'd started repeating himself to God, too. Breathe in, breathe out. Breathe in, breathe out. He wanted to believe Annie Jo: *Everything will be all right.*

"Focus. Stay in the moment. Trust God."

CHAPTER FOUR

*"Be strong and courageous. Do not be afraid or terrified because
of them, for the LORD your God goes with you; he will never
leave you nor forsake you"* (Deuteronomy 31:6 NIV).

"Okay," said Bethany, sitting across from Annie Jo. "Spill it. I'm done waiting for you to tell me what happened that made you late for Starbucks."

Annie chuckled at her friend. "Poor thing. You wanted to know so badly, you totally ignored me to spend time with that hunk, Mr. Gerard, then waited until I was asleep before you came home last night."

"Ha ha, very funny. Now, spill."

Annie stepped into the kitchen and over to the Keurig coffee machine. "Not before at least one cup of coffee. You might want to have one yourself, the story is that good. You need to be fueled up to take it all in."

Annie's tummy churned just thinking about James Baldwin. She had rushed home from town the day before then spent hours online, learning so, so much about the handsome cowboy. But it appeared to be all business related. Not one personal article had been included on his website or even from the Google search she had poured over until her vision blurred, and sleep dragged her under. All she really knew for sure was that he was rich. And handsome. And private.

But there had to be something. No billionaire this side of the Atlantic could glide through life without some sort of personal story. Whether juicy or tragic, something must have happened to James Baldwin that meant more to him than how many zeros defined his bank account.

Bethany plopped down in the seat across from Annie Jo with a cup of cream she had added a little coffee to and a huge cinnamon roll.

"How can you eat like that and stay reed thin?" said Annie, with a shake of her head. Annie was by no means overweight, but model thin seemed beyond ludicrous. Yet, Bethany pulled it off without the slightest effort.

"Generations of great metabolism. No more stalling. Was I right? Is it a guy?"

Annie felt heat crawl up her neck and warm her face, an entirely different kind of awe making her aware of every hair that stood up on her arms.

"Not just a guy, Bethany, a full-grown, gorgeous man, with deep brown chocolate eyes and longish but styled hair, a captivating smile, and tailored western-wear. A man with manners and a sense of humor."

She took in a shuddering breath and started to speak again when someone started banging on the front door.

"Do what?" said Bethany. "It's seven a.m."

"I'll go," said Annie. "At least I'm fully dressed." She grinned at her friend who wore animal print pajama bottoms and an oversized sweatshirt.

Bethany shrugged, clearly unconcerned. "What? I'm between gigs. Send them away so we can get back on topic. I hope you took this guy's picture."

"Oh, you," said Annie, waving a hand at her friend. The banging came again. Harder. Faster.

"Coming!" said Annie, frustration building inside her. "Hold on to your shorts." Who in the wide world would crash her breakfast? Even her brothers didn't pull stunts before the morning chores were done.

Annie reached for the door but stalled when Austin hollered from the other side. "Open up, AJ. I know you're in there!"

Annie looked at Bethany and said, "Call Dad. Right now."

"Dialing. Just don't open that door," said Bethany, her eyes wide with alarm.

The door rattled in its hinges and Austin shouted a string of obscenities that made Annie blush. What was wrong with this guy? She had already wasted too much breath trying to get through his thick skull. Did he think cursing her would be the way back into her good graces? She had tried to be his friend, but she'd finally given up on that. He was just too volatile. And crazy. Could he be drunk at seven in the morning? It was Tuesday. He should be doing chores at his dad's ranch, not pestering her.

"Go home, Austin, before you get yourself in a heap of trouble." Now she was mad.

"I'm not going anywhere until you talk to me. You owe me, AJ!"

Owed him? Was he nuts? She had been his friend, since early childhood. She had tried to be his girlfriend, longer than she should have. Nothing romantic had ever clicked in her toward him. But she did not *owe* him anything.

"Ha! You're delusional. I'm not talking to you, Austin, not about anything. Now go home before Dad gets here and finds you on my doorstep."

Gee, Annie thought her problems with Austin would be over by now. She had made herself perfectly clear. Not only had he cheated on her, he had shoved her into the wall and slapped her across the face when she walked up on him doing unmentionable things in *her* horse trailer, at a rodeo, with the girl Annie had won against that very day. If he'd been her friend, especially her *boy*friend, he would not have dropped his guard and been caught red-handed with his pants down around his ankles.

Maybe she should have filed assault charges. That might have at least gotten his attention.

Annie's cell phone rang. She glanced down at it. Austin. Really?

"Hang up, Austin," she yelled through the door. "I'm not answering."

Austin swore again, followed by a growl, and an attempt to open her door, even though it was plainly locked.

Annie saw dust fly up in the distance and peeked around Austin's shoulder. Yes! Her father *and* brothers were racing up both sides of the driveway on horseback at a fast gallop. The instant they reached the railing at the end of the steps, Mack jumped off Silver and stormed up to the expansive porch. Annie watched with bated breath.

"I thought we settled this matter months ago," said Mack, clapping a hand on Austin's shoulder. "AJ has spoken her desire to not be your girl, Austin. You need to go home. Now. Don't press your luck or try my patience."

Although they didn't know the real reason she had ditched Austin, only gratitude filled her as they stood their ground in her defense.

Annie stayed inside but didn't take her eyes off the scene. Her brothers and dad were all taller and broader than Austin Anderson. He rode bulls and was tough, sure, but he couldn't hold a candle to the Parker brothers.

"Now, don't get all riled up," said Austin, placating, annoying as all get out. "I ain't done nothin' wrong."

Josh slipped up next to Mack, with Dad settling a few steps to Mack's right, where he had a clear view of Austin and could get to him without plowing over either one of her brothers. She appreciated their united stance. Austin had verbally abused her for years then escalated to physical violence when she didn't give in to his demands. So yeah, she had spoken her desire to not be Austin's girl, rather vehemently, and with no regrets.

"Better start praying for Austin," said Annie over her shoulder. "He might need it."

Bethany left the table and joined Annie at the door. "He's such a scumbag."

"Turned out that way," said Annie. "But sometimes I miss the kid he was when we were growing up. His mother's death sent his dad into a downward spiral and Austin jumped in right after him. I'm not sure either one of them will ever fully recover."

"Yeah, I liked Mrs. Parker."

"Everyone did," said Annie, her heart breaking a little more for Austin and for his dad, too. "She was the glue that held that family together. Obviously."

Raised voices on the other side of the door interrupted their conversation.

"Go home now, Austin, or I'm calling Sheriff Nelson." Dad. Good, maybe Austin would listen to Dad. "This is your first and last warning, or I let Josh and Mack loose on you."

"I'm goin'," grumbled Austin. He said the words but didn't make any effort to head down the stairs. "But I'm not giving up. Annie Jo is my girl!"

At that, Annie yanked the door open, letting it slam against the interior wall, and got right in Austin's face. "Have you lost your ever-lovin' mind, Austin Adam Anderson? Get on out of here. Now! Before I call the sheriff myself."

Josh, Mack, and Sam all took a step back and gestured with their arms in a motion that indicated they had made the path clear, and Austin had best take advantage of their patience and generosity.

"I made a mistake," said Austin, reaching out to touch Annie's arm.

She jerked away from him and shuddered. She caught the look of surprise in her father's eye and knew she would have to be forthcoming about what had happened between them. And soon.

Mack, however, didn't need an explanation in order to act.

"Okay, that's it," he said, taking two long strides forward. He hauled Austin up by the waist at the back of his jeans and dragged him across the porch, down the steps, along the sidewalk, then out to his pickup truck. With one swift movement, Mack slung Austin toward the driver side door. With a wide stance and hands on his hips, he glared at the unwelcome intruder. "Git, Austin. Go now, before I lose my temper."

The Parker family and Bethany glared as Austin climbed up behind the wheel of his truck then sped down Annie's driveway.

Shivering in the cold morning air, Annie stood with her back stiff, her limbs taut. They watched Austin until he squealed off her property and raced up the highway, fishtailing and speeding along, seemingly undisturbed that he could take his own life, or the life of another.

Once the bed of his pickup was out of sight, Annie turned to her brothers and dad. "Can I offer you some coffee and fresh cinnamon rolls?" She kept her voice light, like it didn't matter in the least that Austin had disturbed her coffee time, screamed and cussed at her on her own front porch then had the audacity to try and touch her again.

"Punkin," said Sam, his voice calm and consoling. "Let's go inside and have a little chat."

The consoling sound of her father's voice made Annie take note of her own inner turmoil. The reality struck her. Austin was still a threat. If her father and brothers had been out of town, how far would he have gone to get to her? Was her stubborn pride putting Bethany in danger, too?

Annie had wanted so badly to be on her own, perhaps she had rushed her father into getting the house finished. Bullied him into getting her way. He'd always been a gentle giant. A man of integrity and strength that most who knew him admired. Maybe not Austin. But for years now, Austin seemed only able to hear his own voice.

He wanted the Parker ranch. That's what he wanted. And he'd figured out a long time ago, that he could have a share in it, if he had Annie Jo.

The peace of the morning had been shattered. And telling Bethany about James Baldwin would have to wait.

But then, under the circumstances, that was the least of her concerns.

Inside, Annie rushed to the kitchen. She put on a fresh pot of coffee and stuck another store-bought package of cinnamon rolls in the oven. She had never taken the time to ask her mother to teach her how to make them from scratch. Another dig of guilt raced through her. There was just so much guilt one person could carry without collapsing into a pile of despair.

Her nerves felt exposed, every little touch like fire on her skin.

"Punkin," said her father, standing behind her, his hands on her shoulders. "What are you not telling us?"

The concern in his voice pushed Annie over the edge of control, into a flood of tears. Once the oven door was closed, she turned toward her father and settled into his embrace, her head against his chest. She let herself cry, while his embrace consoled her, much as he'd done when Glory passed away.

The loss of her horse, her long-time friend, and now being forced to tell the awful truth about Austin's treatment of her, had combined to pull her into an emotional funk. She couldn't even conjure up a mental picture of James Baldwin.

This was bad. And it would necessarily get worse before it got better.

She should have told her family the truth about Austin, long ago. A very long time ago. After this latest outburst, they had to know something beyond frustration with his attitude had pushed her past wanting to be his friend. Made her cringe at his touch.

Her father's warm, large hands on her back soothed Annie's soul, to some degree. Her father loved her. Her brothers, too. She owed them the truth. This wouldn't be easy. She'd kept the secret from everyone, even her best, best friend.

But Austin was out of control. If she didn't tell her family, and her roommate, the truth, she could be putting all their lives in jeopardy. And she didn't want that on her conscience. No way.

The time had come to tell them all the whole ugly truth.

CHAPTER FIVE

She'd had the hard talk with her family. They'd been shocked. Appalled, even. And promised to support her if Austin ever gave her trouble again. It had gone better than she could have hoped, and she had felt a little foolish. Austin must have really done a number on her head for her to think it wasn't possible to tell her family that he had been abusive toward her. She would have to wait now, praying with all that was within her that he would behave himself.

Her brothers had wanted to go after him and teach him a lesson. Right then. Wanted her to file charges against him for laying a hand on her. For hurting their baby sister.

"It's been over a year since all of that happened," she'd said. "Right before Austin lost his mother. When Mrs. Anderson passed away, I couldn't bring myself to put anything else on their family. He dislocated my shoulder, sure, but he didn't break my arm. I got over it. I just don't ever want to be alone with him again."

And so, the matter had been dropped—unless Austin pulled another stunt. Hopefully, he would be stopped before anyone she loved got hurt.

She decided to trust God to handle Austin and get on with her life.

Especially now that Austin knew that her father and brothers would come at him if he made any attempt to bother Annie Jo. Ever.

She pushed all that junk to the side and turned her attention to training Bluebell for the Taylor County Thanksgiving Classic. As Glory had gotten older, Annie had faced the fact that she would need to train someone else to race barrels. Bluebell had won, hands down, the weekend she had spent hour upon hour testing the three possible replacements.

They had named Bluebell after her grandmother, Blue Satin, but also because, as a colt, Bluebell had a tendency to steal anyone and everyone's ice cream cone. No apology. And it had taken months to break her of the habit before she got sick or too heavy to make it around a barrel. By the time she had reached two years of age, she had gotten the message, and Annie Jo had started training her in the basics of barrel racing. Now, a year later, Bluebell was ready to compete at the higher levels.

James had seemed surprised that a woman of Annie's maturity would need to introduce a new beau to her family, before she would follow through with a date. But he didn't squawk or back off, so she counted that as a good sign.

Thankfully, she didn't have to think of a way to get James and her family together before Friday. They had all been busy with ranching necessities and the matter had slipped her mind.

So, when he called on Thursday morning, asking if she had any information about ranches for sale in the area, she was both embarrassed that she had forgotten, and relieved that he had a legitimate excuse to see her—without going on an official date.

She knew of a ranch for sale, all right. An expansive, well-established spread that began where her fence line ended. Right next door to her father's ranch. They could be one big happy family.

The idea came to her then. She would direct James to the BB ranch, introduce him to the grouchy owner, Mr. Blankenship, then figure out a way to get him to make the short trip to her parents' ranch and get this introduction thing out of the way. She wanted to go on a real date with James Baldwin. And introducing him to the family was the only way that was going to happen.

It probably sounded ridiculous to him, but she couldn't worry about that. If meeting the family spooked him, she was better off without him. Annie Jo was the baby in a family filled with over-protective men. Meeting James before she dated him would have been a requirement, even if she had never had trouble with Austin.

Sometimes it bugged her—being the baby—but her family loved her, would do anything for her. Introducing a man before she went out with him was a small thing, when compared with all the ways her family stood by her.

She tugged on the braid that hung over her shoulder, uncomfortable with the idea of losing James's affection before she'd had a chance to experience an evening out with him, the feel of his hand wrapped around hers, or find out what it would be like to kiss him.

Now she was just being silly. He had taken the initiative to see her before they engaged in a real date. That had to be a good sign. Surely, he'd be man enough to meet her over-protective family.

If he knew about Austin, her family's paranoia would make more sense. And she supposed that sordid story would have to come out, at some point. Ugh. She didn't want to think about Austin, much less reveal his arrogance to a prospective, dare she say, boyfriend?

Stop it, girl. Take one step at a time. Don't borrow trouble before it even happens. Get a grip.

Around eleven Thursday morning, James picked Annie up at her house then followed her directions to the BB ranch. She had said great things about it and had his curiosity piqued. How sweet would it be to own property so close to Annie Jo? From all he had to go on at this point, he thought it would be better than a triple chocolate fudge cake with chocolate icing. Sweeeet.

"Turn right here," she said. "The BB ranch entrance is up this road about five miles."

When they turned toward Mr. Blankenship's gate, James scanned the area. It seemed the man had gone to great lengths to turn this mostly flat land into an oasis. Massive pine trees lined each side of an extra wide paved driveway. *Must have one heck of a water well.*

Once they reached the massive entrance gate, flanked by a ten-foot-high rock fence that stretched a good ways down each side, James's mouth began to salivate. The security expert in him sprang to life.

He could see himself living here. A strange thought suddenly, unexpectedly, entered his head. A picture of Annie Jo on the back of a horse that matched the color of her hair, racing across the prairie, that glorious mane of hair flying behind her—on *their* land, near *their* house, with *his* wedding band fitted snugly on her left ring finger.

The fear James usually associated with the thought of marriage didn't come. Odd, he had been nervous just calling her and asking her out. And now, his mind had gone to forever?

His stomach didn't sour, and sweat didn't pop out on his forehead, either. Really? He'd met the girl less than a week ago, and already thought of her—as his. And they had yet to go on even one date.

For JB Baldwin, that was moving at warp speed. He'd never met anyone who made him hope for a future with a woman. A wife, and maybe even a child or two.

"What do you think?" said Annie, her voice rich and sweet, like melted chocolate. More chocolate. How much chocolate could one person consume before they keeled over?

He let the sound of her voice settle over him for a moment before he disturbed the peace that came with it. He looked at her then and realized he wanted to know everything about her. To experience her, to share the same space with her, for a lifetime.

"Gorgeous," he said, looking straight at her, and unable to stop the words. He meant it. Yeah, the ranch was gorgeous, but it couldn't hold a candle to the lady sitting across from him.

Her eyes widened in surprise, as if she knew he was referring to her, more than the ranch. Their gazes locked and held for several long seconds.

Long enough for James to notice the smattering of freckles across her nose. Long enough to realize she didn't need a ton of makeup to enhance her natural beauty. She probably didn't need makeup at all. Long enough to look into the depths of her soul. An innocence radiated off her and he wanted to take her in his arms and kiss her. Pretend it would be her first kiss—which made no sense. A woman of this caliber probably had men lined up at her door. Suddenly, he wanted, needed, to know the answer to that question.

"The ranch seems ideal for what I had in mind, from what I can see," he finally said, without taking his eyes off her. "But before I make any inquiries in that regard, there's something I'd like to know."

One shoulder went up in a shrug, before Annie said, "I'll tell you, if I know the answer. I've been Mr. Blankenship's neighbor my entire life, so I know a lot about his spread. What is it you would like to know?"

He'd find out about the ranch, later.

"Are you in a committed relationship with anyone?" He asked the question in earnest, not caring about the stats on the acreage stretched before them, or the number of head of cattle it ran, or the pedigree of the horses he'd seen grazing in the distance. This first inquiry took precedence over all of that.

Those big green eyes sparkled as a perfect smile slowly filled her face, reaching all the way to her eyes. A sincere smile that took his breath away.

"No. You?"

James's heart started racing, like the horse he'd entered in last year's Iroquois Steeplechase. It hammered against his ribs. His mouth went dry, and he couldn't have stopped the wide grin that settled on his face, if he'd tried. Might not be able to stop it, all day.

"Not yet."

Annie could hardly believe what was happening. She was falling for a virtual stranger. She'd seen good looking men in her life, but not one of them had ever looked at her this way, or made her blood pump so hard, or made her limbs jittery, or her heart swell with hope. She didn't understand exactly what was happening here, but she definitely wanted to find out.

"Can I be honest with you?" she said.

"Please."

Annie unbuckled her seat belt and leaned across the console between them. She held this gorgeous hunk of a man with her eyes, searching for words. Stalling, really, for she had no idea what she was about to say. She had offered him honesty, but what would that look like? Should she tell him that she had somewhat of a history with Austin Anderson? A semi-relationship that had ended abruptly, when he'd been caught in the back of Annie's horse trailer with the second-best barrel racer in the nation? Should she tell him she didn't want him to buy the BB ranch, because she wanted it for herself, and didn't even know why she'd brought him out here to see it? Or did she tell him that she thought he was extremely handsome and wished she already knew him well enough to climb over the console, snuggle onto his lap, and kiss him?

Good grief, AJ. Calm down.

"You'll probably think I'm crazy."

"No one has a market on that. Trust me."

"Well, I think I like you. A lot. Which sounds crazy, I know, since we just met, not that long ago."

"I like you, too," said James, before Annie got out another word. "How about we take one day at a time and see how things play out. And in the spirit of honesty, I feel like I should tell you, I never planned on anything like this happening to me. I never intended to fall in love and get married. Have a family. But now. Anyway, one day at a time? What do you say?"

The blare of a horn interrupted them before she uttered a sound.

Annie pulled her eyes away from James, unable to get his words out of her head. Thankful for the distraction, she turned toward the gate and let a frown bring her brows together.

Barry Blankenship, in his shiny new, silver Cadillac pickup, sat on the other side of the massive electric gate, glaring at her. Without saying a word, Annie climbed down out of James's truck and marched over to the gate. She didn't look back but heard James's door shut and felt him come up behind her. Not the way she wanted the two men to meet. Didn't want Mr. Blankenship to know she was involved, in any way, with a prospective buyer. He was just stubborn enough not to sell to James, if he had any sort of relationship with Annie Jo Parker.

If she'd been thinking, they would have pulled off the road, just close enough for James to see the outlying edges of the BB ranch. She should have just given him Mr. B's phone number and left it up to him to make contact. Couldn't be helped now, though. They were already here.

Mr. Blankenship dropped out of his truck and stomped over to the gate. But did not offer to open it.

Why would he? Barry couldn't stand the sight of Annie Jo, even though he'd known her since the day she was born and had wanted her to marry his nephew, which was laughable. He looked the same as always. A hard glint shone in his eyes and a chewed-up butt of a cigar stuck out of the corner of his mouth. She had never known if he smoked them or just kept one handy to smoke it later. Either way, it was a nasty habit. The dark brown juice on his lips seemed at odds with his impeccable dress and shiny new pickup truck. But to each his own.

Then there was the fact that James was a stranger.

"Good morning, Mr. Blankenship," said Annie, forcing kindness into her tone, much as it grated on her nerves. "I'd like to introduce you to a prospective buyer, James Baldwin." She paused, turning toward her companion.

James stepped around Annie Jo and faced Mr. B. "You have an impressive set-up here, Mr. Blankenship. I'd appreciate a tour some time if you could work it into your busy schedule."

And like magic, Barry Blankenship cracked a smile. Annie's jaw dropped.

Seemed that James's smooth, respectful manner affected Barry much the same way it had affected her. Shaking her head, she took a step back. If she didn't draw attention to herself, maybe Mr. B's dislike for her wouldn't come up. Wouldn't interfere with James's interaction with the man who might just be willing to sell him the ranch next door.

Sixty seconds later, James headed back toward his truck. Annie skipped ahead to get in front of him. Walking backward, she said, "That was amazing. I didn't think Mr. Blankenship had a soft side."

"Likes to be respected, is all."

"Amazing. I've never seen anything like it, in all the years I've known him."

Annie hurried to get inside James's truck before Mr. Blankenship came to his senses and changed his mind. James settled in and Annie waited until they were back on the road before she mentioned the BB ranch again.

"Really, Mr. B has been stubborn about holding onto his ranch, convinced his nephew would come back and take over."

"Come back from where?"

"If you can believe it, he's a broker on Wall Street in New York City. Wild, huh?"

"Does sound strange. What made Mr. Blankenship think his nephew would be interested?"

"Kind of a long story."

"Care to share?"

"In the spirit of honesty, yes. When I turned eighteen, Mr. B decided his nephew Joshua and I should get married. That way, his ranch would stay in the family, if something happened to him. Apparently, my dad had mentioned to him that I wanted to own the ranch myself. But he would only talk about joining the ranch to ours if I consented to marry *Joshua*."

"Ouch."

"Yeah. I was afraid he wouldn't even talk to you when he realized we were together."

Her face blushed pink as she stuttered around *together*.

"I like the idea of us being together."

"What?"

"In the spirit of honesty, and all."

The truth was out there now. James had apparently developed strong feelings for her, in less than a week. Before their first date. Today made the second time they had been in the same vicinity. The first time they had been alone.

If she let herself admit it, she already had strong feelings for James Baldwin, too. She'd been thrilled when he asked her advice about ranches in the area. And she'd known exactly which ranch she thought he would admire. And since Mr. B would never sell to her anyway, it might be handy to have the gorgeous cowboy right up the road. They could build on their relationship, get cozy, maybe get married one day and have a family, like he said.

Wow, if she felt this way before they even had one date, how would she feel if he kissed her? Hugged her? Held her close?

Gee, her mind had jumped a lot of steps ahead. But if anyone pressed her for an answer today, she would have to say she was falling in love. If James asked her to elope tomorrow, she would be sorely tempted to say yes.

"How about lunch at Mom's," she said, instead of asking him to marry her. "You could meet the family. Ask Dad anything about the BB ranch. I doubt there's much he wouldn't know."

She'd made the invitation and hoped she hadn't scared him off already.

"Sounds great," he said.

Her nerves ratcheted up a notch. He agreed to meet the family, but then, he would have to do that, regardless. Even so, hope soared and lightened every burden she had been carrying since Austin had turned nasty and vindictive.

And she prayed the meeting would go well. Oh, how she prayed for that.

CHAPTER SIX

He has made everything beautiful in its time. He has also set eternity in the human heart; yet no one can fathom what God has done from beginning to end (Ecclesiastes 3:11 NIV).

James had meant what he said. He *did* like the idea of them together. On the ranch—Mr. B's ranch, to be specific—which he now very much wanted to buy. He had no real concept of how to make that happen. What would it take to win her heart? He barely knew her. She barely knew him. But he wanted to change that. Starting now.

"Speaking of wild, how would you feel about joining my family for Thanksgiving dinner?"

He couldn't believe the words had slipped out of his mouth. They were barely into September. He had *never* taken a girl home to meet his family. He had no idea if this strange, fascinating pull would even last through their first date.

But right now, he believed it a definite possibility.

When he glanced her way, his obvious vulnerability made him even more appealing. Yes, she liked this man very much. She wondered what her own family would say, if she agreed to skip their traditional holiday dinner to spend time with the family of a man she'd met less than a week ago. A man, however, who intrigued her, fascinated her, and made her blush, in a good way.

At least Thanksgiving was still two months away. They would have some time to get acquainted, date a little. If things were still copasetic by November, she could meet his family. No worries. She wondered about them, on some level. What sort of family did he come from? A person's family didn't necessarily define a man; but might provide some insight into what she might expect. What kind of foundation he'd been grown out of.

James wore cowboy boots and a cowboy hat, but she had learned via the Internet that cowboying definitely was not his regular job. She had discovered numerous facts and figures about his professional prowess. He had risen to a level of success that to most would be impressive.

And she had been, really. But more than his list of accolades, Annie wanted to know the man behind the persona. She wanted to know his favorite foods, his favorite color, his hobbies, why a business tycoon wanted to own a ranch. She wanted to know what he saw in her and whether they could possibly be as compatible as they seemed on the surface.

She wanted to know how he would respond in the heat of anger, if he was patient and compassionate, or if she had created a Greek-like god in her head, only to watch it crumble at the first sign of trouble.

Was he the gentleman he appeared to be? Could she trust him with her heart?

So many unanswered questions.

Even so, deep in her soul, Annie Jo trusted James Baldwin.

"I can't believe I'm saying this, but I'm so curious, I'm inclined to accept your invitation. *If* I can convince my two brothers and parents to let me miss our traditional feast."

"Should I be afraid of your brothers?" A frown wrinkled his brow, and his concern made her grin.

"Maybe." She flashed a smile at him then let herself full-out laugh. She had to tease him a little bit.

Annie's laughter was refreshing. If she were his little sister, he'd do whatever it took to protect her, too.

"I understand. I have two younger sisters, myself. My brothers and I would pummel anyone who mistreated them. I promise to be a gentleman. Will your brothers be present at lunch?"

"No doubt. Dad's ranch butts up to mine, which butts up to Mr. B's. It's not that far from here. I could call ahead and make sure they can meet us at the barn before lunch. You know, just in case."

"Very funny. Go ahead, call 'em."

James didn't hesitate with his answer. He could face two brothers. He'd spent a lifetime doing just that. This enchanting girl had crawled under his skin and planted a tiny seed in his heart. Obviously, to be eligible for Annie's heart he would have to win over her brothers. And probably her dad, as well. Come to think of it, Dad should probably be at the top of that list. And her mother, too. Seemed like a lot to deal with—before the first date.

Grant me favor, Lord. I'm headed for uncharted waters and do not want to go alone.

"All set," said Annie, happy and nervous at the same time. She had never brought a man home to meet the family. Austin had just always been a part of them—a man her family had loved and respected for years. Austin's reputation had been tarnished, for sure. But if her family couldn't trust someone they had known as long as Austin, how would they feel about this outsider whom she knew very little about? How would she explain this insane attraction and convince her family that James Baldwin was a safe bet, when she wasn't sure of it herself? Pretty close, but not one hundred percent sure.

Well, she would soon find out. Her brothers would be waiting in the barn. At least it wouldn't be an ambush.

What had he just agreed to? Annie had two older, protective brothers. James appreciated protective brothers, he had two of his own. Two large, impressive brothers who made him feel like a shrimp. Two handsome brothers with their mother's golden hair and their father's broad shoulders.

In the short drive to the Parker ranch, James let his imagination run away with him. Not only had he let his unending insecurities cripple his self-confidence, but he had also conjured up an inflated mental picture of the brothers he was about to meet. He squeezed the steering wheel until his knuckles turned white.

He felt ridiculous and hoped she hadn't noticed.

Ten minutes later, James followed Annie's directions to turn left onto a wide driveway that provided plenty of room on each side to pull a six-horse trailer, no problem. No pine trees had been planted along the driveway, but the gate alone spoke volumes about the quality and integrity of the family that lived beyond its framework. Impressive.

As they made their way down the broad, paved lane, James took in what, at first glance, appeared to be a "natural" setting. But subtle changes, clever groupings of mesquite, cacti, a man-made pond strategically placed here and there, created a well-balanced combination of landscaping that drew the eye. Large barns, outbuildings, corrals, and a huge indoor arena, calculated quickly through his number-inspired and technology-oriented brain—and impressive seemed too small a word.

"If you'll take this next right, it'll take you to the barn where my brothers are waiting."

James turned up another wide, paved road which led to a massive barn, doors open wide in greeting.

"Here goes nothin'," he said.

"Don't be afraid. They talk big, but they're all mush on the inside. Just follow my lead."

"Your turf, your rules."

James hopped down out of the truck and raced around the front hoping to beat Annie to the door. It opened at the same time he reached for the handle.

"Oh," she said, sounding surprised.

"I was trying to be a gentleman."

Her chuckle made a chill race up his spine. A lovely, deep, alto sound that could feed his ego. Being the source of her joy made him feel special.

"Thank you. You have probably already impressed my brothers, and they don't even know you yet. This should be good."

Annie offered James her hand. With wide eyes and a grateful heart, he latched onto it. They moved forward, together.

Two really tall, broad-shouldered cowboys met them at the opening of the barn.

"James, meet Mack and Josh Parker, my brothers. Mack, Josh, this is James Baldwin, my new friend."

James stuck his hand out toward the brother standing closest to him.

"Nice to meet you. You have an amazing sister."

Annie's brother took James's hand. "I'm Mack," he said, squeezing James's hand with a tighter grip than most social circumstances would require. "She's our baby sister. Catch my drift?"

"Message received," said James, pulling his hand back and stretching out his fingers.

"What he said," said Josh, his thumb pointed toward Mack.

"Okay, guys," said Annie, as she put herself between James and her brothers. "Enough with the intimidation. James is good people, and I expect you to treat him with respect."

James turned as he heard someone approaching from behind. A big man, taller and broader than Mack or Josh. As if that were possible.

"Seems to me we can trust your sister's judge of character," said the giant of a man.

"Dad!" said Annie, rushing into the big man's arms.

James wished his brothers were here to meet Annie's father, the largest male specimen James had ever seen. How did the petite form of Annie Jo Parker come from this galaxy of giants? Then he immediately got his answer, as an exact replica of Annie Jo stepped up to the big man's side.

Mrs. Parker approached James with her hand outstretched. As she drew closer, he realized that her hair was a shade lighter than Annie's, and her eyes were sapphire blue rather than Annie's bright emerald green. But they had the same button nose and full lips and tiny build.

He had stumbled into a family as noteworthy, eye-catching, and imposing as his own. A little more country, maybe, but he felt a kinship, right away. He felt comfortable. Small, but comfortable.

"We were just about to sit down to lunch," said Annie's duplicate. "Won't you join us?"

"I'd be honored," said James. "Thank you."

Annie stepped out of her father's arms and skipped, *skipped* over to James's side. She felt giddy as a schoolgirl and acted on it. The first several minutes with her family had gone well. For the first time in a long time, she let herself hope.

She reminded herself not to compare James with Austin. She couldn't anyway, since there was no comparison. In her lifetime, she'd never met anyone like James Baldwin. She knew Josh and Mack would both Google him, but she didn't care. She felt the goodness in him and wanted to know more. A lot more. She wanted to know everything about him—in an experiential way. And she wanted him to know her.

Her ears perked up when she heard her mother invite James to lunch. *Cool. One thing I don't have to make happen.* She grinned big when he accepted her mother's invitation. Good, he hadn't been scared off, yet.

Conversation lulled as the group moved to their vehicles. Annie rode with James, naturally, so she could show him the way to the house. She wiggled in her seat, unable to contain the excitement, eagerness, and building passion, like a volcano had erupted in the center of her gut and hot lava raced through her veins.

"You okay?" said James.

She turned to face him, her smile broad and telling. She wanted to roll down the window and shout that James Baldwin was coming to the house for lunch. Like he was some kind of celebrity, and the countryside would be impressed.

An idea popped into her head, and she blurted it out. "Would you go to Taylor County with us? For the Thanksgiving Classic? I'd like to bring it up to them during lunch. If you're willing to go. It would mean so much to me, to know you're in the stands. I know it sounds crazy, but it feels like our relationship—just the word sounds nuts. But our relationship feels like it's months, maybe years old, rather than a few days. Really. What do you think? About the trip to Taylor County, I mean."

She paused for a second then started laughing. "I haven't felt this wonderful in years," she said, wiping happy tears from her cheeks.

"Yes, I'd love that," said James, with no hesitation, which made the volcano erupt inside her a second time.

James agreed with Annie. He had *never* felt this wonderful. And he didn't even know what a Taylor County Thanksgiving Classic could possibly be. Didn't much care, since he would be willing to go to the moon for her.

The pact he'd made with himself to never get seriously involved with anyone of the female persuasion now seemed totally ludicrous. If he'd had any inkling that he'd meet a glorious creature like Annie Jo Parker, he'd have planned for this day long ago, and would have had an appropriate diamond in his jacket pocket. As soon as they parked the truck he'd have run around to her door, opened it then dropped to one knee. The impulse to marry her revved up his engine like nothing he'd felt before—more than when his startup company, that exploded over ten years ago, soared to a billion-dollar company, then to a multi-billion-dollar company. And more than any accomplishment or accumulated award of his entire career. They would all pale in comparison to a life-long journey with one champion barrel racer.

His life would be complete when JB and AJ merged as one at the altar, before a reverend, a company of family, friends, and probably the press. Let them come. He wanted to tell the whole world, today, how he felt about Annie Jo Parker.

Lunch was served in the kitchen, which helped James relax. A kitchen two sizes larger than any commercial kitchen he'd ever seen. A ten-man rectangular table sat at one end of the country-style space, complete with a four-foot by four-foot chopping block, oversized refrigerator, walk-in freezer, and eight-burner gas cookstove. The heart of the Parker ranch seemed to pump from right here, in this room.

He felt the stress of the morning roll off his shoulders, as he began to decompress, to feel accepted. In some respects, even more comfortable than with his own brothers. But lately he'd been making a concerted effort to mend that bridge. Things were looking up.

They all shared the chicken fried chicken, mashed potatoes, white gravy, fresh black-eyed peas, piping hot cornbread, and a garden salad, served with sweet tea or lemonade, or a combination of both.

"This must seem like a heavy meal for noon," said Mrs. Parker, that is Sissy, which she had insisted he call her. "But lunch is our biggest meal of the day. Then we snooze for a couple hours before finishing our workload before nightfall. The routine is typical for ranchers, but I thought it might seem odd to you. Or is that how you do business, as well?"

James chuckled at the back-door manner of asking him what he did for a living. She simply wanted to know what sort of man her daughter had brought home for lunch.

"Are you asking me what kind of job I have, Mrs. Parker? Um, I mean, Sissy?"

When her face blushed pink, James knew he'd guessed right.

"Well, I'm embarrassed to admit it, now," she said, which he found endearing.

"It's not a problem," said James. "I'll tell you anything you want to know. I have no secrets. You could probably find out all about me online. There's really not much to tell."

"Good," said Sissy, with a chuckle of her own. "I don't spend any time on computers, and I forbid my sons to invade other people's privacy unless the need arises. And yes, what do you do for a living, James?"

Everyone at the table laughed then.

James swiped the rust-colored cloth napkin across his mouth then placed it beside his plate. It warmed his heart, bringing memories of his grandmother, who had consistently set the table with cloth napkins, indicative of the season or a particular holiday.

"JB Electronics and Security is my baby," said James. "I started it with a small inheritance from my dad when I was nineteen. We're international now, with offices across the US and in thirteen countries."

He didn't know how much he should say, or how extensive would be the background check Annie's family might perform after his confession. But he wanted an honest and open relationship with Annie Jo Parker, so James told them that his father had died when he was ten years old, how he'd thrown himself into his love for computers and all things technology and didn't look up until he'd built something his dad would have been proud of. He told them he had a mom, a stepdad, two sisters and two brothers. And he even went so far as to share his experience with equine therapy, and that he owned several racehorses that waited for him back in Tennessee. Then he reached for Annie's hand, squeezed it and said, "And I'd really like to date your daughter, exclusively."

The room fell quiet. So quiet.

James didn't know if he'd put them all in shock, if they felt sorry for him, or if they were contemplating a polite way to throw him out. He glanced at Annie. She interlaced their fingers in what felt like an encouraging manner. Her eyes glistened with tears. He took in each face around the table. Sissy's eyes were shining, and the boys looked down at their plates. They didn't move a muscle. When James made eye contact with Sam, Annie's dad cleared his throat and looked James in the eye.

"I seem to recall," he began.

But James dared to cut him off. "Yes, sir, I'm one of the Baldwins from Ransom Canyon. My father was Dr. Bradley Baldwin."

Sam cleared his throat again. James waited one beat before he released Annie's hand and pushed his chair back, ready to leave, to get away from the awkwardness. He'd been afraid of the ghosts that might linger in Lubbock County. He hated that his family, in the midst of tragedy, had been put on display. That his grandmother had tried to destroy them all, that she stole his childhood home, and they'd been forced to flee in the middle of the night. It had happened twenty-five years ago, and had been resolved, his family and the homestead restored. Maybe he hadn't dealt with it as well and thoroughly as he should, because the look in Sam's eyes hurt to the core of his being.

"Maybe this was a bad idea," he said, standing. He didn't want to give up on a relationship with Annie. But he also had a limit. His family history was just that. History. Granted, the facts had shaped the man he'd become, but they no longer ruled his actions. He had placed his life in God's hands.

In an instant, everyone at the table scrambled to their feet. No one said anything, but they moved together as a unit. Annie wrapped her arms around James's waist. Sissy stood on tiptoe and planted a motherly kiss on his cheek. Sam reached his hand out in a welcoming gesture, and Annie's brothers stood nearby, quiet but seemingly supportive.

James grabbed hold of Sam's offered hand and returned his firm handshake. Mack and Josh stepped forward, each slapping a hand on one of his shoulders.

A close-knit, weepy moment, like a sappy coming-home television commercial.

Then Mack said, "You can date my baby sister. But if you hurt her, I'll take you down." His mouth smiled but his eyes said he meant business.

James could appreciate the sentiment. He and his older siblings felt the same way about Kimmie.

"Mack Parker," said Sissy. "You behave yourself."

"I'm just sayin'," Mack reiterated.

"That's all well and good, Son," said Sam. "But what say we give this young man a chance, before we start fashioning the hangman's noose."

Hangman's noose? Whoa.

His eyes went wide, but James stood his ground and said, "I'll do my best. I have a baby sister, too. I get it."

Mack gave him a nod then returned to his seat. Everyone followed suit then shared a man-sized portion of peach cobbler topped with Blue Bell Homemade Vanilla ice cream that tasted homemade and reminded James of the essential oil he had smelled on Annie Jo.

The tense moment had passed, and peace settled around them. James felt like the icy part of his heart was melting much like the ice cream on the hot cobbler. He let the feeling wrap him in warmth. These people made him feel like family, like he might have a place among them, a solid place that could last a lifetime.

"Thanks for the lovely meal, Sissy," said James. "I'll get out of your way now."

"I'll walk you out," said Annie.

James shook hands with the men and received Sissy's hug, allowing her warm welcome to massage yet another hardened chamber of his heart. He knew his mother loved him. He did. But it gave him an ego boost for this gentle woman to see that he had value, when she barely knew him at all.

CHAPTER SEVEN

*Dear children, let us not love with words or speech but
with actions and in truth* (1 John 3:18 NIV).

At nine o'clock on Friday morning, Annie and Bethany climbed into
Bethany's sporty-model BMW and headed for town. It was a bright,
sunny, fall day, headed toward a tolerable fifty-five degrees. They were feeling
young and feisty, so they called up a playlist from their high school days and
sang along. In the middle of one of Annie's favorites, Bethany turned the
volume way down.

"What's up with that?" said Annie. "You know that's my all-time
favorite group."

"I just remembered what I know about James Baldwin," she said,
stealing a look at Annie then turning her eyes back to the road. "It completely
slipped my mind until this moment."

Annie swallowed hard. What could Bethany possibly know about
James? What did she mean by that? Annie had guessed James must have
some sort of secret, but how would Bethany know what it is? Would it make
her want to cancel her date with him? It could be something dreadful. Did
she even want to know?

"Do I want to know?" Her voice trembled and Annie laced her fingers
together in her lap, bracing herself for Bethany's next words.

"Sorry, I didn't mean to scare you. It's not bad, but it explains a few
things."

A frown creased Annie's brow. "What kinds of things? What are you
talking about?" Annie was getting a little frustrated with the subject. They

were supposed to be having a relaxing day (if you could call shopping relaxing) not dissing on Annie's hopefully new boyfriend.

"Not bad, as in a flaw in his character," said Bethany. "Let me make that perfectly clear. By all indications, he's a super good guy."

"Okay," said Annie, dragging out the word. She would have a difficult time believing anything sinister could live in the heart of James Baldwin, he was just too good. "But?"

Annie Jo began to doubt herself. Doubt James. Would Bethany tell her that he was really some kind of a monster? That he'd been fooling her, leading her on? Her skin began to itch.

"No but," Bethany insisted. "I mean it. He really is a good guy, Annie Jo."

Bethany sounded sincere, at least that was something. Annie began to breathe a little easier. She sunk into the warmth of the heated seat and waited for the rhythm of her heart to slow down before she tried to speak. "So, what are you not telling me?"

Bethany grimaced, and Annie cringed again, her muscles instantly in a bunch. This was getting ridiculous. "Okay, maybe I don't want to know," she said, her heart sinking again. "Let's just rewind this day and start over."

"You need to know," said Bethany, another glance in her direction. "You really do."

"Gee whiz, Bethany. You're killing me here."

"Look, I'm sorry."

"Don't be. Just spit it out. It's not like I've made a lifelong commitment to the guy. I can find another one." She wasn't sure on that point, however. She already felt like she had made a lifelong commitment to James; and absolutely did not want to look for a substitute.

She sounded snarky, maybe, but she'd had high hopes for James Baldwin for several days now. At this stage of the game, she didn't want to hear anything that might keep them apart.

Or maybe it was better this way. Get it over with before anyone got hurt. But no matter what had happened to James in his past or what he might have done, Annie Jo would *not* be getting back together with Austin Anderson. Not ever.

"It's like this," said Bethany. "James Baldwin's dad was a famous brain surgeon, right here in Lubbock."

"I know. He told us. So, his father is dead. That shouldn't be a black mark against James."

"I agree," said Bethany, her look so serious Annie Jo made herself pay attention. Her best friend had never steered her wrong before. Surely, she wouldn't start now. "And did he tell you that his father died of a brain aneurysm? That he left behind a wife and five kids, the youngest of which wasn't born until two weeks after their father's death?"

"He told us he had four siblings, but none of the rest of that."

James came from a large family. A family that shared a common bond. The loss of a husband and father. And Lubbock County lost a brilliant surgeon. The thought of James losing his dad in such a tragic way at a young age made her nauseous. She tried to imagine how such a tremendous loss would have changed her own life. Would she be the happy, well-adjusted woman she was today, or would she be more like Austin? The loss of Austin's mother had devastated Mr. Anderson and accelerated the self-destructive track his son had started down their sophomore year.

The stark differences between Austin's remedy and the way James had managed his loss were like a storm and the peaceful calm of a gentle brook. But how had he managed it? He'd been a kid.

"Pull over, Bethany. I'm gonna throw up."

Bethany turned on the blinker, slowed way down then pulled off the highway. The instant Bethany came to a full stop, Annie rushed out and lost her breakfast on the side of the road. Poor James. Just the thought of what he'd been through made her sick. She wretched until she had nothing left then inched back inside Bethany's car and downed half a bottle of water. Her whole body ached—for James, his siblings, his mother.

"I didn't know it had been that bad," said Annie with a slow blink of her eyes. She turned her head toward Bethany. "He seems so well adjusted. How did you?"

"One of my model friends, Dawn Somersby, went on a date with James about five years ago."

Annie had seen photos and videos of Dawn, a supermodel that had caused a bidding war for her attention. "Oh, guess I can't compete with that," said Annie, her tone full of self-doubt. Vying for James's affection with the likes of Dawn Somersby could be disastrous.

"Are you kidding?" said Bethany, breaking into Annie's thoughts. "According to Dawn, you are the first woman James Baldwin has had more than one conversation with, since then. Five years, Annie. He doesn't date. Period. He's afraid. Obviously."

Afraid? Why should James be afraid to date? It didn't make sense. Yes, it was beyond sad that his father died young but what did that have to do with dating?

"Afraid?"

"Yeah. Afraid if he gets married, someone will have to call his wife one day and tell her he died. He told Dawn he did not intend to be responsible for that kind of heartache and loss. It's just better not to get involved. She had to coax the admission out of him. But he seemed not to have any difficulty walking away from her."

"James is thirty-five years old, Bethany, and he's been carrying that kind of heartache around with him for all these years?"

"That's right. He needs you, Annie. Listen, James Baldwin doesn't pursue women, they pursue him. And in case you haven't noticed, he made the effort to find you, asked you out, i.e., he's pursuing you. You're special, Annie, and he knows it. You owe it to yourself and to him to give this relationship a fighting chance."

Could she? What if she fell head over heels in love with him just to have him walk out on her to avoid an unknown future? A future neither one of them could control. Should she risk getting hurt by a man who had sworn off long-term relationships?

Annie dropped her head back against the headrest and groaned.

"Still wanna go shopping?" said Bethany, her voice bright and cheery as though nothing had been said to put a damper on their shopping spree.

"I never wanted to go shopping," said Annie, rolling her neck to look at her friend, without making the effort to raise her head off the headrest. "But maybe you're right. If I can free James from the clutches of fear and a lifetime of loneliness, it's my duty, right?" Her friend's upbeat demeanor had brought sunshine to an otherwise dismal morning.

"My point, exactly. Soldier on!" she said, with a fist raised high.

Annie Jo raised her fist in like manner and repeated, "Soldier on!"

Squishy, squirmy things still swam in Annie Jo's belly; but if she worked things just right, James Baldwin might never want to leave her side again, after their very first date.

Maybe.

It could happen.

***

Around eleven-thirty the same morning that Bethany took Annie Jo shopping, Matt and Paul sat across the table from James while they waited for their food at the Cast Iron Grill on 19th. James had picked the restaurant because Matt had an uncanny appetite for their famous pies. Suited James just fine, since his stomach was churning too much to care about the menu.

He probably should have called them sooner, not waiting until the day of his date with an amazing woman. He had put it off for no good reason, really. But he had to face the fact that he was in a new and foreign place in his life and needed their support. They were brothers, close kin, who cared about him. He felt sure they would be thrilled for him. Shocked, but thrilled. And he did not want to go into this relationship blind. At least his brothers had been married for a while now and might be able to guide him. Married? Was he already thinking about marriage with Annie Jo Parker?

Yes.

"Thanks for treating us to lunch, bro," said Matt, as he plopped down in the seat across from James. "You know how much I love the pies here."

James had to laugh. Everyone in the family knew about Matt's preferences in the pie department. "My pleasure."

"But I'm extra curious. Something big shaking in the security business and you need our advice?"

The twinkle in Matt's eye helped calm James's over-active nerves. Matt had always been the happy-go-lucky one in the family. Adventurous, jumping into dangerous waters without fear. His need for speed began early, with his first motorcycle. As he got older, he gravitated toward the air. At the end of his tour of duty as a Naval aviator, Matt obtained a position as a commercial pilot with Southwest Airlines, then married Jessica and eventually settled down in Lubbock, close to the rest of the family.

"I wish it were that simple," said James, hoping he could control his emotions. His brothers would pick up on every little change in his demeanor. After all, they had never seen him interested in starting a relationship with a woman. Not ever, not even in high school or college. He had dated a few times back then, but no one had trumped his devotion to his education and career goals.

Paul raised his eyebrows and a wide grin spread across his face. "It's a girl."

Guess he didn't hide his emotions all that well, after all.

"A girl?" cried Matt, with a chuckle. "You gotta be kidding."

"He's right," James confessed, shoving a fry in his mouth to stop any more words from escaping. He swallowed hard. He could do this, talk about Annie Jo. He could. He hadn't known her long but felt drawn to her like a metal arrow to a magnetic bull's eye. He needed her in his life. Uncanny, but he knew it was true. And he wanted to woo her properly. Respectfully, but with determination. And he had no idea how to do that.

"Wow, this is the best thing to happen in our family since Jessica," said Matt.

"Ahem." Paul cut his eyes at Matt.

"Okay," said Matt with a roll of his eyes. "Since Jo."

James loved these guys. They could joke around with each other and not lose their cool. Their brotherly bond had been revved up since the loss of their father. They had leaned on each other, confessed the hard feelings and disappointments that came with living life. Even in college they had used code to ask for help, especially when it came to their vow to stay pure before God, while dating. They had called it their Honor Pact. James intended to start that tradition up again, today. He had a feeling he was going to need it. His brothers had worn it thin, in college, so it was James's turn to catch up.

Matt crossed his massive arms across his massive chest and grinned at his baby brother. "Who is this lucky lady? Anyone we know?"

"I doubt it," said James. "She's a barrel racer. Wears jeans and boots and a cowboy hat, the whole nine yards."

Paul held James's attention with his eyes for a long moment. "A *champion* barrel racer?"

"As a matter of fact, yes. Why? Does it matter?"

"Not as a requirement, no. But I think I know her. Annie Jo Parker, by any chance?"

James felt his mouth drop open. How would Paul know Annie Jo? He hadn't mentioned her to anyone. Not his family, his colleagues, or even his stepfather. If anyone would understand a secret longing for a lady it would be Tommy Churchwell, who had waited twenty years to marry the girl of his dreams. James had kept his lips sealed shut, hoping the longing for Annie Jo would dissipate and he could return to his solitude. Didn't happen. At this point he didn't believe it ever would.

James felt love in his heart for a woman like he had never imagined possible. Marriage and children and horses and dogs made up his dreams at night. The memory of her eyes, her hair, her voice invaded his thoughts every day. And Paul already knew her? What were the odds?

"That is her name, yes," he said, his eyes wide and curiosity evident in his tone. "How do you?"

Paul slapped James on the shoulder and smiled big. "She volunteers with the youth at my church and teaches barrel racing to the kids at the Cowboy Church. I have witnessed her leading young girls to the saving knowledge of Jesus Christ, on more than one occasion. She's amazing. Our nation's barrel racing champion is humble, God loving, and generous with her time. How did the two of you meet?"

James tried to absorb Paul's news. For a moment, his brain failed him, and he couldn't speak. The all-consuming, sweet-smelling, easy-going lady he'd met at the gift shop was more than just a beautiful woman. She was an accomplished champion, who donated her time and talent to benefit others. Her website focused on barrel racing without mentioning her more benevolent characteristics. Wow.

Bringing his mind back around to the moment, he looked up at his brother. "By chance. Purely by chance."

"Oooo, this is good," said Matt, rubbing his hands together and scraping his chair along the tile, drawing it closer to the table. He leaned forward and grabbed James with his eyes. "What happened? Tell us everything."

James went into a description of Monday morning, how he'd heard the raised voices inside the shop and felt compelled to see if he could help. How he offered his linguistic skills and saved the day. How he pretended to be interested in the China just so he could stand close to her. How all he had managed to get out of her was her name. And how he Googled her and got Terri to look up the phone number to her father's ranch. And finally, that she had agreed to go out with him. He had no idea why; he just knew she had.

"I have reservations at Cattle Baron tonight. I'm supposed to pick up Annie Jo at six-thirty from the ranch where she lives." His voice fell away, and he shook his head, still contemplating all the miraculous attributes Paul had described. "I'm blown away," he said after a long pause. "I was so worried about telling you guys that I've fallen hard for a girl I only met a few days ago. And I find out one of you already knows her. The odds are astronomical." He shrugged then looked back and forth between his brothers. "So, any advice?"

Matt chuckled and Paul shrugged. "Be real with her," they both said at once, followed by dual laughter.

"Just be yourself, man," said Matt. "She'll love it. Be honest even when it hurts. Chicks dig that. I nearly lost Jessica trying to be something I wasn't."

"Cherish her," said Paul. "And respect her. God calls us to love our wives the way Christ loves the Church. It's way harder than it sounds, but it's the only way to have a lasting relationship with a woman. Trust me, I know. Look how close I came to losing Jo, and I was loving her with everything in me."

James stretched his arm across the table and rested his hand on Paul's forearm. "Wife?"

"Yeah. Too soon for that?"

"Maybe a smidge. We have yet to have a date."

"But you already care deeply for this girl, am I right?"

James knew he couldn't deny how he felt about Annie Jo. A line had been crossed. No, he had jumped over that line with both feet. He definitely wanted to know where this relationship might lead.

"I can't deny it," he said, his voice firm and his eye contact with his brother steady.

Matt spoke up then. "All right, that's what I like to hear. We can work with that. If you need us, you know how to reach us."

"Honor Pact?" said James.

The three siblings reached a hand toward the center of the table and stacked them, one on top of the other. Paul counted to three and they pressed their hands toward the table then quickly up again, citing, "Honor Pact."

"Jolly good," said Matt. "Keep us posted, brother."

"We'll be praying, James."

"Thank you. I appreciate it. Frankly, I'm scared to pieces." He and his brothers burst out a laugh at the phrase their nanny had used when they were little. Maggie had loved them to pieces. If they'd heard it once, they'd heard it a thousand times. Affectionate memories always came with the reference.

"Go get 'er," said Matt. "You've got my number."

"Here too," said Paul. "Any time, day or night. Seriously."

CHAPTER EIGHT

*Humble yourselves, therefore, under God's mighty hand, that
he may lift you up in due time* (1 Peter 5:6 NIV).

Annie twirled once in front of the full-length mirror with shining eyes. She'd been on cloud nine all week, waiting for her date with James Baldwin, grateful her family hadn't scared him off.

Bethany had outfitted Annie in an emerald green wrap-around dress with a cowl neck (which, according to her fashionista, contrasted perfectly with her dark auburn hair), three-quarter sleeves and a skirt that swirled in luscious folds around her calves. The low-heeled leather fashion boots with slouched tops made her feel feminine. More like a lady than a cowgirl.

Bethany, celebrated fashion model that she was, lived for shopping. She looked flawless in the perfect outfit—every single day. She had taken up modeling their sophomore year in high school and could have been New York runway great, but preferred print work and traveling. She had been half-way around the world in the past ten years but always ended up back where she'd started. Close to family and friends. Close to her charity work and the church she had attended since grade school. Bethany had attained high-class model status but remained as down to earth as Annie's rodeo crowd.

Guardedly, Annie had succumbed to her roommate's insistence that she be allowed to apply *date makeup* as a gift, which seemed a bit much. But this could be an important night. A man's first impression of a woman could be crucial. But wait, they had already had their chance at first impressions, hadn't they?

"But not alone in a car for an extended period of time, with only a console between us," she whispered to her reflection. With a wink at herself she twirled one more time, feeling brave and blessed as she looked forward to an evening that oozed with possibility.

She'd never felt this way with Austin, whom she had blessedly not heard from since the incident at her front door. Maybe he finally believed he'd lost his opportunity to own a piece of the Parker ranch—to own her, control her, and have his way with other women at the same time. Alcohol and greed and a stubborn will made a lethal combination, and she didn't want to have anything to do with the grown-up, albeit immature, version of Austin.

Sadly, he had not improved since she had dumped him for the final time. His focus had been on himself then, just as it is now. Or on a bull ride, or a night out drinking with buddies. Or another woman.

Annie was suddenly struck with a blessing she hadn't thought of before. God had certainly been with her through the years. For no matter how much pressure Austin put on her, she had never given in to his coaxing. And, praise God, he had never forced himself on her. So, turning to Sylvia had been a selfish move on his part, yes, but had also saved Annie from a fate worse than death. If he had sexually abused her, there would be no chance to renew their original friendship. Rape would have cost her a great treasure; but it might have cost Austin his life. Dad, Josh and Mack would have been hard pressed to not come after him. And there would have been zero tolerance, no second chance, after that.

Lord, thank you for allowing Austin to avert his attention in another direction. Thank you for sparing my dad and brothers the temptation to take a life. And thank you for saving me from Austin's wrath. Protect us all as we move forward, Lord. Show us the way. And I pray for Austin to come to his senses. Send someone who can crack that hard shell and get through to him. In Jesus's name, Amen.

She dropped down on the padded bench in front of the dresser, her mind whirling. Austin had never treated her like a treasure, had he? No. He had taken advantage of their friendship to snake his way into her father's heart. Not out of love for his daughter, but out of covetousness for the Parker ranch. He'd cheated on her with *Sylvia*, in Annie's own horse trailer, at a rodeo. Anyone could have walked in on them. She groaned at the memory.

Even though she had not been in love with Austin, she had considered his actions a betrayal of their friendship. If he'd wanted to have his way with Sylvia, he could have taken her to his own trailer. The very idea that he had chosen to perform his misdeed in her personal property seemed an extra slap in the face. The confrontation had been painful—in more ways than one.

It hadn't been the first time Austin had slapped her or yanked her around by the hair of her head. But it had been the first time he'd drawn blood. The first time he'd dislocated her shoulder. She'd told her parents she'd tripped over the long reins, got tangled up, busted her lip and dislocated her shoulder. They seemed to believe her, thank goodness. She hadn't felt up to facing them with the truth—or dealing with the demons that seemed to possess Austin.

He'd thundered at her, releasing years of pent-up aggravation with her continual rejections—then been caught doing the dirty deed with Annie's professional nemesis. It had been an ugly scene that made for an unpleasant, debilitating memory.

Her body began to shake, as tears filled her eyes. She buried her face in her hands and let the tears fall.

"Please, Lord," she whispered. "Help me forgive him and leave the past in the past."

Five whole minutes passed as she waited for peace to restore her soul.

As she pulled her hands away from her face, she gasped at what she saw. All Bethany's hard work had run together in a kaleidoscope of color, none of which had stayed where it had been carefully placed a half hour earlier.

With a sigh, Annie sent a panicked text to her friend.

She could hear Bethany pounding up the stairs.

Bethany slammed into Annie's room. All she could do was shrug her shoulders, while fighting a fresh onslaught of tears.

"Ah, Annie, what's wrong?"

Through blubbering lips and intermittent sniffles, Annie explained what had destroyed Bethany's handiwork.

Bethany knelt beside Annie and Annie let her friend console her with a hug and tender words of encouragement.

"I feel so stupid," Annie managed to say.

"Well, don't," said Bethany. "Austin is the one who acted stupidly. Now," she continued, gently turning Annie's face toward the mirror. "We need to get you cleaned up and gorgeous for a real man, who seems to care a great deal for you. Think you can do that?"

Annie stared at herself.

"It'll take a miracle," she mumbled.

"And we believe in miracles, right?"

Annie blew her nose while nodding in the affirmative.

"That's better," said Bethany. "Pull yourself together while I work my magic."

"Thank you," said Annie, with a sniff, as she turned to face her friend.

"That's what friends are for," said Bethany, as she popped a Neutrogena makeup remover wipe out of Annie's dressing table drawer and set to work.

Just as Bethany whirled Annie around to see her fresh face, the doorbell rang. Annie whooshed out a breath, closed her eyes and took a moment to thank her friend.

Annie peered at herself once more then whispered yet another prayer that God's will be done in her life. *Now is not the time for wallowing in the past, Lord. Help me be the lady you created me to be. Help me honor your name in all I say and do.*

Just a quick reminder to keep her head on straight and act like a lady.

"You've got this," said Bethany. "I'll run downstairs and let him in. Don't keep him waiting too long."

James stood by the front door, praying. What was he doing here? He had never let any relationship get this far. If the few dates he'd been on could even be described by such an intimate term. Likely not. He hadn't ever let a woman into his heart. Had protected himself from such entanglements. He was already thirty-five years old and had managed all these years without risking anything.

The door swung open, but it wasn't Annie who stood there.

"You're not Annie." Well, that sounded stupid.

The tall blonde laughed. "You're right. Come in. She'll be down in a minute."

He had protected himself, yes. But he had been thinking of others, right? He didn't want anyone to be hurt. He didn't want a family to struggle because of losing him. He didn't want a group of siblings to have to go through what he and his siblings had suffered. His mind whirred with all the good reasons he had abstained from close encounters of the female persuasion. He had done the right thing, the thoughtful thing.

Then Annie floated down the stairway.

Every doubt evaporated in an instant. His mouth went dry, and his hands began to sweat. Then she smiled and his nerves calmed in an instant, his mind settled, and he took a step closer. As she stepped down to the floor, she advanced one brave stride at a time. He followed suit, until they finally reached each other.

"You look, I hate to say beautiful, that's too mundane. But wow, you look beautiful, Annie."

"Thank you," she whispered, her cheeks turning pink, which he found totally adorable. She looked like no one had ever told her she was beautiful. Incredible.

They stood there for an extended moment, lost in each other's eyes.

"I thought you two had reservations," said Bethany with the raise of one eyebrow. "Or are you just gonna stand there and stare at each other all night?"

James had to laugh at himself. Bethany was right. "She's right," he said, his grin spreading across his face. "You still wanna go out?"

"You bet I do," said Annie, her silken voice sending tingles up his spine. "I don't get dressed up like this very often and I want to take advantage of it. If I had no place to go, trust me, I wouldn't get all dolled up."

"Makes sense," said James. "And I'm pretty excited to be seen with you."

She giggled again and James felt his chest swell. This lady was good for his ego. She had agreed to go out with him. She smiled at him, and he'd made her laugh. *Lord, I could get used to this in a hurry.* Made him wonder if any other girl had had similar notions about him and he hadn't let himself see it. But then, he doubted that could even be possible. The dazzling magnificence of Annie Jo Parker could not be duplicated.

"Okay then, I guess we better get started," he said.

"I'm ready."

They made their way to the door, expressed their good nights to Bethany then James safely escorted his date to his SUV.

The now-familiar scent of vanilla filled his nostrils as he helped her up into his truck. He inhaled deeply but discretely, keenly aware of the soft skin from her touch that sent that now-familiar zing up his arm. The charge felt so strong it seemed his heart had been jump-started like a car battery.

Yeah, being around Annie Jo Parker stoked his coals, as well as his ego.

The evening started out magical. The drive into town, pleasant. They talked about the weather for a minute. They talked about the food at Cattle Baron. They talked about Bethany's modeling career, with no mention whatsoever of Dawn Somersby, then shared a few stories from their childhood. Easy, no-pressure conversation. Nothing special. Just normal exchanges between two people.

Annie let herself relax. She'd been nervous about going out with James Baldwin, especially since Bethany had shared his apparent angst about sharing his future with a woman. Any woman. One day she would ask him about that. Morbidly, she even wanted to ask him about dating Dawn. But not tonight. Tonight, wasn't about any of that. Tonight, was about getting to know the man James Baldwin had grown up to be. The man he was today. She wanted to experience this relaxed and low-stress atmosphere, for as long as she could.

A feeling she hadn't experienced with Austin, since high school. Dating him had been a nightmare. He had destroyed their friendship with his drinking and cavorting. It had been a year or more since she had seen him at church. But there her traitorous mind went again. With determination, she blanked Austin out of her head and let the peace of being near a man she could trust surround her.

A comfortable silence filled the space between them. But in the midst of the peace came an overwhelming urge to pray for Austin. She had no idea why, but the message had been loud and clear. *Pray, child. Pray for Austin. To avert tragedy, pray.*

I hear you, Lord. Whatever is happening with Austin right now, please help him through it. Please help him find his way back to you. I think he trusted you once. If he is in trouble, please show him a measure of mercy and grace. And show him and his dad how to heal from the loss of Austin's mother. Thank you in advance for what you are about to do. In Jesus' name, I pray.

"Everything okay?" said James, concern reverberating through his tone.

Annie's eyes popped open, and she turned in her seat to face him. *You're here with James,* she told herself, firmly. *Concentrate.* "Yeah, just praying."

"You don't have to be afraid with me, Annie. I promise. No pressure. I don't do that. Wouldn't do that. I want you to know that I respect you."

Oh my, he thought she was praying her way through this date. So not true.

"It's not that," she said firmly. "Really. I'm not afraid of you. But I have a friend who has been getting into trouble for a few years now, and the Lord impressed upon me just now to pray for him. I don't know what's going on at this moment, but I had to pray."

She wondered how James would respond to the declaration. She was on a date with *him* and praying for another man? True. What would he say? How would he feel about that? Her relationship with Austin had been a complicated thing. They went way back, lived on back-to-back ranches, had performed in rodeos together, had dated for a while—no matter that they had been the most tumultuous years of her life.

She had taken a chance by being honest with him. If he had questions about Austin, she would answer them. She had nothing to hide. Nothing to be ashamed of. But she really didn't want to get into all that. Not tonight. Not on their first date.

"Do you want to talk about it?"

A smile spread across Annie's face, and she silently thanked God for sending this compassionate man into her life. Maybe he was exactly what he appeared to be—the exact opposite of Austin. He had not accused her of anything, jumped to conclusions, or resorted to condemnation. Jealousy did not seem to rule his heart. So yeah, the total opposite of Austin.

"Someday, I'll tell you all about it. But could we just enjoy each other's company tonight? I appreciate having a date with a man I can be comfortable with. I'm so thankful to have met you. So pleased that you asked me out."

A man she could be comfortable with? There had to be a story behind that statement. But Annie had said she didn't want to talk about it. James had seen the pain in her eyes after she'd prayed. Somewhere along the line, a root of something had been planted in her heart. He couldn't discern exactly what that was, but it must run deep and hurt something fierce.

But he would not ask her about it today. They were, after all, on their first date. All the heavy stuff could wait. He decided he'd be praying for her though, and maybe pray for her friend as well. A male friend. James wasn't an ostrich with his head stuck in the sand. Just about everyone in their age bracket had experienced past relationships. He would not judge her for that. Maybe this guy she was praying for had broken her heart. Maybe he was just a friend she cared about. Again, he would not ask her about him tonight.

"I'm good with that," he said, as he took the exit to the restaurant. The traffic was heavy, typical for a Friday night. James didn't dare turn his head from the road, but he really wanted to get lost in Annie's eyes and search her heart. He really wanted to make sure she knew he was serious about not being a threat.

Whether she had saved herself for marriage or not, was none of his business. Tonight, she was with him. If she'd been abused, she would now be able to experience a clean, pure, transparent relationship with a man. If she had saved herself, all the better. Either way, he would make sure she knew that she was safe with him. He'd been raised to be a gentleman, regardless.

"Thank you," she whispered.

James barely heard her and when he glanced over, her eyes shimmered with unshed tears. Oh man, she had been through something traumatic. He could almost read the novel written in those gorgeous green eyes. He didn't know the details, might never know them. But he could show her the way a man should treat a woman. With God's help, she would heal. Whether they became romantically involved or stayed friends, she would know.

God, help me be gentle with this tender woman who loves you. Help me love her the way you love the church.

Their relationship was brand new. James realized that the prayer had been guided by Holy Spirit. He knew, without a doubt. For in the natural he would not be praying about marriage less than one date into a relationship. In the natural he would have run the other way the day he met her. In the natural he would hide behind work and stay single. Just like he had done in the past.

But God had impressed upon him to pray about loving this sweet spirit the way Christ loved the church, the commandment regarding a husband and wife. He would need to meditate on that. For a while.

James parked at the restaurant then raced around the car to open the door for Annie, so he wouldn't sit stunned behind the wheel and analyze his prayer until he had ruined the message. Opening the door for his date was automatic and would give his mind something routine to do. Small things added up to big things, and he wanted Annie Jo to feel special, to enjoy the evening without fear. If he played his cards right, there could be another evening like this in store for them. A few more hours in the company of Annie Jo Parker.

A look of surprise lit up Annie's face when James opened the door for her. "Thank you," she said. "I don't think a date has ever done that for me before." He had opened the door for her at the barn, but that hadn't been a date. And she might have thought he was just trying to impress her brothers.

Her statement had been a shock. If he'd learned anything, it was how to treat a lady. Even the most-rowdy cowboys he knew, said yes ma'am and no ma'am and opened doors for ladies. Who had Annie Jo been dating all her life?

"Well, get used to it," he said, with a wink and his best grin. "I know lots of gentlemanly ways. My mother, grandmother and nanny drilled all of us boys in the art of treating a lady the way a lady should be treated. I haven't had a lot of practice, I admit, but I've observed my big brothers. They both married incredible, godly women, and love them well. So, there must be something to it."

Once Annie cleared the door, James closed it behind her and stretched his hand out toward her. He grinned when she responded in kind. When their fingers touched, he laced them together. When she didn't pull away his smile grew. They stalled for a moment, and he took the opportunity to inhale the scent of fall. Early September could be warm in Lubbock County, but a hint of winter permeated the air. Maybe the *Almanac* had been right, and they were headed into a bleak winter.

Annie shivered at his side, so he slipped his hand out of hers and rested his arm across her shoulders, tugging her close into his side. "Cold?"

"A little," she said. "But isn't it magnificent out here? The leaves are already beginning to change, which is my favorite part of this season. Coming on earlier than the norm. But look around us, James. And do you smell what I smell?"

"Let me guess." He closed his eyes and inhaled, eager to please her. "Let's see. I smell burning fireplaces, wet leaves and smoked beef."

"Exactly," said Annie. "You have quite the nose."

"Right, people rave about it."

They chuckled together then moved toward the restaurant entrance. When they stepped inside, warmth embraced them. James inhaled the aroma of sizzling steaks, which made him hungry. He chuckled. "Just the smell of meat has my tummy rumbling."

"This is one of my favorite restaurants," said Annie, looking up at him. He listened, made eye contact, wanted her to know he valued her opinion. "My family comes here for special occasions. You know, birthdays, new births, dinners after a funeral, that sort of thing. Even some holidays. I have many happy memories of this place."

"Good to know," he said, approaching the hostess desk. He would file that information away and take advantage of it, one day. "Baldwin, reservation for two."

His own family had frequented Cattle Baron on special occasions, as well. A few came to mind. Matt's job with Southwest Airlines was a big one. Their mother would not have to struggle through another sleepless night while her son was deployed. The engagement dinner for his mom and Tommy. And the wedding feast after Kim and Christian married, a few years back. Perhaps he and this splendid woman would one day celebrate a ceremony of their own. Interesting. He had asked her out, she'd said yes. That's a good first step. But he was already wondering about a future with her. A till-death-us-do-part future. The thought settled in his heart, and he left it there to study later.

"Yes, sir, right this way," said the young girl to their right. She picked up two menus and two set-ups then led them to the back of the restaurant to a cozy booth.

They settled in, but before they had a chance to order, a middle-aged man stopped at their table. "We're honored to have you here, Mr. Baldwin. I'm Cody, the manager."

James shrugged and raised a brow then winked at Annie Jo. "We're happy to be here. Thank you." A public appearance, a spark of recognition, and suddenly it was an honor for Mr. Baldwin to dine in their establishment. "I'd prefer to dine in anonymity, please."

"Of course, sir. I'll make sure you are escorted out the back way, just signal when you are ready to leave."

"Thank you, Cody."

"Of course, sir. I'll send your waiter right over."

He left and James laughed again. "Sorry about that."

"Does that happen often?"

"It had become a nuisance in Nashville, but it's been rare since I moved back here. Guess the word is out. If you're uncomfortable we can leave."

CHAPTER NINE

Come quickly to help me, my Lord and my Savior (Psalm 38:22 NIV).

id she feel uncomfortable? James happened to be rich and famous, probably had to deal with this kind of thing all the time. It wouldn't change her life though, would it? They were friends. He probably had a different woman on his arm every weekend. She was merely a barrel-racer. People didn't stop her on the street for her autograph. The press wouldn't even notice her.

"You know what?" she said. "I'm fine. So, you're famous. The pressure is on you, not me. Let's enjoy our meal and pretend you are a normal guy. I know that's not true, though, even if you weren't rich and famous, you are far from normal. I've seriously never known anyone like you."

She ran down a mental checklist of all the men she had ever known. Only three made the top of her list as completely trustworthy—her father and her two brothers. But she had the feeling that she would soon be able to add James Baldwin to that list. He carried a confidence that set him apart. A vibe of goodness that rang true. Maybe she had already added his name to her short list of trustworthy men.

"From what I saw on your website, you could give me a run for my money in the famous department. I am very impressed with your accomplishments. What say we pat each other on the back then just enjoy our evening together?"

She held her breath. Had she gone too far? She liked this man. A lot. But she didn't want him to think she expected him to change his whole life for her. Well, maybe she did. But this was their first date. What must he think of her?

"I'm game," she finally said. Good, maybe he hadn't let notoriety go completely to his head. He seemed humble. Comfortable in his skin—and those luxurious clothes. She decided she really did like him, and his attitude.

"Trust me, I'm normal," he said, breaking into her thoughts. "Anyway, I have quirks and hang-ups like most people. Heck, I made my fortune because I was determined to make something of my life, build a life my father would have been proud of. Sometimes I miss him so much I can hardly breathe. And he's been gone twenty-five years."

The pain in his eyes made Annie Jo's heart break for him all over again. She had seen that same pain in his eyes when he'd shared part of his story with her family. It still hurt to think what that must have been like for him. What could she say? She needed to be real with him, to let him see her heart. To know she would try to understand.

"I can't imagine what it must have been like to lose your father as a child." Tears sprang to her eyes, and she couldn't look away.

"Are you ready to order?" chirped a young, blonde waitress, who seemed to have appeared out of nowhere.

"What?" said Annie Jo, shaken. She had forgotten where they were and had to tear her eyes away from James's gaze.

"Are you ready to order?" the young girl repeated.

Annie glanced at James.

"Sure," he said. "We probably should, don't you think, Annie Jo?"

She smiled a sad smile, nodding in agreement. "If we're going to eat, that's probably a good idea." It would take her a minute to shake off the gloom.

"I'm glad you agree. What sounds good? Or do you need a minute to review the menu?"

Annie chuckled, more herself now that she had broken eye contact with her date. She had drifted into a world that contained only the two of them, while the restaurant noises faded into the background. "I pretty much have the menu memorized. How about you?"

"Well, not memorized, but I know I want a steak, medium well, with baked potato and a salad with ranch dressing."

"You read my mind," said Annie Jo.

James wanted to thank the waitress. She had broken up the difficult moment with a lighthearted countenance. Maybe the talk about of his father's death would be over. Maybe they could move on and focus on each other.

He liked, very much, that Annie had ordered steak and baked potato, rather than a house salad with nothing else. He'd been irked by women who made a big show of eating light, then mooched off his plate throughout dinner.

He observed later that Annie Jo had consumed two dinner rolls slathered with butter. And she appreciated sweet tea. His kind of woman. She probably worked out, too. Would just about have to, to maintain her level of fitness and still have a hardy appetite. The thought amused him. Maybe they could work-out together, sometime. Wouldn't that be sweet?

"I've been racking my brain to think of a way to prolong the evening," he admitted, unwilling to let their date end with dinner. "I didn't research very well, I'm afraid, and I'm drawing a blank. Any ideas?"

Annie wrinkled up her nose in the most enticing way. Her thinking face? Maybe. Anyway, he entertained himself by watching the process unfold. When she smiled openly at him from across the table hope filled his heart. Aha, it appeared she had thought of something.

"How about a stroll through the park? There's a lovely one just up the street. Well-lit, tranquil, and boasts a body of water with a lighted fountain in the center."

"Sounds grand. Let's get going."

James paid the bill and allowed the manager to escort them out the back way. He'd been embarrassed for the extra attention earlier but getting out unnoticed could be a blessing. He didn't want to waste time with crowds of people. He wanted to be alone with the gorgeous champion barrel racer. Alone with Annie.

They made their way along 82nd until Annie said, "It's just up here on the right."

"Yes, I see it," said James. "I think I remember it from when I was a kid. If I'm not wrong Dad used to bring us here to feed the ducks."

"Most people feed bread to ducks, thinking they are being kind. Did you know bread is actually not good for them?"

"Is that right?" James internalized the grin that threatened to escape. It intrigued him that Annie Jo knew this little tidbit. He hadn't heard it before.

"Yeah, Dad looked it up once. He says that even the bread that birds don't eat is bad for them: Rotting bread, you know, that people leave behind, can grow mold. The mold is what makes ducks sick. But it also grows algae—which can kill lots of different animals—which in turn attracts vermin that spread disease to birds and humans alike. It's a bigger deal than most people think."

"Wow, I had no idea. It's a good thing we ate our rolls, then."

"Ha ha, you're a funny man."

"Just teasing a little. I am glad to know the truth, so I never harm another duck, for as long as I live."

"Okay, that's enough of the trivia," said Annie Jo, amusement lighting her eyes. James appreciated the effect and silently vowed to give her more reasons to smile. She really was a gorgeous cowgirl. He enjoyed being around her. Relieved that the girl he'd met in the novelty shop had been a genuine representation of the everyday version of Annie Jo Parker, he let his imagination carry him into the future. A future filled with sunlight, smiles, and the shining eyes of this lovely, godly woman.

It might take some getting used to, but he had wandered into new territory without a map, or a guidance system and he didn't want to lose his way. Didn't want to steer them in the wrong direction or rush into something he couldn't handle.

But being close to Annie Jo seemed as natural as breathing. His heart told him he had found his soulmate—possibly the only woman on earth who could fill that role.

"But if you ever need my sage advice in the future, I'd be happy to keep you duly informed."

Her voice broke into his musings, and he jerked back to reality, grateful he hadn't missed what she'd said.

"Good to know," he said, glancing toward her then back to the road. "I'll keep that in mind."

He was enjoying the banter, the inside jokes they were racking up. Enjoying her company, her wit, and her beauty.

James made the exit then parked. They sat in the car and watched the moon light up the water fountain. "It's really something," he said. "I don't think I've ever seen it at night. I should come here more often."

"There's a veteran memorial too, if you'd like to see it," said Annie.

"I would. But not tonight. I'll come check it out sometime during the day so I can read the names at my leisure. There should be a few of my relatives on the wall and some of my grandfather's service mates. It would take some time, I think. Precious minutes I don't want to distract me from you."

"How gallant," she said with a chuckle. "Come on then, let's walk a little."

Annie Jo had proven to be a breath of fresh air. God willing, he looked forward to a long, happy life with her. The foreign concept was beginning to grow on him. A lifetime with Annie Jo suddenly didn't seem like long enough. "Yes, ma'am. I'm coming around to get your door, so please wait."

They made eye contact and the message in her eyes filled him with hope. She looked, well, happy. Like opening her door could be construed as significant. The same look she had given him at the restaurant. He was still blown away by her innocent surprise.

The air felt crisp with a touch of humidity as they strolled down the concrete path. James stopped for a moment and looked up at a clear sky shimmering with stars. The clouds had separated and left a magnificent view of God's handiwork.

"Breathtaking, isn't it?" said Annie Jo.

"Almost as breathtaking as my date," said James, reaching for her hand.

"You're a funny man, James Baldwin."

"I'm not being funny, Annie Jo. I'm serious. Breathtaking."

In a quick motion, he slipped his hand out of her grasp and snaked an arm around her waist, hugging her to him. He noticed that a cinnamon scent had been added to the hint of vanilla, as he kissed the top of her head. The combination made him want to kiss her.

Romance filled the space around them as Annie Jo relaxed in his arms and rested her head against his chest. For the first time in his life, James Baldwin was falling in love. If he'd known it would be this grand, he may have tried it earlier. But then again, maybe not. He had never met anyone even close to the caliber of Annie Jo Parker.

I'm ready, Lord. Hold me up, teach me to love this lady with my whole heart.

Annie began to shiver in his arms. "I'm sorry, sweetheart," he said. "Come on, let's go. I'm getting really cold myself."

"You're leaving for my benefit, aren't you?"

A chuckle escaped his throat. "I confess. I can't deny it. You're shivering and I feel guilty. I wanted to stretch this out, but not at your expense."

"Okay, I give. I really am cold."

"Thought so."

James led Annie back to his Lexus SUV, opened the passenger side door and offered his hand as she climbed up into the seat. As he watched her, it occurred to him again that Annie had a tiny frame and sported hair that probably outweighed her head. He smiled at the thought. Watching it in motion in one of her barrel-racing videos had taken his breath away. One of the few where she'd let it fly, rather than lacing it into a long braid.

As she settled behind the seatbelt, James offered a wink, stepped back then closed the door. He made his way around the front of the truck, grinning all the way. Words would be an affront to the heart-stopping moment, so he kept his lips sealed and whispered a prayer of thanksgiving.

She's glorious, Lord. Really. Don't let me scare her off by moving too fast.

James pulled out onto 82nd Street then headed east to take the exit to North 87. Without warning, in the middle of a gentle tinkling laugh, the blare of a horn and bright lights in the rearview mirror shattered the peace. James jerked forward then slammed back against the seat. He grunted and glanced at Annie Jo.

"James, what's happening?" she said, the fear in her eyes pushing his anger button.

"Someone is trying to run us off the road. Just sit tight, I'll try to get away from him."

"Can you see a face?" Her voice trembled, which made him furious. But nothing could be done about it now, except try to keep her safe.

"No, only the high beams of headlights."

He sped up and managed to put a margin of space between the vehicle and his own bumper. A few seconds later, he yanked the wheel to the right and took the 4th Street exit. Tires squealed and the guard rail scraped the side of his truck, but he held on tight. A quick glance in the rearview mirror revealed that a pickup that looked to be some shade of red under the streetlight, sped past the exit and continued up 87 at a high rate of speed.

James slowed at the traffic light then came to a complete stop, waiting for it to change. His chest heaved with the rush of adrenalin. Breathing deeply, he turned to face Annie. Tears streamed down her face. Indignance rushed through him. Taking in the surrounding area, he decided to turn left at the light, then pulled off the road at the first opportunity.

Slamming the door shut behind him, he raced around to Annie Jo. When he opened the door, she fell into his arms, weeping, clinging to him. He wrapped his arms around her and held on. "It's okay, love. I've got you."

For a full five minutes, James held Annie in his arms. He consoled her as best he could, a helpless feeling making his limbs tremble. Who had come after them? Why would anyone care if he had a date with Annie Jo Parker? He could have some business enemies, he supposed, but they only wanted his invention secrets, not his women. And surely, Annie would have no adversaries. Not a sweetheart like Annie Jo.

When the shuddering slowed and Annie's breathing became more even, James held her at arms' length and said, "You okay?"

"I think so. Nothing like that has ever happened to me before. You?"

"No," he admitted. "But I'll be investigating, or at least get someone else to investigate. It's not something I'm willing to overlook. It feels personal and could escalate into something more dangerous, maybe deadly. I don't know, but I'm not taking any chances with your life. Or mine, for that matter."

There had to be a reason they had been tracked down and threatened. It felt like a threat, anyway. "Let me make a quick call then I'll get you home. You'll be safe, I promise."

"Who are you calling?"

"My security team is on call 24/7. We'll only have to wait about five minutes. You good with that?"

"Totally."

At ten-fifty p.m. a large, black Suburban filled with two armed and very hulky guards stopped in front of Annie Jo's house. The two men jumped out of the truck, displaying their weapons. They canvased the area while James and Annie approached the front door. Once Annie had unlocked it, she let the men inside, ahead of her and James. He noticed right away that she did not appear to have a security system. That would change, tomorrow.

The guards searched every room then checked the doors and windows. Once cleared, Annie and James entered the front room, still holding hands. He had been reluctant to let go of her. Keeping her close to his side gave him a measure of assurance that she would be safe.

"My men and I will be staying the night, Annie Jo," he explained, squeezing her hands, holding her attention with his eyes. "They can be trusted. I have placed my own life in their hands, many times. I'll take the couch, but Eric and Britte will not be sleeping. Please let me do this. Please. I need to know you're safe."

The thought of something happening to Annie Jo on his watch made his gut wrench. He had never had such intense feelings for a woman. And he did not contribute it to the circumstances, alone. He cared deeply for this lady he was just getting to know, to appreciate and admire. Maybe even love. He knew enough to recognize genuine affection, godly compassion, and a humble spirit.

He would do everything in his power to keep her safe.

When James squeezed her hand, Annie smiled up into his face, loving him, here, at the end of their first date. It had taken about an hour to solidify the feeling that had begun in the gift shop on Monday.

Her feelings grew as she sat back in amazement and absorbed each kind look, compassionate phrase, and occasional wink they shared during their date. He took her breath.

Then, in the face of danger, he had taken control, remained calm, and managed to save them. He had called in the troupes and made sure she arrived home, safe and sound. She had met the proverbial knight in shining armor and fallen for him, without question.

"Who's arguing?" she said, still shaken.

She managed a slight grin, but it was weak, and her lips trembled.

James draped an arm across her shoulders. "Should we call your father?" he whispered, close to her ear.

She closed her eyes and tried to think. What would her father do? Her brothers? Insist she live with her parents? Be run out of her home, for her own good? Would they become vigilantes? Storm the sheriff's office? Release the dogs?

"I live on a lot of acres," she said. "But out here, it's like a very small town where it would be impossible to keep a secret. They probably already know I was brought home under escort. So yes, I'll call him. Would you mind standing at my side while I talk to him? He'll probably be here within five minutes of the call."

"You'd have a hard time getting me to leave," said James, which instantly increased her affection for him.

Someone had come after them—whether as a target or a lark. But James had taken steps to make certain no harm came to her. He would stick with her, rather than bale at the first sign of trouble. *Thank you, Lord, for getting us home safe. Watch over us as we find our way along this new road, a road we share as more than friends.*

Annie's phone buzzed in her hand, and she jumped, visibly shaken. It was getting late, who would be texting at this hour? When she looked down, she breathed out a sigh of relief.

"Bethany," she said, showing James the face of her phone: *Staying in town tonight. You know, in case you and your hot billionaire want to be alone.* Annie's face burned with embarrassment and awareness.

James tugged her ever closer, which made her heart speed up. "Guess that won't be happening tonight."

Annie let herself lean against him, grateful for the strength of his presence, so moved, so affected by the warmth of his embrace. She silently thanked God that they would *not* be alone. She needed him close, but out of the range of temptation. She was scared, which made her vulnerable to affection. God had saved them from a tragic car wreck. That's where her focus needed to be. Grateful for his watch-care over them. Grateful no one had been hurt.

"Let's sit in front of the fireplace," she said. "If you'll get a fire going, I'll call Dad."

<h1 style="text-align:center">CHAPTER TEN</h1>

I pray also that the eyes of your heart may be enlightened in order that you may know the hope to which he has called you, the riches of his glorious inheritance in the saints, and his incomparably great power for us who believe (Ephesians 1:18 NIV).

"**G**ood morning, sleepyhead," said Annie Jo.

James blinked his eyes open, temporarily disoriented. But he came fully awake, fully aware, as he gazed into the same green eyes he had dreamed about. "Annie." Her smile made him want to wake up to her every morning, for the rest of his life. "Something smells delicious."

He had slept on the couch because the spare room had been claimed by Annie's parents. His security team had done their jobs, and patrolled the area around her house, while they slept.

Annie's father had demanded to stay, and James did not wish to stand in his way. Sam Parker had proven to be quite formidable, at least six foot seven in height and broad enough to challenge even Matthew Baldwin.

"Mother."

"Ah, so you don't cook?" He grinned, wondering how she would react. He didn't much care if she had cooking skills, they would manage, either way.

"I have limited skills in that department, I admit. I grew up on the back of a horse. Being confined to housework and stuck in a kitchen frightens me more than a runaway steed."

Annie Jo on the back of a horse sounded amazing. He would happily learn to cook if he could watch her ride every day.

"Point made. In that case, I'm thrilled that your parents opted to stay the night."

"Ha ha," said Annie, punching him in the arm. "Time to get up, buster. The bathroom is momentarily available."

"Here I go then."

He jumped up from the couch, inhaling bacon and what he recognized as scratch biscuits. Nothing smelled better than scratch biscuits in the oven. It had been ages since he had smeared butter and jam on one. "Yum," he whispered, as he turned the hot water knob in the shower.

But after breakfast, he would have work to do. Someone had targeted him. Or maybe even Annie. He needed to get to the bottom of this. Annie had been in danger, under his care.

And now, he would have to make a choice. Stay far away from her until the mystery was solved or not let her out of his sight until the guilty party had been apprehended.

The night before, James had arranged a meeting with his security team for ten this morning. He would decide what to do after that. But for now, he intended to enjoy bacon, eggs, and biscuits with the most delightful girl in the world.

***

Come Monday morning, James sat across his desk from Martin Hornsby, waiting for the details of his investigation into the vehicle that had rammed into the back of his SUV on Friday night. It would only be a few minutes more before the truth would out, they could deal with the perpetrator, and life could get back to normal. And Annie Jo would be safe.

"What did you discover, Marty?"

"Well, not a lot. But I'll tell you what I know."

"Please do." James tapped a pen atop the glass-covered desk, clicking away, until Marty focused on the pen, without saying a word about the case. "Oh, sorry," said James, setting the pen down. "I'm anxious to know the truth."

Marty shrugged then said, "We know you were hit by a red pickup truck."

"Marty." Irritation laced his voice. James had seen the red pickup truck in the glow of the streetlights. He didn't need Martin to tell him that.

"Yeah, sorry. Details. You were hit by a 2018 red dually pickup truck. Apparently, the body shop on Frankford remembered repairing that make and model on Saturday."

"Perfect. Call the cops and let's get this guy arrested."

Marty paused, uncertainty and guilt penetrating his words. James had heard that tone before. Less than good news was coming, he could feel it. "We don't know who the owner of the pickup is."

"Why not?" This was ridiculous. Wouldn't a repair shop keep vital information regarding the vehicles they serviced? Weren't there guidelines for such a thing? "Marty, what are you not telling me?"

Marty stood and began to pace.

James watched him for a moment, then circled around his desk and stopped in front of the private detective. Marty didn't look up until he plowed into James's chest. The frown on James's face must have loosened Marty's tongue, because he began to rattle on until James wanted to shake him.

"Look, it's like this," he began. "I spoke to the manager of the shop on Saturday afternoon. He said they did repair a red 2018 pickup that morning."

"I understood you the first time," said James, crossing his arms and glaring at Marty.

"Well, it seems a new guy got caught stealing tools provided by the body shop." The tremble in Martin's voice revealed he didn't have good news. If they didn't catch this guy right away, the coming weeks would be fraught with worry and danger—especially if the damage had been caused by someone aiming to hurt Annie or himself.

But getting to Annie would be difficult, James would see to that. He had the resources and the manpower to guard her day and night until the truth could be discovered. And, if necessary, the perpetrator put behind bars where he couldn't hurt anyone.

"They literally caught him on his way out the back door, arms loaded."

Martin paused then walked over to the window and stared out. When he spoke again, he kept his back to James, which tripled his annoyance. "According to the manager, the kid took a bribe. Whoever brought the pickup in for repair paid him off, to do the work off-book."

James could feel his impatience scale rising by the second. "And?"

Marty spun around then. "Mr. B, it would take lots and lots of man hours to trace the owner of every 2018 red dually pickup truck in and around Lubbock County. Especially since we don't have a license plate number and can't even be sure of which shade of red we'd be looking for. This is ranch country, after all. And that's if the owner was even from Lubbock County. We literally have nothing going for us."

James stomped over to his desk and lowered himself onto the chair, his hands balled into fists, frustration boiling in his veins. This sounded like a deliberate coverup. Unless they were dealing with a simple case of random bullying, which he highly doubted. An idiot who made a game of harassing other drivers on the road. A drunk or a kid on drugs who had laughed through the entire ordeal. At this point, they had no hope of nabbing the suspect. People became victims of drunk drivers all the time, without being a specified target. It could mean the danger had passed, for now, but also that justice would not be served. But what if it had not been random and someone came after Annie Jo again?

"I was hoping for more," he said, making eye contact with Marty.

Following James's lead, Martin took a seat on the other side of the desk. However, sun rays broke through the clouds and aimed straight for Martin's eyes, causing him to wince. "We'll keep digging, if that's what you want," he continued, his hand blocking the glare.

James pushed a button to close the blinds behind him.

"Thank you."

"But you think that would be a waste of time," said James with a nod, resting his back against his office chair.

"Honestly?"

"If we don't have that, we don't have anything," answered James, with a stern look. "I thought we established that a while ago. Is there a reason I should question your honesty, now?"

James observed Martin with a keen eye. He had made the move to Lubbock with James and been working for him for the previous eight years. He had no reason to doubt Martin's integrity, his methods, or his motives. Unless something had changed.

"No, sir. No way," said Martin, with a force James appreciated. He sounded sincere, maybe even shocked that James would suspect him of being less than forthright. "I would never intentionally cause you harm or give you reason to doubt me. I'm inclined to think you've been the victim of a prank. Maybe some rich rancher's kid who didn't want to get in trouble with the law. Honestly, I think you have much more significant matters to concern yourself with."

A frown creased his brow and James glared at the desktop in front of him. At this point, they had no hope of catching the punk who had put Annie Jo's life in danger. And James couldn't be sure if Annie was safe now, especially if this turned out to be the beginning of something more sinister. Something they might not see coming.

"I hate not knowing the whole truth," he finally said, tapping that pen again.

"Yes, sir."

"But I'll set it aside for now. To a point. Make sure five of our best guys are on call day and night, until the foreseeable future. I will send a crew out in the morning to upgrade the security at Annie Jo's house. Be sure to schedule a rotation of men to keep surveillance, round the clock, in a discreet location, until further notice. I don't want Annie to be frightened by their presence, but I'm not gambling with her life either. Do you understand?" James made certain to express himself strongly enough to leave no room for doubt. He was serious about keeping Annie Jo safe. Whatever that looked like, at whatever cost.

Martin stood to his feet. "Yes, sir. I'll inform the men immediately."

"I would appreciate daily reports," he responded, as a form of dismissal.

James and Martin had an okay working relationship, but they weren't buddies. He preferred to keep a definite line between boss and employee. He tried to be fair, but not too personal.

"Yes, sir."

Martin turned toward the door and James ejected him from his mind. He needed to call Annie. Make sure everything was okay at her house. Find out if anything more had happened.

Guide me, Lord. Help me stay alert and keep Annie out of harm's way.

***

Three weeks passed quietly, with no sign of an intruder, no odd phone calls or messages.

Annie Jo had begun to relax, accepting the premise that the accident had been the result of a prank or a careless driver operating under the influence of drugs or alcohol.

But now they faced a new concern. If the rumors could be believed, Austin had increased his consumption of alcohol and broadened his appetites to take in the red-light district.

"I'm worried about him, Dad," said Annie Jo. "I mean, I'm mad at him, but I don't want him to drink himself to death or die of some dreaded disease he picked up on the wrong side of town. Have you spoken to Mr. Anderson lately?"

Her father looked down at the floor. "You haven't?" Annie pushed.

"I'm ashamed to say it, but no, I haven't. I've been meaning to get over there."

The look in his eye made Annie wary. There had to be a good reason for Sam Parker to neglect his friend. Ignoring a friend in need was out of character for her father, so she pressed a little harder. "Do you know something I don't?"

Mr. Anderson had been her father's best friend since before Annie or her brothers had been born. Their families had been like extensions of each other. Even though it broke her heart to think she had been the reason for that connection to fall apart, she wouldn't take anything back. She did not owe Austin one single thing. Her lack of a relationship with the brute shouldn't cost her father a dear friend. So why would her dad not know what was going on at the Anderson ranch? She was almost afraid to ask.

When Sam looked up, his eyes shimmered with unshed tears. "Dad, what's going on? Has something happened to Mr. Anderson?" Alarm rushed through her. More bad news for Mr. Anderson could be devastating. He had already buried his wife and struggled with Austin's rebellion. How much more could he take?

"I don't know. I've been avoiding him."

Annie's brows shot up. What was going on here? Her mother joined them at the table. She sat next to her husband and slipped her hand in his. Annie recognized a gesture of support when she saw it. She had been observing her parents her entire life. They had a marriage like she longed for. They had loved each other through every storm, forgiven each other without keeping a record of wrongs. They had consistently walked the talk and had raised their children to do the same. A love unshakable, with God at the center. Something must be very wrong for her dad to turn his back on his friend. His best friend.

"Not because of me," said Annie, stunned. "It's been weeks since I've even heard from Austin. I don't want to come between you and Jake. Surely you know that."

Sam gripped Annie's wrist and rubbed his thumb on her forearm. "It's not you, baby girl."

"Should I believe that?" Annie knew her father well enough to know he would sacrifice anything for her, for anyone in their family. She draped a hand over his where it rested on her arm. She waited, a deep fold gathering between her eyes, waiting for him to disclose the whole truth.

"Well, it's not all you," he said, breaking eye contact. And of course, that couldn't be a good sign either. Sam had hammered it into their heads to look people in the eye when they spoke, a sign of being open and honest. "I don't trust myself right now. If I show up over there, I'm liable to punch Austin in the face. And we don't need that kind of drama. It could cost me my friendship with Jake, for good. I need to cool down."

It had been four whole weeks since Austin had showed up at her door and made a scene. Why would her father still be mad about that? She had gotten over it. What was he not telling her?

Sam's cell phone rang, buzzing and bouncing on the table. Annie glanced down at it. Sheriff Nelson? She kept her lips tightly closed but listened to every word, straining to pick up both ends of the conversation. Did Sheriff Nelson just say Austin? Okay, that did it. She was not going home to finish her chores or ride Bluebell or even stop for lunch until she knew the truth behind that phone call.

"Sure thing, Noah. Thanks." When Dad disconnected, he scrubbed a hand over his scowling face, his eyes full of hurt.

Annie felt her stomach lurch. "You have to tell me, Dad. I'm not a little kid anymore. And I heard Sheriff Nelson say Austin's name. I repeat. What are you not telling me?" Annie steeled herself. "Has Austin been hurt?" She couldn't spend all day guessing, he needed to confess what he knew.

"No."

Okay, so Austin hadn't been hurt, that was good. Mr. Anderson would be crushed if his son couldn't help around the ranch. He'd lost his wife suddenly with a heart attack that no doctor had seen coming. Jake hadn't done very well with the loss. Annie hadn't seen him or Austin in church since the funeral, and now her dad seemed unwilling to be supportive of his long-time friend, which seemed preposterous. Something must be terribly, terribly wrong.

"I'm listening," she finally said, braced for the news, but firm in her resolve.

Out of the corner of her eye, Annie saw her mother shift. She now stood behind Sam with a hand on each shoulder. Annie looked up. A tear traced a trail down her mother's cheek. Alarm shot through her, and Annie moved her gaze to meet her father's, once again.

"What gives?"

Sam looked into his daughter's eyes for several seconds. He had to tell her the truth, there was no way around it. But he didn't want to. He'd rather face Jake than Annie Jo, right now.

Austin had already shattered the family's image of him. Messed up the only chance he would ever have to become a percentage owner in the Parker ranch. Jake and Sam had talked about merging their ranches, since their kids had been in junior high school. That dream had died with Austin's insane behavior. And it could never be resurrected again.

"You went out with James on a Friday night, right? The night someone chased you down and nearly ran you off the road?"

"Yes, sir. You already know that."

Revealing the truth hurt deep in his core. He squirmed in his seat; but forced himself to look Annie in the eye. "Ahem," said Sam, forcing the phlegm out of his throat. "Sheriff Nelson says that Austin was arrested for DWI that night."

"Okay, that's nothing new. When we were in high school, he got away with driving under the influence almost every weekend. He's way overdue for getting caught."

His head hurt. She didn't pick up on what he was trying to tell her.

"He confessed, Annie Jo. Austin followed you and James to the restaurant and the park, then rammed into the back of him on 87."

There, he'd said it. Jake had confronted Austin at the sheriff's office, forced him to tell the truth. "I'm sorry I didn't tell you before; and now we need to tell James."

"Thanks, Dad. I really appreciate it." She stood all the way to her feet, ready to walk out on this ridiculous conversation.

"Now, wait a minute, young lady," said Sissy. "Sit down and hear your father out."

"Please, Annie," said Josh.

"Please," said Mack.

"Please?" said Sam, a question in his voice.

Sam held his breath and didn't relax even a little bit until Annie lowered herself back down. Steely silent, but she'd stayed. *Help me here, Lord. I really don't have a leg to stand on.*

His mind took him back to the last time he'd met with Jake…

"Come in, Jake," said Sam. While Sam let Jake in the front door, Annie slipped out the back. A good thing. Annie didn't need a reminder of Jake's son. Not this morning. She'd been through enough because of him. Sam couldn't imagine what Jake might have to say. But Jake had been his best friend for a big chunk of his life. He didn't want to lose him. But he also had a tremendous loyalty to his own family. It would take a lot of explaining for Jake to get under his skin, to redirect him away from filing charges against Austin. He longed for the days when the man in front of him had been strong in the Lord, whole in his family, and ready to help a neighbor in a pinch.

Sam and Jake sat at the kitchen table. Sissy served coffee and homemade cinnamon rolls then sat down next to her husband. They joined hands and waited for Jake to speak.

"I came to beg for mercy," said Jake. "For Austin."

"Why does he need it?" said Sam. "And why from me? From us?" It had to be more serious than Austin pounding on Annie Jo's door. Jake probably didn't even know about that little trick. So, why was he here today, when he hadn't darkened Sam's door for months?

Sam squeezed his wife's hand and looked Jake in the eye. This better be good, man.

Sam observed his friend. Sweat popped out on his forehead, he wrung his fingers together and had trouble looking Sam in the eye. This was not the man

Sam had grown up with, raced horses with. Not the man who had served as Sam's best man. Not the man who had shown up in the middle of the night when one of Sam's horses was having a difficult delivery. Not the man who had come over and sat with the boys when Sissy had to have an emergency c-section when Annie had been born.

The man who sat across from him today, was a broken man. A man who had lost his wife, lost his grip on his faith, and been embarrassed by his son's outrageous behavior. He had to ask himself how he would act, where he would be—if he'd lost the woman he loved, and had no children left that he could count on. He couldn't imagine it. Any of it. So, he let his friend plead his case and tried to listen with an open mind.

Sam reached for Annie's hand. She let him coax her back into the chair she had vacated. She let him guide her, disappointed with herself for crying and giving in. Disappointed with her father for letting Austin get away with reckless endangerment. Mad at herself for not storming out of here and getting to the man she loved. Stupid, that's how she felt. Stupid.

"I don't have a good excuse," Sam began.

"Okay, maybe I've heard enough," said Annie, ready to leave, again. Ready to head straight to James's house and then to the sheriff. "I'm not sure I even want to hear it. You do realize you let a man go free who rammed the back of a vehicle that *I* was riding in, probably drunk and laughing the entire time. You do realize he could have killed me, James, and himself. You get that, right?"

She sounded disrespectful, which had never been tolerated under her parents' roof. She was a little sorry about that. Her dad had raised her to respect her elders, to trust her parents to tell her the truth, and teach her how to live a godly life. So why hadn't he told her the truth a month ago?

"Sweetheart," Sam tried again. "I'm trying to tell you that Jake is a broken man. I agreed not to press charges *if* he kept Austin on the ranch, and away from you."

Annie fought the urge to roll her eyes. Like Mr. Anderson could *make* Austin do anything. He'd been running wild and free for at least a dozen years. It would probably take something disastrous to stop him, at this point.

She closed her eyes and tried to focus on her father's concern for his best friend. Tried to make herself believe that her dad believed he had done the right thing. Tried to breathe.

"I don't really know what to say to that," she finally said, blowing out a breath. "I can't imagine Austin obeying his father's edict. But I'd hate to see someone get killed before Austin is put in his place."

Sissy started to speak but Annie raised a hand to stop her. With a shake of her head and a pleading look, she tried to convey that the discussion was closed. Austin was out of control. The sooner everyone accepted that fact the sooner they might be able to slow him down.

"I'm going home now," said Annie. "Please give me some time to absorb the shock. And pray from me, because I have to tell James that my family ignored the fact that Austin put his life in danger."

She stood then and moved toward the door. Thankfully, no one followed her. No one said another word. When the cold, outside air hit her, Annie let the tears fall. She walked woodenly out to her truck, climbed up behind the wheel then robotically drove herself home.

CHAPTER ELEVEN

*You will be protected from the lash of the tongue, and need
not fear when destruction comes.* (Job 5:21 NIV).

Annie sat across the breakfast table from Bethany, sipping her second cup
of coffee. She'd been thinking about Austin, which made her stomach
gurgle with unrest, like a geyser just before it blew. But since learning the
truth, guilt had built inside her until the burden had grown wearisome.

There had been no repercussions for Austin running into the backend
of James's Lexus. One or both of them could have been seriously injured or
killed, if things had turned out differently. And it wouldn't have taken much
for the incident to end in a fatal crash. Just one slip of the wheel or one
wrong turn at high speeds.

A frown creased her forehead. Wrapped up in building a relationship
with James, she had let herself bury the matter. But this morning, it was
bugging her. A lot. She hadn't even told James that Austin had been
responsible for the damage to his SUV.

"Something wrong?"

Annie glanced up and smiled at her friend. She'd been missing her, of
late. Bethany had been on the road almost the entire time Annie had been
dating James. She'd been to Europe for three weeks and just returned home
the day before, still catching up from jet lag.

"Have I told you how glad I am that you're home?" said Annie. "My
parents insisted I stay with them while you were gone. I've missed you. I've
missed my house, my own space."

Bethany raised a brow.

"What?"

"I asked if something was wrong, and you started talking about me coming home."

"I am glad you're home."

"I believe you. But that doesn't tell me if something is wrong. You had a pretty deep scowl on your face. You know I can't stand not knowing stuff. So, spill your guts. Do I need to put Austin in his place?"

Of course, Bethany would connect Annie's frown with Austin. And, in a manner of speaking, she was right. Annie Jo felt guilty because of Austin, but he wasn't her main focus, never would be again. True, he had invaded their privacy not long before Bethany left for Europe. Made sense, she would think of him first. He'd been problematic for years, now.

But Annie Jo did not want to talk about Austin.

"We have a lot to catch up on," said Annie, with a grin. She fiddled with the handle on her coffee mug, swiveling the cup from side to side. She chuckled then glanced up at the sound of Bethany's voice.

"Not all bad news, huh?"

"No."

Annie felt like James's name glowed in neon lights on her forehead. Their relationship had grown by leaps and bounds while Bethany had been gone. But intermingled with the joy of a new love was the fury she felt with Austin and the sadness connected with the loss of Glory. Losing her best friend, her life-long, trusted barrel-racing partner, would sting for a while.

Bethany had grown up in the same schools with Annie Jo and Austin. She had witnessed the silly playground antics, as well as the acceleration from friendship to dating and its disastrous outcome. Annie Jo couldn't fool Bethany on any account, so she decided to begin at the beginning, take her time, tell Bethany the whole sordid, yet treasured story.

Following Annie's long explanation, Bethany winked at her, while something between a smile and a frown crossed her face. A myriad of emotions shadowed her eyes.

"Man, Annie, I don't know whether to hug you out of congratulations or hold you and let you cry."

"Just stay home for a while. I've laughed and cried so much in the past month I could use a good dose of normal."

"Speaking of normal, what do you have planned for the day?"

Annie wanted normal, really. But normal would have to wait. Today, Annie Jo intended to confront her father. And come clean with James. She had kept the secret as long as her conscience could tolerate it.

A whirlwind of activity had caused Annie to push the matter of Austin to the back of her mind. And now she had to tell James that she knew who had tried to run them off the road a month ago. She wasn't sure *I forgot* would cut it. How would he react to the news? Would he blow his top and tell her he couldn't be with someone who would lie to him, even a lie of omission?

"Let me set this Austin mess straight then maybe we can talk about normal," said Annie. "You do realize I'm going to have to get serious about practice, like tomorrow. The Taylor County Classic is scheduled for Thanksgiving weekend, and I've been acting like a schoolgirl with a crush. Did I mention that James is looking to buy the BB ranch?"

Bethany clunked the mug back onto the table and chuckled. "How in the world did that happen?"

"You wouldn't have believed it if you'd been there to see it. I was, and I can barely believe it myself. James spoke to Mr. B for about sixty seconds—and Mr. B smiled. Can't remember the last time I saw Mr. B smile." She had been totally impressed with James's negotiation skills. He had charmed Mr. B in record time. Witnessing the miracle had left a lasting impression.

"I'm not sure anyone has seen him smile in decades."

"That's probably true. Anyway, James has an appointment with him the Monday after Thanksgiving. He is really, really charming."

"And handsome."

"Totally." Annie remembered then that Bethany had told her more about James than James had told her—until lunch with her family. She had learned a lot about him, that day. It thrilled her to know that he loved horses, on a level to match her own. She loved that he hadn't bragged about his accomplishments or his racehorses or his famous family. So far, she loved everything about James Baldwin.

"Is he a good kisser?" Bethany broke into Annie Jo's thoughts. Annie turned crimson with the question, she could feel the heat in her face.

"We haven't kissed, yet."

"You what?"

"Yeah, but I have a feeling it will be well worth the wait. He's nothing like Austin, Bethany. Nothing. A total gentleman."

"Well then, maybe I'd better start praying for you. You won't know if you really like him, in a long-term kind of way, until he's kissed you."

"Greatly appreciated. I really want him to kiss me." And her face heated up a second time.

***

James formed a megaphone with his hands and shouted, "Go deep, Travis!" He paced in a small rectangle among the players who stood on the sidelines. No one sat on the bench this close to the end of a crucial game, especially with the promise of victory, at hand.

Mark released the ball, and it went soaring through the air, a perfect spiral. Travis jumped, both arms extended toward the ball, grabbed it then cradled it close to his side, a mere five yards from score territory.

"Stay inside the boundary lines, buddy," whispered James. As blockers did their job better than they had all season, excitement overtook all other senses. He didn't feel the cold, and lost any sense of his surroundings, as he focused on that one player.

The second Travis crossed the goal line the ref blew his whistle and both arms went straight up. A roar filled the stands, whoops and hollers, clapping and stomping.

The last play of the last game, and the Tigers had squeaked by the Hawks, winning by one point. Two sets of college kids from different faith-based churches out for a little fun. Serious fun.

The crowd left the stands and rushed onto the field, shouting as they high fived every player, slapped backs, and jumped around like little children. They had every right to celebrate.

The Tigers hadn't won a game against the Hawks in three years.

"Hey coach!" Travis called, his fist pumping the air. "Good game! Woo-Hoo!"

With two thumbs up, James laughed as the other players lifted their star running back onto their shoulders then carried him off the field.

Football. James had never thought he'd be involved in a team sport, much less be tagged as coach. The thought made him chuckle. It felt good.

Better than good. Amazing. Who knew? Well, his brothers knew. They had competed with one another throughout high school. Football for Matt. Baseball for Paul. But James had grown up a loner, a geek who got his workouts in a gym.

Now, God was using him to influence young men who would one day lead their country, their state, city, their own families. *Thank you, Lord, for pulling me out of my shell. For giving me a chance to live life to the full. And thank you for these boys who have welcomed me.*

Turning away from the fray, he searched the crowd for one face.

James hadn't seen Annie Jo except on Sunday mornings in three weeks. He'd been working non-stop to get ready for the annual, worldwide conference set for November first, in Paris, France. A mere twelve days away. He'd been preparing Sunday school lessons and participating in youth activities on Wednesdays and Fridays.

And Annie Jo had devoted six days a week to gearing up for the Taylor County Thanksgiving Classic. He had no idea it would take that kind of preparation for a barrel racing competition. But any championship required diligence and hard work. He did know that much.

They had, however, shared long talks over the phone, each tucked away safely in their own beds. More than once, he had fallen asleep with his cell still in his hand. Like a satin pillowcase, her words had soothed and comforted him, called to him, pulled him deeper and deeper into a fantasy that he prayed would come true. A home, a family, a life, with this enchantress.

Then he spotted her coming down out of the stands. She had sacrificed a Saturday to be here. Made him feel special.

Their eyes connected as he rushed toward her. When she smiled, he broke into a run. Man, she looked good. As he got closer, he realized she hadn't come alone. Josh, the second youngest, stood next to her, towering a foot above her. A broad grin filled his face.

James had been praying for a connection with Annie Jo's brothers, and this looked like the best progress he'd made so far. *Football.* He snickered again at the irony. His brothers would be proud. Maybe next year, he would invite them out to watch. He'd take a ribbing of course, but their approval would be worth it. He could almost feel Matt slapping him on the back, and suddenly wished he had invited them, today.

Next year resonated in his soul. Coming home, putting down roots, falling in love. *God willing, I'll buy Mr. B's ranch then offer Annie Jo a home. God willing, we'll build a life together. God willing.*

"Glad you could make it," he said aloud, switching his full attention to the beauty who had come to watch his guys play. He wanted to swing her around in a circle and kiss her full on the mouth, but not yet. Some things shouldn't have an audience. "Isn't it a great day?" The exuberance in his voice matched the bounce in his step. Winning a game of football could be exhilarating.

"Great day, nothin'," said Josh, with a clamp on James's shoulder. "That's an understatement. You led these guys to a win against the *Hawks*. I'm impressed."

If he had any claim to such an accomplishment, James might have been proud. But he knew that God had revealed every word of encouragement, every play that came to mind, every life lesson that had surfaced, after hours and hours of studying the playbook alongside the Bible. No, he couldn't take credit for today's win. Not even a little bit.

"Don't be, I have no idea what I'm doing," James confessed with a chortle. And he meant it. He had never coached football before and had only played with his brothers in the back yard. "God deserves all the credit. Plus, they're good kids, which is half the battle. Besides, I had a lot of help."

"Don't be so modest." Annie Jo slipped her hand around his bicep, and he felt the tingle all the way to his toes. He had to make himself *not* flex, just to impress her. "I hear really good things about your coaching style, mister. Positive and encouraging. The kids are pumped. If you could hear the chatter in the stands, your head would swell."

"Thank you for saying so." He rested a hand over hers and squeezed. She winked and his breath caught. *Thank you, God.*

His chest puffed out, full of gratitude and peace, as he and Josh gathered gear and stashed it into the back of his truck. A gust of cold wind grabbed at his cap, and he had to be quick to save it. But he didn't care, not really. The wind felt chilly, but it had blown back the clouds to let dull rays of sunshine break through. A fitting backdrop for this tremendous day.

Slowing down and now drained of the adrenaline rush, he shivered, suddenly hyper aware of the cold. Pushing remote start on his SUV, he turned to Josh. "I promised the guys pizza—win or lose. Can you stay in town long enough to join us?"

"You bet."

"Pizza Hut on 82nd."

"Got it. Go on with James, Sis, and I'll meet y'all over there."

James adjusted the baseball cap that had helped warm his head during the game as a plan came to mind. A repeat of the vision of Annie Jo on a horse, on their land, solidified his determination to purchase BB ranch and make it his own. The idea of them starting a family together rang true. James believed God had revealed the plan to him. If he'd heard right, his next step would be in the right direction. A step toward home.

A short caravan of five vehicles made their way down Quaker Avenue then up 82nd to the Pizza Hut. The same location where James had consumed the delicious pie as a child, when his father would bring them here on Saturday afternoons. They'd been a noisy group, full of excitement and joy, after playing in the park with their dad. A good memory he cherished and held close to his heart.

Much like now. He chuckled at the noise level when everyone piled out of their cars at the restaurant. He would add this day to an ever-growing list of stored-up treasures.

"They sound happy," said James, holding Annie's attention with his eyes, planning that first kiss. It needed to happen soon. Real soon.

"They have every right to be excited," she said. "You've given them a super good reason."

He shrugged, pulled the restaurant door open, and fist-bumped every player as they entered. His snug grip on Annie's hand felt like a lifeline. He hadn't fully realized how much he'd been missing her, until this moment. Time for another date as soon as they could work it in.

Her brother brought up the rear, so James pulled the door closed behind him. Up close, Josh could be intimidating. Tall and broad, like his own brothers. Six-four, if he remembered right. He wanted to stay on the good side of Josh Parker.

Being self-conscious and feeling like less-than-a-man, had been a concern for James, what with over-sized brothers of his own. And now, his girlfriend's brothers and dad were every bit as tall and broad. *Cut it out, man.*

Get a grip on yourself. God made you exactly how he wanted you to be. Get happy in the frame he molded you in.

A man's stature doesn't make him more or less of a man. Stand tall in your own shoes and keep your head up. He could almost hear his grandmother's voice in his head. He'd been internalizing her advice for many years and thought he had conquered his insecurities. Even so, the feeling still plagued him, at times.

The guys pushed four rectangular tables together, making sure everyone had a chair, then formed a line at the restroom door. For the next half hour, conversations stacked on each other, crossed one another, and blended into a cacophony of joy. The best sound, ever.

Moisture filled his eyes as James absorbed the goodness around him. Smiling, he reached for Annie Jo's hand beneath the table. She moved their joined fingers to rest on his thigh and hope roared through his body. *She seems to like me, Lord. And you know I like her. So much. I might even love her, already.*

He cleared his throat then coughed, hoping the sound would mask the scraping of chair legs as he inched closer to his girlfriend. *Girlfriend.* His first. And hopefully, his last.

Annie Jo glanced up at him with a mischievous gleam and he knew he hadn't fooled her. With a shrug and a wink, he settled in to eat pizza with one hand. Being accepted by her made him feel like a super-hero. He could eat one-handed, no problem.

Once the crew had gone through the buffet and drinks had been served, James tapped a spoon to the side of his plastic glass filled with Dr. Pepper, to get everyone's attention. "I'm so proud of you guys. You all played well today."

"Coach, coach, coach, coach," the team chanted in unison.

He sniggered at that then held up a hand to silence them. "Thank you," he said, again aware that God had led him through every play of every game, and thankful that no one had been injured. "Now, dig in and celebrate!"

It had been an exceptional day. Truly.

CHAPTER TWELVE

Do not be anxious about anything, but in every situation,
by prayer and petition, with thanksgiving, present
your requests to God (Philippians 4:6 NIV).

The peace shattered a moment later when the door slammed open, like the wind had gotten hold of it. Glass rattled and metal clanged. At the same time, Annie Jo dug fingernails into James's jeans, her features frozen in fear. Confusion and concern conjured up his protective instincts. Scooting to the edge of his seat, he paused, ready for a confrontation, when Josh shoved back his chair hard, and stood, glaring across the room.

What was happening? He followed Josh's stare to a muscular man who stood about six feet tall. Anger blazed in the man's gray eyes, barely visible beneath unkempt, long, dark-blond hair and a well-worn cowboy hat. The intruder stomped over and stood in front of Josh.

"This ain't your concern," he said, jabbing a finger at Josh's chest. "AJ has no business snuggling up to this clown. I'm taking her with me."

James sprang out of his seat, pulling Annie Jo up with him. He gently shuffled her behind him. He'd keep this stranger away from her, no matter what it took. A physical altercation didn't scare him. Judging by the tight grip she had on the back of his shirt, it seemed like she did not want to leave with the hothead, anyway. Her small body trembled against him.

Josh growled and his hands balled into fists. "What's wrong with you, Austin? Get out of here before I kick you out. I think you've caused enough trouble. If it were up to me, you'd be behind bars. Besides, Sis has moved on, so deal with it."

Austin. So, this is the guy Annie had been praying for, on their first date. Moved on? Had she and this character been an item? Seriously? She had called him an old friend of the family. But was there more to it than that? He'd been curious at the time, but the name hadn't come up again, so he'd let the subject drop. After this disturbing display, he'd have to ask.

And what did Josh mean by suggesting Austin should be behind bars? This was getting more and more curious.

Austin rushed forward then, fists flying. But Josh easily overpowered him, blocking the blows with little effort. In one swift movement, he grabbed Austin by the shoulders, twirled him around, and pulled his arms behind his back. With a firm grip, he ushered the angry man toward the door.

Stopping under the Exit sign, Josh turned and asked, "Take Annie Jo home for me?"

"Sure. I got her," said James. "You need any help over there?"

"Nah, he's just mad. I'll see that he gets home without hurting anyone, including himself."

Once the door closed behind them, the room fell eerily quiet. No one stirred for a full minute.

"Coach?" said Travis.

James turned toward him, forcing himself to focus. "I'm sorry, didn't see that coming. Everybody okay?" He looked up and down the tables, making eye contact with each man. Nods of affirmation came in answer. His team looked as puzzled as he felt. Thankfully, no damage had been done to the restaurant, and no one had been hurt. But he had no idea what to tell them. Didn't know himself, where Annie stood, or what his own role should be. He'd go after the guy without hesitation, if she gave the nod. Almost wished she would.

"I apologize too," she said, a soft quiver in her voice. He looked down and saw tears swimming in her eyes. The hair stood on the back of his neck. Something had happened to her that he knew nothing about. Made his blood heat up a little. "Austin has a hot temper."

The players pushed back their chairs in a synchronized movement, encircled the two of them, and offered encouragement and understanding. His heart filled with so much love he thought it might burst.

Thank you, Lord. Give me the nerve to ask what role Austin plays in Annie Jo's life. I care a great deal for her, want a future with her. But should I get out of the way and let her work things out with her old flame? The pounding of his heart cried 'no.' *Grant me wisdom and courage, Father. I place the matter totally in your hands.*

***

The drive to Annie's would take half an hour. James prayed it would be long enough for his nerves to settle, so he could voice the question that wouldn't leave him alone. He felt compelled to ask, even though he was afraid to hear the answer. His palms sweat and his gut churned.

No matter what she revealed, the thrill of a possible relationship with Annie Jo made him a little lightheaded, like he'd spent the last month twirling around in a circle with his arms extended to the sides. His brothers had played human helicopter with him on a regular basis when they were children. He could see them in his mind's eye, all piled in a heap on the floor, giggling like schoolgirls. He hadn't felt that level of freedom since his tenth birthday.

He glanced at Annie. She had turned sideways in the seat, one knee pulled up to her chest and her back against the door, watching him, and grinning. Not what he'd expected to see.

"What's on your mind, cowboy?"

He shrugged. "Just thinkin'." That look of affection in her eyes made him sweat.

"Watcha thinkin'?"

Despite the angst, he snickered, twisting his fingers around the steering wheel, grateful she had mellowed after the disruption in the Pizza Hut—and wishing he could.

"You can tell me, you know," she said, in the sexiest whisper he had ever heard. Oh brother. He would gladly give this woman his whole heart. Right now. No regrets. The twinkle in those beyond-green eyes, the tiny freckles that trailed over her nose, her glorious auburn hair. Her active, live-out-loud love for the Lord. Her vulnerability that filled him with a need to protect her and be there for her, forever. The accolades could go on for a while. Simply put, he was sunk. *Dear Lord, help me out here. I think I'm falling in love.*

100

"You make me dizzy," he admitted. Good grief. He must sound like a complete idiot.

Annie reached across the console and squeezed his bicep through his black leather jacket. Call him goofy, but he loved when she did that. "How delicious," she said. "I've never made anyone dizzy before. Tell you what, I'll give you Dramamine before we go riding, so you don't fall off. It'll be fine."

James laughed out loud at that, letting her sweetness wash over him.

He'd thought she would be shaking in her boots all the way home, worried about the other cowboy. But no, she seemed to be over it, like once he'd gone, the fear left with him.

Oh yeah, he could take a lifetime of this brave, charming, sweet, innocent woman, positive it wouldn't be nearly long enough. A few seconds of comfortable silence passed, and he decided to take a chance. He wanted to know more about her, more about her past, more about *him.*

He cleared his throat then put it out there. "Would you consider telling me about Austin? You know, someday." He shut his mouth and held his breath.

She removed her hand from his arm and his heart sank, just as his heartrate skyrocketed. Maybe he had asked too much too soon. Maybe it was too painful for her to talk about. Maybe he'd like to kick himself for even bringing it up.

A quiet sigh escaped her lips and he watched in horror as tears began to drip down onto her clenched hands. Perfect, he'd made her cry. *Way to go, JB. Now you've done it.*

Gently, smoothly, tenderly, he placed his large hand over her clenched fingers and said, "I'm so sorry. Forget I brought it up. It's none of my business, anyway." He said what he thought she'd want to hear, even though he believed the moron's (a term he rarely used, because it had always made his nanny frown at him) involvement in their lives, was very much his business.

When she didn't respond, or move at all, James started to panic. In one swift movement, he pulled off Highway 87, parked, leaving the engine running to keep the interior warm, then jumped out and ran to the passenger side door. As soon as it opened, he reached inside, unbuckled her seat belt and wrapped her in his arms. She snuggled there, her face pressed into his neck, her head on his shoulder, sniffling, snuggling closer. He held on tight, rubbing small circles on her back, mumbling, "It's okay, babe. It's okay.

I'm sorry. Please forgive me." Over and over until she stilled in his arms, shuddered out a breath, and pulled back to look into his eyes.

He thought he'd ruined everything that had grown between them. But the eyes that looked back at him were not angry. Sad, but not angry. He kept his lips zipped, waiting, afraid of what he'd done, what she might say. When she spoke, her words surprised him.

"Thank you," she said. "I haven't told you everything. My family loved and trusted him, and I just couldn't tell you the whole truth. It has been difficult for my family to think that Austin might be less than he appeared to be."

Her family must be acquainted with a completely different man than the one James had witnessed at lunch. There didn't seem to be anything noteworthy about the goon. Cocky and rude—not at all the gentle, romantic yet manly man his girl deserved. He shivered as a blast of winter-like air came sweeping through the open door between them.

"Gee, that wind's cold," she said. "Get in, before you turn into a popsicle. I'll tell you. I promise. No secrets. Thank you for caring. It means a lot."

"Yes, ma'am. I didn't mean to make you cry. I never want to make you cry." James didn't dare breathe, didn't look away. He really needed her to know he did not want to hurt her feelings or pry into her business.

Still wanted to hear the skinny on Austin, though. And he really wanted to kiss her. But he shook that thought off, knowing the timing would be all wrong. What would she think? That he was pushing himself on her? Being like Austin? Not even.

"I know. I *do*," she said. "I'm fine. By the way, thanks for destroying my makeup. I was trying to impress you. But this day did not turn out anything like I'd hoped."

"Sorry." Her makeup was of no consequence. A natural beauty like her didn't need paint. However, his mom had emphasized the right of a woman to look her best. Men could just wait for them and be glad God had created such a wonder for their eyes to behold.

Regardless, her heart mattered a great deal. It had been bruised and he wanted to massage it back to life. Wanted to love her so much that the past seemed like someone else's story. Just a tall tale that could never again disturb the calm peace of her soul.

"Shut the door, would ya?"

He smiled at this stunning, tiny woman he wanted to never let out of his sight. So, she wanted to impress him, huh? Well, the feeling was very much mutual. He wanted to impress her all the way to a promise of matrimony. His soul longed for it. His heart resounded with the truth as he pondered what their life would look like. What exceptional children they would produce.

"Well?" she said, shaking him out of his reverie.

"I'm goin'," he said, amused by her spunk. It seemed this sweetheart had a lot more in common with her mother than just her outward appearance. From what he'd witnessed, Sissy could command a room with just a tone and a look. A room full of big, strong men who could destroy her, with little effort. But her husband had raised his children to respect their mother and obey her. From his viewpoint, Mr. Parker would have confronted his boys before he would allow them to disrespect his wife. A fine husbandly trait. James wanted to be a trustworthy, loyal and protective husband, himself. The Lord had provided him with three great role models. If he were smart, he'd pay attention and learn from their example.

James felt taller and stronger and braver than he'd ever felt in his life, as he made his way back around the SUV. He climbed in, relishing the warmth, and sat angled toward Annie, waiting. He made a silent vow to let her tell the story in her time, in her way. And not interrupt with stupid questions.

He promised himself that once she finished, he would calmly drive her home rather than whipping a U-turn and going after Austin. He instinctively knew that the-poor-excuse-for-a-man had hurt *his* Annie. He just didn't know to what extent. Had it been a continual verbal assault like he'd witnessed today—or had the goon branched out and physically harmed this dazzling, sensitive woman, who owned his heart? Anger swelled within him, but he pushed it back down. Hard. *Be patient. Don't get ahead of yourself. Assault is still against the law, you know.*

He scrambled then, searching for a tissue. In the console, that's right. He remembered putting them in there the week before. Popping it open, he pulled out the small package and offered it to his sweetheart. Premature or not, that's exactly how he felt about her.

"Thank you," she said, a hesitant smile on her face. "You ready for this?"

"Lay it on me." Yes, he was ready for this, touched that she had decided to trust him. One day, his own complicated story would be revealed. He searched his heart, suddenly okay with that. Trust ran both ways. And if his future lay with this gorgeous woman, he didn't want any roadblocks to stand in their way.

Annie Jo accepted the offered tissue and blotted the last of her tears. She must look a fright, after letting a simple question throw her into a tailspin. But James's voice had been soft and tender, caring. He'd asked about Austin. Of course, he'd be curious after that scene at the restaurant.

She'd have to be selective here, though. Unveiling the life and times of the Anderson's involvement with her family could take a week. Austin's dad owned a ranch; his son rode the backs of bulls—because he liked it. A control-freak who got his thrills subduing thousands of pounds of muscle and rage. Not much different, in or out of the arena.

They'd grown up participating in the same rodeos, tirelessly competing, bunking down in horse trailers when the nights got late or windy or stormy. They'd been tagged a couple by both sets of parents long before either one of them had entertained such an idea.

"I'm not really sure how we even became an item. I just woke up one day and that's how people perceived us."

She wrung the tissue in her hands so tight it began to crumble. Avoiding his eyes, she kept her voice low and her head down. "Really. To me, he was just one of the guys. There were several of us, male and female, who grew up together and participated in rodeo events. But when Austin and I started winning on a regular basis, our parents encouraged the union. Saw partnership written all over us."

Another pause. She cautiously raised her head to look him in the eye, and offered the slightest shrug, as though there were no other words to explain Austin's claim on her.

"Did you love him?"

She heard, and appreciated, the hesitancy in the question. "No," she was quick to say. "No," she repeated with a little more force. "We tried dating off and on for a couple years, but." She paused without offering any further explanation. "Anyway, it didn't work out. I admit, I'd let him kiss me after an especially difficult win. More routine, than romantic. But there were no sparks. Not ever. I'm certain of it, now that I know what real sparks feel like."

She ducked her head, again. But she'd meant the words. Even though James hadn't kissed her yet, he did things to her that she'd never felt before. He made her heart swell, filled her with hope and wonder and joy. He oozed a tenderness that made her feel valuable, like a porcelain doll in the hands of a dollmaker. And in her world of rodeo, such a feeling was practically unheard of. Rodeo-riders were not delicate or soft. Even the reference seemed other-worldly.

"Hey, don't be shy about that," said James, bringing her around, reaching across to caress her hand. "I'm flattered. The sparks were so strong the morning we met, I had to turn my attention to the store clerk, to keep from pulling you into my arms and kissing you like we'd been together for years. It felt so natural, I couldn't believe it."

She let her best smile shine through. "Wow."

"Yeah, it might sound lame now, but I was a goner. Right then."

She giggled—certain her face had turned the color of pickled beets. But she held his gaze, relished in the admiration that looked back at her. Yeah, she'd never experienced anything remotely close to this feeling with that other man, the one who had humiliated her and smacked her around.

Their friendship had been strained, even before high school graduation. Then, for her anyway, their tenuous relationship had completely disintegrated seven years ago. Not a shred of their previous camaraderie had survived the fray. She just couldn't make him understand. *You can't have me and every other woman out there. You have no right to a piece of my dad's ranch. And you have no right to hurt me. I dang sure wouldn't give you the satisfaction of owning me. You're the most stubborn, hardheaded man ever born.*

He'd never truly wanted her, the way a man wants a woman, loves a woman, cares for a woman. No, he wanted to own her, but be a free man. He wanted to control her and establish a place for himself in her family. It seemed to have become his obsession.

"Anyway, things escalated, but not in a romantic way," she continued. "Austin took every opportunity to ridicule my racing technique, even after a big win. Like he'd groomed me and coached me and encouraged me. What a joke. But he never bullied me in front of our parents. He was very careful about that." She jolted at the memory, immediately assuaged when James placed his hand on her forearm.

A sad look passed between them. "He'd sneak behind barns and duck inside trailers to have a fling then accuse me of cheating on him. I repeatedly said no to physical relations outside of marriage. He didn't like that, even a little bit. Gradually, he became more aggressive, started shoving me around and stuff."

James jerked then and she rushed on before he could respond. "I wanted to tell my parents a long time ago. Really, I did. But I was struggling. I felt abused and totally alone. I didn't think they would believe that Austin would hurt me.

"And not until today, when Josh escorted him out of the Pizza Hut, did I feel I could have the full support of my family. Like they might listen. If you can believe it, I've been trying to get Austin out of my life for seven long years. I avoided the conversation for five of them, before I confessed to Mother that I would never give Austin my heart. Praise God, she didn't push for some big, long explanation.

"I had to come clean, somewhat, after our accident, when Dad told me Austin had confessed to causing it."

CHAPTER THIRTEEN

*Be joyful in hope, patient in affliction, faithful
in prayer.* (Romans 12: 12 NIV).

"Wait. What?"

Annie Jo sucked in a breath, as she realized what she had just said. She had meant to tell James the truth about the accident, but they had both been so busy. She hadn't kept it from him, on purpose. She just hadn't told him she knew the truth.

"Oh. I've been meaning to tell you." Fear snaked through her. This one fact could cost her everything.

"How long have you known?"

"Well, today is Saturday. Dad told me on Tuesday or Wednesday a couple weeks ago. I'm so sorry. I should have called as soon as I found out. I was just so angry, I wanted to calm down first. Then I. Well, there is no other excuse. I just got busy and didn't do it. I hope you can forgive me." She held her breath, watching the different emotions shadow his eyes.

"I can understand that," he finally said, even though a frown marred his handsome face. "But I'm curious about why no charges were filed. Austin is obviously running around loose. And he seems like a danger to others."

A calmer reaction than she had expected. But her explanation would sound just as lame as to why she hadn't called him. Sweat pooled at the small of her back, so she pulled both feet up into the seat to avoid the warm air that rushed out from underneath the dash. Yeah, today hadn't turned out anything like she had planned.

"You won't like it," she managed.

She hadn't told him the reason, but she could tell, instinctively, that he wouldn't like it.

He closed his eyes, and she wondered if he was counting. Only three seconds passed before he looked at her. She saw patience and concern mingled together, in that look. She would do anything to make this right. She'd been angry herself, so there would be no defense for her dad making a deal with Jake. And there was certainly no excuse that would hold water when it came to Austin. She would just have to do the best she could with the challenges as they presented themselves. She did not, however, want to lose James Baldwin.

"Look," he said, reaching for her hand. She grasped on to his like a drowning girl in need of a life preserver. "I can't pretend to be happy that Austin endangered your life and got away with it. Obviously, there is some family dynamic that I am not privy to."

She jumped in here, needing to set things straight.

"Oh, James. I don't want any secrets or grudges between us. My dad made a deal with Austin's father, who is my dad's best friend. He agreed not to press charges if Jake would keep Austin confined to the ranch. Dad is trying to convince Mr. Anderson to take Austin to a rehab facility. But, as you witnessed today, Austin isn't likely to obey his father or voluntarily go into rehab. It's a sordid mess, and I'm sorry I got you involved in the junk that complicates my life."

Annie Jo was crying again, talking like she thought he'd be better off without her. Austin could run into his truck ten times, and it wouldn't keep him from wanting Annie in his life.

"Whoa, stop right there." He shifted, leaning across the console, and spread a hand across both of her knees until she made eye contact again. He would not let her get away with that nonsense.

When she looked at him, he wanted to cry, too. She looked so stinking sad. So defeated.

"Babe, I don't give a hoot about my truck. I don't even care that your father made a deal. It sounds like he and Austin's dad are trying to help him. I understand how it feels to want to defend a family member, even a close friend. Sometimes our actions don't make sense to anyone else.

"And I'm not going to fight against those decisions, even if I don't agree with them. My truck is fixed, you are safe, and you're here with me. That's all that matters. My focus is on building a relationship with you. And I'll stand beside you, come heck or high water. Don't ever doubt that."

A hint of a grin lit up her face and James relaxed, just a smidgen. Moving forward, he would be on the lookout for Austin Anderson. He didn't believe for a second, that Annie Jo could trust him to leave her alone.

And if it came to that, he'd be there with his security team, to defend her.

Annie wanted to take James in her arms and never let go. But she knew this conversation wasn't over. There were still important matters to discuss.

"Are you for real?"

"If you pinch me, it hurts," he said with a grin.

"I think I love you, James Baldwin."

"The feeling is mutual."

With her heart hammering in her chest, Annie Jo beamed across the car at this incredible, handsome, loving, patient man. She would hold on to him with every fiber of her being.

For years now, every encounter with Austin had been a negative one. Why couldn't he just go away? Fall in love (if he were even capable of such a thing) with someone else whose daddy owned a ranch. Be happy in his own skin. Ride a bull to work out his frustrations. *Something*, anything, to keep him distracted.

Her story hung between them. She waited while James absorbed her words and hoped with all her heart that he didn't opt out of their budding connection—because she came with baggage. Because staying with her could mean trouble for him too. Hoped he could understand the position she'd found herself in, how trapped she'd felt. But then, he'd said he loved her. Even after she had shared her sordid, ugly story.

Maybe everything would work out, after all.

But no matter what James decided, she had two inciteful events on her side: (1) Her father and brothers had witnessed Austin's outrageous behavior on her porch and had all the details about his abuse; and (2) Josh had defended her in public against a life-long friend of the family.

The whole ugly truth had now been told and her family knew what she had dealt with for years.

The unpleasant scene at the Pizza Hut would serve as further evidence that throwing a fit on her front porch had not been an isolated incident. That Austin's issues had metastasized like a growing cancer. And just like that, he could cause an untimely death, whether he intended such a thing, or not. He had grown careless and reckless—a bully without a harness and a conscience that seemed to be napping.

She would deal with her family, be open and honest with them, from now on. She would.

But if she could just keep her grip on this handsome cowboy, she could count this year an especially great one. Never mind the seven previous years of bad luck, as though she'd smashed a relationship mirror and now tiptoed through the broken shards, trying to avoid getting cut to ribbons.

Just as he'd thought, Austin had abused this darling girl, to the point of getting physical with her. James had witnessed the verbal abuse, believed Austin would stoop low enough to push around a much smaller woman and still feel free to flaunt his talents as a womanizer. The very idea that she'd been mishandled made his blood boil. Suddenly, the damage Austin had caused to his vehicle was of no consequence. None, whatsoever.

A low growl escaped his lips, and he squeezed his eyes closed. Tight, tight, trying to control a surging impulse to turn the truck around, seek out the moron, and teach him a lesson. A lesson he would not soon forget.

James gripped the steering wheel with both hands, twisting and twisting, trying to decide what he should do. Confront the guy and stand up for his girl? Punch his lights out and watch him fall? Report him to the authorities? What heinous act would Austin have to commit for Annie Jo to file charges against him?

Although he had struggled with some insecurities about his less-than-impressive height, it hadn't kept him from training with his larger brothers, day after day, since he'd been big enough to lift a five-pound weight. He could hold his own in a fight, and would relish the opportunity to practice, with Austin as a sparring partner. He couldn't recall a time in his life when he'd been this angry.

"You okay?"

Her sweet voice brought him around. He didn't answer right away, but kept his eyes closed while he counted, slowly, to ten. It would take that long to trust his voice. Tears pushed against the backs of his eyelids.

When he looked over at Annie Jo, his imagination put pictures in his head of Austin's hands on her. Fury like he'd never known raised the hairs on the back of his neck and burned through his veins.

Shake it off, man. Before you get into deep trouble. With the law.

"I'm so sorry," he managed to say. A single tear slipped down his face, and there was nothing he could do about it. "I won't let him hurt you again. Not ever."

Her murmured "thank you" drifted across the cab of the truck and his ears barely picked it up. A quiet sentiment that broke his heart.

He reached both hands across the console and waited for her to place her smaller ones in his. He grabbed her with his eyes and said, "You have my word."

Gazing into the eyes of James Baldwin, Annie realized she had settled for the familiar with Austin, when she should have waited for her own champion. A man of honor, comfortable in his own skin, who'd been raised a gentleman, and appeared to be everything Annie had been educated to expect from a godly, loyal man.

Time would tell, of course. Time would tell all. But today, in this moment, Annie Jo Parker imagined a future with James Baldwin. A good, long, delicious future.

***

Another two weeks passed. The temperatures had dropped below forty, making November unseasonably cold.

On the Tuesday before Thanksgiving, James joined Annie's family for lunch, which had become a weekly thing with them. He felt grounded while in her parents' home, accepted and loved. His heart beat faster, just thinking about introducing her to his mom and siblings and their spouses.

This holiday would be the best he'd had in years. As a child, in Nashville, after his father's death, he had learned to let Tommy Churchwell into his personal space. A kind, compassionate, and patient man who had helped shape the man James had grown into. The man who had introduced James to equine therapy, which had made all the difference in learning to live without his dad.

James wanted to be that man for other youngsters.

Once the closing happened on the BB ranch and he had taken the plunge to find out if Annie Jo would be his wife, he planned to discuss incorporating equine therapy into the workings of his new ranch. He didn't know much about how to make that happen, but he could do research as well as the next guy. Hopefully, Annie would love the idea, too. It would give them something to look forward to, once she retired from barrel racing. Give them a purpose, even in the short-term.

The more he thought about it the more he liked the idea.

Once the table had been cleared and the dishes loaded in the dishwasher, Annie led James out the front door. She grinned as she walked beside him to his pickup truck, a purchase he had made since observing all the benefits a truck could afford him on a ranch. He had thanked her profusely for filling him in on the myriad of ways her family utilized said vehicles. They would make a cowboy of this tech genius, one day, she had teased him. He seemed to want to learn, and that thrilled her. She realized that ranching would never be full-time for him, but there would be a lot of activities they could share as a couple, if they were both into horses. Her dad and brothers had already volunteered to help him, in any way he might need.

Things were looking up in her world.

She had fallen hard for James Baldwin, and he seemed to feel the same way about her.

Standing next to said pickup, James took Annie's hand, pressed it into his chest and kissed her knuckles, the brim of his hat resting on top of her head. Her breath hitched as he lingered with his lips on her fist.

Seconds later, he straightened, and his words squeezed a single tear out onto her cheek.

"I'll be forever grateful we ended up at that novelty shop at the same time. I'm feeling things I never thought possible. In the past, I refused to let anyone get close, because I carried the loss of my dad like a dead weight around my neck. I didn't want to be the cause of pain for a wife or children. Like the coward I was, I sprinted away from women who wanted more than a date or two.

"And then God dropped you right in front of me, and suddenly I'm willing to endure any pain, any challenge, any roadblock, just to spend another day with you. I don't want to scare you, Annie, but I feel a powerful draw toward you. And I'm telling you now, after just a couple months, that forever doesn't sound like long enough to be with you. You set the pace, because we'd be engaged by now, if it were up to me."

Engaged.

The word hung in the air between them. Annie felt a tiny bit of alarm at the fact that she hadn't been alarmed that she'd just met James Baldwin two months ago, and he was already talking about marriage. If she were honest with herself, she'd been thinking along those same lines, herself.

In the years she had been linked with Austin, considered a couple by all the ranchers and rodeoers in the state of Texas and beyond, not once had she felt an urge to *marry* him. Marriage was a big deal. Huge. She'd expected it to take years to fall hard enough for a man to even think about marriage. But now…

"No pressure," said James, taking a step back. He seemed to have misinterpreted her hesitancy to respond.

Annie almost panicked. Her silence had given him the wrong impression. He was pulling away. *No!*

"James," said Annie, slipping her hand inside his leather jacket and tugging on his shirt, pulling him closer. "I don't feel pressured that way. More like I'm in a pressure cooker. If I don't turn the burner off the explosion will be epic. At the same time, I'm afraid to be away from you. Afraid the past weeks have been a dream and I'll wake up tomorrow and wonder if any of this is real."

A flash of Austin and the second-best barrel racer sneaked into her mind, but she shoved it right back out. Their break-up might have been her own fault. She'd had a tendency to treat Austin like a brother, since it was easier than getting into it with him about boundaries and long-standing morals she intended to honor. Now that she thought about it, relief might have been the chief emotion that had pumped through her when she'd caught him doing things with Sylvia that Annie never would have agreed to, right there in the horse trailer, while she'd been gone to get feed for Glory.

"I don't know if I'm making sense," said Annie. "But for a lot of reasons I trust you. I admire a man who recognizes that the past affects us, and we have to deal with the aftermath.

"I love the way your hair curls up in the back and hangs half-way over your collar. The color of your eyes makes me weak in the knees. Your voice sounds like melted chocolate to me. I love that you made something of yourself, to honor your dad. I can see the love of Jesus in those sparkling eyes. And if my dad and brothers wouldn't go ballistic, I'd take you up on that engagement thing. Today."

In the next second, James's lips captured hers, and she soaked him in like a dry sponge soaks up water. The most glorious kiss of her life. She wanted to never let go, never stop kissing him. She ran her hands up his back and raised up on tiptoe, to get closer to him.

If this was what Austin and second-best had felt, no wonder they'd given in.

James blinked twice before he realized what had just happened. Before the kiss or Annie's words had registered in his head.

He turned to find her watching him, one hand up in farewell. He'd been stunned when she'd run off. But when the dust settled, he was grateful for her quick thinking. He thought he'd been pushing it when he pressed his lips to hers. But she had responded, matching his passion with her own. He hadn't imagined that. He was sure of it.

He was grateful, too, that Annie hadn't merely tried to slow things down, but instead had slammed on the brakes and put distance between them.

"I'll text you," she said, smiling, a bright, can't-wait-to-see-you-again smile, then made her way up the steps and across the wide porch to the front door.

James shook his head to clear it, his grin still in place then reached for the handle on the pickup. He didn't open the door though. The glower on Annie's face made his blood run cold. But it didn't seem to be aimed at him.

The rumble of an engine caught his attention and he looked around for its source. There, near the barn they'd been in earlier, a four-door dually pickup, a red one, came roaring up the paved road that connected with the driveway.

Annie placed one hand on her hip, frowned deeper then raced down the steps back toward James.

"It's okay," she said, once she reached him. "Don't pay attention to anything he says. I can't believe he had the nerve to show up here, anyway."

Austin.

James let his instincts take over. He didn't think about it. Didn't ask permission. Just swept his hat off, pressed it into her back, and kissed her again like their future depended on this one kiss. And again, she kissed him back.

They didn't break away until someone harrumphed behind them. When James pulled back, he held Annie close with one hand and settled his hat back on his head with the other, positioned a little higher in the front, open for confrontation, or whatever.

He winked at his sweetheart then gently turned so they were both facing this new player. In his peripheral vision, he grew keenly aware of Annie's family, who had gathered on the porch.

James had no idea what to expect. If he would be fighting for his life, for the right to claim Annie as his own, or just what. But he didn't release his grip on her. If a fight was coming, he wouldn't back down. But he wouldn't start one, either. His brother Paul, the preacher, was non-combative by nature but had learned to handle himself in case a loved one, or anyone for that matter, might need his help. Especially after his wife had narrowly escaped becoming a rape victim. And then there was Matt, a fighter-pilot hero that oozed "don't push me; I push back." James had settled somewhere in between.

It took the guy about five seconds to climb down out of his truck and stomp his way over to Annie Jo and James, his eyes blazing.

"What the heck?" he yelled. He actually sounded surprised, like he had never seen them together before.

James pulled Annie closer, watching for any sign that this overly aggressive moron (yeah, moron) might come at her.

"What are you doing here, Austin?"

He would defend her to the end. And he would not be giving Annie up, ever, unless she made it abundantly clear that she didn't want him in her life.

"The Classic is this weekend. What do you think I'm doing here?" Austin barked at her. "And who is this clown, and why are you kissing him? Sheesh, Annie Jo."

This guy must have a couple screws loose. He'd seen enough in his short time connected with the Parkers, that Austin had lost the respect of Annie Jo's father, of Josh for sure, and maybe the entire family. How could the punk forget all that? Just act like he and Annie Jo were still an item. That he had some kind of claim on her. It didn't make sense.

James noticed the second that Sam made quick work of the space between the porch and Austin, who seemed comfortable making a scene in front of Annie's family. Like he expected them to take his side and run James out on a rail, tarred and feathered.

But James didn't budge or say a word, especially when Annie's nails dug into his side, and he felt her small body shaking. Poised and ready for action, he would wait for Sam to say his piece. If James's assistance was required, he would jump in the fray without hesitation. This blockhead would never lay a hand on Annie Jo again.

James had sized up the cocky cowboy when he'd come around the front of his truck. Of course, he was taller than James, but only an inch or so. But he wasn't as broad, and had reckless endangerment working against him. Long years of holding in crippling emotions had been honed to perfection. James could stand toe-to-toe with this guy and not break a sweat.

"Well!?" Austin yelled at Annie again, slapping his hat against a dusty jean-clad thigh.

James took one step forward as he smoothly and swiftly shifted Annie until she stood slightly behind him. Just as he opened his mouth to speak, Sam said, "Austin." Low and deep, his intent undeniable.

Sam Parker meant business. If Austin didn't listen to Sam, James had a feeling the guy would be picking himself up out of the dirt before he knew what hit him.

Two beats passed. Austin's attention shifted from Annie to Sam.

"Sir," said Austin, as his whole demeanor changed. James could see what Annie Jo had meant when she said Austin acted differently in front of her family than he had in private.

The small measure of respect surprised James. He had managed an about-face in a matter of seconds. Seemed to be a well-practiced move.

"I spoke with your dad earlier today," Sam continued. "We won't be able to accommodate you with the mare you inquired about last spring. I'm sure you understand."

Wow.

And just like that, the fuse that had lit up Austin's anger fizzled to nothing. Snuffed out before anybody got burned. The adrenaline eased out of James as well, as he watched Annie's father defend her honor, dismiss the boy, and clarify their future business association. In one short paragraph.

James almost, but not quite, felt sorry for the guy, as he positioned the well-worn cowboy hat back on his head and said, "Yes, sir." With one more, less-glaring glance in Annie's direction, he turned away.

Not until Austin had climbed up behind the wheel, backed out then started up the driveway, did Annie's grip on James's shirt loosen, even a little.

"You okay?" James kept his voice low, even, with more compassion than he'd ever felt for anyone, ever.

"I am now."

James didn't believe in fooling around, anymore than he believed in sexual relations before marriage. As hot as his blood flowed when Annie Jo touched him, he would not be breaking that vow.

He would never forget the night Matt had come home from a date, at sixteen, and called for a brother-bond. A pact they would hold each other accountable to—and not just because their mother, grandmother and youth minister had driven the point home, on several occasions. But out of pure, unadulterated fear. They all had sense enough to know they were not ready to be a dad, and they absolutely did not want to contract some indescribable, unmentionable disease. They all carried cell phones—and used them—all the way through college, when their resistance would begin to wear thin. No wonder they were all buff, they'd all lifted a ton of weights, year after year, until God introduced each of them to the love of their lives.

James was lifting still. Waiting, for what, he didn't know. Scratch that. He'd kissed Annie Jo Parker today. Had fallen all the way in love with her, without shame or regret.

The standards he lived his life by would remain in place—but his willpower would definitely be stretched to the limit.

Sam stepped closer to them, and James moved to the side so Annie could see her father.

"Annie?"

"I'm okay, Dad," she said. She let her father cradle her in his arms. "Really. He's delusional. Thank you for putting him in his place."

James took in a calming breath. He had been privileged to see the beginnings of restoration for Annie Jo and her family.

Sam released her, still holding her at arm's length and looked into her eyes.

"I'm so sorry we ever doubted you. I had no idea who he'd become. I mean, hearing about it and seeing it in person are two very different things."

"Shhh," said Annie, stretching up to place two fingers on her father's lips. "It's okay. You thought Austin would be part of this ranch one day. He did a good job of keeping the ugly out of your sight. So, in light of that, I'm a little glad he showed up here today. He kinda forgot to put up the front he's worked so hard to master."

James watched with interest as the big man let tears slip down his face. With intrigue, as Annie's mother and two brothers encircled Annie and her father. With an even greater depth of compassion, as this strong family wept together.

The question came to him: How long had the charade gone on? How much humiliation had Annie suffered at the hands of a less-than-honorable cowboy? Without her family's knowledge. His heart broke for her and all that she had endured.

He stood by silently, uncertain what would be expected of him. Should he slip away quietly, and leave them to heal their wounds, in private?

But starting the truck would be disruptive, so he waited. For a while. A full five minutes.

When Annie stepped out of the circle of her family, she looked straight at James.

"I'm sorry you had to see that."

"I'm sorry I didn't meet you first."

CHAPTER FOURTEEN

I will praise God's name in song and glorify him
with thanksgiving (Psalms 69:30 NIV).

THANKSGIVING DAY

James parked in front of the Parker's house at eight-thirty on Thanksgiving morning, eager to spend another day with Annie Jo. Their first holiday together. They had texted the day before, all afternoon and into the night like junior high students with their first crush. He'd met with his family to explain that he'd invited a girl for Thanksgiving dinner. He chuckled, remembering the pats on the back, the startled looks and squeals from his mom and sisters.

"I love her, Mom," he'd said. "You will too."

He blew out a breath and made his way to the front door. As he reached for the bell, the door swung open from inside.

"James," said Mack. "Come in. Annie's in the kitchen with Mom. Go on back."

"Thank you, Mack. Happy Thanksgiving."

"You too."

Mack clapped James on the shoulder as he passed and hope filled James's heart. He felt accepted, even though he had just met Annie two months ago. Two months that had changed his life, elevated him onto some unnumbered cloud that made everything look perfect and rosy and surreal. But he had no intention of looking for flaws or trying to figure out how he got so lucky, or how long it would last, or question if this could be *the* relationship, the last one he would ever need to have. He wanted more than he'd ever asked of a girl, er, woman, and more than he'd ever asked of himself.

"Happy Thanksgiving, Mrs. P. Annie. It smells so good in here. Mom's house smells about the same way. You ready to meet my family, Annie? There's a lot of them, so I hope you're ready for that."

Annie giggled like she was ten.

"What?"

"Nervous much?"

Yeah, he was nervous. He hadn't brought a girl home to meet the family. Ever. Part of him was glad everyone would be home at the same time. And part of him hoped Annie wouldn't go screaming from the room, inside the first hour. All of them at once could be a bit overwhelming, even for him, and he was one of them.

"Look, my family will love you. I promise. There's just a lot of us. And I've never brought a girl home before, so they're going to be curious, and probably tease me a little. At least you already know one of them, so maybe that will help."

Annie stretched her arms around James's waist. "Don't be afraid," she said. "I'm not. It'll be fun. And you're right, I admire Paul and the work he and his wife do for the Lord."

"I'm glad you feel that way. So, you about ready? I promised Mom we'd."

"I'm ready," said Annie, with a wide grin that made his heart start hammering. How had this happened? He was standing smack-dab in the middle of his own personal miracle. And he'd be forever grateful.

Annie hugged her mom, grabbed her purse off the kitchen counter then stepped into the great room. Standing in front of the television to get her brothers' attention, she said, "We're off. I'll be back by four. Get your nap and be ready to work."

"Aye, aye, Captain," Josh and Mack said, in unison, with a salute in her direction.

"Yeah, yeah. Very funny. I'm not kidding."

Mr. Parker, waiting by the front door, said, "Annie, don't worry. I'll make sure the boys don't sleep through their chores."

"Thanks, Dad." On tiptoe, she planted a quick peck on her father's cheek.

"Sir," said James, as Sam released Annie Jo. Ever mindful of the fact that he'd been accepted into Annie Jo's family, welcomed, even though he'd been afraid he wouldn't measure up. Afraid he would mess up and lose Annie Jo forever. At the moment, he felt engulfed with humility and gratitude.

Good grief, Baldwin, get a grip. You're being pretty sappy, here.

Sam man-hugged James, and the gesture brought with it a wave of longing for his own father, and a warmth that melted the doubts he'd had about fitting in with this amazing family.

"Have fun, kids," said Sam. He let go of James with a look of understanding that buoyed him up and put a confidence in his step that meant more to him than a standing ovation at a tech convention. A feeling of home that encompassed more than just a father's hug.

"See you this afternoon."

"Yes, sir," said James. "Thank you."

"You're welcome."

"Bye, Daddy," said Annie, reaching for James's hand. "See you later."

James grasped hold of Annie's hand like a lifeline. The feel of her hand in his gave him a focal point, so he wouldn't break down and cry like a baby. How could a man be totally aware of the gaping hole left in his heart at his father's death and yet be so full of love at the same time? A miracle. It's the only explanation that fit the scenario.

James pulled up in front of the house at 106 Arrowhead Drive at 9:45 a.m., killed the engine, and made his way to the passenger side to help Annie Jo down. She looped her hand through his arm as they started up the sidewalk, and his heart filled with pride and love and eagerness.

They walked toward the house, slowly. He took the time to tell her what this place meant to him. About the happiest years of his childhood. Then suddenly, they were standing at the door.

"It's a long story, Annie. I'll tell it to you sometime."

"I look forward to it."

James rang the bell and opened the door at the same time.

"Mom, we're here."

Catherine came out of the kitchen wiping her hands on an autumn-patterned apron with a welcoming smile already in place.

Annie stared at James's mother. She did not look the least big haggard or disheveled, the way Annie's mom always did on Thanksgiving morning. She wore a spotless *white* jumpsuit with a long, sheer covering decorated with the deepest colors of fall, the same pattern as the apron tied around her waist. Her shiny blonde hair hung in a long braid, draped over one shoulder. Only a few strands had succumbed to the graying process. Her skin appeared flawless, which made her look more like James's sister than his mother. She greeted Annie with a dazzling white smile that Annie would have thought had been reserved for movie stars, and a warm hug that brought tears to Annie's eyes. When Catherine pulled away, Annie felt captured by her deep blue eyes that also seemed to hug her. When they'd come in the door, Annie had been super curious about the interior of this magnificent home, but when she met Catherine the stuff that surrounded them didn't much matter.

"I've got a few minutes to spare," said Catherine. "Come on in. James and I will give you a quick tour if you're interested in that sort of thing. We wouldn't want you to get lost. It'll be easier before everyone gets here."

A light, tinkling laugh, reminiscent of a fairy, floated out of Catherine's mouth and Annie felt like she was standing in a palace, in front of royalty. So different from her parents' ranch house, which was clean and respectable—but nowhere near the grandeur of 106 Arrowhead Drive.

Annie glanced up at James, afraid she would be under-dressed and wouldn't fit in. Afraid she would say the wrong thing or do the wrong thing. She felt like a country bumpkin, like a cowgirl at a gala where everyone else wore a ball gown.

"Mom, I think I smell something," said James, scrunching up his nose. "Why don't you check while I show Annie around."

The look on his face made Annie want to hug him. He'd read her concerns and come to the rescue. She relaxed against him and let him support her with his arm draped across her shoulders.

"You know what?" said Catherine. "I almost forgot it was time to baste again. You kids go ahead. We'll catch up later."

James steered Annie away from the kitchen, back toward the great room and said, "This is the great room. As you can tell, Mom prefers an open concept."

Annie stood still, taking in everything around her. To her right and up two steps stood a dining table that would seat twenty guests. Its dark wood with medieval like chairs had been set for company and stood in front of a massive bay window.

Directly in front of her and down two steps, a great room, quasi-octagonal in shape, had no ceiling until the top of the second story. Mauve colored leather pit couches, two of them, and four cream-colored armchairs with matching ottomans took up most of the space. She noticed the room did not contain a television set, whereas she'd had to stand in front of theirs to get her brothers' attention. The thought made her smile and wonder what this family did for entertainment. The mansion had been situated on what might be a five-acre estate, all perfectly manicured, but without barns or any sign of animals. She marveled that her family's ranch was a mere fifteen-minutes away; yet seemed worlds apart from this estate.

How had James ever gotten involved with horses? Not a single deer head had been mounted in this home, no peacocks squawked from the barnyard, and no chickens pecked the ground outside the back door. She felt sure of this point, even though she had yet to see a back door. At her parents' home, you could see the back door from the front door.

She shook her head and tried to pay attention as James walked her through the massive home, full of grandeur and antiques and champagne carpeting. She'd been impressed, she had to admit, by several unique features she hadn't previously seen in anyone's home. She admired the open concept, with a wide staircase that led up to a second-story landing that filled three sides, like an indoor porch. The landing contained row after row of movies, shelf after shelf of books, and oddly enough, a restored antique barber chair had been placed up there, for no particular reason that she could discern. If she didn't pay attention, her mouth would be hanging open and she'd be drooling like a fool. It was a sight to behold—like a homey museum, if such a thing were possible.

On the opposite side of the great room the entrance to the master bedroom beckoned them. It stood to the right of another raised platform that contained a full-size organ at one end and a grand piano at the other. Maybe this was the answer to the entertainment question.

"Should we go in there?" said Annie in a whisper of awe. She was curious, for sure, but did *not* want to catch Tommy Churchwell in his underwear—or worse.

"Let me check." James stepped inside the open door. "Tommy? You in here?"

Annie heard Catherine from behind them. "Tommy is up at Mrs. Applebee's, James."

Catherine approached, chuckling, wiping her hands on a cup towel. "You know Mrs. Applebee. She's not about to inconvenience Canyon security on a holiday when Tommy is just a few doors down—and never tells her no. You're welcome to look, my dear, especially upstairs in the study. It's very unique. Anyway, I'll get back to the kitchen. Make yourself at home."

"Thank you," said Annie. "I'm curious about the study, now." She stepped inside the master bedroom and was stopped in her tracks at the sight of an imposing, life-size portrait of Catherine and four children. All dressed in immaculate white, they posed, not with stoic faces, but with telling looks of personality that glowed through each one of them.

"Tell me who's who," she said, staring at the portrait.

"Okay." James pointed to the mother. "This is Mom. Obviously. The tallest boy is Paul, the oldest."

Annie was mesmerized. Paul was the spitting image of his mother.

"This is me. This is Matt, the mischievous one."

"I can see it in his eyes," said Annie, with a chuckle.

"He's the largest of us all now, but still the most fun and relaxed, despite his deployments for the Navy. Anyway. This is Brooke. As you can see, she and I have Dad's coloring and darker hair. And Kimmie hadn't been born yet."

"You're all so perfect."

"Angelic, in that picture," said James with a laugh. "No telling what happened five minutes after they turned us loose."

Continuing the tour, they began with the study that sat at the top of a winding stairway, just beyond the large portrait, inside the master bedroom. The study contained a double, back-to-back desk, leather sofa and chair, and every wall had been filled top to bottom with books. Double French doors opened out onto a small patio that overlooked an enormous garden area and swimming pool. She gasped at the picture-like perfection of the gardens, so far removed from her mom's vegetable garden, it stunned her. She stared at the view so long, James finally gripped her elbow to get her attention.

She looked up at him, eyes filled with tears.

With alarm in his voice, James said, "Annie. What's wrong?"

"Nothing," she said, smiling through her tears. "It's magical here, James. I feel like I'm in a fairytale, complete with a palace and grounds and my own Prince Charming. I must sound ridiculous to you."

She shrugged and looked down at her feet.

"Annie," said James, his voice deep but whisper soft. "If I'm Prince Charming then you are my princess."

Eyes wide, her head popped up. He gently brushed away a tear with his thumb, and his touch ignited a fire inside her.

"But how?"

James pulled her in close and wrapped his arms around her.

"Sweetheart, a house is just a house without the people living inside it. The Baldwins have worked hard and been financially blessed. But we're just people, with hang-ups and hardships and heartaches—just like everyone else."

He held her at arm's length and looked at her with so much love she thought she might swoon at his feet.

"Without you, the stuff and the money, and even the horses, don't mean anything."

"Oh, James," she started. But he covered her mouth with his own and she snuggled into him, just in case her legs gave way and she'd need him to hold her up.

Magical.

As they made their way through the house, Annie counted five bedrooms, the master being the only one at ground level. The third story above-ground consisted solely of a game room, with a shuffleboard, a full-size basketball court, a ping-pong table, and closets filled with shelves of every toy imaginable. It must have been an adventure to grow up here. The entire floor contained floor-to-ceiling reinforced windows on three sides that overlooked the Olympic-size swimming pool.

James led Annie back downstairs then through a short hall that opened into the kitchen on one side and a stairway that took them to yet another level underground. On one end a bedroom and kitchenette had been furnished for a live-in maid, whom Catherine had given the rest of the week off to spend with her own family. James explained that the downstairs room was where the family nanny had lived, when James was young. But she had since passed on.

James then opened a door that led into the theatre room. It contained a drive-in theater-size movie screen and plush lounging chairs with cup holders. Large, framed posters of vintage films filled the spaces on the walls. A pool table beckoned at one end and a phone booth from days gone by stood in one corner.

"This room was my personal favorite," said James, with a sigh. "I discovered John Wayne movies in here. And lots of other cowboy flicks. I wasn't born into a ranching family," he mused, "but I love everything about it. It took the practiced art of persuasion to talk me into leaving Tennessee and my horses."

Annie touched his forearm and smiled up into his eyes.

"I'm so glad you did," she whispered.

James looked down at her and she read hunger in his eyes that she knew must be glaring from her own. She raised up on tiptoe and gripped his biceps. Pausing there, she silently invited him to kiss her. When he lowered his head and their lips touched, Annie drank him in. She'd been kissed some, but never like this. The kisses they had shared before had been delicious, but this one set her skin on fire. Even the earlier kiss on the balcony that had weakened her knees paled in comparison. Maybe it was the solitude of the underground room, a special place for James. Or maybe she had invited him to kiss her deeper, longer.

Whatever it was, they needed to dial it back a notch before things got out of hand. She could hear the voice inside her head but kept pushing it away.

Just when the heat got to the boiling point, Catherine called down from upstairs.

"Tour's over, kids. Come mingle with the family."

Annie pulled away, breathing hard, but laughing. "She has good instincts."

"It can be annoying," said James. "But I'm actually grateful right now, if you know what I mean."

"Pretty sure I could guess. Come on, let's go, before we get into trouble."

"Yes, ma'am."

James called up that they were on their way. Annie followed him, still glowing. She touched a finger to her lips and smiled.

CHAPTER FIFTEEN

"Very truly I tell you, whoever accepts anyone I
send accepts me; and whoever accepts me accepts the one who
sent me." (John 13:20 NIV).

"**Y**our family is amazing," said Annie Jo, as she and James headed back toward her parents' ranch. The day had flown by, filled with good food, laughter, and a little ribbing.

Apparently, James really had never brought a girl home to meet the family. Puffed her up a little bit.

"You think so?"

"Don't you?"

"Well, yeah. I guess. We're like most families, I suspect."

Annie didn't think so. One, they lived in a mansion on an estate. Two, the mother had lived in the spotlight as a career concert pianist, most of her adult life. Three, the oldest son was a preacher with seemingly unlimited resources. Four, their stepdad was a down-to-earth veterinarian who loved his wife, all of her children and his daughter, unconditionally. Five, one of James's sisters was a heart surgeon, the other an attorney. And six, James owned his own security/software company and several winning racehorses.

"I don't think so, Tim," she said, quoting Al from the sitcom *Home Improvement*, with a roll of her eyes. "And I can't believe you're related to Samuel White! My parents adore him and contribute to a few of his charities. I have to be honest with you, James, when you pulled up in front of that mansion, I was instantly intimidated."

James scoffed. "Really? I felt the same way at the ranch."

Annie laughed out loud then. "We're a pair, aren't we?"

"That's my goal," he said.

When he winked, Annie felt heat creep up her neck and burn her cheeks. So far, she felt like they fit perfectly together. And Bethany had been right. Annie had felt a future with James come to life in his kisses. Passionate, but with set boundaries built of love and respect. Alluring yet gentle. His kisses left her wanting more. She could no longer fathom a life without James Baldwin at the center.

She had been loved more in the past two months than in all the years Austin had tried to force her to be his girl. What a joke. How she ever considered such a union, boggled the mind.

James may have come from a more polished background than her—and she'd love to see him in a pair of Wranglers and a western shirt, sans the tie and western cut jacket—but she really, really liked this cowboy.

She wondered what it would be like for them to spend three whole days with her family. Especially since Austin and his dad were sure to be in Abilene, as well. All she could do was pray about that situation then trust God, her dad, and her brothers to keep James safe. She did not trust Austin Anderson as far as she could throw him.

They pulled up beside the barn at 3:45 that afternoon. It was already buzzing with activity. They would need to get on the road by five the next morning in order to offload everything and make the first round of competition.

Annie jumped down out of James's truck, almost stomping on his feet. He'd come around to open the door for her.

"Oh," she said, "I'm gonna have to get used to being around a gentleman. And not just when we're on a date."

James grinned and tipped his cowboy hat. The new addition to his wardrobe added more sex appeal than she'd thought reasonably possible. He wore it perched on the back of his head so she could see those chocolate brown eyes. *Whew.*

She had been around cowboys her entire life, but not one of them set off fireworks in her tummy like the tantalizing man standing in front of her.

"Point me in the right direction. I want to help."

He had removed his custom cut jacket, left his bolo behind and rolled up the sleeves of his no-telling-how-much-it-cost dress shirt, to just above the elbows. Annie stared at the muscles that pulled his shirt taut and rippled down his forearms. The wind had mussed his hair just enough to make it look like he'd planned it, and his five o'clock shadow sucked the air out of her lungs. She swallowed the lump in her throat.

"You okay?" he said, eyebrows raised in question.

A slight shake of her head and Annie could think again.

"Uh. Yeah. Sure. Right this way." She cleared her throat to re-set her vocal cords then continued. "There's a checklist on the wall, right over here."

She was amazed she could get the words out, her throat suddenly bone-dry. They passed a galvanized tub filled with ice and bottled water. Despite the cold, a body got thirsty working in the winter, just like it did in the summer.

During the hot months of the year, however, they kept water and Gatorade on ice. The loss of electrolytes could be dangerous. And this dry country could prove sweltering, and suck the salt right out of a body, before a careless cowboy knew what hit him.

Annie grabbed two bottles of water and passed one to James. She quickly uncapped the second and sucked down a third of the refreshing 8.8 pH water, infused with electrolytes, for taste. She could do this. Nothing to it.

"Okay," she said, feeling more like herself. "Here's the board. See, there are three checklists. We use a whiteboard, so we can rub off the checkmarks from previous trips and fill in the blank squares with new ones for the current trip."

Mack walked up behind Annie and rested his chin on top of her head. "How was dinner at the Baldwin mansion?" he said, in a goading tone.

Annie stiffened. She could feel James watching them. Was this her brother's way of saying he had looked up the Baldwins, and wanted James to know it? Not that she cared, one way or another. 'Cause no matter what image Mack had conjured up regarding the Baldwin family, Annie had spent the entire day with them—and knew they were good people. Wealthy, yeah, but good. Money had not corrupted them. And the few stories she'd heard today had convinced her that money had not protected them from hardship, either. They had stuck together as a family and developed an unbreakable bond. Their faith had kept them strong, so when the storms came, their house had withstood the onslaught against them.

"Mighty tasty," said Annie, not giving him anything to work with.

Josh came up beside her, retrieved a dry erase marker and checked off the last item on the first list.

"You've been busy," said Annie.

"Yeah. We're recording a couple bowl games. Maybe we can watch them on the road tomorrow."

Sam came around the corner of the barn then stopped when he saw the gathering at the white board.

"You're back. Good," he said. "I thought you might want to practice some before it gets dark, little one. What do you think?"

Annie looked up at James. "Wanna come?"

"Very much," he said. "But why don't I help Josh and Mack finish up here first? I'd like to get familiar with the equipment and the way everything works together. I really want to understand. Could I catch up to you in a bit?"

Annie beamed when her brothers both dropped their jaws and witnessed the smile of appreciation that spread across her father's face. James had impressed all three of them, just by being himself. He had an inquisitive mind and a strong work ethic. Two things they had never witnessed in Austin Anderson.

Good grief. Quit comparing Austin and James. There is *no comparison.*

"All right then," said Sam. "Josh, Mack, show James where everything is and answer whatever questions he might have. James, we'll meet you out at the arena once the equipment is loaded. Sissy has made up the guest room for you and we'll have supper once all the chores are done."

"Yes, sir. Thank you."

Annie skipped over to James, raised up on tiptoe and kissed him on the cheek. "You're amazing. Have fun and I'll see you out at the arena."

When Annie approached him, James pulled her into his side and let the scent of her hair fill his senses as she pressed a kiss to his cheek.

When she slipped away, he followed her with his eyes, until she disappeared around the corner.

A large hand clapped him on the shoulder. He turned to see Josh grinning at him. "Follow me. We should be able to whip this out in about an hour. It's a matter of rote learning. Repetition. Anyway, it's not hard. Just requires muscles, effort, sorting and stacking. You'll see."

Mack went one way. Josh and James went the other.

James relaxed a bit when Josh didn't comment on his interaction with Annie Jo. Maybe the huge, protective brothers were getting used to the idea of James and Annie as a couple. He sure hoped so, because he wouldn't allow himself to think of a life without Annie Jo in it. The fact that she was in his life at all, still amazed him. The mere thought of a lifelong partner had once sent him running for the hills.

No more. His heart belonged to Annie Jo Parker. For a lifetime. He held onto that hope with his whole being.

Once the lifting, sorting and stacking were done, James better understood what it took to get a barrel racer and two ropers on the road and ready to compete. The equipment list had been long and included everything from harnesses to Band-aids. They packed more horseshoes than tires and more liniment than lassos.

Steeplechase racing had been a far cry from a working ranch. James had enjoyed the formality and societal positioning that came with Steeplechase racing, at the time. But this ranching lifestyle, the sheer exhilaration of combining brawn and brain, made him wish he'd known about the benefits, years ago. He suddenly felt reborn. A part of something special. Something no amount of money could buy.

He loved his family. He really did. But he had always felt a little outside the box with them. Like he had a gene that grew sideways, or something ridiculous. His success in security and software had filled his bank account to overflowing. But until he'd observed, then participated in, a working ranch, sweat and laughed and wrestled with two brothers on a whole new level, something inside him had been dead. Today, in the course of one afternoon, that something had come to life.

He had an appointment for Monday afternoon to see the BB ranch. He'd made the appointment on a whim, not long after he'd met Annie Jo. Suddenly, owning the ranch next door to her felt imperative. Urgent.

Mack came up behind him. "Ready to watch her run?"

James turned to face him. The image he'd had of Annie on the back of a horse, her hair flying behind her, was about to come to be manifested in real life. The thought sent a shiver up his spine. He closed his eyes and sucked in a breath.

"So ready."

Josh, Mack and James stood in a row on the lower rail of the arena fence. James kept his eye on Annie and prayed. Anything could happen at any time. He knew as much from being an owner with a stake in Steeplechase races.

He knew it because he'd lost his father at age ten.

He knew it because Austin had put Annie's life in danger, and still remained a threat.

He knew it because the devil and his minions never let up. Ever. And they hated, absolutely hated, all born-again believers.

Bad things happened to good people every day, but James wasn't about to stand back and hold the door open for any of them. Not today. And especially not when it came to Annie Jo Parker.

The three of them stood along the side view fence. James observed three barrels set up in the middle of the arena, a gate at the far end, and Annie Jo sitting tall in the saddle, to the right of them. Mack explained the set-up while James listened intently, though in continual prayer mode.

"Okay," said Mack. "The idea is to stay in the saddle, race around the barrels, a clean run, without bumping, scraping or knocking over the barrels. She'll be racing against the clock, fast enough and clean enough to beat every other competitor. That's the goal."

Mack pointed at Annie then to the first barrel. "There's 60 feet from the starting line, called the scoreline, to the first barrel. Then 90 feet between the first and second barrels. The distance increases to 105 feet from the second to third barrels. Then she'll open up all the way at the end, to get across the last 25 feet to the gate at the back fence.

"It takes a tremendous amount of concentration—hours, weeks, months, and usually years to become a serious contender. Annie Jo is currently the reigning national champion. We're very proud of her. And you know what? I personally believe that practice alone doesn't get the job done. Without heart and soul and a sincere desire to be a champion, it wouldn't come together. To develop an uncanny rapport with her horse. A sync so incredible it's difficult to put into words."

Mack stopped speaking then and James could feel his eyes staring at the side of his face.

James turned toward Mack, but only because Annie had not begun her final practice run.

"I assume you know about Glory."

"Yes."

"AJ and Glory were practically inseparable from the time Glory was born. Annie was six at the time."

"Is there a message in there?"

"Look, AJ is quite taken with you." He held up a hand when James started to say something. "I'm not here to threaten you, man. Just asking you to be sensitive. I don't think she has completely grieved the loss of Glory. It could mess with her head, ya know?"

Just then Annie Jo thundered around the first barrel. James held up a hand toward Mack and nodded, but kept his eyes riveted on Annie. Seeing her ride in person? At least a hundred times better than his imagination.

The practice run went fast, so fast, and he felt himself fill with euphoria, the adrenaline so intoxicating he could hardly breathe. It was glorious. Thundering and dusty and extraordinary.

He was hooked. In love with a barrel racer, who loved barrel racing.

CHAPTER SIXTEEN

*Rescue me, Lord, from evildoers; protect me from
the violent* (Psalm 140:1 NIV).

Black Friday dawned cool, but clear. A good sign. If the weather held, the arena at Taylor County Expo would be perfect. It would be an educational day for James. He had never been to a rodeo and looked forward to witnessing each of the events Josh had told him about at dinner the night before. He loved horses and he'd been the only one in his family to take a professional interest in them. Not that animals and technology had much of anything in common. He could thank Tommy Churchwell, his veterinarian stepfather, for introducing him to their magnificence and the calming effect their larger-than-life presence had had on his life.

The family had moved to Nashville, and been there a little over a year, when James's older brother Paul had helped James confront the agonizing grief surrounding the loss of their dad. They had blamed each other, blamed themselves, for his death. They'd been kids, Dad had a brain aneurysm. The boys had played zero part in its formation or its eruption. But the three of them, Paul, James and their dad had had a heated argument the morning their father died. Their last words had been said in anger.

True or not, it had *felt like* the hostile words had brought on enough stress to kill their father. The notion had been incorrect on a scientific level but had seemed true enough. It had been a lot to deal with. A heavy load for a kid to carry.

Tommy's plan had been genius, really. He knew horses, and he knew James, a tender-hearted brainchild who needed a non-traditional form of therapy. So, he introduced them to each other. James and horses. The bond had been strong on day one. James's healing began to manifest itself by the end of day two.

Tommy bought James his first horse.

James built an empire and was still buying horses.

But not rodeo horses. And not barrel-racing horses. He had a lot to learn. And wanted the amazing Parker family to teach him. Wanted personal, up-close-and-personal, lessons from AJ Parker, herself.

Today, he would get his first full exposure to competitive barrel racing. He would have a spectacular view and the emotional support of AJ's family. It had happened quick and gone deep. He could feel the root sprouted in his heart. If he could find the equivalent of romance Miracle-Gro he would stock up. A lasting relationship with Annie Jo Parker felt right. She could be the answer to years of anxiety, speculation and fear that had plagued him. He hadn't thought it possible.

Then, in the course of a few short weeks, he'd fallen so hard for a girl, he dared hope for a future. A future with a family. His heart told him he was right. His head told him to take it slow, make sure this was real and not some whirlwind romance that would fizzle out as fast as a West Texas dirt devil.

Someone knocked on the guest bedroom door as he pulled on his second boot. His thoughts sped forward to the present day. His first rodeo.

"Breakfast is served, cowboy."

Annie. Just the sound of her voice set his heart to pounding.

"Coming."

He crossed the room and pulled open the door. Suddenly, he had no saliva and his tongue stuck to the roof of his mouth, as if a spoonful of peanut butter had grown there, overnight. Her smile beckoned him, her eyes twinkled, and her hair begged him to touch it. Man, he wanted this girl to be his.

"Cat got your tongue?" she said, grinning like she had a secret.

James tried to swallow. No spit. None. So, he returned her smile and stepped out of the guest room. It took a minute for him to recover.

"More like a lioness," he mumbled, rubbing his damp palms down the front of his jeans.

Annie laughed. A carefree, unfettered chuckle that lit a fire inside him. They walked side by side to the dining room, their fingers brushing. He wanted to clutch her hand in his but didn't have the confidence to be so forward in front of her family. Even so, he had to concentrate, in order to keep his hands to himself.

Rather than wrap his harm around Annie Jo's waist, he focused on the smell of bacon and coffee, the sound of her brothers teasing one another. Anything to distract from the magnetic draw of the girl at his side.

The tactic worked. Somewhat. He managed to relax, to a degree, and pulled an oak dining chair out for Annie then lowered himself in the chair next to her. There, he'd done it. No one could accuse him of acting untoward.

A quick glance over the country fare made him think of his grandmother. She had always gone out of her way to keep family bellies full, which further insured that he and his brothers held to a regular workout schedule. Grammi had often said that feeding the three of them was akin to feeding an army.

Breakfast at her table would be much like the dishes set before him now: scratch biscuits, fresh-squeezed orange juice, bacon cooked to the consumer's preference, some floppy, some crisp, a large bowl of fluffy scrambled eggs, homemade jam, some peach, some blackberry, fresh-brewed coffee, ice-cold milk and *real* butter—no plastic substitute would do. He chuckled at the memory. He missed Grammi. Would miss her always, until he saw her again in heaven.

"What's funny?" said Annie, poking him with her elbow.

"I was just remembering my grandmother. This breakfast looks like she set the table. She was a special lady, who loved to feed people. A nice memory. I miss her."

Josh said, "I know what you mean. We had the same grandmother."

The next little bit passed with sharing grandmother stories, some funny, some sentimental, until Sam set his napkin atop his plate and stated the obvious next step. "All right, boys, let's double check everything, one last time."

"I'll load the luggage," offered James, realizing everyone probably had assigned duties they had performed, year after year. But he wanted to help and thought the mere fact that he carried heavy bags and loaded them might relieve someone else of the duty, and free them up for more important tasks.

"Great," said Sissy. "That will give me plenty of time to take care of the kitchen and pack some lunches. Thank you, James."

"Yes, ma'am," he said with a grin, aware once again that he had pleased Annie Jo's mother.

"I'll load Bluebell," said Annie Jo. "We need to have a talk, anyway."

"Let's get started then," said Sam, pushing back his chair and standing to his feet.

An hour later, two trucks and two trailers had been double-checked and hitched, and the short caravan headed east on Highway 82. James and Annie rode with Sam and Sissy, with Bluebell in the trailer behind them. Josh and Mack were not far behind, with the luggage, each of their horses, and all the tack the men had loaded the day before.

"Are you nervous, Annie?" said James, a safe, respectable distance from her, lawfully strapped in, and itching to reach for her hand. Not with her mom and dad in the front seat. No way.

"I'm not sure nervous is the word. I get all tingly inside, for sure. But I feel ready. I know Bluebell is ready, so I'm excited for both of us. Of course, there are no guarantees. But I'm not afraid."

She paused then and smiled that gorgeous smile, but he detected mischief in that look, too.

"Not my first rodeo," she said with a wink.

"Very funny," said James, even as Sam chuckled from the front seat.

"Very amusing," said Sissy. "Just don't get too cocky. You don't want the Lord to humble you in front of a big crowd, do you?"

"No, ma'am. I certainly do not."

She sounded contrite but winked at James again, and he got the feeling that humility had kept her on top of her game through the years. That she came prepared but not arrogant. So special and unique. He'd never even imagined anyone like her existed in the world. She wore her performance garb, a stunning turquoise cowboy hat, a shimmering silver-studded western-cut shirt with pearl snaps, form-fitting jeans and boots the color of her hat. This outfit, though stunning, had been enhanced by the wearer, not the other way around. For even in plaid flannel, worn jeans and scuffed cowgirl boots, Annie Jo Parker oozed confidence and remained stunning.

She had captured the dark auburn tresses of her hair in a long thick braid that hung over her shoulder. Her large green eyes held his gaze and he longed to kiss her—thoroughly.

The trip took a little over two hours. They made one pit stop along the way, swapped childhood stories, laughed, and solidified the romantic feelings that had begun a mere two months earlier. Two of the best months James had ever known. The more they shared, the more he dared believe he had met the one woman on earth, who could tame his stubborn heart.

Once they arrived at the arena, James took in the sites. Gravel crunched beneath the wheels of the truck. Theirs, and many others. Dust swirled around the boots of those who made their way from horse trailers to the arena. He cracked the window, so he could hear the sounds and smell the odors that accompanied the scene.

Rumbling wheels, laughter, locks being unlocked, a breeze that stirred dry leaves and dead grass, a horse rattling inside the confines of a trailer. And another. And another.

"It's hypnotizing," said James.

"No kidding," said Annie. "I've been addicted since I turned eight."

"Such a different world than a businessman in the city, or even a horse owner at Steeplechase. It's raw and wild, like the Old West has been tamed a little bit. But not too much."

"That's a pretty accurate description," said Sam. "Okay, here's our spot. Annie, you handle Bluebell, and we'll take care of everything else."

"Yes, sir."

Sam and Sissy exited the vehicle then Annie reached for the door handle. But James rested a hand on her arm, a silent request that she wait. She stalled then faced him, curiosity evident in her eyes.

"I'll be praying," he said.

Tears filled her eyes in an instant. Alarmed, James unbuckled the seatbelt and closed the gap between them. He reached for her hand and gave it a squeeze. What was happening? Had he upset her? But how? He didn't think an offered prayer would cause such a reaction.

"Is something wrong?"

Annie swiped at the tears, even though she gave him a tender, gentle smile.

"No one has ever said that to me."

"Oh. I didn't mean to offend."

"No," she said quickly. "No. I'm not offended. I'm touched. Don't think less of my family, please. We are believers. All of us. I guess we've just been doing this for so long, we act on autopilot. And Austin never."

The look on his face must have stopped her from finishing that sentence. She leaned closer and kissed him on the cheek.

"Thank you. So much."

"Annie Jo, get a move on!"

"Mack. He gets impatient sometimes."

"I'll apologize to him."

"Don't you dare," said Annie. "I can handle Mack. Thank you again."

"Is there a 'break a leg' for barrel racing?"

Annie laughed, a full, intoxicating laugh. "Not that I know of."

"Okay, but I'll be praying, non-stop."

Annie blew him a kiss then scrambled down out of the truck. It would be another couple hours before the barrel racing event. He would sit in the stands with Sam and Sissy while Mack and Josh wrestled steers, team roped and made their parents proud. Their efforts had been rewarded, practice proven to make, as nearly as possible, perfection.

A break came for the boys before the barrel racing event. They joined James, Sam and Sissy in the stands. It wouldn't be long now, and they could watch Annie in action. James sat on the cold, uncomfortable stands, his right leg bouncing, his palms sweating, his lips moving in a whispered prayer.

In the midst of high-fives and happy hooting, Austin Anderson appeared in front of them. Or more specifically, in front of James.

"Keep walkin', Austin," said Josh.

"That's good advice," said Sam. "There's nothing here for you."

Austin whirled away from James, waggled his finger in Sam's face, a daring move that left James speechless. Austin wasn't tiny, but James felt certain he would be no match for Sam Parker. James watched in amazement while Sam calmly looked Austin in the eye while he ranted on and on.

"So, you're just going to let this city slicker weasel his way into this family and take my girl? After what, two months? Like years and years of my loyalty to this family have suddenly become worthless!? I'm not impressed, Sam Parker. And you're wrong if you think I'm going to sit back and take it."

The entire section where they sat had gone silent. An odd silence, in that the chaos of the rodeo carried on in the arena, about twenty-five yards in front of them. James kept his mouth shut, anxious to see how one very large, very calm cowboy would handle the situation. To his left, Josh popped up.

Sam stretched his arm out across James, and pointed at Josh.

"Sit down, Son."

Then calmly, and with purpose, Sam stood up, unfolding like a giant climbing out of a cave or a Volkswagen. Anyway, his 6'7" frame towered over Austin Anderson. James tried not to snicker as Austin took a step back, while his head bent back, and he looked up at Sam. He was still glowering, but wisely waited in silence.

"Austin, your family and mine have worked closely together for a lot of years. But that's business, and I'd be happy to continue that relationship with your father. There can be a little give and take in business. Not so with family. You crossed a line when you hurt the one person who could secure your place in this family. Then tried to hide it. Makes me sick to think how many times she tried to tell us."

Sam stepped up on the seat in front of them, pushing his height to over seven feet. Austin took two more steps back. "I never," he started.

"Save it," said Mack and Josh, in unison, as they joined their father.

The three of them made a high wall of intimidating muscle. Like a troop of Navy S.E.A.L.S. on mission to protect the freedom of the United States of America.

James stood, as did Sissy. She stepped closer to him and looped her arm through his crooked elbow.

The stand-off lasted about thirty seconds, before Austin ground out between clinched teeth, "This ain't over. I earned a place on that ranch!" But he didn't stay for a rebuttal and was down the steps and out of sight inside another thirty seconds. The pounding of his boots against the metal stairs echoed eerily in the silence.

Once Austin disappeared around the corner, the people around them slowly began to clap. Technically, these people didn't know what was going on. But it was obvious, even to strangers, that Austin was acting like a complete jerk. He'd lied to Sam, in front of witnesses. He'd riled up Annie's big brothers, something James vowed he would never do—not on purpose, anyway.

Sam turned to the crowd, held up his hands then motioned for everyone to hold it down. He made a formidable picture of fortitude and strength. He oozed confidence and impressed James with an unfathomable degree of patience.

"I apologize, folks. Just a little family situation. No need to concern yourselves. Let's just watch the rodeo and forget this little incident ever happened."

Sissy stayed at James's side, so Sam settled on the other side of her. Josh and Mack returned to their seats, and all eyes returned to the arena. The tie-down roping had ended, and barrel racing was slated as the next event.

James blew out a breath, amazed that the confrontation with Austin had not turned into an altercation. If James had been in Austin's shoes, he couldn't imagine standing up to Sam Parker, especially with Josh and Mack there to back Sam's play.

He'd never been much for fighting, beyond wrestling with his brothers. His interest in technology had confined his workouts to a gym, rather than working out his frustrations on the football field or a baseball diamond or even a tennis court. His brain thrived on numbers and expressed itself best in binary code. He'd kept his nose to the grindstone and his heart incapsulated for all of his 35 years. Until Monday morning, September 11, 2000, when he'd met Annie Jo Parker in a novelty shop on 82nd Street. Her large green eyes, long, dark auburn waves and captivating smile had cracked his binary code wide open. Her laughter and obvious innocence awakened a long-cold spark of possibility and gave him hope. A hope he'd never considered might one day become his reality. She sparked romantic once-in-a-lifetime love in him. And he longed to experience their together-forever journey.

Then he heard her name announced for the final competition of the day in barrels: "AJ Parker from Idalou. Let's give a round of applause to this spunky young lady, who is here defending her championship."

The applause was thunderous as it echoed through the indoor arena. People stood to their feet, whistled, and screamed out her name. It seemed AJ Parker had made a name for herself.

And she was his girlfriend.

Had been for a few weeks now.

CHAPTER SEVENTEEN

Be on your guard; stand firm in the faith; be courageous;
be strong (1 Corinthians 16:13 NIV).

James could scarcely take in the enormity of emotion that washed over him. Annie's final time had been shouted over the crackle of the speakers. Thirteen, flat. He had no idea, on an experiential level, if thirteen seconds could be considered great, but everyone else in the stadium seats, those watching along the fence, and the announcers, sure did.

With victory under her belt, AJ raced to the finish, guaranteed the win, as she had bested every other rider's time.

Before James realized what was happening, he heard Sissy cry out, "No!" He glanced her way then followed her line of sight. Just inside the back-fence line, he spotted a body on the ground. A jean-clad body in a silver top and turquoise boots! Her hat lay a foot or two away.

He jumped up and headed down the metal stands. He and Annie's family raced toward the scene. The stand-by ambulance arrived just after he and the Parkers did.

The flashing lights sent eerie slashes of red across the faces of the gathering crowd. He had no right to approach her. He was her close friend, maybe even her boyfriend. But not her fiancé, not yet. No one would give him the time of day. He stood nearby, but to the back of Josh's elbow. He wanted to be close enough to hear what was going on, but blend in, remain inconspicuous. If he stayed quiet, he might learn something, observe something that might give them a clue as to what might have caused Annie to fall off her horse, of all things. He didn't, for one second, believe it had been an accident, or rider error.

His ears perked up when he heard Annie's voice. Gratitude rushed through him. She could speak. Her voice sounded weak, but she had to be conscious to talk at all, right? In the next few minutes, EMTs laid her limp body on a gurney and loaded her into the back of an ambulance.

He felt a hand on his elbow. "Come with us, James," said Sissy, quietly, with a tinge of sadness that broke his heart and filled his chest cavity with alarm. "We're headed to the hospital."

"Of course," he said, automatically. He kept the myriad of questions locked in his head until they made it back to the truck. In route, he observed everything around them. Faces, many faces, he didn't know, everywhere.

He searched for clues, for suspicious looks, for Austin Anderson, in particular. AJ Parker was a seasoned pro, a champion. She didn't just fall off her horse, willy-nilly. Something was going on here that he didn't like.

There. He spotted Austin, less than ten feet from where Annie had fallen. Odd, he was holding hands with a girl. A girl dressed much like Annie, only with a red hat. He glanced down at her feet. Right, red boots. Her top favored Annie's as well, only cream-colored. She had her eyes fixed on Austin, then leaned forward and whispered in his ear. For some reason the sight irked James. Austin had practically threatened Sam in one breath and was now cozying up with someone who was *not* Annie, in the next.

But Annie had already told James that Austin tended to stray. He felt ridiculous—why would he think Austin should be faithful to Annie, when he didn't want Austin anywhere near her? So, why would Austin try to bully his way back into the Parker's business? His behavior did not make sense.

James shifted his thoughts, so he could focus solely on Annie, find out how badly she'd been hurt. Was it an accident or had someone sabotaged her rigging? Had they intended to do more harm than met the eye? They might never know the answers, but right now, it didn't matter as much as getting Annie Jo to the hospital.

Sam, Sissy and James reached Sam's truck. James climbed into the back seat, his heart sinking as he glanced over at the empty seat where Annie had been that morning. He sent up a prayer for her injuries to be minor, her healing miraculous.

Josh and Mack would follow them to the hospital. Answers would have to wait. But he could at least ask what they knew, so far.

"What did the EMT say?" said James, working to control the tremor in his voice. He would never get the sight of her lying there on the ground, out of his head.

Sissy shifted to look at him. "Looks like a broken fibula, but they won't know for sure until after x-rays. If something had to be broken, the fibula is much easier to heal than the femur or tibia."

"Hopefully, that's all it'll be," said James, swallowing back the bile that rose in this throat.

He sat back for the short ride to the hospital, unable to stop wondering what had really happened to cause Annie's fall. It just didn't add up that she would fall off her horse, seconds after a win. Although he had to assume such a thing were possible. In his estimation, it did not seem probable.

The drive to the hospital seemed much longer than real time. Sam pulled into a parking space as near to the emergency entrance as possible. They all scrambled out of the truck and raced for the door, Josh and Mack close behind them.

Sam approached the sliding glass window, while the rest of them stood nearby. Only Sam and Sissy had been allowed to follow the route to the curtained-off area, where a doctor would examine Annie. Josh, Mack and James stayed in the emergency waiting area. All three of them remained quiet, each stuck in his own head, wrestling his own thoughts.

James needed to ask, though, "Did either of you see how it happened?"

Mack and Josh shifted to look James in the eye. Mack broke the silence. "I didn't, but I spoke to the EMT before they loaded Annie on the gurney. He said it looked like the cinch on her saddle had been cut. Said it was a miracle it didn't break in the middle of her run."

James's entire body stiffened. Just as he'd suspected. Foul play. Someone had gotten to Bluebell before Annie's ride. Someone with the initials A.A., if he should chance a guess. Austin had access to areas of the rodeo grounds where only participants could go, as would the blonde who'd been clinging to him at the scene. How they would prove such a thing, was another matter altogether.

"I'd like to accuse someone in particular," James groused, unwilling to give Austin the slightest break. He just plain did not trust that man. Especially when it came to Annie Jo. "But there's no way I could prove my suspicions."

"Yeah," said Mack. "That's the problem. A hundred different people could have gotten to Annie's horse before her run. Barrel racing is a highly competitive sport. Could have been anyone. But I get where you're coming from," he said, with a hand resting on James's shoulder.

"Thanks, man. Maybe the truth will out, and the guilty party proven guilty, all without me having to thump anyone."

Josh chuckled at that. "If we knew who did this, you'd have to stand in line."

An hour later, the three men's attention shifted to the double doors where Sam and Sissy had disappeared earlier. James sprang to his feet when he caught a glimpse of the wheelchair behind them. *Annie.* Her left leg stuck straight out, encased in a cast below the knee, including her foot. He rushed toward her, Josh and Mack on his heels.

He squatted next to the wheelchair and said, "You okay?"

"I'm fine," said Annie. Anger rang through the last word, which she spat out, with an emphasis on the "f."

"You don't sound fine," said Josh. "What's going on?"

Sissy turned and pressed a hand on Josh's arm. "The doctor wants to keep her overnight for observation. It's a routine precaution after a fall. They're getting a room ready for her."

"It's ridiculous," said Annie, rolling her eyes. "I'm fine."

Sissy's hand moved from Josh's arm to Annie's shoulder.

"It's one night, Sweetheart. We don't want to take any chances. Would you please just calm down and cooperate? We already had hotel rooms booked for the night, so it's not a hardship on us. And you'll be out of here in time for lunch tomorrow."

Everyone fell silent, waiting for Annie to respond. James held his breath (he'd been doing that a lot lately). He didn't want Annie to leave the hospital and put her life in jeopardy. But he also didn't want to leave her alone, in the hospital. What if she had a bad reaction to some medication, or fell trying to get to the restroom, and broke her other leg? Or hit her head on something and made things worse?

Only a few seconds passed, but it seemed much longer, before Annie heaved a big sigh and said, "I guess that makes sense. I'll stay. I won't like it, but I'll stay."

"Thank you, Dear," said Sissy, patting her daughter's arm in what James read on her face as relief.

There it was again. It amazed him how little, tiny Sissy Parker could command obedience from her children with just a look or a touch, never out of anger or any other obvious method of control. Just love and a steady, consistent display of how important it was to do the next right thing. A reminder of how God took care of his children and always provided a way out of difficult circumstances.

Kneeling beside Annie, James whispered, "May I stay here with you? I can't bear to leave you."

Annie looked up at her father, pleading evident in her eyes. "Would you arrange it, Dad? I don't really want to be alone, but there's no reason for all of you to stay. Please?"

The look in Sam's eyes could only be described as unconditional, whatever-you-want-I'll-make-it-happen, love. The smile that spread across his face, and the warm glow that covered his countenance made James appreciate Sam, even more. He loved his daughter. Would do anything for her. Made him think of his own father and the many attributes he had admired in him.

"Of course, Punkin. Then we'll go get a bite of supper and bring y'all back something. How does that sound?"

"Amazing," said Annie. "Thank you, Dad."

"Everything's gonna be okay, Sweetheart. You just concentrate on healing. Great win today, by the way."

"Thank you."

A round of applause echoed through the waiting room as Sam made his way over to the sliding glass window. The lady behind the glass buzzed him in and he disappeared behind the double doors again. The family hovered over Annie, everyone talking at once, finally beginning to relax, since they felt confident Annie had passed the danger point.

Sam returned in about fifteen minutes and announced they had a room ready for Annie. A nurse came in behind him.

"I'll show you to your room, Miss Parker," she said. "We set up a cot in there for your fiancé, so you'll both be comfortable for the night."

All eyes riveted to Sam, wide with shock. He simply shrugged his shoulders and grinned. "Only immediate family is allowed to stay, you know."

James looked at Annie with trepidation, afraid of what she might say or do. The family seemed to hold a collective breath, until Annie started laughing. She laughed until tears rolled down her cheeks.

"Annie, you okay?" said James, when she finally calmed down.

Her eyes swiveled to meet his. She smiled tenderly at him, suddenly serious. "I've never been more okay. How about you?"

James didn't stop to think or try to censor his words, just blurted out, "I'm in love with the most amazing barrel-racer in the world."

Taking her hand in his, he held her captive with his eyes, until someone behind him cleared his throat. Mack. Of course, Mack would challenge this entire situation. Mack, the practical, by-the-book, all-columns-are-straight-and-must-balance, one.

James stood and faced him, keeping a tight grip on Annie's hand, as Sam approached them on James's right.

"It's okay, Son," he said, squeezing Mack's shoulder. "This isn't the time or place."

Mack didn't look at his dad or take his eyes off James, for an excruciatingly long moment. James kept his mouth shut but didn't back down. He had told the truth. In a span of two months, he had fallen completely in love with Annie Jo Parker. Nothing Mack, or anyone else said, would change that.

Sam nudged Mack at the same time the nurse said, "I really should get Miss Parker to her room."

"Of course," said Sissy, edging in front of Mack and Sam. "We'll go and get out of your way. Mack, come along now. It's time to go."

Two more beats passed before Mack broke eye contact with James and followed his mother to the exit. The longest James had witnessed anyone delaying obedience to a command given by Sissy Parker.

"We'll see you two in a bit," whispered Sam, with a conspiratorial wink. "Hope I didn't stir up trouble. It's the only way they'd let you stay, James."

"No apology necessary," said James. "I'm tickled." He winked at Annie, and she giggled.

"We're good, Dad," she said. "Just don't forget my cheeseburger and curly fries."

Engaged. James liked the sound of that. He went so far as to hope it might one day be the actual truth. Be real. His reality with Annie Jo

Parker. The thought should have scared him senseless, just like he'd always expected it would. He waited for the fear to fill him. It didn't come. A Bible verse emerged, instead: *Perfect love casts out fear.* The perfect love of God commands us to love one another. From familial love to agape love, all love comes from God, for God *is* love. James understood that romantic love fell on the familial end of the love scale, and he was okay with that; but he also understood that a man is called to love his wife "the way Crist loved the church," which he understood could only be done well with an agape kind of love. No wonder people were afraid to get married. God took marriage pretty seriously. Even with that thought, fear did not come. Just a peace that he allowed to flood his soul.

James sucked in a deep breath. He and Annie had time to develop a deep, abiding love. He believed they were well on their way, even if their relationship was only two months old. And now that the idea of marriage had been put out there by Annie's dad, maybe it wouldn't be so farfetched when he proposed to her. For real.

But for today, he had permission to stay in the hospital, overnight, with Annie Jo. For today, that was good enough.

Cheeseburgers had settled and sleep had taken Annie to dreamland. James at last let himself relax and take advantage of the opportunity to rest. The day had been both entertaining and emotional. Gratefully, Annie had shown no signs of a concussion. The small abrasion on her head had proven superficial, and the prognosis had been good. It looked like it would just involve the normal four to six weeks for the fracture to heal.

Thankfully, mercifully, the break had not splintered or separated the bone into parts. The doctor had emphasized how fortunate Annie had been to fall on grass, rather than rock; that she'd fallen, just right, to avoid a more serious break. He'd even acknowledged that the hand of God must have intervened, protecting her head from a concussion and her bones from a worse fate. They were blessed to be able to take her back to the ranch, without need of any surgery.

The doctor fully expected to release her in the morning. Essentially, they were home free.

James let sleep overtake him, even though part of him thought he should stay awake, keep vigil over his girl, until morning. But he was tired, and confident Annie would be safe and able to rest. They were in a hospital, after all. What could go wrong? And help was only a panic button away. So, he closed his eyes, whispered yet another prayer of thanksgiving and praise then pulled the light blanket up to his chest, and fell asleep.

In the middle of the night, James awoke, startled at the sound of boots stomping into the room. Alarmed, he jumped to his feet, instantly alert. His eyes went wide, and his hands instinctively formed into fists, as he planted himself between Austin and Annie Jo. He could scarcely believe that Austin had the nerve to show his face here, especially after boldly confronting Sam about his place in the Parker family, then minutes later making a public show of affection with someone other than Annie Jo. The guy's audacity made James's skin crawl. He made eye contact with Austin and didn't look away. When Austin moved to step around him, James moved with him. Austin would have to get to Annie *through* James. He wouldn't have it any other way.

Austin glared at him. "Look, I don't know who you think you are, but you're not part of this," he said, gesturing between himself and Annie. His words slurred and the odor of hard liquor escaped on his breath.

Super. Austin was drunk and obnoxious, a lethal combination. No matter. James wasn't about to back down.

His instinct to stay with Annie had proven beneficial. He could provide a buffer and keep Austin from getting his hands on Annie Jo.

"She could have broken her neck, you lousy coward," James growled, his stance wide, his hands fisted at his sides, at the ready.

The look Austin gave James made him brave and wary at the same time. But he knew in that moment, somehow Austin had been responsible for Annie's injury. Even if he hadn't cut the cinch himself, James would bet Austin knew who did. Wouldn't put it past him to get his on-the-side girlfriend to do his dirty work. What a sleaze.

James didn't cower away from the bull rider but didn't want a fight to break out in the hospital, either. Annie's family had gone to the hotel to get some rest, since Annie had been pronounced out of danger. James felt extra satisfied that he'd stayed with her. If he had his way, Austin wouldn't get any closer to Annie than the three feet that currently separated them.

A hot, melting anger burned in Austin's eyes, his mouth twisted in a sneer. "I didn't put AJ in here," he said. "And you *will* step aside. She's been mine for a long time and there's no room here for the likes of some sissy wannabe cowboy."

Austin shoved James in the shoulder and tried again to step around him.

"You're pushing your luck, mister," said James, his eyes narrowed, his stance firm.

Just then an older, seasoned nurse came barreling into the room. She pushed the two men apart with apparent ease and approached the bed.

"What do you need, sweetie?"

Annie raised the call button she still held in her hand and pointed it at Austin. "Please make him leave," she said, her voice breaking. "Please."

"Consider it done," said the nurse, straightening her shoulders. "Now, get back to sleep, child. I'll take care of everything."

CHAPTER EIGHTEEN

*So do not fear, for I am with you; do not be dismayed, for I am
your God. I will strengthen you and help you; I will uphold
you with my righteous right hand* (Isaiah 41:10 NIV).

"You can't be serious, AJ. What are you thinking?" shouted Austin,
trying to shove his way past the nurse.

James stayed put and let Nurse Ivans handle the bully of a bull rider.
If he didn't, he would deck the guy, which would likely make things worse.

"She's thinking she wants you to leave," said the stout nurse, standing
her ground, hands on her hips, her eyes glaring at Austin. "That's all there
is to it."

It took all of James's willpower to not laugh at the scene before him. It
was plain that Austin would not win this battle. It was over before it really
got started. James knew it, and he felt sure Austin knew it as well. He was
in a hospital, ripe with security, and not one of the doctors, nurses or guards
would give a flip about the bull-riding history of Austin Anderson.

Austin backed toward the door, the guardian nurse close behind him.

"This isn't over, AJ!" he yelled, sounding threatening. But the bite in
his tone didn't mesh with his abrupt departure. Nurse Ivans had him on the
run.

Under other circumstances, the scene would have been comical.

But with Annie Jo's injuries and obvious emotional distress, James bit
his bottom lip to keep his mouth from forming a grin. It felt great to see
Austin put in his place.

At least Austin was gone. The echo of his footsteps faded into the
distance.

Annie flopped back on the bed and James rushed to her side.

"What is wrong with that man?" she said with a groan. "He never truly wanted me, so why is he acting like a complete jealous idiot?"

James slowly dragged a chair closer to the bed, racking his brain, stalling, searching for a reasonable explanation. He could only come up with one plausible reason—and love had nothing to do with it. Control. Greed, maybe. But not love. Not even lust, he'd fulfilled that need elsewhere.

"Well?" said Annie, her eyes filled with a raw anxiety that broke his heart. "What do you think?"

"Honestly?"

"Of course."

James scrubbed his face, stalling yet again. He did not want to say anything that might hurt Annie or make her feel like it was even remotely possible she might not be a desirable woman.

"First of all, I want you to know that you are the most gorgeous, fascinating, amazing, and enticing woman I have ever met. Hands down. I'm so crazy about you already that I wish what Sam told the hospital was true. I'm falling for you—hard."

James cleared his throat (something else he'd been doing a lot of lately) but managed to not break eye contact with Annie. Part of him felt like he didn't know Austin well enough to diss on Annie's life-long friend. But part of him felt certain he had Austin pegged for the type of man he had evolved into, over the years. With all the good, hard working, ethical ranchers surrounding him, Austin had still managed to detour off the road less traveled and allow himself to become a self-centered bully, for lack of a more sophisticated term.

"But?" said Annie.

"But," James repeated. "I don't think he loves you with a pure heart. I think he loves the ranch your father owns and wants part of it for himself. You're the only way that could possibly happen. I'm sorry if that's wrong or unfair, it's just the vibe I get from him. Plus, what I've seen of him, so far. His temper. His arrogance. His deplorable manners."

Annie turned on her side to face him. The look in her eyes made him cringe. Maybe he had overstepped. But she had wanted his honest answer, and he'd given it to her.

"You're not wrong," she whispered, as a tear slid down the side of her face. Several followed it and soon made a wet spot on her pillow.

"Are you crying because you love him, Annie? Because even though it might mean the death of me, I would step away. I'm not the type to come between two people."

She sat straight up then, like she'd been shot out of a rocket. He winced when her hand went to her head, like it hurt from being jostled too quickly.

"James Baldwin, don't you ever talk like that again. I couldn't bear it."

James popped up then and joined her on the side of the hospital bed.

"I'm sorry. I just don't want to stand in your way. I don't ever want to hurt you, Annie."

Annie leaned her head against James's shoulder and sniffed.

"We're something, aren't we?" she said.

She had said that before. And he was inclined to agree with her. They really were something. Something great.

"The best *something* I could imagine," he muttered. "Better than anything I could have ever thought up on my own. I think we fit perfectly well together." He tilted his head to rest against hers and sighed with relief. She didn't love Austin.

"I couldn't agree with you more."

They sat that way for several minutes, just quietly enjoying one another's company. Until Nurse Ivans poked her head in the door and suggested they both get some sleep.

"Yes, ma'am," said James, with a chuckle. He had seen Nurse Ivans in action and had no desire to tussle with her. "Thank you so much for your help earlier."

"Yes, thank you," said Annie.

"You're welcome. He's long gone, and I don't think he'll be back tonight. So, get some rest, sweetie, so you can go home feeling refreshed in the morning."

"Good night, Nurse Ivans," said Annie. "Will you be here in the morning before I leave?"

"Yes, my shift ends at seven. I'll stop by and check on you before I go home."

"Thanks."

"Welcome. Now, good night. Get some rest."

Annie chuckled. "Yes, ma'am."

And Nurse Ivans left them alone.

"I think she could hire out as a bodyguard," said James, grinning, but serious. "She's right, you know. I'll leave you alone now, so you can get that rest. I love you, Annie. Really. As crazy as it might sound to anyone else, it's the truth."

He leaned forward and pressed a kiss to her lips. His words might surprise anyone who knew their story. Heck, it surprised him. For all his adult life he had fought against the idea of getting romantically involved with anyone. As he looked into the eyes of Annie Jo Parker, however, the very idea of living a solitary life now seemed ludicrous. He had not seen any of this coming. Had not prepared his heart for the sweet, precious jewel he'd discovered in the novelty shop, never so happy that he could speak Chinese. The band that squeezed his heart tightened as he thought of their future together.

"Good night, sweetheart," he said, forcing himself to stand. "I'll see you in the morning."

"Good night, hero," said Annie, even as her head dropped back on her pillow.

"Right. Call me anytime I can come between you and Austin. I'll be there in a heartbeat."

"Good to know."

His chest filled with a combination of longing and expectation. He had a chance with Annie Jo Parker.

If Austin could be restrained, or convinced to pursue someone else, the road ahead would be straight and filled with promise.

But if today was any indication of what they were up against, they'd have to stay alert and be ready for anything.

Austin wasn't stable, more than a little arrogant, and determined to have Annie Jo, simply because she would come with a percentage of ownership in the Parker ranch.

"I'm turning the light out now," James whispered. "Get some sleep."

The room settled into a peaceful quiet and James shook off the unpleasant feeling that Austin had left in his wake. He closed his eyes and waited for sleep to come. No doubt, it wouldn't come easy.

Before long, he heard Annie say, "I never loved Austin that way, James. But I feel like I lost him as a friend a while back, and that hurt a little. Just wanted you to know."

He blew out a breath, filled with such awe, he could scarcely think straight. She had considered Austin a friend. And he understood how much it hurt to lose a friend. His heart hurt for her.

"I understand, Annie. Really. I'm sorry you lost a friend, that always stings. But I'm glad I get the latter part of your life. The best part. I want to be the last boy you ever kiss."

Annie took in a shuddering breath and James waited—afraid he'd made her cry again.

"That's the sweetest thing anyone has ever said to me. Good night, James."

Whew. Maybe he'd said the right thing, after all.

"Good night, my love."

He'd been wrong. With the love of a good woman sealed in his heart, sleep claimed him with little or no effort. A peaceful sleep, filled with pleasant dreams.

Morning came. The doctor signed the release papers, and they could at last take Annie Jo home. Sam and Sissy, and their sons, came to the hospital early, all packed and ready to go, in anticipation of Annie's release. When the four of them came barreling into the hospital room, James felt a rush of relief that Austin had not followed them. It would really be a huge bonus if they could put his theatrics behind them. For good.

"Good morning, Annie," said Sissy, as she approached the bed. Her eyes shone with love and affection. James felt the same. He loved Annie beyond mere affection, though. It was all he could do to keep from kissing her good morning.

"Did you sleep well?"

"Oh yes," said Annie, sitting up tall. "But I'm so ready to get out of here. I feel sorry for anyone who has to endure an extended stay in the hospital. I miss the blue sky and the smell of hay. And I miss my horse."

Sissy chuckled. "Have you eaten? We brought you a breakfast burrito." Turning swiftly to James, she said, "And we brought two for you, young man. Thank you for keeping watch over our Annie."

James grinned at his girlfriend. He loved the thought of that. "It wasn't a hardship. And I thank you for the food. It smells delicious." He faced Annie, determined to get the topic out there, so it could be dealt with. "Do you want to tell them or should I?" he said with raised brows, staring straight at Annie.

He felt a little bad when Annie's countenance fell. But he didn't think it wise to keep secrets from her family. Especially when it came to Austin. He and Annie had talked about it, and last night she had agreed. But right now, he wasn't sure if she still felt that way. It surely wouldn't be pleasant. And maybe he should have waited until later to bring it up. But it was too late for that now, so he would just have to deal with it.

"Tell us what?" said Sam, stepping closer to Annie's bed, his arms crossed. The look in his eyes said he expected the truth, the whole truth, and nothing but the truth. Her hand rested on a Bible would be implied. Sam's deep scowl reminded James of the same look a judge would render in a court of law.

Annie looked around the room, making eye contact with each brother, her mother, father and finally, James. Then swung her eyes back to Sam, wishing they didn't have to talk about Austin. Knowing she had no choice. Her dad wouldn't let the subject just drop. For certain.

"I don't want to make a big deal out of it, Dad, just in case it's over. But James and I agreed that we should disclose everything that involved Austin."

"Austin," said Sam, with a grunt, widening his stance and dropping his hands to his hips. "What has he done?" The timbre in his voice sounded like the growl that precedes a wild dog attack.

"He came in here after visiting hours and started making demands," said Annie, rushing through the story. "You know, like I'm his and he has earned a part of our ranch. The usual smack-talk. He insulted James, dismissing him altogether. I had him escorted out. So, nothing bad happened. He was just mad and mouthing off. You know how he is."

No one in the family could argue that point. Austin had always been a hot-headed bull rider. Proud to the point of believing himself indestructible. The Andersons had been neighbors to the Parkers for as long as Annie could remember. She and Austin had learned ranching and riding, and rodeo, side by side. She missed that friend. But not for a long time now.

The friend he'd been for many years. Until something inside Austin snapped. He started winning, earning bigger pots, and greed took over. It seemed he'd set his sights on owning a piece of the Parker spread long before he realized he would have to have Annie in order to get that done. When Annie caught him with second-best and officially ended their relationship, he'd gone ballistic. Hopefully, he wouldn't do anything beyond spouting off threats. But somehow, Annie knew he'd meant what he said: "This isn't over, AJ!" She believed him. And she was afraid. Afraid for every person standing in front of her—especially James.

"You had him thrown out?" said Josh, with a chortle.

"I certainly did. He was being belligerent. And Nurse Ivans gave him the old heave-ho. I was so proud of her." Her eyes shifted to James, and she winked. "Thank you for not punching him in the face. I know he deserved it."

James nodded and winked right back. She blushed, could feel the heat climb up her neck and into her face. He was so strong, and good, and kind. *Thank you, God.*

A rap on the door grabbed everyone's attention. Good, maybe they wouldn't have to talk about Austin anymore. She didn't care if she never heard his name again, no matter how unlikely that wish might be.

"You're free to go, Miss Annie," said a cheerful nurse's aide. "I've brought a chair to wheel you out. Hospital policy, you know. We can't have you getting reinjured on our watch, now, can we? Are you ready?"

Thus, the subject of Austin Anderson had instantly been tabled. But Annie believed this weekend wouldn't be the end. She suspected her dad would confront Austin through Jake, try to settle things amicably. Just like he'd tried to do after Austin had rammed his pickup into James's SUV. That kind gesture hadn't solved anything. And now, Austin was at it again. Mouthing off, making threats. She didn't know how all this might end but did not look forward to its coming to a head. Someone could get hurt, way beyond a broken leg.

If he didn't cool his jets, someone might even die—which would complicate everything. Bring them around a bend from which there could be no return.

Please God, stop him. Make him see reason. End this. Please, Lord.

Jake Anderson was still her dad's friend, after all. But she also knew, at least now, that her father would not hesitate to sever all ties with their long-time neighbor, if he did not take control of Austin. It could get ugly. And she hated that. But she was no longer willing to take Austin's abuse, just to keep peace with their neighbor. The truth was out, and she relished the fact that her family would stand by her. No matter what.

Austin had made choices he couldn't unmake. And it would take a lot to restore relations with the Andersons. A *lot*.

On the ride back to the ranch, Annie rode with her cast propped up on pillows and her foot on James's lap. He rested his hand on her foot, even touching her toes occasionally. Nervous, wondering what would come next with them. They had talked about riding together, but that would be impossible until after Christmas. He wondered if he would be allowed to visit, if he would be invited, or would have to invite himself. If Annie would go out with him, on crutches, or if they could spend time together at her house, watching a movie or something. He would gladly bring dinner. But he also had to get back to work. His companies wouldn't run themselves, although he trusted the head of every branch in every country. But checks and balances were in place for a reason, and he refused to let go of the reins completely. He didn't trust anyone that much.

"Are you going to stay at your house while you recover?" he said, his finger resting on Annie's big toe sticking out at the end of the cast.

"I don't think so," said Sissy, at the same time Annie said, "Of course."

"Annie," said her mother, with that universal I'm-your-mother-and-I-know-what's-best-for-you tone. James held back a chuckle. It would be interesting to see who won this little disagreement. Two strong-willed women at odds over the same thing. James wanted Annie to be safe and well cared for, but also wanted to be able to visit with her—alone.

"Mom," said Annie, matching her mother's determination. "Bethany will be with me, and you're right next door. It's not like I'll be bedridden and can't do anything for myself. I'll be fine. Really."

If Annie used that tone with him, James would obey her, without question.

Sissy turned in her seat, twisting until she could look Annie in the eye. "Are you sure?"

James cringed at the deep scowl on her face and the aching tone in her voice. She just wanted to take care of her daughter. His own mother would do the same thing.

"Totally," said Annie, making an "x" over her heart. "I promise to call if I need help."

Sissy frowned but didn't say anything. She also didn't turn back toward the front of the truck. She stared hopefully at Annie Jo. James could almost hear his mother's voice when Sissy spoke to Annie. That same caring, motherly tone, known worldwide.

"I promise, Mom," said Annie, hope and sincerity ringing through her voice.

"Well, I'd rather take care of you myself. So, don't fuss if I bring dinner over."

Surprised but pleased, James kept his ears open, and his mouth shut. This could be a good thing. Maybe he should offer his services, endear himself to Annie Jo's mother. Get an "in" with the family and spend more time with Annie Jo, all in one fell swoop.

"Yes, ma'am."

Contrite, sweet, perfect.

"I plan to help, too," he chimed in. "I'm a fair cook, or I could bring dinner. Hopefully, Annie will allow me to spoil her a little."

He gave her a wink and she giggled. He loved that sound, above all other sounds.

"Could be fun," said Annie Jo. "See, Mom, I'll have extra help, too. But your dinners are always welcome. So, relax. I'll be in good hands. You know Bethany will treat me like a helpless child. And you've witnessed how caring and capable James can be. The time will fly by, and I'll be under your feet again in no time."

Sissy paused, glanced between Annie and him, then said, "Well, if you're sure." She might have been convinced. James certainly hoped so. Helping to take care of Annie would be a privilege. And a delight.

"Yes, ma'am. I'm sure."

"Well, okay then." She twisted in her seat and looked straight at James, as if she were commanding one of her own sons. "I'm counting on you to be a man of your word."

He liked it. Made him feel accepted, like part of the family. When a parent trusts a guy with their daughter, it serves as a show of confidence. An opportunity to earn the trust Mrs. Parker placed in him. He would enjoy gaining that trust. Immensely.

"Yes, ma'am," he said, heavy on the sincerity. "I'll keep in close contact with Annie Jo, in case she needs anything. I promise. And I'll call you if anything unexpected happens. You can count on me." He placed an "x" over his own heart, completely serious. He meant every word.

James kept quiet, too, about Annie's cinch being cut. He didn't want to upset her right now. She had enough to deal with. Mack would likely share that little tidbit with Sam, and Sam would deal with it.

Hopefully, an investigation would ensue and the culprit responsible would be brought to justice.

CHAPTER NINETEEN

They will receive blessing from the Lord and vindication
from God their Savior (Psalm 24:5 NIV).

J ames spent most of Monday morning catching up at the office. It seemed
many of his associates and employees around the globe had worked right
through the holiday—and expressed concern that he had taken off Tuesday
through Sunday. Although he might feel bad that they felt bad—he didn't
feel bad that he'd taken off work, shopped for a ranch, attended a rodeo—
and fallen in love with the most incredible woman he had ever known, or
could have imagined. A small woman with a heart as big as Dallas.

He'd struggled through meeting after meeting, trying to keep his mind
on his work, and off Annie Jo Parker. He found her face popping into his
head in the middle of a few serious video chats, and he'd had to work at
keeping a straight face. Gee, he'd never thought a woman could imbed
herself so deeply into his psyche that he couldn't focus on work. Now, he
knew better.

He'd stopped just short of running his hand through his hair to redirect
his nerves. His colleagues and potential customers had yet to see him sweat.
And he'd like to keep it that way.

Thus, James blew out a breath of relief when he blackened the giant
screen on the TV above the fireplace in his office. He'd been hard at it since
seven that morning. All he wanted was to take Annie some lunch then scoot
over to the BB ranch to keep the appointment he'd made to view it, with
an eye for purchase. Maybe as his forever home with Annie. Maybe have a
kid or two.

Reel it back in, JB. You're getting ahead of yourself again.

He chuckled, pulled out his phone, and sent a text to Annie to confirm lunch. Then put in a call to Mr. Blankenship to solidify their appointment, expecting that Mr. Blankenship would not appreciate doing business, via text. Relief flooded through him when he discovered that Mr. B had not changed his mind, had not sold the place out from under him, and the New York nephew had not decided to move to Texas. None of those scenarios had come to pass.

His plan to purchase a forever home just might come to fruition, after all. Another first in his life. Although he had lived in Nashville for a lot of years, he had not replaced Lubbock in his heart. Lubbock County had been "home" in his soul. But returning meant facing a painful past mixed with the best memories of his life.

If he admitted it, he would have to acknowledge he'd already been able to heal on a couple levels. His family had gathered under one roof, in the family's original home. And he'd been growing closer to his brothers, which healed a few holes in his heart.

Emotional healing had opened his eyes to greater possibilities. Enter Annie Jo Parker. Exposing his heart to familial love had changed his attitude. He now wanted what the other members of his family had: security and trust in relationships.

Annie Jo made a forever relationship conceivable. She made him want to be a better man. His focus had shifted from being totally about himself to putting someone else's needs above his own.

Rather than running from involvement with a member of the opposite sex, he now embraced hope and love as a real possibility. Whatever risk came with it, they would deal with, together.

He wanted to live life to the full, not in fear of what he could not see, could not predict, and could not control. He'd done enough of that, thank you very much.

Rather, he gently lay his future in God's hands and declared his trust and faith that God loved him and wanted to bless him.

Tears misted in his eyes as he realized that his own stubborn pride had been blocking God's every attempt to bless him with a good woman—for years.

"Forgive me, Lord," he whispered.

With a contented sigh, James locked the office door—a long-standing habit that had begun after a trusted employee had stolen his laptop then tried to sell his latest security program to a competitor. It had taken months to clear up that mess, prove his patent pending then confiscate every computer and all backup equipment from his adversary—followed by weeks of annoyance during a very public trial. He had no desire to walk down that road again. So, not only did his office door remain locked in his absence, but important documents and equipment were kept under triple safeguards, within his office sanctuary. All meetings were held in the conference room. You had to be someone James would trust with his life, to meet inside his office. It was a very short list.

James raised his hand to knock on Annie's front door, just as it swung open from the inside.

"Hey, Bethany. I come bearing lunch. Is Annie here?"

Bethany opened the door wider and held her arm out. "Come in."

"I'm here," said Annie, from somewhere down the hall to his right. "Takes me a minute with these darn crutches. "Oh," she said, her eyes wide once she came fully into view. "You look beautiful."

James and Bethany glanced at each other.

"Thank you?" said Bethany, with a raised brow and a chuckle, even though Annie Jo was not looking at her.

"And I thought she was talking to me," said James, with a smug grin. "I seldom get pegged as beautiful, though, I must admit."

James made his way over to Annie and pressed a quick kiss to her lips. "I brought barbecue from J&M. Sound good? And you look beyond beautiful," he said, dropping his voice to that husky sound he knew made Annie get the chills.

"Thank you," she said in a whisper.

James turned toward Bethany. "There's plenty for three, if you'd care to join us."

"I appreciate it, but I'm running late for a luncheon in Ransom Canyon and really need to get. Maybe next time."

"Of course. Thank you for being here for Annie," he said, resting his arm around her waist, not only to support her, but to draw her closer to him, which made him hyper aware of the light scent of vanilla emanating from his sweetheart, who seemed to want to be with him. The thought warmed him to his toes. "She doesn't like being slowed down, even a little bit."

"You're telling me," said Bethany, with a laugh. "But she's really no trouble. She's so stubborn and independent, I have to force her to let me help."

"Hellooo," said Annie in a sing-song voice, waving her hand in the air. "I'm right here."

"Sorry," said Bethany, with a wide smile. "But you are."

"I know," said Annie, grinning back. James enjoyed their interaction and secret way of communicating more than what was said. "And you love me, just the way I am."

"Yes, I do. Well, you two have fun. I really gotta run." She made her way to the front door. "I don't want to miss a single number Mrs. Churchwell plays. She's fabulous."

"Catherine Churchwell?" said James, certain Bethany must be referring to his mother. He had always been proud of her accomplishments.

"Why, yes. Do you know her?"

"Catherine Baldwin Churchwell is my mother."

"Wow," said Bethany, her voice sounding in awe of the fact. "You come from good stock."

"Yes, I do. Thank you." It pleased him no end to hear someone else brag on his mom. She had struggled for years after she'd lost her husband and their home. But she hadn't let anything keep her down. She'd gathered her chicks under her wings and carried them to safety then increased her concert appearances and provided for herself, her mother, the nanny, and her five children.

God had rewarded her faithfulness, as she now lived in the homestead she'd lost, enjoyed the fruits of her deceased husband's restored estate, and held her head high in public places, still giving back to a community that had once misunderstood and shunned her. So yeah, he was super proud of his mother.

Bethany winked at Annie. "Hold on to this one, AJ. He's a keeper."

Annie laughed then darted a look toward James. "I intend to."

Two o'clock was approaching way too fast. James and Annie had spent two hours together, eating, visiting, snuggling, and even managed to work in a few kisses. But at one thirty, James forced himself up out of the comfort of Annie's supple leather sofa then pulled her up next to him.

"Are you sure you don't want to come with?"

"Do you want to purchase the BB ranch?"

"If it looks as good on the inside and on paper, as it does from the outside, I'd say yes. Plus, it has a lot going for it—just being next door to you."

He ran a finger down the side of her face and along her jawline. When she closed her eyes, he took that as permission to kiss her again. So, he did.

"Trust me," said Annie once he released her lips. "You have a better chance without me."

He wondered about that but didn't have time to delve into it. Maybe he would remember to ask her about the disharmony with her neighbor, later.

"If you say so." With another quick peck on her cheek, he said, "Anyway, I gotta get. Don't wanna be late."

He made his way to the door then turned to face the love of his life again. Still in awe that this could be his reality. Still stunned by Annie Jo's beauty, and blown away by the fact that he, Mr. Independent who doesn't need anybody, wanted to get married.

"Are you available for dinner out? With me?"

"I'd go anywhere with you, James." And the look in her eye solidified the sentiment of a forever union. The woman standing before him was the only woman for him.

"I'll text you when I'm done next door. I love you, Annie."

He closed the door behind him to keep from prolonging his departure, then jogged to his truck. If he stayed one minute longer, he wouldn't be able to pull himself away from her. And he didn't want to miss this appointment. And he definitely did not intend to give Mr. Blankenship an excuse to pull out, before he had even been given the grand tour. So, he sucked in a sobering breath and made a beeline for his truck. His pickup truck, with its four doors and short, wide bed, that he had grown to appreciate a little more every day.

Pulling up to the gate at the neighboring ranch, James called Mr. Blankenship. Thirty seconds later, the gate swung open. He clocked two miles from the gate to the circle drive, where Mr. Blankenship stood on the front porch. The man didn't growl at James as he came up the steps, but he didn't smile either. A knot formed in James's gut. Had something happened since their last conversation to make Barry change his mind about selling the ranch? He'd just talked to him a little over two hours ago. He wasn't having second thoughts about selling to *him*, was he? James prayed that wasn't the case. Before he'd even seen it, James wanted to own the ranch adjacent to Annie Jo.

He swallowed hard before trying to speak. A lot was riding on this being a successful interaction. There weren't that many ranches in the area that could offer so many of James's requirements, i.e., quality of workmanship, evidenced by the few amenities he had seen so far; proximity to Annie Jo; and now that he'd had a glimpse of the exterior, a magnificent house. Yeah, he didn't want to blow this encounter. He felt like Mr. B was scrutinizing him, even more than James was inspecting the ranch.

"Good afternoon, Mr. Blankenship. It's good to see you again." He kept his voice light, sincere, respectful.

"Call me Barry." Well, that was one good sign.

"Yes, sir."

James waited for Mr. Blankenship, that is, Barry, to make the next move. He could sense he was standing on shaky ground with this guy. He didn't know why, but the reception he was getting today seemed much chillier than the consideration he had enjoyed back in September. *Barry's* attitude matched the late November chill in the air.

Barry zipped up his jacket and said, "I'll drive."

James still didn't speak, just followed Barry to his truck then climbed up into the passenger seat of the silver Cadillac pickup. Cadillac, in general, had never been James's favorite, but he couldn't very well judge a man for what truck he chose to drive, now could he? Not out loud, anyway.

Once Barry began the tour, pointing out massive barns, corrals, an indoor arena, manmade ponds, and strategically placed landscaping, the atmosphere in the cab of the truck began to thaw. Barry was a proud man. Proud of his accomplishments. Even so, he seemed to carry a weight of melancholy that affected his countenance, making him appear grumpy. But James suspected he was more sad than mad.

It took two hours for Barry to show James the high points of the ranch. Once they'd parked in front of the house again, Barry said, "I guess you'd like to see inside the house."

"That would be great," said James. "If you have the time."

"I got time." With that, he climbed out of the pickup and led James to the double wide, ten-foot-high front doors.

James followed Barry inside, but stopped just inside the door and let out a low whistle.

It was like Barry Blankenship had seen the sketches James had been working on for years. From the high vaulted ceilings to the choice of colors and flooring, James was staring at *his* house. He didn't voice this fact, but it reverberated deep in his soul. Surreal. Miraculous. Magical.

As much as James admired the look and size of the ranch, the house sealed the deal for him. Right then. And he had only seen the great room/kitchen/dining area combined in an open format that gave a man room to breathe. A large room that would easily accommodate his extended family for visits or holiday gatherings. Another foreign concept he had not considered before.

This house had been built for a growing family. The thought made James wonder why Barry lived here alone, in this expansive mansion, and apparently, he had no one to share it with.

"Follow me upstairs first," said Barry, still a little on the cool side.

James made his way behind Barry up the broad staircase that contained one wide landing on the second level, lighted by an oval window, before it continued up to a third floor, a constant prayer in his heart.

Level two contained four bedrooms, all roomy, and two full baths, one sandwiched between each pair of bedrooms. The third level included a conference room, an office, and a game room, complete with a pool table, big-screen TV, pit leather couches and a game table.

Perfect. James was happy to note that the space did not contain a wet bar. Good, people could not automatically assume he would condone drinking in his home, which he decidedly would not.

When they came back downstairs, Barry crossed the great room and led James down a long hallway then into the master bedroom. The furniture was large, the bed massive, and the master bath contained dual sinks, showers, and walk-in closets, with a large garden tub in the middle. One closet could hold his own personal, somewhat extensive wardrobe, three times over. On the back wall of the restroom, he took in a breathtaking view of the ranch through windows situated above the tub. Throughout the house were scattered expansive bay windows that brought in light from every direction. His heart raced with anticipation. It would be a joy to share the space with Annie Jo.

Mr. B broke into his thoughts, sobering him in an instant. He didn't own the space, just yet, and needed to get his head in the game.

"That's about it," said Barry. "Except for the back yard. I'll get us some coffee. We can sit out there and chat. Maybe it's not too cold. We won't stay long."

"That would be nice," said James. "Thank you." They seemed to be progressing, although the weight that Barry carried on his shoulders glowed dark in his eyes—like the light had been snuffed out and he hadn't found his way to the switch, so he could f lip it back on.

James could only hope he could work his way around that, maybe help cheer the guy up. His honed negotiation skills would be called upon. Something had broken this man, deep in his core—a feeling James could identify with. Dealing with him would require delicacy and compassion.

James and Barry sat in silence for several minutes, as James took in the surrounding area. He was somewhat surprised to see an Olympic-size pool nestled among the myriad trees, bushes and fall-happy flowers, in what Barry had referred to as the 'back yard'. James estimated that the fenced area consisted of approximately two acres, surrounded by an eight-foot stone and wood fence. The covered deck where they sat had been built with the same materials as the privacy fence and sported a full outdoor kitchen of gleaming stainless steel. They shared a table that would seat eight people, built of redwood, with a tabletop covered with thick glass.

"I guess you're wondering why an old man lives here, alone. It must seem ridiculous to you."

James shrugged one shoulder. "I have a feeling it's much more complicated than it looks."

"Yeah." Barry swiped a stubborn tear off his face.

James kept quiet. If Barry wanted to share his past with him, he would. If not, he would leave the subject alone. It wasn't easy for men to speak about what burdened their hearts, and he'd only known a handful who would let another man see him cry.

CHAPTER TWENTY

*I called to the LORD, who is worthy of praise; and I have
been saved from my enemies* (Psalm 18:3 NIV).

Barry remained silent—a full five minutes—sitting still and staring at his boots. But then he started talking, as if he'd forgotten that James was a stranger. Or maybe he felt safe to share *because* James was a stranger.

"I haven't always lived alone," he said. "I inherited this ranch then built it up, expanded my borders and had the house finished before I got up the nerve to ask Melissa to marry me. Melissa loved this place. She would spend hours in that swimming pool. She was a champion swimmer, not a country girl, at all. I think the pool is what convinced her she could live out here." He chuckled then, even as another tear slipped down his cheek.

James didn't know what was coming, but his heart already broke for this man.

"We were married seven years, before Mel conceived. A boy. Barry, Junior. Or he would have been, had he lived. It was a difficult pregnancy for Mel. I felt guilty the entire time. Still do. I lost them both during childbirth."

James felt tears of his own trickle down his face. The shock had jarred the tears loose. He couldn't have stopped them if he'd tried. He held his tongue, lost in thought.

Finally, Barry looked up at him. "Don't know why I got into all that," he said with a deep frown. "I've never talked about it before. You'll just have to forgive me."

James straightened in his chair and forced the tears to stay at bay. "No need. I am so sorry for your loss. I can't even imagine."

"Thank you," said Barry, clearing his throat then slapping a hand on his thigh. "Anyway, I knew this place needed a family to fill it up. And I was determined to keep it in my family line. But that's not happening. I only have the one nephew, and to hear him say it, 'He wouldn't live out in the sticks, for any amount of inheritance.' He's a big muckity-muck on Wall Street in New York City. I thought if I could get him interested in Annie Jo, they could settle here, and make this house a home."

He laughed again, but it held no trace of humor.

"But that's not happening, either. So, I have no choice but to retire, and no choice but to sell. Anyway, forget all that. Can you handle my asking price?"

Finally, they were getting down to the bottom line. At last, speaking James's language. A surge of hope rushed to his head and made him a little dizzy. He'd been given some insight into this sad, wealthy man's heart. He might not agree with everything Mr. Blankenship had done, how he had handled a long-time, innocent neighbor for one, but that wouldn't stop him from buying the man's ranch. He wanted to close the deal and have something tangible to offer Annie Jo. A house they could make into a home.

"Yes, sir. I can offer you cash and can close before Christmas. If that timeline would suit you." He held his breath, hoping Barry didn't feel too rushed, pushed even. The timing had to be Barry's idea. James just wanted him to know he could pull off a quick closing date.

Barry swallowed the last of his coffee that had turned cold while they conversed then faced James. "Honestly, I'd rather not spend another night alone in this house. I can't believe I've waited this long, hoping my nephew would change his mind. How soon can you move in?"

James's jaw dropped. He could feel it hanging open. "Do you have somewhere to go?"

"Yes. I made arrangements, in advance, just in case you decided to buy. Even if you didn't, I'd be leaving tomorrow. A truck is coming in the morning for my clothes and a few personal items. Everything else stays."

"Including livestock and ranch hands?"

"Sure."

Surprise raced through him. He could scarcely believe what he was hearing. Mr. Blankenship, Barry, must be struggling emotionally more than he'd first imagined. He seemed to want this chapter of his life closed without further delay.

How heavy must his heart be? But then, he had lived with loss most of the time he'd owned this ranch. Sad memories had overcome the good ones and spilled out onto the people who tried to get to know him. No wonder Annie disliked him, she had only seen the grouch, had no idea what had turned this sad man's heart to stone.

But now, having spent a little time with him, James knew the truth. Barry didn't have a heart of stone, he had a heart filled with grief and regret, guilt and misery.

"In that case, I'm upping my offer by another hundred thousand. What do you think?"

"Sounds more than fair. Can you meet me here in the morning around ten? We can close the deal and I can start figuring out a new life for myself. It's long overdue."

"Yes, sir. I'll bring a cashier's check." James had been planning to purchase a ranch, at some point, and had been saving for fifteen years. Hadn't figured on it being in Lubbock County, but now, with Annie Jo in the picture, he couldn't imagine being anywhere else.

A cashier's check would be doable, under the circumstances. If the bank gave him a hard time, he would pull all his money out and deposit it somewhere else. He didn't believe that would be necessary, though. James had made multi-million-dollar purchases before without any grief from the bank.

"Great. Then I'll instruct my attorney to draw up the paperwork today. I'll make sure all the keys are labeled and at the ready. My attorney will be here, and he'll bring a notary. There will be a deed to the property and a bill of sale for everything else. We'll keep it simple."

Yeah, James could hardly believe this was happening. *Thank you for granting me favor, Lord. Help me give you all the praise and glory. Now, and always.*

***

James stood on Barry Blankenship's doorstep at 9:45 the following morning. He pulled his long woolen duster tighter around his middle and shivered. An unexpected shower had dropped cold rain on everything the night before, which caused a light frost to cover the trees and grass.

The forecast predicted a long, cold winter, with plenty of snow and ice. If today were any indication of things to come, he needed to get his horses relocated and into a warm barn before the worst of it hit. A longing snaked through him. He hadn't seen or ridden or brushed any of his horses in months. If not for his trusted trainer, he'd be lost. *So, quit worrying about it. You have good men looking out for them. They're safe and well cared for.* But that thought wasn't enough to settle the matter in his heart, so he determined he would call his trainer as soon as he finished business with Barry. *Please watch over my friends and livestock in Nashville, Lord.* "Do not be afraid, for I am with you," whispered through his spirit, causing a warm feeling of satisfaction to take root in is heart.

Everything would work out in accordance with God's will, he just had to trust and believe. Listen and obey.

It had taken some persuasion and juggling with his investment portfolio to transform such a large amount of money into disposable income, on short notice. But now that it was done, and he literally stood on the doorstep of opportunity, a warm feeling of satisfaction blossomed on the tree of excitement that had taken root in is heart.

The door swung open in front of him, and Barry stood there—smiling! And no sign of a stogey. Things could be turning around for Barry.

James had not seen that expression on Barry's face in the few short hours they had spent together. A nice change. It lightened his eyes and made him appear like a personable human being. Perhaps getting away from the years of depression and shattered dreams that had kept him company for many, long, lonely years would change his life for the better.

"Come in, my boy. Everything is laid out on the dining room table."

"Thank you. It's beginning to feel like winter is upon us."

They had taken a few steps inside when James rested a hand on Barry's arm. "Barry," he said, his belly aching to help this man feel better—beyond today.

Barry stopped and gave James his full attention. No words, just a raised brow. James hesitated, in case Barry might not be receptive to the idea.

"I was hoping you would share your forwarding address with me. I'd like to stay in touch."

Both of Barry's eyebrows eased up, and his eyes misted with tears. "I'd like that," he said.

"Thank you." That being said, he was ready to get this show on the road.

He followed Barry into the dining room, where the simple, yet lucrative, closing would take place.

Barry introduced James to his attorney and his assistant, Richard Worley and Beth Sawyer.

"I'm sure there will be no surprises here today," said Richard, making eye contact with James. That "lawyer look" that some in his profession used to intimidate people, to maintain control. It almost made James want to chuckle. This guy, who thought so highly of himself, had no idea who he was dealing with. Today's transaction paled in comparison with a long list of closings from James's lucrative past.

"I understand you are willing to forego title insurance," said Richard, still in awe of himself.

But James wouldn't let on about his true net worth. He recognized a scoundrel when he saw one, and this attorney had that look in his eye. No need to ruffle anyone's feathers. The less said, the better. He could close this deal and take the next step toward making a family with Annie Jo—and Barry could get on with his life. He did, however, make a mental note to not engage Richard's services in the future. Arrogance did not appeal.

"Yes, sir," he said pushing a measure of respect into his tone. "Barry has had the place for a number of years, and I'm confident that any title issues were cleared up back then."

Mr. Blankenship nodded to affirm the statement and another sigh of relief escaped, as James had been concerned about the mental state of the man the day before. He felt stupid that he hadn't brought it up himself, yesterday. It was good to know. Even though Barry had been melancholy, he had not been mindless, and had taken care of business properly. The closing could proceed, without delay.

"Okay then, here is the deed," said Richard. "Please, take a moment to look it over."

James read through the document then gave Richard a nod. Standard Texas deed language he'd seen many times before. Although he hadn't considered moving to Lubbock on a permanent basis, until recently, he had been stock-piling commercial investment properties in the area, for the past five years, which he had entrusted to a reputable management company. The action had scratched an itch to set down mental roots in and around his hometown. And each investment had turned a tidy profit. However, having the Midas touch could be a cold way to live. Now that he knew the difference, a warm woman with a good heart was "worth far more than rubies", just like the Bible said in Proverbs 31:10. Another verse that Paul had quoted at his wedding drifted into James's mind. *He who finds a wife finds what is good and receives favor from the Lord.*

The attorney's voice broke into the pleasant reverie. "I assume you have brought good funds."

That uppity tone again. But no matter. He served a purpose today. Then James would be done with the man. Pulling out the certified funds for forty million dollars, he set it next to the deed.

Barry examined the check then picked up the gold Cross pen Richard had left on the opposite side of the deed. He signed his name with a flourish then autographed the bill of sale. He then stepped to the side so Beth could notarize the deed.

The house was filled with the background noise of men carrying Barry's personal belongings out to a large moving truck. The sounds of change. The shifting from one reality to another. While the moving crew bustled around them, Richard picked up the signed and notarized deed, reviewed the document then tucked it inside his leather briefcase.

Pushing aside all thought of the lawyer, James took note of the amazing transformation in Barry's countenance. Still smiling. At peace with his decision. Excellent.

James felt the same way, peaceful, reticent, enthralled about what lay ahead for him. For him and Annie Jo, God willing.

"I'll take this directly to the courthouse and get it filed for record," said Richard. "The clerk will get it back to me in the next few days, then Beth will mail the original to you, James, and a copy to Barry. So, it might be next week before you have the deed in hand, but I assure you, it will be safe in the courthouse, and likely filed for record by tomorrow afternoon."

"Thank you." Enough said. The attorney had simply done his job. No further accolades need be used to feed his over-plump ego any further.

"Thanks, Richard. Beth," said Barry. "I appreciate you making the trip out here on short notice." He laughed then. "It's not like I haven't been trying to prepare you for this day. I can't tell you how relieved I am. You know where to send the bill."

"Yes, sir. We sure are going to miss you around here. I hope you won't stay a stranger."

Now *that* sounded sincere, although James couldn't be certain if the attorney would miss Barry, the man, or the billable hours their association represented.

"I appreciate the sentiment. We'll just have to see how things go."

"I understand. Well, take care. We'll be going now. Wish you the best."

Barry walked Richard and Beth to the door then stopped to give instructions to a couple of movers, before returning to James, who had been staring out the dining room window.

"I hope you're planning to have a family," said Barry, joining him. "This place could use a little racket, the laughter of children." He paused for a long, insightful moment. "Well, you know what I mean."

James turned his head enough to acknowledge Barry's words. "Yes, sir. It is certainly my hope. One day. I'll invite you out, so you can witness it for yourself."

A daydream would have consumed him, if given the chance. This ranch now belonged to him. Every square inch of it. And he was thrilled beyond words. Just needed a bride to share the master bedroom, then go from there.

"I'd like that."

They stared out the window for a few minutes, each man lost in his own head. Barry likely lost in the past. James, in the future.

Suddenly, the front door slammed open, and shouts of obscenities tainted the momentary peace.

"Barry Blankenship, what is going on here?! Have you lost your ever-lovin' mind?"

Barry glanced at James then turned toward the offensive noise.

Austin Anderson. Really? Unbelievable.

"What are you going on about, Austin? And how did you get inside my gate?" The anger that filled Barry's tone told James that his new-found friend knew something troublesome about Austin, as well. Relief helped him relax. At least, Barry didn't appear to be Austin's buddy.

Austin Anderson. James could scarcely believe this latest caper. Had Austin really just crashed the real estate closing that transferred the BB ranch into James's name? Hadn't he caused more than his share of trouble already?

There hadn't been enough concrete evidence to charge anyone with willful intent regarding Annie Jo's injuries at the Thanksgiving Classic, even with the severed cinch. No discernible fingerprints. No DNA. No foreign fibers. Nothing.

So, once again, Austin had slipped through their fingers. But now he was on James's property, and if it came to a head here, he would gladly call the sheriff and have him forcibly removed.

"I'm talking about the insanity of you selling to this greenhorn, when I've had my eye on this place since I was old enough to ride. Don't pretend you didn't know it," he growled, puffing out his chest and breathing hard. "And as far as getting inside your gate, I just told Richard Worley we had an appointment. Easy-peasy. He and I went through the gate, simultaneously. He went out and I came in. My timing couldn't have been better." His voice was loud, disrespectful and annoying. He slurred his words, per usual. Was the guy ever sober?

This was the first James had heard about Austin being interested in purchasing the BB ranch. He'd been aware of Annie Jo's feelings on the matter, but Austin had not been mentioned in any of their discussions. And Barry hadn't mentioned even one other serious contender.

He had a feeling this new revelation stemmed from pure old jealousy. James wanted Annie Jo, so Austin determined to keep her for himself. James wanted the BB ranch, so Austin threw a fit to have it.

Austin's gaze shifted from Barry to James. His eyes narrowed and he stomped a step closer.

"There you are. You snake. How dare you move into my territory, take my girl, and now take my ranch!"

CHAPTER TWENTY-ONE

*Your right hand, LORD, was majestic in power. Your right
hand, LORD, shattered the enemy* (Exodus 15:6 NIV).

Austin pushed past Barry but went sprawling across the room, sliding to
a stop at James's feet, when Barry casually slid his booted foot out in
front of him.

James stood perfectly still, holding in the burst of laughter stuck in his
throat.

Coming up beside James, Barry glared down at Austin. "You best get
back on home, Austin, before I call your daddy."

Austin scrambled to his feet, staggered, before squaring his stance.
Rage flashed in his eyes and his hands balled into fists. "My *daddy* ain't got
nothing to do with this!"

And so, the short streak of being free of Austin Anderson, ended.
James had half a mind to call 911, without asking Barry's permission. He
had witnessed Austin in action, knew his presence could only mean trouble.
The boy seemed not to be bothered by a conscience.

"I don't much think he would agree," said Barry, smooth as butter,
hands on his hips, like he'd been given a fortifying shot from the fountain of
youth. That did make James smile. "I have a feeling the price of this ranch
isn't tucked inside that cowhide of a wallet sticking up out of your back
pocket. Now get, before I call the law *and* your daddy. The sale has been
finalized, and I'd advise you to keep your distance."

Austin morphed into a boorish man, resembling the bulls he rode on a
regular basis. Wild, out of control, beyond angry. He even huffed his breath
through his nose, in a similar manner. James wanted to laugh this clown out

of the house; but miraculously managed to keep a straight face. He was in Barry's home, technically, since the deed had yet to be filed for record, and he'd respect Barry's right to handle this intruder in his own way. He made a mental note, however, to have his team inspect the security at the house and the perimeter of the ranch, as soon as possible. Especially the gate.

Man, this Austin character had a temper, and he didn't appear to have absorbed any part of a good raising.

"I'll go for now," Austin growled. "But you ain't seen the last of me, James Baldwin!"

"That's unfortunate," said James, keeping his feet firmly in place.

Austin made a pitiful sight. A notion pricked James's heart. A reminder that he had promised the Lord that he would pray for the annoying little man. He had not been faithful in that regard. *But I tell you, love your enemies and pray for those who persecute you.* The Scripture from Matthew echoed in James's head. *I may need to be reminded, more than once, Lord. This unruly man appears to have no redeeming qualities. No character. Help me pray for him, with sincerity. I know you have a good plan for his life—if he would just listen.*

"Time's up, Austin," chimed Barry, as if speaking to a derelict teenager. "Get on home, now."

Barry held the door open for Austin to leave. He stood on the porch and watched him climb into his pickup and tear off up the driveway. He stayed there until the black smoke of diesel disappeared, and the gate closed securely behind him.

James joined Barry on the porch.

"I'd keep my eye on that one," said Barry. "He's got a burr under his saddle."

***

James left Barry to finish his moving and hurried over to Annie's. He was getting hungry and hoped she would feel up to celebrating with him. However, his throat constricted when he pulled up in front of her house and found Austin's dusty pickup parked in front of it. *What in the world?*

When he heard Annie scream from inside, sweat broke out on his forehead and his heart hammered in his chest. His imagination ran wild as he raced to the porch.

"Darn that guy, he's gonna make me fight him, yet."

Thundering up the steps, he crossed the wide veranda then slammed the door the rest of the way open.

Austin had Annie pinned to the couch, clawing at her, holding her head back with a fistful of hair, trying to kiss her. The challenge of praying for the stinker, just got harder.

James didn't stop to talk sense into the punk. He was past that point. Way past. Rather, he fisted a big chunk of Austin's shirt and hauled him up off the couch, dragged him over to the door then booted him out onto the porch.

"Get out of here, Anderson," he roared. "I won't hesitate to call the sheriff. This is your only warning."

"You can't tell me what to do!" Austin screamed, raising a fist in the air, his face dark red, his eyes flashing fury. He sounded like a child, yelling at a stepparent.

Austin didn't take off toward his pickup but didn't charge at James either. The point being he didn't leave. Without hesitation, James whipped out his phone and dialed 911.

"Yes, this is James Baldwin. I'm calling from Annie Jo Parker's residence. There is an intruder here. Yes, sir. Be happy to."

James was shocked that Austin still stood there, as if calling the law would be of no consequence. He really should have run. Swiftly shifting from the tolerance he'd managed at Barry's house to determined guardian, he was done coddling this brute. Maybe his daddy still saw him as a victim, but James considered him a menace.

Austin's eyes got wide when James rushed forward and fisted the front of his shirt. He slammed Austin down on the top step and forced his hands behind his back. It had taken all the strength he had in him. A bull.

The element of surprise gave him the advantage. Austin, a champion bull rider, was both strong and mean. But James held him. A new level of gratitude for two older brothers' training filled him. All those years of working out together were paying off today.

"Annie," he hollered over his shoulder. When she appeared in the doorway, he said, "Have any rope handy? The sheriff is on his way, but I want to secure this joker until he gets here."

Annie stood there, seemingly in shock, leaned against the doorframe on one side and her crutches on the other. Tears flooded her cheeks and fear filled her eyes. She clung to her crutches like a lifeline.

"Annie?" he said again, a little louder, but with a question in the word. Was she hurt? Had Austin done more than try to force a kiss from her? The scene flashed before his eyes, making his grip even tighter where he held Austin down. Had Austin assaulted his precious Annie Jo? Had he dared punch her? "Annie," he said, his voice now pleading. He needed to get through to her before Austin mustered up the energy and resolve to fight back.

Annie shook her head then made eye contact with him. A good sign. She seemed to recognize him. "I want to comfort you, sweetheart," he said. "But right now, I need a piece of rope to hold this bull down. Can you help me?"

A new light shone in her eyes.

Thank you, Lord.

Annie offered a slight grin then glared past him and scowled at the back of Austin's head. Then turned to go back inside. "I know just the one," she said, sounding more like herself.

She had come around, much to his relief. He didn't know how long he could hold Austin at bay. He was strong, and big, and mad. And still a little drunk.

For the few minutes Annie was gone, James called on his full strength to keep Austin in place. He prayed, and prayed some more, ignoring Austin's cries of protest, the curse words that flew out of his mouth. It took everything he had in him to subdue the tyrant—as if Austin were a steer and it was James's job to hold him until the rope restrained his limbs. Conjured up a whole new level of respect for Josh and Mack's rodeo performances.

His hands soon began to hurt from the strain and the cold.

The second Annie returned with a solid length of rope, James securely tied Austin to the porch post then flopped down on the boards to catch his breath and rest a minute.

Once he could feel blood pumping through his hands again, he stood, then led Annie over to the double swing. They snuggled close and spoke in low tones. He pulled a blanket off the back of the swing and wrapped her in it.

James held his sweetheart close, as he pondered the past several minutes. Angels must have come to help, as Austin remained tied fast. No amount of wiggling granted him freedom. When the sheriff stopped in front of the house, Sam pulled in behind him. Josh and Mack, next to Sam.

"What's going on here?" said Sheriff Nelson, stepping out of his vehicle and hurrying toward the porch.

James stood and made his way over to the sheriff, Annie right by his side, her arm looped through the crook of his elbow. He managed to keep a lid on the anger that threatened to explode out of his mouth and through his fists. He could feel Annie tremble at his side, could hear her sniffling, could only imagine the level of violation she must be feeling. Man, he wanted to hurt Austin Anderson. He had attempted to rape a woman with a cast on her leg, a woman smaller than himself, and alone in her house. A woman who was supposed to be his friend.

Sheriff Nelson gave a nod in Annie's direction. "Miss Annie."

"Sheriff." Her voice came out as a squeak, wrapped in fear. Made James want to knock the stuffing out of Austin.

Sam, Josh and Mack stood just beyond the sheriff. James kept his focus on the matter at hand, rather than wondering what the Parkers might think of him tying up their long-time friend and neighbor. But James had had his fill of Austin. No matter what anyone thought, he would do the same thing all over again. In a heartbeat. No regrets. No apologies.

"Get me out of this rope, Sheriff," shouted Austin. "I'm fightin' mad."

"Then maybe you're better off, right where you are. What started this mess?"

"First of all," said James, his tone demanding an audience, "Austin wriggled his way onto Mr. Blankenship's property, crashed in through the front door and started mouthing off. He was obviously inebriated. When Barry threatened to call you, Austin left. Boiling mad, but he did leave. Once my business with Mr. Blankenship was concluded, I came over here." He stumbled over the next words, shaken to the core. "And found Austin attacking Annie."

"Attacking?" said Sheriff Nelson, his attention shifting to Annie.

"Attacking?" said Josh, Mack and Sam, simultaneously, racing up the porch steps to stand behind her, showing total support.

Annie drew in a deep breath then pushed out the words. "Yes," she said, her voice firm, without hesitation, and without a trace of doubt. "He accosted me, and I believe he would have raped me, if James hadn't come when he did."

Sam put a hand back to ward off his sons, then skipped down to the lowest step, where he knelt eye to eye with Austin. Sam grabbed the boy/man by the collar and said, "You better thank your lucky stars the sheriff is here, buddy, or you'd be begging for your life, right about now."

Sam shoved Austin away from him, so the sheriff could handcuff him, before the rope came off.

Where Austin had gone ballistic at James, he had been subdued by a father's seething, yet sincere, promise. Messing with his daughter would not be tolerated.

Maybe Austin would finally go to jail, where he belonged.

"Let's go, son," said Sheriff Nelson. "I'll call your dad on the way to the office."

Sam, Josh, Mack, James, and Annie stood on the porch while the sheriff helped Austin into the back seat of his SUV then got behind the wheel. Josh jumped off the porch and ran over to the driver's side window of the sheriff's vehicle.

"I'll see that his pickup gets home," said Josh. "Please tell Mr. Anderson for me, when you call."

"Will do."

The Parkers and James went inside Annie's house, where they sat around the kitchen table. For a few minutes, everyone just sat there, stunned. Until Mack said, "I'll make some coffee, and some hot cocoa."

"Thanks," said Annie, smiling up at her big brother. "You know what I like. And there are fresh-baked cookies in the jar."

James thanked the good Lord that Annie had calmed down, had not been injured…or worse. This had to be the straw that broke the camel's back, right? Surely, charges would be filed, and Austin would be punished.

"Good. I could use a snack," said Josh, with a chuckle. James appreciated Josh's attempt to lighten the mood in the room. But no one at the table smiled. Annie had been attacked. They couldn't take that lightly, no matter how long they had known Austin. Surely, justice was not long behind this latest incident.

Once each of them had a beverage and a snack, the conversation turned to Austin. Of course, it did. Something needed to be done. Even Mr. Anderson would have to agree, Austin had gone too far.

"I'll start," said Sam, his voice still on the angry side. He turned the coffee mug slowly, back and forth for several seconds before he continued. "What happened at Barry's place?" He steadied his gaze on James.

"I bought his ranch," James said, simply. "We had the closing this morning. Not long after Barry's attorney and his assistant left, Austin came barreling in through the front door. Said he and Richard Worley came in and out the gate at the same time, so we had no warning. He said he'd had his eye on Barry's ranch for a long time and Barry didn't have any business selling to a greenhorn. Then he started threatening me. Barry humiliated him, offered to call Austin's dad and Sheriff Nelson, then ordered him off the property."

He paused then, thinking about what came next. The scene would never fade from his memory, as long he lived. He considered rape one of the lowest forms of criminal activity, right below sexual abuse of a child. Forgiving Austin would take some doing. A lot of prayer. A long, serious talk with the Lord. And some time. Maybe lots of time.

"He must have come straight over here because I left Barry's not long after Austin did. When I got out of my truck, I heard Annie scream. So, I barreled my way in and pulled Austin off her. I was livid. He's lucky I stopped at tying him up."

His voice quivered, his palms sweat, and the hair on the back of his neck stood up. He gripped his hands together in his lap, a technique he'd learned to focus pent up anger to one spot. The move had allowed him to control his temper, sitting across from more than one unreasonable foreign dignitary.

CHAPTER TWENTY-TWO

*May integrity and uprightness protect me, because my
hope, Lord, is in you.* (Psalm 25:21 NIV).

The room went deathly quiet, with only the sound of the wind outside. It stayed that way for a long, drawn-out, excruciating moment.

"Are you hurt, Annie? Did he?" Sam started, tears filling his eyes.

"No, he didn't have control of me that long," she said, reaching for James's hand, prying his fingers apart. He held on for dear life, never wanting to let her out of his sight again. Unrealistic, yeah, but that's how he felt.

"I almost feel sorry for him," said Josh, in a whisper.

"What?" cried Annie, surprise and hurt making the word sound pinched and full of hurt. "How can you say that?" She came half up out of her chair but reseated herself before her fingers slipped out of his grasp.

"It's just, I can't imagine losing Mom, ya know?" Tears filled his eyes, but James wasn't entirely moved. Yes, losing his own mother would be devastating—but he had proven he could build an honest life after the major loss of a parent. It was a matter of character. What is in a man's heart determines his actions, even his words. People made choices that were followed by unavoidable consequences.

"Things have not been right between Austin and Mr. Anderson since they buried her," Josh continued. "It's like he lost both of his parents at the same time."

From what James understood, the entire county knew the wife and mother had been the glue that held the Anderson family together. She had been a classy woman, strong, and kind, and godly. She had helped her husband build a ranch from nothing. Their dream had been to raise a passel of kids, but the good Lord had only blessed them with one. Austin. Even so, Mrs. Anderson did not lose her kind demeanor or turn bitter and ungrateful. Annie had told him several stories about Mrs. Anderson. She had loved the men in her life with all she had in her and provided a hot lunch for the ranch hands every day. Often, supper, as well.

Annie Jo sighed. James appreciated her deep well of patience. Marveled at how well she held herself together. She'd just been attacked, could have been badly hurt, or worse, and her brother was defending her attacker. He wanted to smack Josh, himself.

"I loved Mrs. Anderson, Josh. Really. I spent a lot of hours at her kitchen table. We bonded. She even taught me to cook, a little. I miss her, sure, but I don't owe my life to Austin, just because he feels lost without his mother. And I don't think her death justifies anything Austin has done. Remember, he treated me poorly, cheated on me, and pushed me around, long before his mother passed away. I hurt for him, yes. But I don't think we should ignore the cold, hard facts, here."

Good girl, Annie Jo. Stand up for yourself. James wanted to do more than speak his mind, he wanted to make sure Annie's family understood exactly where he was coming from. To what great lengths he would be willing to go to protect her, whether her family supported him in that regard or not.

Annie was a beautiful girl. But more than that she was a victim. Austin didn't see her beauty, only what he could get for himself, if he controlled her life. He wanted to be a big shot rancher with money and land and control. It seemed to always come back to control.

"I realize I am the new guy in town," James spoke up, determined to be heard. "But I have to agree with Annie. And now that I have a ranch of my own, I'm going to have to make a trip to Tennessee to arrange for the transfer of my horses and equipment and set up movers to bring the rest of my things down here. Before winter sets in. I need to put my house on the market. There's so much to be done, I could be gone a week or more. And just the thought of Annie being left here at Austin's mercy makes my stomach hurt."

One glimpse at Annie tightened his stomach even more. She looked crushed.

"Please consider staying with your folks, Annie," he continued, with a squeeze of her hand. "At least while I am away. I'd sleep better at night, knowing you're safe."

Sam stood and rapped his knuckles on the table. "You won't have to worry about that. We won't be asking Annie's opinion this time. Until things are settled, one way or another, with Austin, and until Annie is back on her feet, she most certainly will be staying with us. No question, no discussion."

"Dad," Annie started, a whine in her voice.

"Did you hear me say we won't be asking your opinion this time?" One eyebrow rose and his voice hardened. James had never heard that tone when he spoke to Annie Jo. He was seriously…serious.

The look Sam gave his daughter made James think of when he was a teenager and his mother put her foot down, then brought Maggie, the nanny, and Grammi in, for reinforcements. He could tell this would be much the same, for Mack and Josh would stand behind their dad, and soon Sissy would be in on what happened today. Then James felt certain the decision would be made, regardless of any protest from Annie Jo.

"Are you going to press charges?" said James, his voice gentle, encouraging, pleading. "You have every right. You know what his intentions were."

Annie frowned and scooted her chair even closer to James. His heart sank. Not again. Would she really let him get away with assault?

"I don't think so. It would just make him madder."

"What?" said James, his eyebrows raised. He leaned closer to her with his arm draped across the back of her chair. "And who cares how mad he is?"

"I can't really accuse him of a rape he didn't commit."

What was wrong with this picture? Why didn't her family demand justice be served?

"No," he said carefully, pulling patience from deep within. "But he is guilty of assault, at the very least. And should be charged with attempted rape."

"We'll stand behind your decision," said Sam.

James couldn't believe what he was hearing. Was Annie's family really considering *not* filing charges? Austin had already proven that he had no respect for Annie or for authority. His gut told him that Austin needed to be put away. And the sooner the better.

"Or go after him, if that's what you want," said Mack.

Now, you're talking, thought James. He'd be pleased to go after Austin himself, teach him a lesson, and give him a dose of his own medicine. Maybe if he got whipped and spent a few days in the hospital, he'd get the message. Maybe if he got convicted by a jury of his peers and spent some time in prison, he would get the message. Maybe if his father would act like a dad, he would stand up to his son with the Parkers, and make sure Austin turned himself in and owned up to his deplorable actions. All of them. A lot of maybes to hope for.

But James knew he would not provoke Austin, go after him without warning and beat him up. He knew God would frown on that behavior. He even heard Grammi's voice in his head: *Two wrongs never make a right, sweetie. If someone bullies you, find the principal or a teacher and let them handle it. Revenge is not our right; it belongs to the Lord. You're a child of the King, kiddo. I expect you to act like it.*

"Nobody's going after him," said Sam, affirming what Grammi would have said. "But whether or not you press charges, Annie, I intend to have a serious talk with Jake. His son can't go around bullying everyone and get away with it. It's time he took control of his own family.

"My heart breaks for him, at the loss of his wife. It does. I can't even imagine such a thing. But Austin needs to be stopped. If Jake can't or won't handle him, then we will get the law involved, and be available if the sheriff needs our help.

"Now, I think it's time we get Annie's things together and get her out of here. Soon as she's settled, I'll go see Jake. He may need someone to talk to, especially in light of the grief Austin has been dishing out. I've neglected our friendship, hiding behind the fear of stirring things up. Making life harder for him. It's time I stopped that nonsense and faced him."

It took a half hour for Annie to decide what all she would need to take to her parents' house. James had been given the privilege to drive her over, but his heart ached with the thought of leaving her. He had no choice, really. Winter was coming on fast. If he didn't get his things moved soon, it might be spring before the task could safely be accomplished.

"I hate that I have to leave you right now, Annie."

"Yeah, I hate it, too." The sadness in her voice didn't make him feel any better. He was tempted to take her with him. But that thought left as soon as it came. The trip would be busy, all over the place. Tiring. And right now, Annie Jo needed to recover, yet again. She needed her family close. He knew that, but he would rather be selfish.

"Have you talked to Bethany?"

"Not about this, no. But she left yesterday for Hawaii for a photo shoot. I'll tell her when she calls tonight. I don't want her to stay at the house alone, either. Hopefully, all this will be over before she comes back. But if not, I'm going to insist she stay with either her parents or mine, until it is. I think Austin would be less likely to show up at Dad's, knowing he would be met with opposition from three big men, who are all mad at him right now."

The fact that Austin had come after Annie at all kept James's blood at the simmering point. He could feel the heat under his skin. The man had to be deeply disturbed, controlled by an evil spirit that had a tight grip on him. *Pray for him.* James knew that voice. God was suggesting, no telling, James to pray for the man who had just attacked the woman he loved.

That was so much like God. He didn't want us to hate our enemies, but expected us to love them, commanded his people to pray for those who spitefully used them. It had to be a message from the Lord, because James knew he wouldn't even entertain the thought, unless Holy Spirit had prompted him. *Yes, sir.*

James promised God, yet again, that he would pray for Austin. He didn't know exactly what that might look like, but if the guy did not know the Lord, he needed prayer. He needed conviction and realization. He needed to surrender.

You're in control, Lord. I want your will for our lives, above all else. Please protect Annie Jo while I am away. "I got this," whispered through his spirit. James chuckled, grateful that God spoke to him in a way he could understand, with everyday words and thoughts that made the message clear. His heart swelled with gratitude that he had been raised in a Christian home, that the Lord had captured his attention and welcomed him back into his good graces. *Thank you, Lord. I'm so grateful that you are faithful, and loving, and compassionate.*

"When will you leave?" said Annie, breaking into his thoughts.

Her voice filled him with liquid fire. He loved this woman, her heart, her touch. He loved her enough to leave her here and go to Nashville to take care of business. "As soon as I am certain I have done everything I can from here, and the jet can be ready to go. I'll only be gone a week, tops. I intend to handle as much as possible through email and phone calls. But some things I need to be there for, like sign paperwork at the stables and look my trainer in the eye. And put the house on the market. I need to pack my clothes and some personal books and artwork I want to handle myself. I trust the people who work for me, but they can't do everything. Well, anyway, some things I'd just rather take care of myself."

Annie giggled, the most beautiful sound in the world. "I would have never guessed."

"Very funny." They hadn't known each other a terribly long time, but Annie already knew him better than anyone else. Maybe even better than his brothers, even though they were close. Very close. But James had offered a part of himself to Annie Jo that no one else would ever see. She had healed a long-time wound in his heart.

He parked in front of the Parker home then turned in his seat to face Annie Jo.

"Feeling better?"

"Some."

James left the engine running. He needed to get started with his plan of action, before the first snowfall, before sleet or freezing rain caused the airport to shut down. He reached across the console and offered Annie his hand. She grabbed on tight. "I'll miss you so much."

"Come back as soon as you can, James." Tears shimmered in her eyes, and it hurt. It hurt like crazy. If he had a choice, he wouldn't leave her.

"Promise. Look, I don't want to sound pushy, but please consider filing charges against Austin. He's gone too far. Really. Makes me sick to think what might have happened if I hadn't gotten there when I did."

He searched her eyes, held his breath, tried to convince her, without words.

"I promise to think about it," she finally said.

"I'll be praying every minute," he said, his hand resting on her arm. He was struggling not to lose his temper. He loved this woman and couldn't understand, even a little bit, why her family wouldn't press charges, whether

Annie Jo asked them to, or not. How did her brothers stand by and tolerate the fact that Austin had attacked their baby sister?

Because Sam and Jake were old friends? He simply did not get it.

"You know I love you, right? There isn't anything I wouldn't do to keep you safe."

"I know. I love you, too." Her eyes, tone, and body language rang with truth, and he relaxed a little bit. A little, not a lot. He would worry about her the entire time he was away.

"Call me when you get to Nashville?"

He sighed, realizing she was changing the subject. She might file charges; she might not. Either way, he wasn't going to find out before he left. Might as well acknowledge that fact and get on with it.

"Of course," he said, anyway, resigned, but not happy. "Try not to worry, I'll be back before you know it." *If everything goes as planned. If the weather will cooperate. If everyone in Nashville followed his instructions to the letter. If, if, if.*

"Yeah, well, I won't worry if you don't," she said, a little sass back in her tone. A good sign that she was feeling more comfortable in her skin. Which was a good thing. But he didn't feel any better. He decided to not bring it up again. Leaving her behind was killing him. He'd be gone and couldn't help if Austin came after her again.

"I'm really trying to trust God with the whole mess."

"I knew I liked you, the day we met," she said, leaning over the console. James moved toward her, unable to resist. "I can't tell you how much it means to me that you have a personal relationship with the Lord. It's like God knew exactly what type of man I longed for. Like he protected me from making a permanent mistake with Austin, so I would be available when you came along. Like he knew what I needed, before I did."

James felt a smile fill his face. "Yeah, God's like that. I'm trusting him to work everything out for our good. And for the record, I don't believe, for a second, that you would have let yourself make a permanent mistake with Austin. You're much too in tune with the Lord for that to happen."

"I'm praying, too, James. And thank you for believing in me." She lifted his hand to her lips and pressed a kiss to his knuckles, just as he'd done with her, several times. He closed his eyes and let her touch fill his soul. He would take that feeling with him to Nashville.

"This mess with Austin reminds me of the scripture from Sunday school last week. It didn't register with me then, but today it seems so clear. I still don't like it much, but I think I understand a little better what God was preparing me for. He knew what was coming and what I would need to get me through it. The scripture was from Romans 5, verses three through five. I memorized it over the past few days."

"What does it say? I might need this myself since we're going through this together."

Gratitude filled his heart for this gorgeous woman whom God was trusting him to love. *Thank you that she is listening to you, Lord, even in this deep valley.*

"It says: *We can rejoice, too, when we run into problems and trials, for we know that they help us develop endurance. And endurance develops strength of character, and character strengthens our confident hope of salvation. And this hope will not lead to disappointment. For we know how dearly God loves us, because he has given us the Holy Spirit to fill our hearts with his love.*

Annie was right. The scripture fit perfectly, considering the turmoil that had chased them over the past few months. A band of angels fighting demons. Waging war for the good of God's people. It would serve as an excellent reminder that God makes a way for his people and walks through the valley with them. Sometimes alongside them. Other times, he carries them when they are too weak or frightened to find their way in the dark.

"I'll make a point to memorize it, too," he said, feeling the truth, deep in his heart. They could trust the Holy Spirit to be with them through whatever Satan threw at them. No matter what Austin contrived, planned, or executed.

"Thank you for sharing, Annie. Now, much as I hate to say it, I'd better get you inside and get going, so I can get to Nashville and back in the shortest time possible. I really want my horses in a safe place before the first big winter storm. Plus, I don't want to be away from you any longer than I have to."

Closing the gap between them, he kissed her again, a soft, slow, undemanding kiss, he hoped gave her confidence that he would never force himself on her. Would never step beyond the boundaries of respect and honor he held for her. He wanted her to know the depth of his love, without any measure of fear.

"Come back soon," she whispered against his lips. "And be safe."

He stole another kiss, a lingering, thorough kiss that did not belie his need to hit the road. He reluctantly exited the truck then made his way around to the passenger door to help Annie maneuver her way to the ground, across the asphalt, and up the steps to her parents' front door.

Snuggling her close, he whispered, "Goodbye, sweetheart. I'll call you when we land in Nashville."

"See that you do," said Annie, lifting up on tiptoe. James received her kiss with a soaring heart.

This was the stuff dreams were made of.

CHAPTER TWENTY-THREE

James hugged Annie one last time, before heading to the office to take care of some last-minute business that couldn't be left undone.

By three in the afternoon, he had made arrangements for the horses to be transported, for the movers to meet at his house, and for the realtor to get the listing paperwork ready. He'd done all he could possibly do from Lubbock. And now, in about two hours' time, he would board his private jet and head back to Tennessee. The angst that settled in his gut had nothing to do with moving. That anxiety had been replaced with joy, the day he'd met Annie Jo Parker. But now, strange as it felt to recognize, he did not want to be in Tennessee. He belonged here, in Lubbock County, on his new ranch, with his sweetheart.

But it was too soon for that. So, he settled his mind on what needed to be done in the moment, leaving his beloved behind, in the capable hands of her family. In the watch care of his heavenly Father.

James punched the intercom button to call Terri. "Would you come in here for a minute, please?"

"Yes, sir."

When she entered, James indicated with a wave of his hand that she be seated across from him, realizing that he had yet to tell her how much he appreciated her work ethic. He spent so many hours behind closed doors, in meetings and on conference calls, they only spoke if he had a specific assignment for her. He knew she did a multitude of tasks to keep the office running smoothly. But he rarely thought about it.

"I think I owe you an apology."

"Sir?" She looked more scared than eager, which made him feel worse. He really should have been more forthcoming with her. Shown at least a measure of acknowledgment. The change in him had come on over a few weeks. He had noticed subtle differences since he'd renewed his relationship with the Lord—since he'd fallen in love.

The world looked different now. The sky seemed bluer. The grass greener. He saw people differently, as well. Not just as pawns in his game of adding more billions to his account.

He needed to practice his observation skills and show his assistant that he knew she had worth. That he appreciated her efforts, her consistent work ethic and punctuality.

"You have done a great job as my assistant, and I've never really thanked you," he said, his voice oozing with sincerity. A sincerity he didn't have to fake. Not anymore. His life was real. Exciting. Abundant. He actually looked forward to the future. To being "trapped" in holy matrimony—a feeling he had avoided his entire adult life. "Anyway, so, thank you."

It felt good to say it out loud.

"You're welcome," she said. But she still seemed apprehensive.

"Now that you know how much I appreciate you—I need to ask you to take on more responsibility." Hopefully, he didn't sound gruff or too bossy, but there was a lot on his mind, and he needed to be able to count on her. He was out of time. He believed she was competent, had paid attention and been well trained. If she was made of the stuff he thought she was, she could handle what he was about to ask of her. If he didn't think so, he wouldn't ask her to manage the office in his absence.

"I'll do my best, sir." Her voice trembled and fear still radiated off her body.

Gee, he really needed to work on his social skills. He did not want his personal assistant to be afraid of him, how ludicrous would that be? He could sympathize with her, but he didn't have the time or patience to deal with her insecurities. "Please. Call me James," he said, trying his best to evoke some level of camaraderie. "We need to be able to trust each other. I want you to be comfortable."

"I'll try, sir."

"James."

"I'll try…James."

She smiled then and James relaxed against the back of his chair. "Good. I want to tell you about a girl I met."

He told Terri about Annie Jo, about the ranch, and about his upcoming trip to Nashville.

"So, in my absence, I want you to feel free to call me at any time. This is new, so there will be questions. Don't hesitate to ask. If a supplier calls and you don't know what to tell him, call me. If a conference call needs to be scheduled, call me. If anyone gives you a hard time about my being out of the office, call me. You don't need to let anyone talk down to you. I won't have it. You are a valuable employee. And together we will be able to handle what needs to be handled. We can do it. Do you understand?"

Terri's eyes got big, and James grinned at her. Not in a flirty way at all. He'd been convicted that he had neglected his personal assistant. He was trying to fix that. Nothing more, nothing less.

Terri paused for a long moment. Concern and curiosity snaked up his spine.

What was happening? Would she quit right now when he needed her the most? Time was of the essence—he had to get out of here and finish packing. His personal jet would be sitting on the runway, waiting for him. But making Terri feel comfortable was also important, especially if he expected her to manage this entire place in his absence. She had value as a person. He wanted her to know that she had a place in this company that mattered.

"I appreciate your kind words, uh, James," she finally said, reaching for a tissue. She blotted her forehead and beneath each eye then sucked in a deep breath. "And I'm up for the challenge. I've been trying to work up the nerve to tell you that I needed your input on my job duties and performance. I thought I might even tell you that you have neglected me. Sorry, that sounds a little childish."

He chuckled in spite of his angst to get on the road. "Well, you're absolutely right. I struggled with moving back here. And I suppose I've been rebelling a little bit. But from this point forward things will be different. I want you to feel free to speak up when I mess up. I want your input."

Terri sat up straighter in her chair, like he had pumped her full of helium. She looked grateful, yes, but ready to take on this new and foreboding task. *Thank you, Lord, for making me aware. I trust you to keep me on my toes, so I do right by Terri and train her efficiently. I really need her to not fall apart in my absence.*

When, at last, James climbed aboard his jet, he settled into the same seat he occupied on every flight. Gazing out the window, he admired God's artistic handiwork. The sun hung just above the horizon, casting a rainbow of color across the tops of evergreens, bathing the city in an orange glow, mixed with a palette of color that blended into one gorgeous sunset. An incredible reminder that God is still in control. The entire universe obeys his every command. Whether people believed the truth, or not, did not change the truth. The truth was the truth. Period.

With that kind of power on their side, he and Annie could trust that God would work everything out—even when it seemed the odds were against them. Especially when the odds were against them.

Even so, leaving Annie Jo behind strained against his will. Pulled at his heartstrings and left him exhausted with worry. "Keep her safe, Lord," he mumbled. "Forgive me for worrying, a trait unbecoming to a believer. Help all of us to know what to do about Austin. He is truly a menace."

***

A freak winter storm blew in overnight, covering the territory with four inches of snow. A pleasant surprise in some ways, since the land had been overly dry during the fall. Cold, but dry.

Annie knew her father would be both pleased and annoyed. Snow meant messy fields and challenges with the water storage tanks, discouraged ranch hands, and a threat to weak places in the outbuildings.

It didn't affect Annie so much this year, seeing as she would be zero help. A burden, really. Someone her mother felt compelled to take care of—every minute, day and night. It was enough to make a girl stir-crazy, uncomfortable, and self-conscious.

But Annie Jo refused to lay in bed all day and feel sorry for herself, so she pushed the covers back, dropped her feet onto the plush rug that protected them from the cold hardwood floors, and hobbled her way to the restroom.

An involuntary shiver overtook her. The room was cold. Too cold, like the heating system had gone out. Mom usually reset the thermostat before starting breakfast. Maybe she had gotten a late start and would figure it out soon. Annie decided not to investigate until after her shower.

She turned the water on to warm up while she brushed her teeth. She hated taking showers with a cast on her leg. It had to be wrapped and protected, which was a major pain, while trying to position her lower leg outside the shower curtain and still manage to wash her hair, not to mention the rest of her.

Getting dressed was no fun, either.

Right after the break, her mom had taken a few pairs of old sweats and cut the seam up to the knee so the cast would be exposed, and air could circulate through it. Not Annie's favorite fashion statement, but it meant she could dress herself without assistance. She wore her normal shirts but paired them with zippered sweatshirts that matched the bottoms. Again, not ideal, but she could be seen in public. If she dared. Wearing long skirts on Sundays hadn't been difficult, just colder. She managed. Dealing with the cast every day kept the accident fresh on her mind. Dad had finally broken down and told her the cinch had been cut, so accident had been replaced in her head with incident. Someone, and she shuddered to think it could easily have been Austin, had sabotaged her gear.

Trying to force her to marry him, yet not caring whether she lived or died, made no sense. Could he be so desperate as to hire someone to hurt her? If he wanted to redeem himself to her family, that would be the way wrong approach.

Get out of my head, man.

With a concerted effort, Annie shoved Austin's antics to the back of her mind. But more and more often now, she found herself wondering if James was right—they should file charges against Austin then worry about helping Jake with the ranch, later.

Once clean and dressed, Annie made her way downstairs, surprised again that she didn't smell bacon frying, or even see a light on in the kitchen. Panic struck, and she shuffled to her mother's bedroom. The light was off there, too.

"Mom?" she said into the darkened room. No answer. Odd. Very odd. Her mother had been an early riser as far back as Annie could remember. Full of energy and enthusiasm, she encouraged the sun to rise, every morning.

The shutters in her mother's room were closed, blocking out the magnificent sunrise, a sight Sissy cherished. Mom didn't live that way. Nothing kept her down for long.

"Mom?" Annie said again, a little louder.

Her mother groaned but didn't speak.

Okay, that's bad. "Mom!" Annie cried, shuffling to her mother's side. "What's going on?"

"Please call Dad, sweetheart." The words came out garbled, difficult to understand, but Annie had heard 'call' and 'Dad', plain as day, in an agonized tone that ripped Annie's heart in two. Whipping out her phone, she called her father. He answered on the third ring. "Dad! Something is wrong with Mom. Come home. Now!"

She hung up without waiting for an answer then turned her attention back to her mother. So still and quiet.

"What can I do?" said Annie, lowering herself on the very edge of Sissy's bed. She leaned her ear close to her mother's mouth so she wouldn't strain to be heard.

"Wait."

Hopefully, her dad would make it back to the house in record time—before her mother…she couldn't think that way.

"Yes, ma'am."

She didn't like this. Not one little bit. Something had happened to her mother, and she couldn't do anything about it. She felt helpless. But more than that, fear crept up her spine and wrapped itself around her throat, nearly choking her.

Hurry, Dad. Please hurry. And Heavenly Father, have mercy on us. Please protect Mom from the evil one and his minions. By the power of the Holy Spirit, please perform a miracle in my mother's life.

Annie heard the backdoor slam and her father's pounding footsteps as he raced up the hall. He only moved that quickly when his stress level was through the roof. When a mama cow or horse was in trouble, during labor. When one of her brothers broke a bone, or Annie had fallen off her horse, early in her training days.

"What's going on?" he barked, rushing to her mother's side. Agony like Annie had never heard laced through the words.

"I don't know," said Annie, holding back a sob, standing, and taking a step back to make room for her dad. "She wouldn't say anything except to call you."

"Call 911 and Doc Brown," he snapped. "Do it now."

"Yes, sir."

Annie's hands shook as she pulled the phone out of her pocket, called for an ambulance then punched in Dr. Brown's number, amazed she could manipulate her way through both calls and still keep a grip on the phone. "I don't really know," she said, answering Doc Brown's question. "She's just lying in the bed. I called for an ambulance and Dad said to call you."

Josh and Mack came barreling into the room just as Annie disconnected from the call.

"What's happening?" said Mack, sounding more like a scared kid than their ranch manager.

"Not sure yet, Son," said Sam. "You kids wait in the living room and let me know the instant the ambulance gets here."

"Yes, sir."

Mack led the way, followed closely by Annie Jo, and Josh followed behind her, tears rolling down his face. He had always been the more tender brother, but Annie had a feeling the entire household would follow suit, if anything put their mother out of commission.

The air hung heavy in the living room, as the siblings waited. Annie's heart ached and her eyes leaked tears, as fear threatened to consume her. They couldn't lose their mother; she was too young. It was too soon. They weren't prepared for this.

Suddenly, an image of Jake and Austin filled her mind. A trace of compassion echoed in her spirit. She embraced it, accepted the reality that she had not really understood Austin's rebellion. He evidently did not know how to deal with the loss of his mother. When she died, Austin turned his back on God and the church. Refused condolences, shouting that he didn't need anyone's pity. *Oh, Lord, keep us strong in the faith. No matter what happens next, help us rely totally on you.*

"Doc Brown said he would meet us at the hospital," she told her brothers. "I wish I knew what was going on. I don't mind saying, I'm scared."

Josh mumbled something Annie didn't understand, and Mack patted her on the knee then said, "We need to keep the prayers going up on her behalf."

"For sure."

The three siblings joined hands while Mack led them in a moving prayer for the health and welfare of their mother. For the ambulance to reach them, without mishap. For the doctors and nurses as they worked on her. And for strength for their dad.

CHAPTER TWENTY-FOUR

And the prayer offered in faith will make the sick person well; the Lord will raise them up. If they have sinned, they will be forgiven (James 5:15 NIV).

The ambulance arrived a long, torturous fifteen minutes later. Sam rode with his wife in the back of it, and the kids followed in Sam's pickup, each one of them silently pleading for their mother's life. Each one filled with dread and hope at the same time. Each one dwelling on fond memories of their mother and clinging to the hope that there would be more memories to be made, in the future.

Annie pressed 1 on speed dial and waited for James to pick up. She didn't know what she could report yet, but she needed to hear his voice.

"Annie," he said, his voice bright and happy, deep and engaging, just like she remembered. Tears rushed to the surface, in sheer relief that he'd been available. "I'm so glad you called. How are you? Everything all right?"

Tears escaped the second he answered. He sounded close enough to touch. It took Annie a few seconds to find her voice. She missed him so much, needed him with her, needed to feel his strength, to lean on him, and know he would be there for her, no matter what.

She had never felt that way about a man, other than her dad. But she knew the truth now, she needed James in her life in a more powerful way than she had relied on her father. It was a mystery how love works, but she couldn't deny the magnetic pull, the emptiness she felt without him.

"We're on our way to the hospital," she managed to say, her voice trembling. "Something has happened to Mother and we don't know what it is. I don't have a report yet, but I needed to talk to you, to ask you to pray for her. Please."

There, she'd gotten the words out. A chill raced up her arms and across the back of her neck. The truck was warm, but Annie felt cold. Consumed with concern for her mother, she had a hard time being patient. Some snow had accumulated on the road but remained passable. Her heart raced and she clung to the phone, as though she could feel James's hand at the other end.

"Oh, Annie, of course I will." And right then, he launched into a heartfelt prayer on behalf of Sissy Parker. The sound of it made Annie's heart swell, and confirm, yet again, how much she cared for this godly, handsome man she was falling in love with. How right he was for her, and for her family.

"I wish I were there with you," he whispered. "I can't imagine how anxious you must be."

"When can you come home?" said Annie, sucking in a deep breath, trying to level out her emotions. To get calm and stay rational, for her mother's sake.

"I'm scheduled to return Wednesday morning. But if you need me, I'll head that way right now. I can always finish what I need to up here, some other time. Nothing is as important as you. Just say the word, and I'm there."

Annie glanced over at Mack, behind the wheel. He nodded, indicating they would back whatever decision she made. It seemed obvious that he had followed the gist of her conversation with James.

"No, that won't be necessary," she finally said, admitting that it would be selfish to ask him to come back before they had any news of her mother's condition. Before his business had been concluded. "Not now, anyway. But if something happens." Her voice broke, just thinking about what that might mean. She sniffed, took in a shuddering breath then pulled herself together. Again.

She was not alone. She still had her brothers. They would be fine, until James finished his business in Nashville. They would. "Anyway," she continued, a little steadier than before. "I'll let you know if Mom takes a turn for the worse. If that happens, I definitely want you here. But for now, just get done what you went up there to do, so you never have to leave me again."

Tears rolled down her face and dripped off her chin, but Annie paid them no mind. This was her mother they were talking about. Life would never be the same again if she. But that was not going to happen. Not yet. She had to believe that. Had to have faith that God would heal her, protect her, and bring her back home to them, good as new.

"Only if you're certain," said James. "But I'll keep the jet on standby. If you call, I can be there in a couple hours. I promise."

"Thank you, James."

"I'm so sorry, sweetheart."

"Yeah, me too. Listen, we're approaching the hospital now, so I'll let you go. We'll talk soon, okay?"

"Sure. Hang in there."

"I will. Love you."

"I love you too, Annie. I'll see you soon."

The Parker family sat in silence, awaiting word from the doctor. Sam didn't like one bit that they had his wife back there, where he couldn't go. The people in command had made them wait over an hour, without an update. When Dr. Brown entered the room another half hour later, Sam jumped to his feet and met the doctor three steps inside the door.

"Now calm down, Sam," said Dr. Brown, his hands up in a gesture of good will. "The news isn't bad."

"What *is* the news? Tell it to me straight, Roger. I'll know if you're lyin'."

Her father's imposing height and stance would encourage anyone he interrogated to tell the truth. They wouldn't know, just by looking, that he had a gentle, compassionate spirit. It just came in a really large, intimidating earth suit.

Annie, Josh and Mack joined their dad. Annie placed a hand on her father's lower arm and Sam jumped. "It's okay, Dad. We're all here with you."

"I appreciate that, Annie, I really do. I'm just antsy right now."

"So," said Dr. Brown, clearing his throat, "Sissy has had a mild stroke."

A collective intake of breath could be heard through all four of Sissy's family members. Sam recovered first and took a step closer to Dr. Brown, bending down a little so he could look Roger in the eye.

Annie frowned. Her mother had had a stroke and Dr. Brown had said the news wasn't bad. How did those two things go together?

"What do you mean by 'mild'?"

Annie could feel her heart pounding. How long had it been before Annie found her? Would there be permanent, debilitating effects? Would she die? What caused a stroke, anyway? Blood clots, maybe. Is that what she'd heard? She tightened her grip on her father's arm and started praying. All the questions would be answered in time. And they would face them together, as a family. No matter what they had to deal with. They'd do it. God's Word promised he would never leave them or forsake them. That he would walk with them through the storm. Carry them, if necessary.

Living by faith wasn't always easy. When the wind is whipping around you, accompanied by loud claps of thunder and deadly bolts of lightning, a Christin had to trust God to either calm the storm—or calm the man, in the midst of the storm. And no one can know, in advance, which way the Lord would handle each new set of challenges.

Our human frailty would prefer that our Savior calm the storm, every time, so we don't have to endure the wind or the thunder and lightning. But it doesn't always work that way.

Our faith grows stronger when we experience God's peace, even through the blinding rain. When we push forward against the raging winds, with lightning striking all around us.

"I *mean*," said Dr. Brown, calm and consoling, breaking into Annie's head. "You got her here fast, which is always good. I *mean*, she will recover completely, and there are likely to be no permanent disabling effects. I *mean*, she is overworking herself and may need some medication to deal with possible blood clots. I *mean*, in effect, that she is fine. No paralysis. No speech impediment. No lasting effects. However," he continued, his face stern, not backing away from the giant of a man who stood in front of him, which told Annie he was being totally forthcoming with them. "You must find a way to relieve some of her workload, take some of the stress off her. She won't like it, I know. Probably wouldn't even admit she is stressed. But complete rest is necessary for her complete recovery. Do I make myself clear?"

"Crystal," said Sam, his shoulders relaxing, just a bit.

At least a few of Annie's questions had been answered. Her mother would be fine. Fine being a relative term. There would likely be some sort of rehab to build up her strength, some sort of medication. But nothing that could not be worked into their normal schedule. So, they would have to get some help around the house. Compared to losing her mother, it was nothing. *Thank you, Jesus.*

"Good. I expect to see her again tomorrow, when I'll order a few more tests, in order to verify my diagnosis. I'll be calling in a specialist to double-check my double-check. We will leave no stone unturned in order to prevent a reoccurrence."

"Thank you, Doc," said Sam, completely calm. Annie decided he accepted Doc Brown's words and realized they had been most fortunate. Considering the fact that Sissy could have died, they were most fortunate, indeed. "Can we see her now?"

"Yes, but only two at a time. We don't want her torn in too many directions at once. She needs quiet rest, and plenty of it. Now, if you'll excuse me, I'll see to her prescription and schedule that specialist."

"Thanks again, Doc," said Sam, reaching out his hand.

Doc Brown accepted the handshake and offered a warm smile. "She'll be back on her feet soon. She'll want to overdo it, like she's always done. I'm counting on all of you to make sure that doesn't happen."

"Count on it," said Sam.

Doc Brown took in each face, as he released Sam's hand. "All of you," he said, again.

"Yes, sir," the three siblings said, in unison.

They'd do anything to help their mother get well. Anything.

Doc nodded, seemingly satisfied, then left the family alone.

They all stood looking at each other for a moment, smiles and tears mingled together.

"Thank the good Lord," said Sam.

"Amen." The kids answered together, again. Sometimes, only one word would suffice, and they all knew it.

"So, you boys be okay with me taking Annie in with me?" There would be no questioning the fact that Sam would go first.

"Sure, Dad," said Mack.

"Yeah," said Josh.

With a heart filled with shaky gratitude, Annie walked on wobbly legs alongside her father to see Mom. *She's fine.* Annie repeated the mantra all the way to Sissy's room. She needed to get that message to her heart and her brain. She needed to believe it.

The lighting in Sissy's hospital room seemed dim, no doubt brought on by the cloudy weather, and the fact that the only light came from a lamp on the bedside table. Annie squeezed her father's arm, an automatic reaction to the pale, still form before her, who didn't resemble her mother in the least. It hurt her heart to realize just how fast she could have been taken from them. But she shoved that thought aside, yet again. Her mother had *not* been taken from them. She was alive and would recover. She would be going home with them soon. Good as new, or close to it. She had to. Annie wouldn't be able to handle any other outcome.

In that moment, she wished James wasn't in Tennessee. But she knew it would be wrong to ask him to come home before his work had been completed. She had promised to let him know if things took a turn for the worse. But that wasn't the case at all. She had her family with her. She could wait. It wasn't like she was alone in her misery. But without James, life seemed harder, bleaker, darker.

But Dr. Brown had been optimistic about her mother's recovery. They could handle lightening her load much easier than planning a funeral. Everything was going to turn out okay. Better than okay. Great.

A flash of understanding for Austin zig-zagged its way through her system. His mother *was* gone and would never be back. Granted, he'd chosen destructive ways to deal with the loss. Had been rebellious and reckless, long before her death. It seemed the loss exacerbated his rebel ways and made him even more self-destructive.

But now that they had come so close to losing Sissy, Annie had some inkling of what he must be going through. Especially if his father wasn't coping, either. His entire support system had been yanked out from under him. She decided then and there, that even though she could no longer safely have any sort of relationship with him, it was still her duty to forgive him. To pray for him. *Yes, Lord, I'll pray for Austin and his father. I'll pray for peace, for them to find their way back to you. And I'll rest in your unfailing love, trusting you to help me forgive Austin for being a total jerk.*

Following three days of testing, Sissy was granted leave to go home with her family. Three long days in the hospital had just about worn them out. Hours and hours of waiting and wondering had taken a toll on them, emotionally. However, no one complained about the wait, or the driving back and forth, or managing chores. They just wanted Mom and wife to be well. To be able to enjoy life to the full again. They wanted her home with them, whatever that might require of them.

Annie sat on the sofa, her casted leg resting on a pillow, her phone clutched tightly in her hand. She had spent the past hour haggling with an agency that supposedly specialized in placing domestic help.

"Finally, I think we may be able to use this lady. Please ask her to come out by nine tomorrow morning to meet Mom and get the lay of the land."

"Someone coming in the morning?" said Sissy.

Annie placed her phone atop the coffee table then turned to face her mother. An inspiring sight. Mom was getting around well and behaving herself. Which had surprised everyone.

Sissy was a strong, independent woman who took pride in her role as mother and wife. For her to take a step back, spoke volumes. The mini stroke must have taken its toll.

"Yes, ma'am. She sounds perfect. Even so, I have my fingers crossed. The holidays will soon be upon us and there's so much to do. It irritates me to pieces that I'm stuck in this cast. But, trust me, I don't intend to let it slow me down so much that I can't be of service."

Sissy walked slowly to the coffee table in front of the couch so she could face Annie. She moved Annie's phone to the side and lowered herself onto the table, reaching for Annie's hand.

"You listen to me, young lady. I'm so impressed that you have kept up with everything here, while visiting me at the hospital. That you got up early this morning and made breakfast for everyone. I know how frustrated you are, being cooped up in the house, which makes your good attitude and help, even more impressive. So, listen, young lady, I don't want to hear you say another negative thing about my daughter. And thank you for helping to find someone to take the bulk of the chores off both of us."

Annie let her mother go on and on about her good qualities and outstanding performance, with a hint of hidden amusement. Arguing would be a waste of breath, and part of her liked hearing the accolades, especially thrilled that her mother spoke clearly, without a hint of slurring. A huge blessing.

Dr. Brown and the specialist had agreed that Sissy had had what they called a TIA. Annie had looked it up on the Internet: *A Transient Ischemic Attack (TIA) is often called a mini stroke, but it's really a major warning. TIA is a temporary blockage of blood flow to the brain. Since it doesn't cause permanent damage, it's often ignored. But this is a big mistake. TIAs may signal a full-blown stroke ahead.*

The hospital had taken the warning seriously. Annie's family would do the same. What Sissy needed Sissy would get. Annie smiled across the space, making sure her mother knew she was listening. Her heart swelled with the enormity of the miracle that now sat across from her.

Annie and her mother had always been close—to a point. When it came to domestic engineering, however, Sissy excelled where Annie preferred horses and barns. She had heard her mother say, when she thought Annie was out of earshot, that she sometimes felt like she was raising three boys. It had made Annie chuckle at the time, for she did consider herself a Tomboy, although totally female, at the same time. She loved horses, everything about them. She loved riding them and brushing them and racing them. But she also loved and respected her mother, revered her and admired her skill at running a household, all while meeting the individual needs of her husband and children. Of course, she had noticed. She wasn't deaf, dumb, or blind. Annie had decided long ago, despite her shortcomings in this area, that she would be teachable. As a result, she had mastered a few recipes, could scrub toilets with the best of them, had perfected the art of laundry, and owned enough dresses to make a decent showing at church on Sundays. So, she wasn't terrible, just less than enthralled about engaging in domestic chores than her accomplished mother.

"I'm praying we love her, and she loves us, *and* that she has a real talent for housekeeping and cooking. That she enjoys domestic engineering. And you, my dear mother," said Annie, "will follow your doctor's orders and be a lady of leisure, at least until after the holidays."

Sissy opened her mouth to respond but was stopped by the doorbell.

"Are you expecting anyone?" said Annie, with raised brows. It was rare for anyone to make the trek from town, especially during inclement weather. Or to even use the front door. Except their pastor, who always did.

But they weren't expecting the pastor. He would have called ahead, even if he'd been nearby.

"No. You?"

"No," said Annie, pushing up off the couch and reaching for her crutches.

"Don't get up. I'll go," said Sissy, standing.

Annie followed her mom's progress, noticing she walked slower than yesterday. That she favored her left leg, like she had to concentrate to get its cooperation. She made a mental note to bring it up to Dr. Brown. Something was going on that Sissy had not chosen to share with her family. Annie really wished she wouldn't do that. Could be a costly mistake. It could cost her life. She needed to get over the pride issue and be real with them.

When the door swung open and she saw who was standing there, Annie yelped and pulled herself the rest of the way up and grabbed both crutches at once, nearly tangling herself up in them. She managed not to fall, as she heard her mother exclaim, "JB Baldwin, you little stinker! You didn't tell us you were back. Get in here out of the cold."

"Hello to you, too," said James, with a chuckle, taking her up on her offer. He took his boots off at the door, per usual, before he responded. "Mrs. P, I hope you are doing as well as it looks like you are. I'm so sorry I couldn't be here any sooner, at least for moral support, if nothing else."

Annie reached them then and slid an arm through James's crooked elbow, staring up at him, her eyes full of love and wonder. Her James was back. Safe and sound. Her world had righted itself in an instant.

"I'm better than I can get my family to believe I am. They're all treating me like I'm made of glass."

"Just as all treasures should be treated," said James, with a wink.

"Aren't you sweet," said Sissy. "Come into the kitchen, Son. We have coffee, some leftover bacon and eggs, if you're hungry. I think I even spotted a cinnamon roll in the bun warmer."

James followed Sissy to the dining room table, holding Annie close to his side, while she maneuvered on crutches. Awkward, but doable.

Annie wasn't about to let go of him, and nudged herself as close as possible, without knocking them both off balance.

"I'd love some coffee. But I had breakfast on the plane."

"Good enough. Annie, please show James where everything is. I think I'll go lie down for a bit."

When Sissy had turned away, Annie couldn't stop the frown that took over her face. Her mother was tired, and it was only eight in the morning. Not good. She couldn't be digressing, could she? *Dear Lord, help her rest as much as her body demands. I pray for complete restoration and healing. And help us know what to do and when to do it.*

"Okay, Mom," she said, forcing a brightness into her tone she didn't feel. Her cheerful sing-song effort probably didn't fool anyone, but she needed to put up a front, so her mother didn't suspect that Annie saw more than Sissy knew. "I'll come check on you in a little while."

"Fine. It's nice to see you again, James. I'm pleased you made it back safely."

As soon as James heard Sissy close the bedroom door, he pulled Annie into his arms and grinned as she let the crutches fall and leaned into him. He'd missed this. Missed holding her, the scent of her. The sound of her voice and the very essence of her. His soul hummed just being close to her again.

"You feel so good in my arms. It's been a long, lonely week."

It had taken a day longer than James had anticipated to put things in order and be ready to move. Nashville employees had the Christmas Spirit, well enough, just not the spirit to work. Multiple phone calls followed by multiple visits, bordering on threats, had left him drained.

But it wouldn't be long now until everything he had accumulated in Nashville would be here in Lubbock County, on his ranch, with him. Paul and Matt had jumped right in, overseeing the construction of a new barn where James's racehorses would reside.

He'd only been gone eight days, but the new structure had been framed in. Insulation and the interior walls would be finished this very afternoon. It had cost him, what with weather challenges and grumpy construction workers. But the obstacles had been jumped, thanks to Matt's intimidating presence, which still made James smile. He longed to see the finished product, of course. But not as much as he'd craved seeing Annie. She would remain his number one priority, as far into the future as he could imagine. It made sense to stop at her house first. He had to pass it to get to his and his truck refused to bypass her gate. It headed straight for the love of his life, like a homing pigeon.

"I know what you mean," said Annie, giving him a squeeze that made his hopes soar. "It took a lot of willpower not to beg you to come back early."

"Then you should have called. I would have come," he said, pulling back enough to look her in the eye. "Everything else could have waited."

"No, I should not have called," said Annie with a grin. "I needed time to accept the fact that Mom is going to need help. I needed time alone with God. I even took time to let myself forgive Austin and pray for him and his dad. It was excruciating. But necessary. I missed you lots, but God knew what I needed to do, and he was gracious enough to nudge me in the right direction."

A glow filled her eyes and James hugged her again. "I'm very proud of you, Annie. I had to do some of the same. You're a little distracting, for quiet time."

Annie laughed and pushed back from him, stretching her arms to pick up her crutches. "Yeah, God knows what it takes to get our attention then keep it for a few minutes. So, when will all your things be home?"

Bending over to help her get situated with her crutches, he said, "Let's sit at the table and talk, okay? I'd really appreciate a cup of that coffee your mom mentioned."

Now balanced, she said, "Oh, of course. Let me get it for you."

James rested a hand on her shoulder. "Two crutches and a cup of coffee? I know you could handle it, sweetheart, but let me this time, please? I'm here to help, not sit around while you wait on me."

"Don't have to tell me twice." A big smile filled her face as she made her way to the kitchen table. "Make yourself at home, darlin'. Holler if you can't find something."

James was home, for wherever Annie was, felt like home. He would catch her up on all the latest then fight the weather and traffic to his office. Catch up with Terri, in person, and look over everything she had accomplished in his absence. Then he would go home, check out the barn, and take a nap. A long nap. If he got his way.

CHAPTER TWENTY-FIVE

Then you will go on your way in safety, and your foot
will not stumble. (Proverbs 3:23 NIV).

"I need to go see Jake," said Sam at an emergency family meeting he'd called on short notice. One of the ranch hands had been sent to fetch Josh and Mack.

Once the meeting got under way, Sam continued. "I heard he came down with the flu. They may need some help over there."

"Help?" cried Josh. "Why would you help them after all that has happened with Annie? Austin came close to *raping* her. In case you've forgotten. I can't believe what I'm hearing."

The outcry seemed out of character for Josh. The same Josh who had offered to return the skunk's pickup on the day Austin had attacked his sister. The same Josh who had made excuses for Austin, when the rest of the family had been ready to string him up. Not literally, but they'd been extremely angry after the assault. The only reason Austin wasn't rotting in a jail cell right now was because his father had promised to keep him on the ranch, with the understanding that if he stepped out of line one more time, in any capacity whatsoever, the Parkers would come down on him, hard. Sam had trusted Jake in that regard, and the Parker family had not seen or heard from Austin, since. Hopefully, he had calmed down and accepted the fact that he would never own the BB ranch, any part of the Parker ranch, and controlling Annie Jo Parker would not be part of his future.

But lately, Josh had spent some extra time getting to know his sister. Had made himself sit and listen to the entire story about Annie's long-running association with Austin. He had apologized to her, begged her forgiveness, and promised to watch over her, like he should have been doing all along. That bully would never lay hands on her again. Never.

She could see that same fury in his eyes, now.

"I understand your concern, Josh. And I respect your opinion. But let's ask Annie how she feels about it, shall we?"

Annie gasped. "Me? I wouldn't be any help. I'll be stuck in this cast at least until Christmas."

"Sweetheart, I'm not asking you to perform manual labor," said her father with an edge to his voice, as though desperate for his family to understand where he was coming from. "I'm asking if you object to my helping Jake out of a tight spot. How you feel about it matters to me. I won't go if it's going to cause conflict in my own household."

Annie ran a hand over her face. She really needed some time to think about her answer. "I'd like to think about it while you conclude other business. I can't afford to spout off something I'll regret later. Please excuse me to my room."

"Good idea," said Sissy, standing. She met Annie at the end of the sofa, with a soft smile. "I'll come get you when we're done here."

Even with all the stress the family had endured, Sissy had been making good progress with the physical therapist who had come out to the house. She was getting her strength back and could walk with a sure foot. The TIA had been a scary wakeup call. But now that they knew how to best prevent a second occurrence, the atmosphere at home had begun to relax. If they just didn't have to deal with the Anderson family, life would be next to perfect.

"Thank you," whispered Annie. She dragged herself upstairs, one clunky step at a time, beyond tired of being saddled with a cast and a set of crutches. She might just toss them into a bonfire—the second that blasted cast came off.

Inside the privacy of her old room, Annie crossed over to the window seat and lowered onto the deep emerald-green velvet cushion. She could see the barn and the indoor arena, and a few horses and cattle huddled together under a group of evergreens.

The thought of the family meeting slammed back into her mind. The problem needed to be addressed and apparently her family respected her opinion. Cared that their actions would affect her. So, how did she feel about her dad and brothers helping on the Anderson ranch? How would she feel if her own family were in dire straits and Mr. Anderson offered his help?

The obvious Christian thing to do would be to man up and show up. Obviously. But it didn't seem that simple. Could the rift between the two families be mended with thoughtful gestures? Or would they be sending a message of invitation to Austin? *You hurt my child. Stay away from her. Then, oh, never mind. It wasn't that big a deal.*

With her cast resting on the window seat, Annie Jo's other leg began to bounce, an outward display of inner turmoil. Hurting her had been a big deal.

The human reaction would be to let Mr. Anderson suffer the consequences for his son's outrageous behavior. It was, after all, his big idea to show mercy and let his guilty son walk. They deserved some hardship for what she'd been through.

That thought alone should have been all the insight Annie needed to tell her father not to go. But she couldn't find peace with that answer—struggled with the *right* thing.

Pressing her head against the cool glass, she began to pray. "Not my will, Lord. But thy will be done, on earth as it is in heaven. Give us this day our daily bread and lead us not into temptation but deliver us from the evil one. For thine is the kingdom and the power and the glory forever. Amen."

A simple prayer. A plea. The words came straight out of God's holy word. The only prayer that came to mind at the moment. She did want God's will above her own. She did want to love her neighbor as herself.

"I'm feeling pretty human right now, Lord. Mr. Anderson has had a tough time of it. First, his wife's death. And now, Austin is adding to that grief. When Janice passed away, with no time for her family to get used to the idea of living without her, the world took on a dark countenance for Jake and Austin, leaving them in the throes of grief.

"Give me the mind of Christ, so I will say your words and perform your deeds."

As she closed the prayer, tears slipped down her face. As peace settled in her soul, a knock sounded at the door.

"We're ready when you are, sweetie." Mom. At least she felt ready to face the family now.

"I'm about there," she said, allowing a smile to soften her voice. Mother would hear it and remain calm as well. "I'll be down shortly."

"Okay, then. I'll see you in the den?"

"Yes, ma'am, just a few more minutes."

Annie went into the restroom, splashed water on her face, patted it dry, and reworked her braid. She was stalling, but it really had begun to unravel. She looked herself in the eye and said, "You got this. Not Josh, nor anyone else, can talk you out of doing what's right. Thank you, Lord, for clarity."

***

Sam pounded on the Anderson's front door. He waited a long five minutes, hammering and ringing the bell every few seconds. When no one answered he ran around to the back, hollering along the way. He stopped to suck in a breath when two cowboys came running from the barn.

"Where's Jake?" said Sam, panting. The scare he'd had at the front door had come close to making him panic. He had imagined Jake inside, struggling to breathe, burning up with fever, and nobody there to help. "I haven't been able to rouse him." His breath came in short spurts as he managed to stand to his full height. "I'm afraid he might be in a bad way."

Jake's ranch hands were looking at him like he was off his rocker. What was going on here? He didn't know how much personal information Jake shared with his hands, but Austin was bound to be shouting his disgruntled feelings at the top of his lungs. Suddenly, Sam thought his life might actually be in danger. A feeling he didn't think would ever happen at the home of his best friend.

"Well, do you know where he is?" Sam said sternly, disguising his fear, when the men just stared at him.

"I'm here," said Jake, buttoning his jacket against the cold and pushing his hat down low over his ears, while tightening the scarf around his neck. "What's got you so riled up, Sam?"

Sam was totally speechless, shocked, embarrassed. Had he heard wrong about Jake's illness? Concern for his friend turned to worry for his own safety. Had he been lured there under false pretenses, so he could be attacked? Some kind of retaliation for demanding Austin's behavior be dealt with. He stared at Jake, not knowing what to expect, and trying to come to grips with the entire situation.

"Sam," said Jake. "Are you all right?"

Sam made his way to Jake, bent down and looked his friend in the eye. "Are you?"

"I'm fine. Look, if you're here about Austin."

"I'm not," Sam was quick to say, his hand raised in an effort to promote peace. "I heard you were sick with the flu. I came to offer our assistance. That's it."

A stiff northern breeze whipped between them and swirled snow around their feet. Years of memories rushed through Sam's mind, making him further determined to renew his life-long friendship with Jake. There had to be a way to fix this mess.

"You guys get on with the morning chores," barked Jake, dismissing the ranch hands. "I'll join you soon."

"Yes, sir," said the two men, in unison. They left without another word but did cast sideways glances in Sam's direction. But he shook off their curious stares then turned toward Jake, when he heard him speak.

"Let's go inside, Sam. I'll make a fresh pot of coffee."

With no sign of resentment in his tone, Sam simply said, "Thank you."

He followed Jake into the house. While Jake made coffee, Sam fiddled with the Texas-shaped salt and pepper shakers that sat on either side of a wooden napkin holder Sam remembered Jake making for one of Janice's birthdays after a disastrous picnic when every napkin and paper towel they'd brought along got carried away with the wind. He was sorting out what he'd say to Jake, if the subject of Austin and Annie came up. Their greatest point of contention couldn't be ignored forever.

"Excuse the mess," said Jake, looking peevish, as he set a mug down in front of Sam. "My heart isn't in it."

"Understandable. No judgment, here." He was just glad they could share a moment of civility. He missed his friend, wanted to set things right between them. Austin or no Austin.

The two men sat in silence for a time then Jake spoke first.

"I suppose I owe you an apology for Austin's behavior. Sadly, I don't have any better control of him than I do this house. I'm surprised he's been sticking around. I think this last misunderstanding with AJ must have really shaken him up. Although he'd never admit such a thing."

The look on Jake's face tugged at Sam's heart. His friend was hurting, deeply grieved, and wounded by his son's rebellion. But still, how could he call the ordeal between Austin and Annie Jo a misunderstanding? Sam had to grip the sides of the chair to keep from snapping at his friend. He didn't want this meeting to go sideways, before it even got started.

Sam's most sincere attempt to put himself in Jake's shoes, failed. To lose his wife, followed closely by a son, his only son, being on the rampage, would be beyond devastating. He couldn't begin to convince himself that his own reaction would have been much improved over Jake's denial and dismissiveness. Sam felt almost desperate to help.

"I can't imagine what you've been through. Is there anything I can do?"

The back door slammed, and Austin roared at Sam, "Yeah, there's something you can do. Get out of our house and off our ranch. We don't need anything you have to offer."

Sam didn't respond but watched in wonder as Jake stood and confronted his son. If he'd had the opportunity, he would have escaped and left them to settle the issues between father and son. But he couldn't get out without plowing right between them, so he kept his mouth shut and simply prayed.

Fifteen minutes later, Sam found himself alone with Jake, once again.

"He's a troubled boy," said Jake, with a deep frown. Tears filled his eyes, and the sight of his friend in agony just about broke Sam's heart. "I have no idea what to do with him. At least I got it through his thick skull that if he didn't stay here, on the ranch, he would be charged with attempted rape, and most certainly go to prison. I'm hoping that threat will work for a long time. At least until Austin can get his head on straight. But he's mad as a hornet, and I worry every minute that he's going to rebel and do something crazy. I'm afraid for his life, Sam. He's reckless and angry, and I suspect he's drinking more than ever."

Sam grasped the coffee mug to keep his hands occupied and give his eyes a place to focus. This conversation could get ugly quick, if Sam said everything that had run through his mind since Austin had attacked Annie. But something needed to be done about the boy's behavior. His temper had turned volatile and dangerous. And now, his drinking had increased? Anger and alcohol made for an explosive cocktail. Jake had every right to worry. *Give me your words, Lord. My friend needs help.*

"Let's start with something simple," said Sam, continuing to pray, even as he spoke.

"What are you suggesting?" said Jake, staring a hole through Sam.

He didn't want to insult his friend, but he cut a look over at Jake, wrinkled his nose then glanced around the portion of the house he could see.

"No offense, but we recently discovered a service that places housekeepers who also cook. Would you like the number?" He was nervous about how Jake would react. But the house had suffered a great deal of neglect. Maybe getting it in order would be a good first step to getting the Andersons' lives back in order. Hopefully, Jake wouldn't punch him in the face for pointing out the obvious.

Suddenly, Jake began to guffaw, loud and long. Tears filled his eyes as laughter overtook him. Once Jake got control of himself, he said, "Of all the deep, dark subjects you could bring up, you're worried about my *house?*"

Sam shrugged and offered a half smile. It really did smell bad.

"Well, I'm concerned about you living in it."

Jake sobered then and made eye contact with Sam. In his eyes, Sam read a myriad of emotions: grief and fear, sure, but also gratitude. He caught a glimpse of his old friend, in that look.

"Thank you for coming today, Sam. I've missed our camaraderie. And yes, I'll take that number. Maybe if we get our cleanliness back, godliness will follow."

Sam didn't hesitate. He pulled out his wallet and handed Jake the extra business card for the maid service that Annie had given him. It had been no accident that he'd brought it with him. This family had been without a woman for long months. A household without a rudder, with no definable direction. And Sam had known how much Jake had relied on his wife to keep order in the house, as well as peace between Jake and his son. Their relationship had always been tenuous. The cushion of security and love had been yanked out from under him. Sam could tell, Jake was still reeling from the shock.

"Thank you."

Sam watched his friend, his heart breaking for him, as tears filled his eyes. "You're welcome," he said, wrestling with his own emotions.

"Want a refill?" said Jake, clearing his throat and pushing back his chair.

Sam could feel the pressure of being gone from home so long, but also could not ignore a strong urge to stay, see what Jake might have on his mind.

"Sure."

Jake silently retrieved the two mugs, went back to the coffeepot, refilled them then returned to the table.

"Thanks."

"Can I ask you a personal question?" said Jake, as he settled in the chair across from Sam.

"Sure," Sam repeated, hoping he wouldn't regret the quick answer. Hoped he hadn't just stepped into a pile of quicksand. Their whole relationship could flip back to estranged in the space of one conversation. He didn't want that. But wouldn't back down from any challenge Jake threw at him, either.

"Is there some reason y'all need a maid service? I mean, I know Sissy pretty well. Never thought she'd let go of the reins and have someone else running her kitchen." He paused, then said, "You don't have to answer that. None of my business."

Without fanfare, Sam said, "Sissy had a stroke."

Jake sucked in a loud breath. Sam waited for him to absorb the news. It had to be a painful reminder of his own loss. It had been less than two years since Janice had died. She'd gone quick, without warning. A heart attack or massive stroke could snatch a loved one out of a family in the blink of an eye.

"Oh, no," said Jake, settling the coffee mug on the table with a shaky hand. "How bad is it, if you don't mind me asking."

"We were lucky," said Sam, as he blew out a breath. "Blessed, really. It was a mild one, no obvious or debilitating effects. But since Annie's leg is in a cast and the doctor has ordered light duty and a lot of rest for Sissy, we hired a lady to come out and take over the bulk of the chores. At least till February, or so."

"Live in?"

"Yeah."

Jake frowned.

"Don't worry, Jake," said Sam, reading a lot into that look. "These are BBB approved women. We couldn't find one single bad report on the ladies this agency has placed. Plus, the assistant is not required to live in. You could just have someone come out two or three days a week, maybe. Anyway, pray about it. I'm sure you can figure out what would work best for you and Austin."

Jake frowned again, and Sam felt him slipping away. With Austin's belligerent attitude, it could be tricky bringing a woman into the house, on a ranch filled with men. At least the Parkers had two other women in the house to help ease someone new into their routine. Women who could train her in all the special ways Sissy ran their household. Here, there would be no one.

"Jake," said Sam, resting a hand on Jake's forearm. "The men's prayer group still meets on Wednesday evenings. Maybe you'd benefit from some spiritual support? Get out a little? We'd love to have you."

There, he'd said it. If he offended Jake with prayer and fellowship, his friend needed more help than Sam had thought possible. Surely, Jake hadn't turned his back on God. A dip in normal activity was understandable. Even a dose of depression after such a great and tragic loss. But no matter what the devil threw at a Christian, he has no authority over God's children.

Sometimes, when darkness seems to hide the light, we need to remind ourselves that the Light has already overcome the darkness, we have already won the battle. The scripture for the upcoming prayer and devotional meeting came to mind: *Be on guard; stand firm in the faith; be men of courage; be strong* (1 Corinthians 16:13 NIV).

Sam quoted the scripture to Jake, pulled his hand back then said, "I'd be happy to pick you up."

Jake's chin dropped, he cleared his throat, and kept his head down for several beats.

Jake Anderson had once been an upstanding member of the community, a deacon in the church body, a man who loved the Lord. *Please guide him back to you, Lord.* Sam's prayer was answered in the span of two seconds.

"I'll call you," said Jake. "I promise."

With those words, overwhelming joy filled Sam's heart. Coming here had been the right thing to do. His friend was hurting and seemed eager for someone to notice. For someone to care—and show it.

Just what he wanted to hear. One step in the right direction would likely lead to another, and another, and another. "Great. I look forward to it," he said.

"And I'll call the service," said Jake, with an embarrassed chuckle. "Gotta start somewhere."

Sam stood, as relief washed over him. "Sounds like a plan. Anyway, I guess I'd better get back. My family is gonna start to worry. I'm glad you don't have the flu, brother."

"Of course," said Jake. "Thanks again for coming. We'll talk soon. And yes, please plan on picking me up on Wednesday. I think I need the extra support."

Sam grabbed Jake in a bear hug. "Best news I've heard in months, Jake. We'll help you through this. Together. Please know, we have not stopped praying for you and Austin, and we're not about to give up on either one of you, now."

CHAPTER TWENTY-SIX

*Therefore, as God's chosen people, holy and dearly loved,
clothe yourselves with compassion, kindness, humility,
gentleness and patience* (Colossians 3:12 NIV).

James sat in his pickup, the heater on full blast, and watched as the moving truck lumbered its way through the gate of his newly acquired ranch. The truck followed him up the long road to the circle drive. This day promised to drag on till midnight, since he intended to unpack every box and hang every shirt before he turned in for the night. The only redeeming factor in the hours that lay ahead rested solely in the fact that Annie had agreed to keep him company. He knew she would insist on helping, which he'd be grateful for. But mostly, the thought of having her in his home sent tingles up his spine. He very much wanted to know her impression, for one day they might share this house as a married couple. One day, they might start a family here.

A half hour later, Annie's voice sounded at the gate. "Good morning," she chirped, cheerful as the birds in spring, even with three inches of snow on the ground. "I come bearing Mom's homemade blueberry muffins."

"Enter at your own risk," said James, with a chuckle. "The place resembles an obstacle course."

He buzzed Annie in then stepped out on the porch to wait for her, suddenly struck with whirling snow and a brisk northern breeze. He shivered, feeling ridiculous for not grabbing his coat. He had time, so he whirled back inside and yanked his winter coat, hat, and gloves out of the coat closet.

His head, full of security upgrades for his new home, had kept him awake half the night. Barry had done a fine job when he purchased a commercial security package, but with Austin's explosive temper and obsession with Annie, James wanted to be prepared for any scheme the annoying man might come up with. His tech team would be out in the morning to do a full assessment and offer recommendations. The upgrades couldn't happen too soon.

Thoughts of Austin fled the moment James made eye contact with Annie Jo. He rushed across the wide porch and down the steps, mindful of the fact that he had remembered to salt them down. He made it to Annie's truck before she could lumber her way out, what with crutches to deal with.

He hadn't seen her for two whole days, since she and Sissy had been busy training the new housekeeper/cook. Drinking in the sight of her felt like a blood transfusion. As he reached her door it swung open.

"Hello, gorgeous. I can't believe they let you drive over here alone." Man, she looked good. Good enough to create a life-size mold and set up her likeness in his living room, so he could see her any time he wanted. That sounded like a great idea, maybe he would bring it up, once the cast came off.

"I begged," she said, a giggle slipping over those luscious lips. "There were two stipulations: drive the oldest farm truck on the place, which I'm sure they thought humorous; and text the moment I arrived, in order to avoid being embarrassed by the entire family showing up to check on me."

"Sounds like Mack's idea," said James, gratified that he was beginning to know her family better.

"Precisely," she said, rolling those gorgeous eyes up at him. A sight to behold.

"Anyway, I'm glad you're here," he said, placing a chaste kiss to her lips then offering his hand to help her down.

"Just a sec," she said, handing him an 8x12 Tupperware container. "Please take these muffins."

"Got it." He popped open a corner of the container and inhaled deeply. "Yum. They smell delicious."

"Mmmhmm. Now, I'll group text everyone, before they send the sheriff out looking for me."

"I'll wait." He'd wait for Annie Jo Parker forever, but he sure hoped and prayed they would be together soon. A married couple, with a house and plans and children.

"There, all done."

Annie shifted in the driver's seat and finagled her cast out the door. Once again, James offered his free hand to help steady her to the ground.

"My crutches are in the back seat," she said.

James put his arm around her while they made the few steps to the back door. She balanced herself on the open door while he reached in to retrieve the crutches. Snow still lingered on the ground, but had, mercifully, only accumulated to three inches. Not too bad for driving or maneuvering equipment.

The ranch hands had voiced their thanks just that morning when James had called them together for hot coffee and a rundown of what would be expected of them during the move-in. It had gone well, he thought. They all seemed to believe that their jobs were not in jeopardy. He had even managed to have a conversation with a couple of them that had nothing whatsoever to do with their jobs. Bo, the long-standing foreman, had been a big help, as he made a point to reinforce his own positive relationship with James, so the other hands would see that he could be trusted.

But right now, he had Annie Jo on his mind, standing right in front of him. Why would he be thinking about ranch hands?

"My lady," he said with a flourish, extending the crutches in her direction, fully back in the moment.

"Thank you, kind sir."

They shared a laugh, like they were a ballroom couple right out of a Jane Eyre novel, then James started slowly toward the porch, his heart swelling once again as the realization set in that he was now the owner of this magnificent house and grounds.

"Are you sure you're up for this?" he said with a grimace.

He wanted her with him, for certain. But he didn't want to cause her pain, or be guilty of pushing her, to the point of exhaustion.

"You have no idea how ready I am to *do* something. Sitting around the house, even walking around inside it, is making me crazy.

"Just point the way, and I'll do all I can to help. At least I've had plenty of practice maneuvering these bad boys," she said, lifting one crutch. "That being said I'll try not to break anything."

"It's all just stuff," said James, his heart so full he thought he just might cry. "Stuff can be replaced. You just take care of you, and don't worry about anything else."

Annie stopped at the top of the steps. Balanced on crutches, she waited while James opened the door.

Once inside, out of the biting cold, James set the muffins on the breakfast bar then made his way back to Annie Jo then helped her shrug out of her heavy coat.

"You smell even better than your mom's muffins."

She hummed and he pulled her closer, unable to resist. "Welcome to my home, gorgeous."

Annie sucked in a breath. "Oh, James. It's magnificent. I had no idea."

"You've never been inside the house?" Surprise laced his words, as if her answer shocked him. She thought he would have noticed that Mr. Blankenship wouldn't even open the gate for her—no way would he let her inside his mansion.

Annie had to laugh. "Goodness, no. Mr. Blankenship reserved that privilege for a precious few and I didn't make the cut. Well, not unless I had come in as his nephew's bride. And no way was that ever going to happen. But enough said about that. Do you have time to give me a tour?"

Her wildest imagination hadn't prepared Annie for the interior of Mr. B's home. The style, the colors and materials were the makings of a dream home. She fell in love with it, with just a cursory glance. Her eyes roaming in all directions, she followed James across the room to the kitchen area.

"It would be my pleasure to show you around. Mind if we start here, you know, where we could consume some coffee and a muffin first?"

Much as she wanted to see the rest of the house, it tickled her to witness a vulnerable side to her sweetheart. He had come to her aid, surprised her with romantic gestures, put up with her brothers' teasing antics, and hadn't run away when Austin threatened them both. He was a man of God, well established in his field, yet humble and unassuming. And oh, so handsome. It still took her breath to realize he cared for her. Deeply cared for her. Had proclaimed his love for her.

But right now, with the opportunity to show off his recent purchase, he just wanted coffee and muffins. Adorable. A keeper, as Bethany had suggested.

"No breakfast, huh? Mom thought as much. Sonya is great, but Mom insisted on making these muffins herself, just for you. A simple housewarming gift to get you started off right. And of course, we can begin here."

"Makes me feel special," said James, placing a kiss on Annie's cheek. "Please tell her how grateful I am."

"You are special, James, in so many ways." Their gazes met and locked, and she would have been content to stay right there and share a frozen moment in time with the love of her life, all day long. Instead, she reached up on tiptoe and placed a lingering kiss on his cheek, then turned away. They were alone and didn't need to start a passionate session that could get them both into trouble.

Taking a seat that faced the floor-to-ceiling bay window that looked out on a large, covered deck, Annie let out a sigh she was sure James probably heard in the kitchen. Which was okay, she was impressed, and didn't mind him knowing it.

"Wow. You have a virtual Eden out there. Even in this winter wilderness. It feels strange to say it, but I've never seen what was on the other side of that foreboding fence." The compliment had taken on a negative tone with that last comment. She shouldn't have said anything remotely confrontational. James owned this ranch now, not Mr. Blankenship. Why start something that could be hurtful, for no good reason?

"Would you like a muffin?" said James, coming up beside her.

Odd, he didn't say anything after her unflattering remark. Never mind, she'd focus on answering his question. For now.

"Sure, nothing like second breakfast, right?" She tried to brighten her tone but didn't feel comfortable with where her mind was going. For her, this place was still stained with Barry's brazen rudeness and rejection.

She wondered why she felt alone in her negative attitude toward Barry Blankenship. Like James had turned a bit cool toward her. Like he had chosen Mr. B's side over her.

Maybe James knew something she didn't. She had written off James's ability to purchase the ranch because of his undeniable charm. Because she loved him and hoped one day they would marry. If James married her, she would get the man of her dreams *and* the ranch she had coveted for ten years.

Whoa, girl, you're getting carried away again. James is not responsible for anything Barry ever did. And he doesn't owe you an explanation. Get over yourself. Everybody has a story. Maybe your ghoulish neighbor has a backstory that would curl your toes. You don't know, so you shouldn't judge him. What man doesn't want his family inheritance to stay in the family?

Her mind was beginning to spin, so she shut it off and entertained herself with the fact that James had busied himself with the cappuccino machine. A thrilling surprise. She enjoyed cappuccino but had never learned how they magically appeared in those cute little cups she had sampled on rare trips to high-end restaurants with Bethany.

Despite her best efforts, her mind wandered back to Mr. Blankenship, searching for an endearing quality to accredit to her neighbor. Try as she might, nothing came to mind. She had only unpleasant memories of the crotchety old man, who seemed bitter and unyielding. As far back as twenty years ago, he had been a grouch, unneighborly, kept to himself, and didn't engage in community activities. Like a wealthy hermit determined to keep people away.

She glanced up at James as he placed a fresh-baked, still-warm-from-the-oven muffin and a steaming cappuccino in front of her. He squeezed her hand and offered her a wink and did not appear the least bit disgruntled. Curious.

"Can I ask you something?" she said, picking up the muffin. She inhaled the sweet aroma in appreciation of her mother's culinary skills and took a bite, savoring the flavor.

"Of course, ask me anything." His voice didn't sound irritated, either. Hmmm.

"It's about Mr. Blankenship." She was hesitant, putting a toe in the water, as it were. How did this lovely man stay so in control of himself, even while she was bristling?

"Okay," he said, his voice even, smooth, open. She loved that about James.

Annie savored the muffin, followed by a sip of cappuccino, trying to formulate her question properly. She did not wish to upset him, but she was suddenly super curious. He seemed so at home here, already. So comfortable talking about Mr. Blankenship.

"Oh, that's delicious!" she cried, suddenly distracted by the drink he had concocted. She looked up then made eye contact with James at his chortle.

"One of my few talents in the kitchen," he said. "The personal assistant I had in Nashville got me hooked on them, so I purchased a machine then spent an entire weekend practicing. It sounds silly now, but I'm glad I learned."

"I'm glad you did, too," she said with a twinkle in her eye. "You can make cappuccinos for me anytime."

A man who could make cappuccinos could be a valuable asset for a girl on crutches. Even a man who seemed to have made a friend of Annie's lifelong nemesis. There he was, back in her head again.

"It will be my pleasure."

"Mmm," hummed Annie, as she took another sip. "So good."

"Did you want to ask me something about Barry?" said James.

"Barry?" Her skin prickled again. How had James become so chummy with Mr. B? They hadn't known each other but a few days. Strange.

"He asked me to call him Barry." Simple, matter of fact. And irritating as all get out.

She couldn't pin down exactly why his reply bothered her, but it did.

James had recently purchased the ranch Annie had had a hankering to own, for years. From a stubborn old man who had shunned her for no good reason. So what, if his nephew wanted nothing to do with the place? It should have worked as an incentive to sell to a perfectly respectable neighbor. But no, *Barry* refused to budge. And now, it would never be hers.

The irritation boiled up inside her, which made the next words out of her mouth sound bitter.

"So, you're friends now? On a first-name basis, and everything." She hoped she didn't sound snarky, even though that's exactly how she felt. Snarky and irritable.

"Working toward a mutual friendship. I hope we consider each other as friends."

Friends? James Baldwin considered Barry Blankenship his friend. In what universe did that make sense? There had to be something he hadn't told her. Something major, that could give him a soft spot for Annie's lifelong adversary. Mr. B had not been kind to Annie, not one day in her life, and now the man she had fallen in love with was his chum? Ugh.

"Why?" said Annie. The remark came out blunt, rude even, but she really wanted to understand James's relationship with Barry. How could he be nice to a man who had shunned her, and belittled her, and refused to sell her his precious ranch?

Annie watched James's facial expression closely. Somehow, his answer seemed important. Could James really be friends with someone she held in such low regard? It didn't make sense; didn't jive with the sort of man she had come to believe James Baldwin to be. But she really wanted a future with him, or so she thought. But regardless, she decided to hear him out, listen with an open mind. But if he picked Barry over her, she would figure out a way to live without James Baldwin. Try to forget his captivating eyes and calming demeanor and steadfast love of the Lord. She would try to set aside the love of a man she had waited for, for a lifetime.

She hung her head and brushed an annoying tear off her face, certain she would likely never get over losing James. When he spoke, she looked up at him, glad she had managed to stop the waterworks.

"You don't know his story, do you?"

His story? Why would she know Mr. B's story? She wasn't sure her parents even knew much about the man. Her dad had met with Barry once, they talked about Mr. B's wish for Annie Jo to marry his nephew, give the boy a reason to come to Lubbock County and keep the ranch in the family. His request had been summarily denied; and that defined the entire Parker family relationship with Barry Blankenship. His nephew refused to even meet Annie Jo and Annie Jo refused to be set up to marry anyone, period. End of story. Mr. B had been standoffish, from that point forward.

"Honestly, I never even thought about it. I guess I just believed he was rich and eccentric, and." A pause, then "And mean." There, she said exactly what she thought of Barry Blankenship. He'd proven to be controlling and stubborn. Not even close to becoming a friend to his neighbors.

"I can see how you would get that impression," said James. "But let me tell you how he got to be that way."

CHAPTER TWENTY-SEVEN

I will bless her with abundant provisions; her poor I
will satisfy with food (Psalms 132:15 NIV).

Annie listened as James explained, in simple yet compassionate terms, how the man she abhorred had built a dream house on a dream estate for his dream of a woman—and how she had been lost to him, along with their child. A tragic story of love and loss that broke her heart. In the course of the telling, Annie's bitter impression of Mr. B softened from a stick of frozen butter to a melted pool of warmth that changed everything.

"Anyway, Barry said I'm the only person outside of the family he has ever told. I instantly wanted to befriend him. He feels totally alone in the world, since his nephew lives so far away, and there are no other relations still living.

"He left me his forwarding address. I intend to keep in touch, and even invite him back for a visit one day."

James looked at her for a long moment, and she tried not to squirm.

"Will my friendship with Barry pose a problem for you?"

With tears trickling down her face, Annie said, "No, I just hope your friendship with me doesn't pose a threat to your friendship with him."

James stretched his hands across the table toward her, palms up. She gingerly placed her hands in his, relieved when he folded his fingers around her smaller hands. Warmth rushed through her and every doubt she'd had, vanished. She pulled her eyes up to meet his gaze.

"No one will ever come between us, Annie. I won't allow it. If Barry, or anyone else, has a problem with you, they have a problem with me. And trust me, that is one problem they don't want to have."

He winked then, and Annie felt heat creep up her neck and into her face. She had to admit, even though she had known this incredible man for only a few months, she had fallen completely in love with him. And wanted to spend the rest of her life with him. After Austin, she had let herself wonder if there were any good men left in the world. Now she knew, there was at least one. And he seemed to like her, as much as she liked him.

"So," said James, downing the last of his cappuccino. "Are you ready for the grand tour?"

He thumbed a trace of a tear off Annie's cheek and smiled, hoping she believed what he'd said. Barry needed a friend, no doubt. But if it weren't in the cards for James to be that person, he would pray for him daily. But under no circumstance, would he be allowed to cause friction between James and Annie. No way. No how.

"I'm excited to see everything," she said. "But afterward, we'd better get to work. All these boxes are not going to unpack themselves."

"Right," said James. "Follow me and we'll check on the progress of the movers. They've been unloading for a couple of hours and might be ready to leave."

Sure enough, mover number one stood waiting by the front door, buttoning his coat, with a sweater cap pulled low over his ears.

"The truck is empty, sir. Gerald is warming it up now. Do you need anything further from us?"

"No, thank you," said James. "I included a tip with the fee, so make sure they give it to you and Gerald."

"You bet I will."

"Be safe on the road. I hear an even heavier snowstorm is headed our way."

James had asked a lot, expecting movers to venture out into the northeast part of Texas in the winter. A freak storm could surprise them and put these willing men in danger. He had made a point to pray for them on their journey here and would continue to pray for them as they traveled to the next stop along the way. One job after the next, for endless miles.

"We'll be careful. We have a crazy December ahead of us. Never understood why people would want to move at Christmas, but it happens every year. Anyway, we'll be on our way. It's been a pleasure, Mr. Baldwin."

"I appreciate your help." James extended his hand and mover number one gave him a hearty shake. Good, a strong handshake and direct eye contact said a lot about a man. He had placed his faith in a man of integrity, with good work ethic.

"You're welcome."

With that, mover number one joined Gerald in the large moving truck. James watched through the front window until they were through the gate, and it securely closed behind them. He had no desire for a repeat of Austin's uninvited intrusion.

"Now," he said, turning to Annie Jo. "Let me show you around."

"I'm almost giddy."

"It's just a house, but I'm glad you're excited about it. It is exactly what I've imagined for years that I would like to build."

James guided Annie through the house along the same path Barry had taken him. They moved into the great room then ended in front of the massive bay window in the dining room, where they had begun an hour earlier.

"What do you think?" said James, joining Annie by the bay window.

"I'm speechless." She turned to face him, and James rested his hand on her hip, anticipating a kiss. "It's magnificent. He really thought of everything, didn't he?"

James leaned forward, his arm moving across her back and gently pulling her toward him. When her head lifted closer to him, he lowered his head and kissed her. A gentle kiss filled with an urgency he hoped didn't scare her. Filled with enough passion to offer promise of more to come. The realization that Annie returned the kiss with equal zeal gave him hope for their future together, in this house, as a family.

Ending the kiss, James placed his forehead against hers, and whispered, "Barry built this house for the love of his life, and I bought it for the love of mine."

***

CHAPTER TWENTY-EIGHT

*"But blessed is the one who trusts in the LORD, whose
confidence is in him."* (Jeremiah 17:7 NIV).

James had been in possession of his new ranch for one whole week. He'd been up and down and all around, inspecting fences and outbuildings. His goal today was to call the hands and foreman together for a strategical meeting. With new security measures in place, they needed to work together to keep the ranch and the people who lived on it, safe and secure. Much of his hopes relied on Bo Mattis, who had been foreman of the BB and stayed on to work for James.

Bo Mattis had been loyal to Barry Blankenship for the past 20 years or so and had been running the BB ranch for about fifteen of those years. James needed to feel him out, see if his loyalties still lay with the ranch, or if new ownership had him second guessing where he belonged, where he wanted to live out his days. James needed a reliable and knowledgeable man.

Running a ranch had more facets than he had imagined. Learning the ins and outs was going to take some time. He had a feeling that where Bo stood, the other men would stand as well. And if James couldn't trust or rely on these men, he'd be in big trouble.

The back door suddenly opened, and James looked up from the kitchen island, where he'd just finished breakfast. For a moment, a shot of fear raced up his spine.

"Bo," said James, relief pushing the air out of his lungs. He reminded himself that he'd made it clear that his foreman could walk into the kitchen without giving any notice, in case of an emergency or an urgent topic of concern. So, he wasn't surprised he'd come, but very curious. The range of things that could go wrong could be overwhelming if he stopped to think about it.

"What can I do for you?"

"I was hoping for a minute alone before we all met together."

"I've got a minute. Have a seat. Coffee?" This could be good news or bad news. He really didn't need bad news. But whatever Bo had to say must be important, or he would not have made a concerted effort to seek him out.

"Sounds good. Thank you." He rubbed his gloved hands together then pulled the gloves off and stuck them in his coat pocket.

James got up to get a fresh cup of coffee and pour one for Bo, praying for a good rapport between the two of them. Praying there had not been a rebellion since the day before. Praying for the right words, the right body language, and even for the right questions, minus any poor attitude or worrisome looks.

"Still mighty cold out there."

"Maybe this will help," said James.

With two fresh cups of coffee between them, James let Bo carry the conversation. Hopefully, he would answer some questions, before James had to ask them.

He'd been praying that the men who had worked on the ranch for years, would give him a chance, an opportunity to show them that he respected and admired them for their hard work. It seemed from where James was sitting, Bo had been a good leader, which confirmed what Barry had said.

James intended to give the man the space he needed to run the ranch properly, without compromising his own role as owner and ultimate boss.

James had spent a lot of years watching his mother, stepfather, grandmother, and even his father, teach by example. He'd been young when he lost his dad, but Dr. Brad Baldwin had used everyday circumstances as teachable moments. Hard work could be its own reward, yes, but it could also pave the way to a secure future. James intended to honor and mimic the lifestyles of the people who had helped shape him into a man, and the men God had blessed him with to run his ranch.

If this group of hardworking men stood by him, they would be able to maintain the established credibility of the BB ranch, although now under a new banner. With some ingenuity, even the brand change would not prove too difficult—from BB to JB. He believed that Bo and the others would be able to figure it out. And soon, James's own horses would be arriving from Tennessee. The last piece of the move would be in place, and he could focus all his attention on his Texas ranch, and the girl who lived next door.

Bo's voice invaded his thoughts that had unwittingly turned to Annie Jo.

"I spotted someone trying to come over the southeast fence in the middle of the night," he said.

Alarm snaked through James as he carefully set his mug down on the table.

"Were you able to stop him? Find out what he was up to? See who it was?"

"I had Sarge with me. He went after him. He's a good dog, sometimes takes care of things before we even know they're happening. Anyway, I didn't get close enough to see the guy's face, but I'm concerned he might come back when no one is there to scare him off. Don't know what his agenda might be, could just be cold and lookin' for shelter. Can't know for sure, though."

James had expected Austin to try something. Maybe not quite so soon, but sometime. Supposedly, he'd been quarantined to his father's ranch for the entire month of December; but that fact didn't offer much comfort.

The extra barbed wire and new power poles would not arrive for another week. Little could be done before then, outside of patrolling the fence lines.

Frustration stirred deep in his gut. With so much at stake, it seemed next to impossible that Austin wielded enough fear in others that James would need to go to great lengths and expense, just to avoid his antics. Made his blood boil a little.

"I'm pretty sure I know who," said James, trying to keep a straight face. A deep frown line could become a permanent facial feature if his thoughts lingered on the selfish, ill-mannered, immature bull of a man. "And I'm pretty sure I know why. It's the how that eludes me. It's difficult to know what to prepare for."

"You know who?" said Bo, with raised brows.

"Pretty sure it's Austin Anderson. He isn't happy with me."

"You're new around here, right? What could you have possibly done to that little hothead?"

James chuckled. "Ah, so you know him?"

"Mostly by reputation. I've been here for a lot of years, seen Austin ride a few bulls, but I don't get off the ranch much. Why is he mad at you? If you don't mind me asking."

James pondered the question for a moment then decided it wouldn't hurt to open up to Bo. Barry had trusted him with everything, maybe James could too. Bo had started working at the BB ranch at starter level, a fresh ranch hand after high school graduation then came back every summer, throughout his college career. James had wondered why an intelligent, accomplished man would settle for foreman, rather than get his own spread. Could just be a matter of capital. But he figured that was none of his business. Who knew what future plans Bo might have tucked away in his heart? Anyway, that would be a discussion for another day.

"Well," said James, following another sip of coffee, "it all started with my attraction to Annie Jo Parker. It seems Austin had his eye on a piece of the Parker ranch. Now, that won't be possible." He cleared his throat, caught and held Bo's gaze then said, "She likes me back. Hard feelings on his part escalated from there. And now that I've bought the BB ranch, he has decided it should be his, as well. Anyway, with the loss of his mother and now being crossways with his dad, Austin is acting out in very destructive ways."

"Destructive and dangerous, sounds like to me."

"Could be. So, how do you feel about sticking around and helping me? There could be trouble, you need to know that up front."

Bo drained his coffee mug, rapped his knuckles on the granite surface, and said, "I'll stand by you, Boss. Mr. B had great things to say about you, even hinted that I'd be doing him a personal favor if I treated you right. I'm sure the boys will go along with whatever I say. Most of us have worked together for at least ten years. Don't want to see anything bad happen to this ranch, and we certainly want to keep our jobs."

James released the breath he'd been holding since he'd posed the question. Relief flooded through him. He felt ridiculous for spending so many hours worrying, when it was obvious God had prepared Bo's heart for this meeting. Bo had voluntarily come to him, eliminating the necessity for James to seek him out, prior to the scheduled meeting with the other hands.

He shook his head at himself, remembering the many times he had heard his mother, grandmother and nanny remind various family members, himself included, that praying and worrying did not go together. *If you're gonna worry, might as well not pray. When you worry, you're basically telling God you don't trust him to take care of you. He knows what you need before you ask him. It's a good idea to ask, expected even. But don't lay a burden at his feet then pick it back up, before you ever leave the prayer closet.*

"You have no idea how relieved I am to hear it," said James, standing to his feet. He offered Bo his hand. They shook and agreed to meet in the office situated inside the barn at ten o'clock. The morning chores would be done by then and the hands would be free to meet.

At nine o'clock, the gate intercom crackled to life. James still had an hour to fill before the meeting with the ranch crew, might as well see who had come calling.

"James, you awake?"

Matt.

"Good morning to you, too," said James. "Would you like to come in?"

"Nah, just thought I'd come check out your fancy gate. Open up, would ya? I have Paul with me, and you're keeping us waiting, for no good reason."

Uh-oh, both brothers at once. This had to be a serious visit. His brothers rarely piled on him at the same time. Well, they had as kids, but that had been siblings, wrestling. Horsing around. Grown-up life had changed things a little.

"Everything all right?" said James, suddenly afraid something had happened to a family member. But no, Matt seemed too jovial for it to be bad news. Maybe he was letting his little-brother paranoia take over. But he pushed that thought aside too, just like he'd been doing since he'd earned his first billion. His brothers might be bigger, but that didn't mean they were better.

Although he knew not to define his self-worth with a dollar sign, sometimes it proved difficult not to do just that. Every Baldwin sibling had inherited a million dollars from their father—even Kimberly, who hadn't been born before he died. What each child did with that blessing was up to him or her. But their *character* development had been the main focus of the parents, granny, and nanny who had raised them.

Even so, James often let his smaller stature make him feel "less than". Somehow, a larger bank account and a successful business helped. Ridiculous. Yeah, he realized that. But sometimes…

"James Bartholomew Baldwin!" shouted Matt, breaking into James's self-reflection. "Open this gate before I drive through it."

James had no doubt his fighter-pilot brother would do just that.

"Okay, okay," he said, pushing the remote that would let his brothers pass through then stepped out onto the porch to wait for them.

Matt's truck stopped at the bottom of the steps in front of the expansive porch. Paul climbed out and started up just as Matt circled around the front of his brand new, gleaming black Denali pickup truck.

"Hey, bro," said Paul, reaching the top step. "It's not any warmer at your ranch than anywhere else in Lubbock County, you know that?"

James man-hugged his brother and laughed. He'd seen both of his brothers on Thanksgiving Day, so not that long ago, which made this visit even more suspect. He tried not to show any outward evidence of the gnawing in his gut.

"Come on in," he said, keeping a firm smile plastered on his face. "The fireplace should warm you up. I have plenty of coffee and some chocolate chip cookies that Annie's mother made." A little mini stroke might keep Sissy from performing all of the duties she had assigned to herself when she married Sam, but no one could keep her from baking. That point had proven non-negotiable on her part. James had been blessed with the edict. It just meant he had to work a little harder in the basement gym.

The three brothers entered the great room together and sat in a semi-circle in front of the fireplace.

"Coffee anyone?" said James, to break the awkward silence, as well as give himself a few minutes reprieve—before whatever had prompted this visit came to light.

"Not me," said Paul. "I indulged at Starbucks this morning with one of those caramel macchiato things that Jo likes so much. Must be enough calories in that one cup to make an entire meal."

Paul sounded nervous, like he needed to fill up the space between them with words that had no real meaning. Not like Paul at all. He was a bottom-line kind of guy and only used up his daily word allotment through preaching or witnessing. Something was going on, and James intended to get to the bottom of it.

"Y'all aren't fooling me," he said with a pfft. "Something's up and I want to know what it is."

"Maybe we just wanted to see your place," said Matt, staring at him with just the slightest hint of humor in the look. "Since you haven't invited us over yet."

"Bull."

The room went quiet. James stared at first one brother then the other, until Paul finally spoke up. "Okay, here it is. Are you in some kind of trouble you haven't told any of us about?"

So, this meeting was about him? He hadn't seen that coming. Why would they think he was in trouble? He'd been on the straight-and-narrow, his nose in a book, and his eye on the goal for most of his life.

"Trouble? Why would you ask that?"

"Are you?" pushed Matt, leaning forward, his bulging forearms resting on his thighs. "Tell the truth, brother."

"What's going on here?" said James, the paranoia swelling up inside, rearing its ugly head, and making him squirm. "You guys sound like you read my name in the sheriff's report in the *Journal*."

Another long pause.

"I'm waiting," said James, pressing for an answer. Agitated, irritated, impatient.

"Okay," said Matt, holding James with his eyes, which made James even more uncomfortable. "Mom and Tommy came out to the Parker ranch for dinner, the night before last."

"Oh," said James, averting his eyes. Suddenly, he knew what was coming.

"Yeah. Oh," said Matt, an uncharacteristic frown forming a bridge between his eyes. The jovial brother evaporated, leaving the warrior brother exposed. "You need me to bring this Austin character down to size? It sounds like he could be a real threat."

CHAPTER TWENTY-NINE

"But blessed is the one who trusts in the LORD, whose confidence is in him." (Jeremiah 17:7 NIV).

James scrubbed a hand over his face, frustration pouring out of him. It's true, he hadn't shared anything about Austin with his family. Finding out from someone else made it sound like he was hiding something or didn't trust his brothers with the truth.

They had always stood up for him or stood between him and any threat. He was their baby brother, and apparently would always be considered as such. Made sense that even now that he'd become an adult and made his own way in the world, his brothers would want to be there for him. Maybe he should have called them, he couldn't be certain about that. But he also didn't need Matt to start a war, before any real harm had been done.

"You're right, I should have said something," he finally said, a hand up in surrender. "However, I'm trying to stay on the defensive, rather than start something prematurely. I have to admit, however, while my foreman, Bo, was scouting fence last night, he spotted someone trying to scramble over on the southeast side."

The room suddenly filled with the static of electricity. It crackled with alert energy. James waved a dismissive hand toward his brothers, trying to keep them from flying off the handle. "Bo's dog ran the guy off, so I have no idea who it was. Could have been Austin, I guess. But I can't say for sure."

"Odds are good though, right?" said Paul.

"It wouldn't surprise me. Look, would you be interested in hanging around for a bit? I have a strategy meeting with Bo and the other hands scheduled for ten. Maybe, between all of us, we can figure out a way to keep everyone and everything safe—and Austin in his place."

"I'm in," said his peace-loving brother Paul, without hesitation.

"Ditto," said Matt, standing to his feet, in that warrior-ready-for-battle stance he had learned in the military. "Or we could just go after him now and forego all the melodrama."

"Hold on there, soldier," said James. "If someone makes a mistake here, I want it to be Austin. I have too much to live for, to cause trouble I can't get out of."

Matt settled back onto the couch and shrugged his shoulders. James relaxed and thanked him for understanding, well aware that Matt didn't, as a matter of course, practice the passive approach. Even so, he had calmed down for the moment, so maybe he would cooperate and act inside the boundaries of the law.

The brothers spent the next forty-five minutes sharing family news, antics about James's nieces and nephews, and proposed plans regarding Christmas.

At 9:55, James led the way out to the barn, where Bo and five ranch hands were already partaking of the Keurig flavors and the muffins Bo had taken with him to warm up for the meeting.

"Guys," said James, "I'd like to introduce my brothers. I've invited them to offer their opinions, so we can come up with the best plan to secure our property and keep everyone out of harm's way.

"Anyway, this is Paul," he said, stretching an arm to his left. "And Matt," to his right. "Bo, Buck, Shane, Tye, Dylan, Nick and Rafe," he said, pointing to each man, in turn. "And this is Sarge." He reached down to offer his hand to the seasoned ranch dog, relieved that he had remembered everyone's name. Sarge let James scrub him behind the ears then moved to settle at Bo's feet.

"Now, let's get this show on the road. Keeping everyone safe is my highest priority."

James stepped up to the white board stationed at the front of the office, next to Bo's desk, picked up a black Dry Erase marker and asked for suggestions.

***

December 12

James and Annie stood side by side, hands clasped in excitement, which made his fingers pinch a little, but he didn't mind. This was a big day for the JB ranch. The week before, every brand on every head of cattle had been conformed from BB to JB, and James had been pleased with the results. The electric wiring had been added to the top of the entire fence line, as well as around the privacy fence in the back yard. The security system at the house had been totally replaced with the latest technology.

Perhaps he'd gone overboard; but if Annie came to live there, Austin would not be able to get to her without a great deal of illegal effort. Prayer had been said over every post and wire, nail and cable. Psalm 91 had been etched on each side of the gate posts. God would be their fortress, even if the natural precautions failed them.

Over the past two weeks, there had been no further incidents of attempted break-ins. Nothing had come up missing, no one had been injured, and all the livestock had been accounted for.

And now, a crew worked steadily to replace the front gate leading into James's driveway. One side of the gate contained the initials JB and the other, three crosses, two smaller in the background and one larger in between them and more toward the front, which proclaimed to the world that James Baldwin was a true believer. The gate could be powered with solar, but also had a backup generator. The craftsman had done a superb job.

Later that afternoon, the horses would be arriving from Tennessee. His heart was so full, he could scarcely catch a breath. Especially as peace reigned and his sweetheart stood by his side. This was home. He had come full circle, back to Lubbock County, back to his roots. Back to the place he'd been born. Home.

"You look stunning today," he whispered in Annie's ear. "Are you terribly cold?"

Annie smiled up at him and his breath caught. The look in her eyes radiated her own satisfaction. A broken leg had not crushed her spirit, even though the authorities had been unable to prove, beyond a shadow of a doubt, who might have cut the cinch on her saddle and caused the injury. Annie Jo Parker was a good, good woman, who held his heart in her hand.

"Not too bad right now," she said. "And the gate is magnificent."

"Thank you. I'm pleased with it. But I'm so excited for the horses to be coming today. I've been itching for them to meet you."

It had been the better part of three months since James had brushed one of his own horses. Since he'd had a conversation with Pilgrim's Pride or fed any of them. He missed them, more than he'd thought possible. A lot of stress had been lifted when the trainer he had engaged in Tennessee agreed to make the move.

James, and hopefully Annie, would still travel to races with the horses and trainer, but it was yet to be seen how well they would adapt to Lubbock County weather, which often had much colder winters than Tennessee. James didn't want to think about giving them up, so he'd done his level best to duplicate the facility his horses had been accustomed to in Tennessee. However, if they could not be acclimated, he would sell them before he would allow them to suffer. Quality horses could be had locally, horses adapted to the climate and the New Mexico race tracks he'd heard so much about from Sam. But for now, his heart filled with gratitude that the horses he had loved for the past couple years would soon be here with him.

"Don't forget to let Dad know when they get here," said Annie, breaking into his thoughts. He gave her a squeeze, so she would know he was listening. That despite all the goings-on around them, she had his undivided attention. "I think he's almost as anxious as you are. He's keen on owning a racehorse, you know. Maybe because he doesn't rope as much as he used to and wants a long-term hobby to keep him busy. He's been turning more and more of the responsibility of running the ranch over to Mack. I hope he can find what he's looking for. He's driving Mother crazy. She thinks he's having a mid-life crisis. But then, a fast racehorse would be preferable to a fast woman."

"Definitely," said James. with a chuckle. He had a feeling that Sam Parker was not the "fast woman" sort of man. He hadn't known Sam very long, but he admired what he did know. "Oh look," said James, pointing. "The crew is finished with the installation. And boy, am I'm glad. The wind is beginning to bite."

"How about some hot chocolate?" said Annie.

"Good idea."

James shouted up to the men coming down in the lift. "Would you guys like to come in for cocoa or coffee, and a treat?"

"Yes, sir," said the foreman, answering for the crew. "We'd greatly appreciate it."

***

Right on time, around three in the afternoon, the driver who had hauled James's horses to the ranch buzzed in at the gate.

"Mr. Baldwin, it's Hank. You ready for us?"

"I certainly am," he said, with the jitters of a boy going on his first date. "Come on in. Is Zachary behind you?"

"Yes, sir. Should be able to get in on my tail."

"Perfect. Come up into the circle drive then I'll guide you from there. We'll indulge on coffee and muffins, while we wait for Mr. Parker."

The horses were here. At last. James made a quick call to Mr. Parker. He had given Sam the code to open the gate earlier, so he could come over when he was ready.

Following a mug of coffee and a break to the necessary room, James and Annie led the way to the gleaming new facility that would house his prized racehorses.

The barn James had had built especially for these horses was ready to receive them. The ranch hands had agreed to keep an eye on them in shifts, around the clock, in case of trouble, even though Austin seemed to be minding his own business of late. It still pricked at James's nerves that Austin had not faced any consequences for the attack on Annie. But it hadn't been his call to make. He had prayed about the matter until he'd been convicted by the Holy Spirit to let it lie. He was still trying.

The snow had slacked off a bit, and a dull form of sunlight lit up the clouds. It was a glorious day.

"Hey, boss," said Bo, stepping out of the new barn. "How's the gate look?"

"I'm pleased with it. Everything okay, here?"

"Yes, sir. All's quiet. The barn is ready. I gave the guys a break. They've been at it since sunup. Howdy, Miss Annie," he said, angling toward her and tipping his cowboy hat. "Good to see you."

Another turn of events that added to James's contentment. Seemingly, Barry had not poisoned the ranch hands against Annie Jo, and she had befriended all of them.

James had impressed upon Bo to make sure the hands knew their place when it came to Annie Jo Parker. She was not to be messed with, and he expected them to treat her with the same respect they afforded him.

"Thank you, Bo. I'm so glad James has you here to help."

"Happy to be here."

The rumbling of tires on gravel interrupted the conversation. James turned to watch the truck and trailer slow to a halt. *Thank you, Father, for fair weather and safe travels. Thank you for good, loyal men who love horses and livestock as much as I do. Thank you for your favor on this place. Help me do and say only what would please you and bring you glory.*

James, Annie, and Bo made their way to the back of the long trailer that held four horses in luxury accommodations. The gleaming white trailer shimmered in the streak of sun that broke through the clouds, as though it had aimed itself right at the trailer, and God smiled down on them. A shiver ran up James's spine as he looked up into the clouds, so grateful for the outward sign of an answer to his prayer. *I see you, Lord. Thank you.*

Hank dropped down out of the truck then met Bo, James, and Annie at the back of the trailer then unlatched the door. He waited for Zachary to exit his pickup and make his way over to them then pulled down the backend.

"Zachary," said James, his hand extended in greeting. "Good to see you, man. Thanks for coming. I know it's a bit of a climate shock, but the people here are good people. My prayer is that you will be at home here with us.

"Let me make introductions. Zachary Little, trainer extraordinaire, this is my girlfriend Annie Jo Parker, national barrel racing champion. You've probably heard of her. And this is Bo Mattis, ranch foreman. I'm sure you'll be seeing a lot of both of them. The ranch hands will be around later this evening and I'll introduce them."

Turning to Hank, he said, "Hank, how long can you stay? Could I interest you in a hot meal and lodging for the night?"

James really hoped Hank would stay. He needed the rest after such a long journey. But it would also be best if he didn't wait more than one night, what with the snowy weather prediction.

His horses were home safe, and James wanted the men who had made that possible to be safe as well. It felt good to have a home of his own. To have a plan. A girl of his own. *Thank you, Lord, for working things out so I couldn't do life my way. I like your plan much better.*

"You bet. Wouldn't turn down an offer that good. I'm not crazy. But right now, let's get these guys settled. They've been on the road a while and would probably appreciate a little wiggle room."

With the horses situated, all introductions made, dinner served, and their guests bedded down, James and Annie snuggled on the sofa in front of a blazing fire and talked of wishes and dreams, about their hopes of a bright future for the JB ranch and everyone who made a living from its many assets.

James told her, in detail, how the new security system worked, where the main control panel had been closeted, how the panic room worked, all the codes necessary to work all of it, and gave her a key to the front door.

"It's a big step, I realize," he said, with an almost bashful grin. "But I have no intention of hiding how I feel about you, Annie. I want this place to be our home one day. I want to make a life with you, build a family with you, love you for as long as I live."

No, he didn't propose, but that's what he meant. He didn't want her to freak out, but he did want her to know that when the time was right, he would put a ring on her finger, marry her, and be the best husband he knew how to be. He wanted her to have time to think about her answer before he asked the question.

He was in love with Annie Jo Parker. Heck, he'd marry her that very day if all had been arranged accordingly. But no plans had been made, he hadn't even bought a ring. It was too soon. He knew it in his bones. But he didn't intend to wait long. He prayed about the timing, every day. And the second the Lord released him to ask her, he would be on one knee faster than Annie Jo Parker could blink. Knowing her made him wonder how he had ever doubted that love could be meant for him. He had never thought so, never dreamed he could let go of the fear that had embedded itself in his heart and mind, at the loss of his father. But the day he met Annie Jo, the wall around his heart crumbled, quickly, much like the walls of Jericho had fallen once the time had fully come.

CHAPTER THIRTY

Annie gazed into James's chocolate brown eyes and saw sincerity and love looking back at her. She loved him, with a sweet, solid, forever love. A love like she had only read about in books, had been dropped right in front of her one unsuspecting Monday morning.

A regular day of shopping. She'd heard the deep, resonating baritone of his voice before she'd seen his face, and it had affected her deeply.

When she turned to look his way, her heart hammered in her chest. Every nerve in her body came to life. Her scalp tingled and she had to work to keep her mouth from flopping open like a door on a broken hinge.

Today, when he entered a room, the sight of him still sent chills up her spine. The man behind those intoxicating eyes held her heart. She had seen his compassion in action. Felt the thrill of his lips on hers and the strength of his arms as he held her. And she loved him, thoroughly.

Love had grown out of trust, and they now sat close together in front of the fire, comfortable and confident in their budding relationship. She accepted the offered key without a shred of a guilty conscience. His gesture had been made in a spirit of faithfulness, and as a promise for a future together.

How she loved him. *Protect him, Lord. I pray you grant him favor. Send angels to guard and guide him, and keep Austin far, far away. Help James and I make rational decisions, timed in accordance with your perfect will.*

"Thank you," she whispered, her heart full. "If you get ill this winter, I'll bring you a cup of homemade chicken noodle soup."

"Yeah, that's exactly why I wanted you to have a key. Why else?"

They shared a laugh. James Bartholomew Baldwin had pledged his love to her, in the only way feasible at this juncture. But a proposal would be forthcoming, she could see it in his eyes, hear it in his voice. And she'd be ready. Ready with a *yes*.

Glancing down at her phone, she sucked in a breath. "I'd better get going, James. The boys will be out looking for me. I didn't realize it was so late."

James stood, but Annie didn't move from her place on the love seat. When he reached for her crutches, she placed a hand on his arm. He stilled, and she patted the cushion next to her, an invitation to prolong their time together. She was simply not ready to leave.

With a grin, he lowered himself next to her. Their thighs touched and Annie shivered.

Something extraordinary was happening between them. Something real and lasting and rooted in God's love. Romance swirled around them. The ambiance in the room heightened her senses.

A large, roaring fire filled the fireplace, sending an amber glow over everything. The oak plantation blinds had been left open, letting in the expansive view of acres of white.

She could be looking at her future. An evening at home alone with James, her *husband*, in front of the fire. Once they married, she would not have to return to her own house, after the fire burned down. For a moment, it felt like she was living in the middle of a dream. A dream she did *not* want to wake up from.

"In case you haven't figured it out," she whispered, stretching to press a kiss to his cheek. "I'm crazy about you."

With a hand on the side of his face, she sighed. The desire she saw in his eyes seemed to match her own.

"Oh, Annie, if you only knew what a miracle you are," he said, covering her hand with his. She leaned closer. "I'd like to kiss you."

She sat very still, holding him with her eyes. He shifted slightly then slipped his hand to the back of her neck and buried his fingers in her hair. She moaned and closed the distance between them.

When the kiss ended, James rested his forehead on hers.

"I'll walk you to the truck," he whispered, his voice hoarse, almost worshipful, which sent another chill down her spine. "Thanks for spending the day with me. I wish you could stay forever."

Annie sighed again, as longing flooded her soul. She rested a finger on his lips then stretched up and pressed a kiss to his neck, just below his ear. She was on the precipice of giving in to temptation. And it wasn't a feeling she cared to entertain. The reminder to remain chaste echoed in her heart. Together, they could resist the powerful pull. But only as a team. If one gave in the other was likely to follow. Staying true to the long-ago vow was still important to her and she needed him to stand strong in his faith, with her. The three-prong cord would be strong enough to wait for the Savior's perfect time. "God's timing is always perfect, my love," she said, forcing herself to pull back.

James followed her movement, which helped her resolve. He would not force the tender moment of passion to work against them. The relief was so strong, she almost cried. This beautiful specimen of a man was honorable and godly. She could trust him with her convictions. Trust him with her future.

"Yeah, but sometimes I'd like to help him along a little bit."

A giggle escaped her throat and she relaxed. They had passed the test.

Oh, she knew he wanted to be with her, but unprecedented respect far outweighed the temptation. The Lord had provided a way of escape. *Thank you, Jesus.*

"I know what you mean," she said aloud. "Anyway, I better get home. Will I see you tomorrow?"

She needed to leave, get back to the safety of her parents' house, where desire could fade into reality, and she could get a grip on her emotions.

Spending time alone with James, at night, in front of a roaring fire, could cost her virtue. No matter how dedicated they were to wait for the marriage bed.

She wasn't ready to break her promise to God. Prayed she would never sin against her own body for a pleasure meant by God to be between a husband and a wife. *The two shall become one* resonated within her spirit, making her tremble with anticipation. She'd made a vow she intended to keep.

"Maybe for dinner?" he said, bringing her back to reality. "My schedule is ridiculous tomorrow and the next day."

His voice worked as a salve to the wound Austin had left on her heart. She closed her eyes, enjoying his close proximity, the scent of Creed, his hand on her neck. He had suggested dinner, she needed to answer him.

"No worries," she managed to say, blinking her eyes open. "Do what you need to do."

It occurred to her then that she hadn't mentioned Christmas. Ignoring the angst at the late hour, she wanted to include James in her family's long-standing tradition. "Today's the tenth, right?"

James lowered his hand and interlaced his fingers with hers. She smiled at the fact that he didn't rush her or remind her of the late hour. She would have to make herself leave soon though, or her brothers really would come looking for her. They had been her shield all through school, warding off boys they didn't trust. Sadly, they had believed Austin to be trustworthy.

"Is the date significant?" he said, squeezing her hand.

Annie returned the gesture and drank in the message from his soft brown eyes. Wow, she loved this man. She sucked in a deep breath to keep herself on track, shook off the resurgence of desire, and managed to answer, coherently.

"We Parkers have a Christmas tradition which begins with a dinner on the fifteenth. We plan everything that night. I'd love for you to be a part of it. Interested?"

"Sounds like fun," he said, without hesitation. He didn't pull out his phone to check the date, didn't make a pondering face, but simply agreed. From such a busy man, it made her wonder. "What does your family do?"

He shrugged. "I only know about gifts on Christmas morning." The simple declaration sounded odd to her. He had a huge family. She thought they were tight. Her family's numerous activities centered around the holidays kept them hopping. How could he not know what traditions had been formed with his own family?

"That surprises me," she said, hoping to get a more definitive answer.

His smile dropped off and he looked away from her for a moment.

"James? You okay?"

He stirred then turned to face her. "For a lot of years now, the Christmas morning tradition is all I've come home for."

Not what she had expected to hear. "I see."

"Don't get the wrong idea, sweetie. I love my family. *All* of them. I harbor no ill will toward anyone."

He paused as tears filled his eyes. It broke her heart.

"I'm sorry," she whispered. "I didn't mean to imply."

He jerked his head up, which made her jump.

"Don't be sorry. You're the reason I am making an effort to change. To trust. To love."

"Oh, James." She pulled him close and slipped her arms around his waist.

"It's true," he said against her hair. "I want to live life to the full—even knowing I can't control the future."

He pulled back. She let curiosity show in her eyes.

"I don't want to miss a thing," he said. "Everyone has to deal with challenges…and death. Getting to know you and your family has helped me embrace the good things and let go of the past that held me in chains, far too long. I love you."

Moisture slipped down her cheeks as joy overflowed.

"Thanks for coming home."

They sat in silence for a full minute, before James said, "I'd love to come to dinner on the fifteenth. But can I take you out tomorrow?"

"You bet."

They both relaxed and the air cleared. The atmosphere shifted back to a degree of normal. They needed to be held accountable to each other and stay in the company of others. For her own good, she had to stay strong.

The longer Annie stayed confined to the indoors, at the mercy of a pair of crutches, the walls in her parents' home seemed to squeeze together. She loved her parents and wanted to be close by for her mother, but now that Sonya had moved in, it felt like Annie could breathe a little easier, and even dare to step out for a dinner date. Her father would not relent on expecting her to remain in their house until the cast came off, she might as well not even ask. But a date with James would be acceptable.

"How's Sonya doing?" he said.

"We actually like her a lot. She works hard and is an excellent cook. So, Mom has acquiesced. I was shocked to hear her admit that someone could take care of us almost as well as she could."

"Good to know. I think I'll give the agency a call, myself. Maybe I'll get lucky enough to find a Sonya."

"The agency has a really good reputation," said Annie, relieved to get out of a heavy topic and move on. James was working through his issues. She'd be there for him when he needed a shoulder and give him space to think or pray when he needed alone time. Adjusting to a new way of thinking, learning to let people in, takes time. She could wait. God would seal their union in his way, in his time.

"I understand from Dad that Mr. Anderson has hired a lady from there, too. She's older than Sonya, probably around Mr. Anderson's age. Dad says she's made a huge difference in just a couple weeks. I hope having things closer to normal will help him adjust to his new life. Figure out how to live without his wife."

"And Austin?"

A stab of guilt hit her out of nowhere, which set off a spark of anger. She had nothing to feel guilty about. She'd had years to accept this harsher version of her childhood friend, but it still hurt to watch him mess his life up—and hurt others in the process.

Pushing out a breath of frustration, she said, "I have no idea about Austin. Dad doesn't talk about him, and I don't want to. I'm just grateful I haven't seen him or heard from him, since the day you came to my rescue."

Just remembering that day made her cringe. He'd given her another reason to press charges; but she'd backed off when Mr. Anderson promised to keep a closer eye on his son. Promised to keep him busy on the ranch. Promised, on his word as Sam's friend.

"You'll tell me if he tries anything, won't you?"

She grabbed her hands together in her lap, forcing all the angst and fear into her fingers, until the pain made her pull her hands apart. Stretching out her fingers, she looked James in the eye.

"Of course. But I doubt seriously he would show up at Mom and Dad's. He's basically a bully and a coward."

Annie made a move to stand, but James rested a hand on her arm and asked, "Not to keep you, but how is Bethany doing without you?"

Annie stood, using his shoulder for balance. Mindful of the hour, she quickly answered. "She's fine. Her friend from work is in transition between apartments and agreed to move in with her. I'm so grateful. I sleep better at night knowing Bethany isn't alone. After all, she moved in with me, so I wouldn't be alone."

James joined her. "All good news. So, I'll call the agency tomorrow. I promise. Hopefully, they won't be out of placements, this close to Christmas."

"Hopefully. Use our name for a reference, maybe it will help."

"Will do."

Together, they walked toward the door, where James helped her on with her coat— and kissed her thoroughly.

"I should go," she mumbled, but not pulling out of his arms. Instead, she rested her head on his chest.

"And I have to let you," he said, gently pulling out of her embrace. "Come on, I'll walk out with you."

"Thanks," she said, grasping his hand. If she didn't go now, she would have a tough time managing it. Which would cause a whole new set of problems.

"My pleasure."

James stood on the porch, huddled inside his lamb-lined jacket and watched Annie as she drove beyond the safety of his gate. Past the confines of the ranch, too far away to touch her. Too far away to hold her. Too far away to feel his lips on hers.

James's eyes got wide while he witnessed the next horrifying moments, as if they had been yanked off the screen of an action film. Annie pulled onto the road and began the left turn that would head her pickup back toward the Parker ranch when another vehicle came flying over the slight incline and plowed into her truck, head-on.

James screamed, "Annie!" even as he raced down the steps, over to his truck, scrambling up behind the wheel. He spoke to the car to call Mr. Parker, explained what had happened, then disengaged to call 911. While he sped up the driveway, he called Bo, just in case they needed his help. He thought it best to make sure his backup was awake.

The gate swung inward to let James pass through just as, yes, just as Austin reached the driver's side door of Annie's pickup and dragged her out. He tugged on her arm, pulling her toward his pickup, the cast dragging behind her, while she screamed at the top of her lungs.

James slammed his truck door open, jumped to the ground, and hurled himself onto Austin's back, but grimaced when Annie tumbled to the ground and Austin landed on top of her.

"I'm sorry, hon," he said.

"Just get him off me!" she shouted, trying to shove Austin off her chest.

James hauled the nuisance up by the beltloops, spun him around, then draped his body over the hood of Annie's truck. "Stay put, you little punk. Don't make me hurt you."

"What makes you think you could hurt me?" growled Austin, struggling to get out of James's grasp. "I came here to get AJ and I'm not leaving without her."

James glared at him, but nearly tripped and fell when Austin shoved him hard. Righting himself, he stopped dead still—staring right into the barrel of a gun.

He'd been in a few scrapes in his lifetime, was not afraid of a fight, felt confident he could take Austin if it came to blows. But he'd never had a gun pointed at him—and really didn't want to experience a gunshot wound. Not tonight, not ever.

"You need to think about what you're doing," said James, his hand out in a non-threatening manner, hoping to talk sense to this troubled hothead. "Kidnapping is a federal offense."

"Nobody's kidnapping anybody."

"You'd have to kidnap me!" shouted Annie Jo, pushing off the truck while bracing herself with one arm on the hood. "I wouldn't go anywhere with you voluntarily, and you know it."

James took a sidestep in Annie's direction, slowly, hoping not to anger Austin further. "Listen to her, Austin," said James, stepping slightly in front of Annie, hoping Austin wouldn't react to the movement. "You're digging a pretty deep hole here. One you might bury yourself in."

Austin waved the gun around in the air like a wild man. "Don't tell me what to do! And get away from her!"

James stalled, took in a slow breath, then said, "Hey, I'm just giving you a chance to save yourself." He didn't want to say anything that would make the guy feel justified in pulling the trigger. "No one here wants to see you get hurt or go to prison. But that's just what will happen if you don't back down and stop this nonsense. Think how your dad would feel, if he lost you to a life of crime on the heels of losing his wife."

"My dad don't give a flip about me," roared Austin, waving that stupid gun again. Gee, did he not have any training in the art of handling firearms? "He's got himself a new woman and couldn't care less if I'm there or not."

A new woman? Could he possibly mean the woman from the maid service? Or had Austin gone over the edge and was talking out of his head?

"Why don't we call and ask him if he feels that way?" said James, taking another step, so he stood between Austin's gun and Annie's body. "You might be surprised how much he cares about you. How much he wants to work the ranch with you, side by side."

Hopefully, he could get through to Austin before his trigger finger pressed a little too hard and shot off a round. If Austin would just listen, James might touch on something that had meaning for the lunatic. Something that would persuade him to put the gun down and realize he had a lot to live for.

"If you call my dad, I'll shoot you for sure," said Austin, the gun shaking in his hand. "Now, get in my truck, AJ. I'm not listening to any more of this rubbish."

Annie's fingers gripped the back of James's shirt. "I told you, Austin, I'm not going anywhere with you." Her words were clear, but James could hear the tremble, sense the fear that laced through them. He had to get control of this situation before someone got hurt.

"I said get in the truck! Or I'll shoot your lover."

"You wouldn't dare," said Annie, her voice pitching up an octave, as she took a step closer to Austin.

CHAPTER THIRTY-ONE

There is only one Lawgiver and Judge, the one who is able to save and destroy. But you—who are you to judge your neighbor? (James 4:12 NIV).

James just about panicked, but shifted an arm in front of Annie, as much to keep her in place, as to form a barrier between her and Austin. Not much else he could do, the attempt more symbolic than an actionable threat. The guy was unstable and wielding a gun.

"You're going to end up in prison, Austin," Annie snapped. "Don't you see that? I know you won't shoot anybody."

"Wouldn't I?"

Austin cocked the hammer and put his finger on the trigger.

"No!" shouted Annie. "I'll go with you. Don't hurt him." She was pleading for James's life, and he wished he could conjure up a weapon with his mind.

"That's what I thought," said Austin, smug, his chest puffed out, motioning toward his truck with the gun.

"Annie," said James, from the depths of his soul. "Do not get in that truck with him." Desperate. He'd learned through years in the security business: If at all possible, never get in a vehicle with a perpetrator. Most didn't make it back alive. "No matter what."

"I'm not going to just let him shoot you," she cried, tears running down her face. "I can't let that happen."

"He won't shoot me," said James, standing to his full height, almost daring Austin to do something stupid. "He's a coward."

Austin let out a roar then ran at James, gun in hand. The second before he pulled the trigger James dove at Austin's feet, knocking him to the ground. The gun went off, sending a bullet flying through the windshield of Austin's truck.

Adrenaline coupled with relief that Annie hadn't been hit, seemed to triple the strength in James's arms. He held Austin in place until the sheriff's SUV squealed to a halt in front of them, followed closely by the Parkers.

From the other direction, Mr. Anderson parked behind Annie's truck. Flashing red and blue lights colored the snowflakes that had begun to fill the midnight sky.

Sheriff Nelson approached the scene.

James relinquished his hold on Austin while Mr. Parker wrapped Annie in a bear hug.

Mr. Anderson jogged to his son.

Voices blended in a whir of conversation, making it impossible to distinguish who said what, until Sheriff Nelson whistled, a shrill sound that hurt then raised an arm to signal quiet.

"I'll need your statements, James and Annie," he said, as the small crowd settled down.

"Of course," said James.

"Happily," said Annie, as she freed herself from her father's embrace.

Sheriff Nelson listened to brief statements from Annie and James, once he had Austin handcuffed and tucked safely in the back of his truck. The snow began to fall in larger flakes, making it more difficult to stay out in the weather.

"You folks get to safety," said the sheriff. "We'll talk more tomorrow."

Mr. Anderson followed Sheriff Nelson to town.

"Help me get these trucks off the road, boys," said Mr. Parker. "Before someone else comes this way. I don't think we should leave them until morning." Turning, he said, "Annie, wait in my truck, where it's warm."

"Yes, sir," she said.

"Hold up a sec, Babe. I'll grab your crutches."

"Thank you."

James walked next to Annie as she made her way through the snow to her father's pickup. Neither of them tried to speak. The wind howled and the mood was somber.

They reached Sam's truck. James opened the door to let her in. but she didn't move.

"Annie?"

She looked up at him, tears spilling over onto her cheeks.

"Oh, sweetheart," he murmured, pulling her close. "It's going to be okay."

Annie sniffed, her tears melding with the snow, her face turned upward. The look in her eyes kindled a flame in his gut.

Tonight could have gone much worse. How could he reassure Annie Jo that he would keep her safe, when she'd been taken, right in front of him.

If he had gone back inside, Austin would have her in his clutches, even now.

Words failed him. So, he just held her. Held her until her father and brothers had pushed both damaged vehicles off the road. Held her until Sam climbed behind the wheel, turned up the heat, then cleared his throat.

"It's time to go, Annie," James said, taking a half-step back. "Get some rest. Call me when you feel up to it."

Annie Jo leaned toward him then raised up to press a kiss to his cheek. "I will. Thank you for saving me."

"Next time, I'll pick you up and drive you home. Austin won't get close enough to touch you again." He didn't try to disguise the ferocity behind the words.

"No, he won't," growled Sam. "Climb aboard, Punkin. I'll feel better when I get you home."

"I'm coming, Dad."

"Good night, Annie," said James, as he helped her up and into her father's truck. "Talk to you tomorrow."

"Good night, James. Don't fret about this all night. Say a prayer and get some sleep."

There was the take-charge, don't-let-anything-get-you-down Annie that he loved.

"Yes, ma'am."

His smile was broad—until the door closed and Sam turned the truck toward home.

But as he stood there in the snow, watching the taillights get smaller and smaller, his smile drooped, and his brows drew together.

The effects of the attack still fresh, James had to force his legs to move. He made his way to his truck, climbed behind the wheel, started the engine, then slowly covered the two long miles to his front door.

He sat there, his head against the head rest, his eyes closed, his lips moving in prayer.

He stirred as the wind howled around him. Coming fully to his senses, he drove on to the garage and parked inside.

On automatic, he shut down the engine, jumped to the concrete floor, entered his house, and reset the security code. Somehow, he remembered to tell his foreman he'd made it back, all was well, and he could go back to sleep.

Still stunned at all that had transpired, he warmed up the shower, brushed his teeth, then stood under the water, letting the warmth thaw his extremities and the drain take away the last of his anxiety.

He'd put the matter aside until tomorrow and give God some time to arrange all things for the good of his children.

Before James reacted badly, hurt someone, and messed up God's perfect plan for his life. For Annie's life.

***

"It's hard to believe the Austin of last night is the same kid who chased me around the barnyard all those years ago, giggling like a schoolgirl," said Annie, sipping fresh hot coffee made with two organic packets of Stevia sweetener and one teaspoon of almond creamer.

She and Mom had gotten up early to converse over mugs with their pictures on them, like they had done every morning since the first day of Annie's senior year of high school. They'd shared secrets, female insights, and tears. It had been here, at this breakfast bar, that Annie had finally convinced her mother that Austin could not be trusted with her heart.

Memories flooded through her that brought tears to her eyes. The Austin of twenty years ago would never think of hurting anyone. The Austin of twenty years ago cared about the same things Annie cared about—family, friends, horses, and fun.

Her family had accepted him as a part of them, especially since Austin had no siblings of his own. A heart condition had prevented his mother from having more children. Mr. Anderson and her dad had had many discussions about the future, how they would one day pool their resources and join forces. The kids would marry, and they'd all be one big happy family.

It had started out as a joke one afternoon when Austin, at age twelve, announced his intention to marry Annie Jo. The speculation had grown into expectation over the years, until both families accepted the notion, as fact.

Then one day, during their junior year of high school, Austin made a new friend. A boy who had moved to Lubbock from San Antonio. A boy who liked to drink beer and chase skirts. Sometimes, he caught them and bragged about his conquests, all over school. Sometimes, Austin did the same. Soon, sometimes became a little more regular, until more weekends than not, Austin drank too much, got belligerent, and wound up hurting himself or someone else. The more antagonistic he became the less Annie wanted to be around him. Keeping him as a friend became difficult. Being his girlfriend, impossible.

Convincing her parents that little Austin Anderson had become a bully, was like arguing with a brick wall. So, she'd stopped trying.

But the night Annie found him in the hay with second best—the night he had slapped her across the face and pushed her hard against the wall—hard enough to dislocate her shoulder—she made up her mind to keep her distance from him. When the time was right, she would try harder to persuade her parents that the man he had become, was not the man for her. That there would be no future for them. That the Parker and Anderson ranches would not join forces—if the merger depended upon her marrying Austin. That simply was not going to happen.

"I know, Dear," said Sissy, with a gentle pat on her hand, where it rested on the counter. "It breaks my heart."

The sadness in her mother's tone stung a little. She understood the sentiment, but they needed to deal with their current reality. Austin was not that kid anymore. He had basically been drunk for a decade, had attacked Annie out of jealousy and anger. She believed he had somehow been responsible for the cinch that had been cut and led to her broken leg. If she had fallen while Bluebell was running at top speed, the impact likely would have killed her.

But Austin's belligerence hadn't stopped there.

His level of harassment increased to the point of forcing himself on her. If James hadn't pulled him off her, she fully expected he would have taken advantage of her, defiled her in her own home.

If he didn't change the course of his life, he was headed for disaster—running in the wrong direction at a hundred miles an hour toward a brick wall.

"I wonder what's going to happen to him," said Sissy, with a sniff. She pressed the napkin to her face to absorb the tears. "Have you decided to press charges?" Her mother sounded torn, like she wanted Annie to do something to stop the madness but wished she didn't have to.

Like a time-machine could fix everything. If they went back far enough, Austin and Annie would be out in the barn, brushing Glory and Charge, shoving each other in harmless play, while their mothers drank iced tea and nibbled cookies at this very bar.

Austin wouldn't be in jail, and they could rewrite history.

"I have to, Mom. He can't keep on like this, someone's going to get seriously hurt."

More hurt than a broken leg or a broken heart. If someone didn't stop him, Austin could kill someone while driving drunk, which would crush his father, all over again. He could get some weak-minded girl pregnant and cause a whole new set of problems. Or he could kill someone and really be in trouble.

"Maybe it won't be too bad," said Sissy. "First offense and all."

Sissy's voice broke into Annie's thoughts. She didn't comment. But a history of drinking and running wild all over the county would not help Austin's case. His rebellion had escalated into attempted kidnapping. He'd gone too far. She didn't believe the courts would show mercy for an attempted kidnapping charge. First offense or not. That notion sounded ludicrous to her way of thinking.

Her poor, tenderhearted mother just wanted things to go back to the way they had been, all those years ago. It was much too late for that.

Annie's phone buzzed on the table. When she glanced down, she could hardly believe what she was seeing. *Jake Anderson*. She turned the screen for a second, so her mother could see the face of it.

James hadn't arrived yet but was due any second. The call came less than an hour before Annie, her dad, and James were scheduled to file charges against Austin. Like he knew what was about to come down, and if he acted fast enough, Austin could dodge yet another bullet.

"Hello, Mr. Anderson," said Annie, her voice tight, but even. Her heart pounded in her chest. What could he say that would possibly help the situation? And why had he called her, instead of Dad?

She tried to concentrate, to hear the words Mr. Anderson was saying, as she watched her mother dash out the back door.

"I'm sorry, Mr. Anderson, I got distracted for a moment. What was that again?"

He had called to ask permission to come over and chat with her family—the morning after his son had tried to kidnap her, for crying out loud. The morning after Austin had waved a gun around and made all manner of threats. Just before she signed her name at the bottom of a witness statement that could put his son behind bars, long-term.

Her skin crawled, like a herd of insects had burrowed their way under the surface and were competing for the finish line.

"Where is Austin?" said Annie, her voice beginning to tremble. Surely, Mr. Anderson had not already managed to get him released. Would he dare bring Austin to her parents' house? Surely not.

Dad burst in through the back door and reached his hand out, his gestures and the look on his face making it obvious that he wanted Annie to hand over her phone. She did not hesitate. The last thing she wanted to do was talk to Mr. Anderson.

"What is the meaning of this?" Sam barked into the phone. "Annie is my *daughter*, Jake. She is *not* to be toyed with. I think she's been through quite enough, at the hands of an Anderson."

Annie made her way to her father's side. He wrapped his free arm around her, and she relished in the security that came with being his princess.

Sissy sat in the chair closest to Annie, while they waited for Sam to end this nonsense with Jake. What could Austin's dad be going on and on about that kept her dad on the line, *listening*. Annie had expected him to cut Jake off at the knees and be done with it.

"I'll insist on James Baldwin's presence," said Sam.

Annie stiffened at the statement. She was going to be required to meet with Mr. Anderson, and possibly, Austin. The thought sickened her.

But Dad gave her a squeeze and a wink, his gesture of assurance that she need not be afraid.

She was thrown back into a vivid memory. The morning a calf had been stuck inside its mother so long, Annie had been terrified he would die. Her father knelt to her five-year-old level, gave her a wink, and pulled her into an embrace. "Don't be afraid, Punkin. Doc Andrews knows what to do. Everything will be okay. Whisper a prayer for the calf, its mama, and for Dr. Andrews. Can you do that, little one?" "Yes, Daddy." So, she'd prayed, Dr. Andrews delivered little Adam, and everything really was okay.

Maybe everything would be okay now, too.

The second Sam ended the call with Jake, the doorbell rang, and Annie said, "Daddy?"

She sounded much like that long-ago little girl; she could hear it in her own voice. But she didn't care. That's exactly how she felt.

"It'll be okay," said Sam as he tightened his grip on her and moved toward the front door.

CHAPTER THIRTY-TWO

And the peace of God, which transcends all
understanding, will guard your hearts and your minds
in Christ Jesus (Philippians 4: 7 NIV).

Sam swung the door open and gestured for James to come in. James took in the three of them, his eyes moving from Sam to Annie to Sissy, and back again. Alarm shot through him. Sissy had a death-grip on her coffee mug. Annie had streaks of mascara on both cheeks, and Sam held onto Annie Jo like he was afraid she would disappear.

"Let's sit down and talk," said Sam.

"I'll get more coffee," said Sissy. But before she stood up, Sonya appeared from the kitchen with a full pot of coffee in one hand and her fingers looped through the handles of four mugs, in the other.

"I heard Mr. Parker say sit down and talk. Thought you might like something to keep your hands busy."

"Thank you, Sonya," said Sissy, settling back down on the chair, with a slight frown that James didn't miss.

He followed Sam and Annie to the dining table, where they joined Sissy. He'd thought they would have had the Suburban warmed up, anxious to get to the sheriff's office. But here they were, sitting down for coffee, like nothing major, identified as attempted kidnapping, had happened a few miles down the road, the night before. To their daughter.

Sonya set a mug in front of each of them, filled with fresh, hot coffee that hinted of hazelnut then said, "I'll be down in the basement, mending that pile of jeans I've been putting off. Holler if you need anything."

And she was gone.

"Sometimes I think she's a little too efficient," said Sissy, once Sonya had disappeared down the stairwell.

"I get how you must feel, Darling," said Sam, squeezing her hand on top of the table. "But really, what would we have done without her?"

"I don't mean to sound ungrateful," said Sissy, seemingly resigned and resentful at the same time. "I just don't know what to do with myself, sometimes."

James tapped a finger on the side of his cup, observing these people he admired. Sissy had suffered a mild stroke not long after Annie's leg got broken in a premeditated accident, which had necessitated in Sonya's presence in their home.

Sissy appeared to be struggling with the transition. And now, they had been slammed with yet another crisis before they'd had time to acclimate to their new reality. It would break a family that didn't have a strong spiritual foundation. The storms had pounded against them, just as they had against the Anderson house, built on sand. The Parker house still stood rock solid, while the Anderson house seemed to be crumbling around them.

A point James did not miss. Now, more than ever, he longed for the future James Baldwin family to mirror the Parker family.

And more than that, to mirror the family he'd been raised in. He was a Baldwin, who had spent years acting less than. Being less than. No more. He owed the love of his life a home like she'd been raised in. Like he'd been raised in.

Annie looked back and forth between her parents, curious how her father would manage the situation. Since meeting, and falling for, James Baldwin, she had found herself paying close attention to how a lady should be treated. Paying close attention to the level of affection, respect, and forgiveness that her parents afforded one another. She wanted the kind of marriage her parents had displayed while they raised three totally different siblings. How they walked the talk, kept their family in church then lived out their faith at home. No setback had kept them down. Not destructive weather or sick cows or the death of a beloved pet or champion barrel-racing treasure. Their faith in God and love for each other, for family, had remained strong, unshakable. Yes, that's the life, the legacy, Annie longed for.

The back door opened then, ushering in a blustery wind, a rush of snowflakes, and the two Parker brothers.

"Dad," said Mack. "What's going on? I thought you'd be in town by now."

"Have a seat," said Sam. "We were just about to get into it."

"I'm getting the coffee this time," said Sissy, standing to her feet.

Annie started to get up.

"Don't you dare," said Sissy, pointing at Annie Jo. "I'm not so pitiful that I can't manage coffee."

"Yes, ma'am," said Annie, keeping her expression neutral. But once her mother headed into the kitchen, Annie gave into the sputtering of quiet laughter.

"Don't let your mother catch you laughing at her expense, young lady," Sam whispered. "I'm pleased to see she's getting her spunk back. It's a good sign."

"Yes, sir," said Annie Jo, instantly contrite.

He was right. Her mother had spent a lifetime caring for others. She had a gift. Born to be a wife and mother. Content to live out her days in service to others, on acres and acres of land, feeding her family, getting up in the middle of the night with sick children, or standing at her husband's side while they shoveled dirt on yet another calf, lost at the attack of a coyote in the lean months of winter.

Annie watched her mother make coffee, expertly arrange a variety of muffins and pastries on a platter Annie recognized as one from a set of dishes that had belonged to her grandmother. Tears filled her eyes, knowing that one day her mother would follow Granny into Glory. She brushed at the moisture on her cheek and forced a smile as her mother turned back toward the table.

Sissy grinned then winked at Annie, balancing the tray with both hands. She set it in the center of the table then turned immediately to retrieve the coffee pot.

A few moments of settling in and declarations of appreciation passed, before Annie said, "You've got the floor, Dad."

Sam pulled in a breath, made eye contact with each person at the table. What he needed to say would be difficult and not well received. He hadn't agreed to Jake's proposal but had promised an old friend that he would talk it over with his family. If they agreed to Jake's plea, they would be taking a calculated risk. But a risk, nonetheless.

Sam fiddled with a toothpick, rotating it end to end, end to end, carefully considering his words. Torn, he both wanted to cooperate with Jake, and to stand firm against Austin and see to it that he faced charges and did prison time.

The one point that tugged his heart toward his friend's suggestion was two-fold in nature: Austin's struggle with the loss of his mother and the revelation that his long-time drinking habit had become a full-blown addiction.

Sam still flinched at the tears in Jake's voice as he confessed his desperation. What if Josh or Mack had succumbed to the temptation of drink in the wake of their mother's death? The thought of losing Sissy, alone, would be crippling. What measure of anguish would come with an empty home, no wife, and a child trapped in addiction?

"Dad?"

Annie's agonized whisper tore at his heart. She was his youngest child—his only daughter, and she had been grossly mistreated by his friend's son. He owed Annie his best efforts, his allegiance. The day she was born he had pledged to protect her with his life. He would not go against his pledge. The decision must ultimately be hers.

"I'm sorry," he finally said. "This is…difficult." He reached for his wife's hand then felt himself relax the slightest bit when she grasped onto it with both of hers.

"We trust you, honey," she said.

"Thank you." The look of genuine love and complete trust in her eyes gave him the courage to continue.

With one more intake of breath and a silent prayer, Sam fully explained Jake's appeal. Their next move would be up to Annie Jo.

***

December 11

James rested a hand on Braveheart's nose, his first acquisition and still the closest to his heart. He needed a sounding board, a safe place to vent, someone to listen, without judgment or reproach.

Tomorrow would be upon him in a blink, and he wasn't prepared for it. Tomorrow the Parkers and Andersons would participate in arbitration to determine what punishment Austin deserved, and hopefully keep the case from going to court. What might be done to appease Jake, while teaching Austin a lesson. Jake had been desperate to keep his son out of prison. Desperate to keep what was left of his family, together.

"Jake wants his son to be free," James explained, as Braveheart gave him an understanding nod. "I can see why he would. But man, I'm having a hard time dealing with it. I really wanted Austin to stand trial, to be humiliated in front of a jury of his peers. This guy that Jake wants us to be lenient with is the same guy who bullied my girlfriend, tried to kidnap her, and pulled a gun on me. Leniency was not on my list of options."

James spent an hour pouring his heart out to his friend but was nowhere near reconciled to what would be expected of him the following day. He had promised Annie he would participate. He had promised and would keep that promise. But he didn't want to. He wanted to punch Austin Anderson in the face.

***

December 12

The sky had dumped six inches of snow the night before. Sand trucks had been out since one in the morning. Traffic, praise the Lord, remained light as they made their way into town. Wind whistled around them, swirling snow everywhere. James had to concentrate not to hold the wheel in a death grip. *Relax, James. It's snow. Not like you've never driven in inclement weather before.*

"James," said Annie, from the passenger seat. The sadness in her voice just about broke him.

"Yeah," he said, nowhere near able to anticipate what she might be thinking. And afraid she would ask what he couldn't answer.

But she did.

"You okay?"

"I'm trying," he said. It was the best he could do under the circumstances. The best answer he could give without lying.

"I'm so sorry." He hated that she hadn't felt free enough to insist things be handled differently. But part of him understood, sort of. She had been bullied and controlled for too many years, at the hands of the Austin character. He made her feel weak. He was still manipulating the people around him. That reality made James nauseous.

"Don't be," he said, unwilling to voice all that and make her feel worse. "None of this is your fault."

"I'm not responsible for the way Austin behaves, I agree. But if not for me, you wouldn't be in this mess, at all."

James fell silent for a long moment. What should he say to that? He did not want Annie Jo to feel guilty about anything. Ever. Especially regarding Austin.

He really wanted this day to be over. He wanted nothing more than to hold Annie close, give her the best kiss of her life, then head straight for the jewelry store so she could pick out her own engagement ring. And put this mess behind them.

He wanted to build a snowman with her and laugh the day away. He did *not* want to spend all day in a room with the Parkers while Mr. Anderson and his son sat in a second room with their attorney, then endure the ridiculousness of Austin's whining and pleading, passed from room to room, through an arbitrator. Then bring down a decision that couldn't even be appealed? Uh—no.

No, he did not want to do any of it. But he refused to put the least bit of pressure on Annie. Nope.

"Without you, Annie," he said carefully, determined for her to understand, "I would be a lonely man, shut up in my office, trying to convince myself that I had everything I could ever want. Trying to convince myself that romantic love was for other people, maybe, but not for me.

"Without you, I would be nothing more than a fraction of the man God had created me to be. I mean that. Please don't think I blame you for anything. I don't. I'm just not looking forward to Austin getting another break. A break he doesn't deserve."

His heart melted as Annie placed a hand on his arm. The warmth raced up his sleeve and straight into his circulatory system, burning through every vein and artery. If she left her hand there for long, he just might burst into flame.

In that moment, the Lord seemed to provide some insight into how this could be affecting Annie Jo. He glanced at her and, for the first time, recognized misery, perhaps years of disappointment, with a mixture of the friendship she had shared with a childhood friend, now lost to her. Forever.

"Forgive me, sweetie," he said, forcing himself to keep his eyes on the road. "I tend to forget that you and Austin grew up together, that you aren't just here to put a bully in his place. I see, now, that unless something drastic happens, you have lost a lifelong friend. I'm sorry for that."

"Thank you," she said with a sigh filled with what sounded like regret. "I'll be praying for all of us, all day."

"Me too," he said.

He rested a hand over hers on the console between them and left it there. Together, each in their own level of meditation, rode together in silence, all the way to the attorney's office where the arbitration would take place.

At eleven thirty in the morning, the attorney's assistant brought in sandwiches from McAlister's, their famous sweet or peach tea, bags of chips, and giant chocolate chip cookies.

James stared at the small feast and didn't know if he could get it down and keep it down. It had been a long, long morning, and promised to be an equally long afternoon. His head had started pounding a couple hours ago. Maybe the tea would help. It could be a headache that stemmed from a lack of caffeine, but he doubted it.

He was beginning to think an agreement could not be reached. And that thought made the hammering in his head worse.

Then, at four in the afternoon, Mr. Arbitrator entered their room with a smile on his face. "I think we have a viable solution that could work for everyone."

James kept his mouth shut tight. Expressing negativity at this point would serve no good purpose. He determined to listen to the man, before he made any rash judgments. For all he knew, something could be worked out that would assuage his anxiety. And if Annie agreed with the proposal, he would make himself accept it. He just would.

When Mr. Arbitrator started talking, James reached for Annie's hand beneath the table. Gratefully, she let him take it. He focused his attention on their connection, shoving aside the sound of the arbitrator's voice.

He did not want to hear the proposal. Rather, he kept his mind centered on the peace that comes only from a loving God. He searched his heart, asking for the strength to forgive Austin for all the wrongs he had inflicted on this lovely woman, whom he loved.

Whatever the Parkers and the Andersons figured out would have to be okay. Maybe life could get back to normal. Once this Austin matter had been settled, Christmas would be a welcome celebration. They could forget about this entire tragedy and carry on with their lives.

He had to believe it was possible or he'd go crazy. And if Austin walked again, James would be hard pressed not to cross a line he prayed he'd never be called upon to cross. Never even have to consider.

Fifteen minutes later, James accepted the offered pen and signed his name at the bottom of the document. A set of notes, really, jotted down by the attorney's assistant. But in a few days, it would be neatly typed up as an official document filed with the Court—binding, lawful, unbreakable.

Once Jake and Austin had left the premises, the Parkers were escorted to the front door. James glanced out and noticed that snow still drifted from thick white clouds that hid the sun. If snow weren't such a mesmerizing natural phenomenon to behold, he would think the day gray and dreary.

But snow had never had that effect on him. Rarely had he witnessed snow in Tennessee, where people routinely closed their businesses, let out school, and spent the entire chilly but magnificent day outside, sledding or building snowmen. He had a feeling that Lubbock County received its fair share of snow, since no one seemed to think it necessary to slow down their normal, productive lives in order to gaze at the wonder of the fluffy white wonder, or even to make snow ice cream, like Maggie, their nanny, had done, each time the snow would drift up against the house, glistening, inviting. Delicious.

The instant James and Annie turned the corner of the building, in a hurry to get to the truck, Austin stepped in front of them.

"AJ," he said, reaching toward her.

The very idea that he thought he could approach his Annie, made James so mad he wanted to take the law into his own hands. They had just signed a document that stated Austin was required to keep his distance. The meeting had ended all of ten minutes ago, and he had already violated that trust. If he touched her, James would come unglued and punch his lights out.

CHAPTER THIRTY-THREE

*For he guards the course of the just and protects the
way of his faithful ones* (Proverbs 2:8 NIV).

"Leave me alone, Austin," said Annie, scooting closer to James's side. "I have nothing to say to you."

"You have to know my heart, AJ." Really? He was whining now? "Please don't let this guy come between us," he said, jutting a thumb in James's direction.

Three things happened at once:

Annie moved to stand behind James.

Mr. Anderson rushed up to Austin.

Sam pushed himself in front of James, making two men who blocked Austin's path. Austin wouldn't get to Annie today.

James stared into the eyes of a man he barely knew, a confused, frightened, and angry young man with little comprehension, if any, of what fear and dread his attitude and bullying had rendered on an innocent girl, who had done nothing but be his friend, while trying to protect herself. What Austin read into her kindness was mind boggling.

He sounded delusional. Sober, at least, but totally delusional.

Annie Jo would never be his childhood playmate again. She would never be his girlfriend, his fiancée, or his wife. And she would never trust him again. She had told him so, herself.

Had he shaken a wire loose in his brain the last time he'd been thrown from a bull? What was he thinking? He had manhandled her, manipulated her, tried to kidnap her. Hadn't he just been reminded of all his indiscretions?

Austin was supposed to be on his way to the sheriff's office to get fitted with an ankle monitor that would alert authorities if he so much as stepped outside the gate of his father's ranch.

"Austin," said Jake, his voice firm and determined. "You are making a big mistake, here. Stand down. I'm taking you out of here and you will cooperate fully. Do you understand?"

"Dad, this is wrong," said Austin, a growl in his voice. "We had plans. Big plans for a future. Me and AJ. This punk has no business messing that up." He sounded like the past years of abuse had never happened. Like the past few months of escalated violence had been wiped from the calendar.

Ignoring his father's words, Austin dashed around Sam and launched his body at James.

Sam stuck his foot out and tripped Austin before he slammed into James.

James pressed Annie against the side of the building, standing in front of her, allowing Austin to fall headlong into the slush of dirty snow that had settled along the curb, next to the attorney's office.

Austin let out a growl like an angry or injured animal. He rolled over on his back in the cold, dirty mess and glared up at Sam. "Who do you think you are?" he shouted, struggling to get up. "You think because you still have a complete family and a fancy ranch that you're better than me! I am sick to death of hearing about what a good man you are! I am sick to death of watching AJ make a fool of herself and destroying any hope for the future we had planned." He got up on his knees, brushing slush from his hands onto his jacket. The gesture didn't help his hands much and smeared more wet dirt on his coat.

"Austin," said Jake, falling to his knees in the dirty snow in front of his son. Tears flowed down his face in rivers. "Son, you can't keep doing stuff like this. You're going to get yourself sent away for years. Or killed. Now, stand up and act like the man I raised you to be. I'm not going to let you ruin your life. Andersons do not act this way. I won't have it. Do you hear me?"

James, Annie, Sam, and Sissy stood close together, hands clasped, and watched as Jake coaxed his son to go with him to their vehicle. The seconds seemed to stretch into hours. The painful reality obvious to James as the two men walked away, shoulders bunched, wet and probably cold—from the temperature, as well as humiliation.

Austin's head hung low, his father's arm around his back.

As angry as James had been with the guy, seeing Austin broken made him sad. Each wrong action Austin had taken in the past few months had pushed Annie farther and farther away from where their friendship had once been. And now, the seal of nevermore had been placed on their relationship with the signing of the agreement that would keep them forever separated. It was a sad reality, a difficult thing to watch.

"Let them go," whispered Sam, shaking James from his reverie. "We will honor our side of the agreement. From here on out, prayer is our greatest weapon."

The ride home proved to be both sorrowful and filled with promise.

"You okay?" said James, his eyes on the road, but his heart in the passenger seat, with Annie Jo.

"I think so," she said, with a shuddering breath. "I feel bad for Mr. Anderson. His son is breaking his heart."

"What do you think it'll take for Mr. Anderson to restore their relationship?"

"I have no idea, except that nothing can be fixed, until Austin admits he has a problem and needs help. I don't know if I've told you, but he's been on shaky ground since our junior year of high school, when a new boy moved to town and influenced Austin in a big way. He started drinking heavily and earned a reputation for getting his way with the girls. I've been avoiding alone time with him, ever since."

Annie twisted in her seat so she could look directly at James. He could feel her eyes on the side of his face. He counted to sixty before she continued. One of the longest minutes of his life.

"I want him to get better, you understand. But I can't be his savior. He is delusional on that point. I think he is refusing to look in the mirror and see the true identity of the man looking back at him. He's an alcoholic and needs help. I'll gladly pray for him, but that will be the extent of my personal involvement, at least until he has fully recovered."

She went quiet then and James followed suit. If she needed time to think about the situation, he would honor that unspoken request.

Just a few miles before they reached the gate to the Parker ranch, Annie spoke again.

"Maybe Dad can help Mr. Anderson through this. I know he is willing to try, at any rate. They have been friends for so long, I can't remember a time when they weren't close. This mess is killing him. The sad part is, Jake has started going to church again, even Wednesday night prayer group with Dad. Things were turning around for Jake.

"Austin was right about one thing, though. Jake and Sylvia have grown close. Dad says Jake told him that Sylvia had been making progress with Austin. He was sober today and has been for at least a week now. I guess he thought not drinking would erase his sins.

"I don't know. I don't get it. Honestly, I'm terrified that this setback will undo all the progress that has been made."

James reached his hand across the console, palm up. Annie glanced over at him then placed her hand in his. He laced their fingers together and applied the slightest pressure. He wanted her to know that he had her back. No matter what.

"I promise to pray for him, too, Annie. I don't wish him harm. And if he doesn't know Jesus as his Lord and Savior, I certainly don't wish him an eternity without God."

"Thank you," said Annie, her eyes shimmering with tears.

"Please don't cry, sweetheart. God has a perfect plan. We just can't see it right now."

***

December 15

For one entire day, the Parker household had known a measure of peace. No lawyers called. Mr. Anderson remained quiet. And no one had seen or heard from Austin since the debacle outside the attorney's office.

Jake had telephoned Sam the night of the arbitration to assure him that Austin had gone quietly to the sheriff's office and was now fitted with the ankle monitor. He said that he'd promised to behave himself--had even promised to consider rehab.

Annie couldn't imagine what might have happened to bring Austin to such a level of resolve. The scene she'd witnessed outside the attorney's office had given her little hope that he would come around and behave himself. Perhaps Jake's new female interest had influenced Austin in a positive way. If so, more power to her. With God and a good woman now welcomed in their home, things could turn around quickly for the Anderson household.

But no matter the explanation, she sighed with relief. Maybe Austin would finally realize how much he needed support and encouragement outside of himself. Maybe he would follow the advice of the arbitrator and check into a rehab program. Maybe he would turn to God himself, on his own initiative, and find a whole new way to live. Without her.

Maybe.

Hopefully, he wasn't just saying what he knew his father wanted to hear. Hopefully, he had realized that ending up in the gutter, covered in dirty, icy slush in front of everyone who had ever had a measure of respect for him, was not the way he wanted his life to end up.

"Yes, Lord, help Austin realize that you are knocking on the door of his heart. Help him see how much he is hurting his father, who loves him above everything else in his life."

Annie pushed through the gathering gloom, determined to make this day a joyful experience with her family. They'd had a meeting the day before and agreed they should move forward with their Christmas shopping spree, Austin notwithstanding.

Sonya had prepared their Christmas planning meal in advance and was now on her way to visit her parents. James would be joining the family at six o'clock to enjoy the fruits of Sonya's labor and be in on the planning stages for the celebration of Christ's birth on Christmas Eve. He had assured her that he would come well informed regarding his own family's plans, so they could coordinate everything. It promised to be a fun, memorable day.

At nine-thirty that morning, the entire family climbed aboard the now warmed-up Suburban and headed for the mall. The parking would be horrendous, and the stores crowded with impatient shoppers, as was typical this late in December.

But none of that mattered. Her family would be together, shopping for each other, some in secret, some giving orders for what they expected to find under the tree. Especially Mack, so focused on what the ranch needed, that he would insist people follow his wish list to the letter. It made her smile, and she would never disappoint him, on purpose. She would, however, wrap a gift that came from her heart and had nothing whatsoever to do with his structured, well-thought-out list.

Josh loved surprises and didn't care what came inside a package, just wanted everyone to be together when the gifts were opened. Shopping for him was a delight.

Dad never asked for anything in particular and Mom declared she had everything she could ever want. Her parents had never turned down a gift, just didn't live for the moment they would receive one.

And Annie's absolute favorite part of Christmas was when their family pooled their resources and bought gifts through Heifer International.

According to the Internet definition, Heifer International is: *"a global nonprofit working to eradicate poverty and hunger through sustainable, values-based holistic community development. Heifer distributes animals, along with agricultural and values-based training, to families in need around the world as a means of providing self-sufficiency. Recipients must agree to 'pass on the gift' by sharing animal offspring, as well as the skills and knowledge of animal husbandry and agricultural training with other impoverished families."*

The mission of Heifer International spoke to Annie's love for animals, and for people. The Parkers had plenty, and sharing was expected of them, according to God's Word: *He who oppresses the poor shows contempt for their Maker, but whoever is kind to the needy honors God* (Proverbs 14:31 NIV). The verse had been repeated by her parents so often throughout her life, she gave without begrudging the expense, and had learned to help others in need. She longed to honor God with gifts to those less fortunate, in countries where good will took some effort to accomplish and government subsidies were unheard of. Christmas, a magical time of year.

Since childhood, the family had given generously through the organization. The anonymous gift they made each year filled Annie with more joy and satisfaction than even the happy faces of her loved ones that she could see as they opened their gifts. Just knowing a family would have an opportunity to not only feed their own family but would be able to bless someone else, because someone far, far away had honored God by sending hope to a child of God on the other side of the globe. The tradition continued to fill her with warmth and satisfaction.

Annie waited patiently while her dad searched for a parking space that would not be a hardship on her with crutches, or on her mother who still was not functioning at full strength. Slush and piles of snow dotted the parking lot. Maneuvering the obstacle course would be a challenge, but they'd manage.

She glanced at her watch as Dad pulled into a handicap spot in front of the Dillard's entrance. *Thank you, God*, she prayed. *Thank you. Be with us as we trek through the mayhem that is the mall this time of year. Give Mother supernatural strength and help each of us find what we have in mind for one another, so we only need to make this trip one time.*

She chuckled, and Josh shoved her elbow. "What's so funny, Sis?"

"I was just praying that we would all get through this, find what we need, and not have to come back."

"Amen to that," said Mack, from the third seat. Poor, long-legged guy. He had lost the coin toss for who would have to ride in "the way-way back." The phrase had been invented by Annie at the age of three and the family still used the term, to this day.

Five hours later, with people and packages stuffed everywhere inside the Suburban, the Parker family returned to the ranch.

The second Sam pulled inside the garage the wind began to howl outside their coveted space. Perfect timing.

"And so, it begins," he said. "I heard this storm was going to be a doozy. Maybe you should call James, Annie, see if he wants to hang out over here with us, and ride out the storm."

"I'll call him, once we have all this stuff transferred inside," she said.

"Okay, you do that," said Josh. "But I hear hot chocolate calling my name."

"Sounds yummy," said Sissy. "However, while we enjoy cocoa and gingerbread, I will expect the full cooperation of everyone present to help finish the decorating, as well as gift wrapping."

"How are you feeling, Hon?" said Sam, his hand pressed lightly on her arm. "Holding up okay?"

"Surprisingly well," she said. "Thank you."

There it was again, thought Annie. A good husband who cared about the wellbeing of his wife. A love that spanned decades reflected in the adoring gaze that passed between her parents.

"One of these days I want a marriage just like yours," she said out loud. She'd had the thought many times through the years, but it had grown in intensity over the past few months, what with meeting and dating James. He had grabbed hold of her heart and she didn't want him to ever let go.

Sissy turned to look at her daughter. "Thank you, sweetie. Such has been our prayer for you since the day you were born. I believe there is hope that your wish will come true."

"And what about me?" said Josh, with a pouty lip. "Do you care about *my* happiness, too? Or just the princess barrel racer?" His voice contained a hint of humor, although Annie sensed that the question came from a tender spot in his heart. It would be understandable, seeing as Annie was the baby who had attained a great deal of notoriety as the reigning national champion. Jealousy could sneak its way into anyone's heart, if given enough fodder to make it grow.

She started to protest but stopped when her father spoke from the front seat. She wanted to hear his response to Josh's concerns. Maybe she had been acting too much like a princess, instead of Josh's little sister. She adored her brothers and wanted them to know it, to be secure in their relationship, as equal adults.

CHAPTER THIRTY-FOUR

You are the God who performs miracles… (Psalm 77:14 NIV).

Sam made eye contact through the rearview mirror, then looked away until he killed the engine. Turning in his seat, he connected with each child, individually. "Your mother and I have prayed for God's intended spouse for each of you since the day you were born. One child is not more special than another, just unique. We'll be happy to let you know when we think you have brought home a proper mate, Josh. No need to wonder about that."

Sam laughed and Josh laughed with him. "Sorry," said Josh.

"No need to apologize. We have encouraged you to come to us with your concerns. I'm glad you spoke up. Now, let's get inside, what say, and get started on the Christmas decorating, the consumption of goodies, and enjoy each other's company, while we look forward to this evening's feast."

"Hip, hip hooray! Hip, hip hooray! Hip, hip hooray!" cried the siblings, in unison, as if they were still small children. It seemed they had all remembered the so-happy-it's-Christmas chant they had been shouting since Annie had turned four.

Annie sighed a happy sigh, filled with the happiness and pure bliss of a blessed day, in the company of her family. The short-lived tension had been eased as they worked together to empty the Suburban.

Once Sissy's directives had been followed and the purchases spread across her parents' bed, still in shopping bags, Annie excused herself to her room to call James.

"Hey," she said with a smile in her voice. "You ready to come help out over here? Dad says a big storm is blowing in. You're invited to hunker down with us, so long as you obey my mother. There's a lot to do and we could use another set of hands."

"Sounds like work," said James with a chuckle.

"I cannot tell a lie; you're right."

"If I can be where you are, I'll sign up for indentured servitude and be glad of the opportunity."

James Baldwin had proven himself, at every turn. Not that there was a test. But wait, there was a test, of sorts. Annie had spent a great deal of time praying over and composing a list of non-negotiable requirements regarding an acceptable suitor, a worthwhile mate.

A quick mental calculation revealed that her boyfriend had met each requirement on that list. A realization made especially sweet by the fact that he had no idea such a list existed, so he couldn't be faking his way into her good graces. He already had character and compassion and generosity that had developed over time, until he made a complete, near-perfect package.

"You might choke on those words, once Mom starts handing out assignments," said Annie, hoping he would hear the smile in her voice. "But seriously, how soon can you get away? The weather already sounds angry."

"I won't be long. Bo has taken up residence in the office at the back of the racehorse barn and the crew has battened down the hatches on every outbuilding on the place. The hands have now shut themselves up in their cabins, barring any emergencies. I'll simply put the JB ranch out of my head."

"Easier said than done," said Annie, not trying to hide the joy that sprung from her heart. "But do your best and we'll see you soon. Plan to stay over, just in case. There's plenty of room and chow."

She disconnected the call and let love for her boyfriend wash over her. She flopped back on her bed and shoved a pillow under her cast. It had been several hours since it had been properly elevated and had begun to ache.

"No pills," she told herself. "Just rest a minute and it'll let up." She closed her eyes and didn't open them again until sometime later, when a tap sounded at the door.

"Annie, you okay?" said Josh, pushing the door open. "Some guy named James is at the front door. Should I let him in?"

Annie blinked a few times, before she could focus on Josh's face. "Do what?" she said, still groggy.

"I said, get up. James is here."

Annie groaned and turned over on her side, facing her brother. Instantly, his brows came together. He rushed to her side and lowered himself next to the bed.

"Annie, you okay?" he repeated, nudging her shoulder.

Alarm coated his words and Annie came fully alert. She fluttered her lashes several times, trying to come out of the fog. She had fallen asleep, hard, and it had taken a bit for her to be aware of her surroundings. She yanked the pillow out from under her leg and sat up.

"Sorry. I was dead asleep."

"Is that all?" said Josh. "Well cut it out. You scared me half to death."

Josh, the jokester of the siblings, rarely showed his serious side, so Annie appreciated that he had exposed a vulnerable emotion.

"Sorry," she said again. "Really. I was just so deep under I couldn't wake up in a hurry."

"It's okay. I can breathe again now. Sheesh."

"Thanks for caring," said Annie, as she scooted closer to the edge of the bed.

"I do care, Sis. I hope you know that. I was just kiddin' around earlier. I know you're the real deal and don't just think of yourself as a princess."

Annie soaked up the moment and stored it in a special memories box in her heart. A private moment alone with Josh, that she would keep to herself. If she exposed his confession in public, he would be deeply wounded.

"I get a little competitive," she admitted, with a shrug and an impish look.

"A little?"

Their shared laugh lightened the mood.

"Anyway, if I am a princess that makes you a prince, by default."

"Yeah, a prince. I like the sound of that."

Josh stood to his feet and reached for Annie's crutches. "Here you go, Sis. Prince *Charming* is at the door."

Annie came slowly down the stairs, one hand on the rail and one looped through Josh's arm, as he helped balance her. James still stood by the door. As she lowered her foot off the final step, they made eye contact.

"Hey," she said.

"Hey."

They sounded like middle school students about to go to their first school dance, But she didn't care. She had fallen for this kind, gentle man and didn't care if the whole world knew it. It took a few seconds to get the crutches in place and get into gear. She felt Josh release her then step away.

"We gotta get your truck undercover," she said, as she reached James, the magic of the moment now gone. "We made a place for it in the barn." She stopped then and looked up at him. "Is that okay with you?" The look of concern in her eyes made his heart melt.

"Of course. I like my truck."

Annie giggled, and his heart began to race. How he loved this woman. He patted the inside pocket of his coat, where the little black velvet box had rested for an entire week.

Maybe she would forgive him for picking out a ring, without her. Maybe she would be okay with him proposing on Christmas Eve-Eve. He did not want to put himself out there like that, in front of her entire family. If she said *yes*, they could tell them together. But for now, it was his secret. Asking Sam for her hand was on his list of must-dos, but he hadn't worked up the courage for that yet, either.

Maybe he'd bought the ring prematurely. Maybe he just *thought* Annie felt the same forever love for him that he felt for her. Maybe.

But then, maybe she loved him with the same deep, abiding love that flooded through him every time he looked at her. Every time he heard her voice or simply watched as her hair floated around her when a breeze got up. Maybe he was crazy. But he didn't think so.

"Here we are," said Annie, pulling James back to the moment. "If you'll pull in through the right-hand door, there is a spot just inside where your truck will fit nicely."

"Thanks," he said, following her directions, trying to keep his mind on the task at hand.

With his truck tucked safely away, James and Annie tightened scarves and pulled on lamb-lined gloves before braving the weather and traipsing through the snow, back to the house.

"Here goes nothing," he said.

"Thank goodness it's not that far to the back porch," said Annie. "I've always been grateful that Dad built the barn close to the house, especially when we're expecting a new calf or foal. Bless his heart."

"I totally agree," said James, stepping out into the snow. "Especially now that I have my own barn and livestock to worry about. Please stay in front of me," he said, changing the subject. When her body stiffened next to him, he worried he had sounded bossy. "Uh, so I'll know you haven't been swallowed up by an abominable snowman, or something." Using humor sometimes deflected away from a verbal faux pas.

"That does sound gruesome," she said, with a giggle.

Whew, maybe she hadn't been insulted, after all. James let her pass him as they stepped outside. He kept his eyes on her back and his mind on the ground under his boots. Icy weather could be slippery at best, and treacherous at worse. His heart rate didn't slow until he spotted the steps that had been treated with rock salt, just ahead of them.

"You can breathe now, James," said Annie, a hint of sarcasm in her voice. "We made it."

He had to listen hard to hear her raised voice, competing with the roar of the wind.

"Praise God!" he said, without an ounce of humor, even though she had made an attempt to lighten the stressful moment. "I hope your mom has some hot chocolate or coffee inside."

Stepping up beside Annie, close enough that their jackets swished together, he looked down into her bright green eyes. She winked, and his heart leapt into his throat. "Wow, you're gorgeous," he whispered. "Can I kiss you?"

"Goodness no," she said with a laugh. "It's freezing out here. Come on in, silly man, and I'll get you warmed up."

"Sounds even better," James mumbled in her ear.

"James Bartholomew Baldwin," she cried.

"Sorry, I'm just teasing you. But I am ready to get warm."

Annie opened the back door and they stepped into heavenly warmth. The unmistakable scent of hot apple cider permeated the air. "Ooo," said James, "can I change my request to cider?"

"You certainly can," said Sissy, pulling a mug down from the cabinet. "Have a seat in front of the fireplace and I'll bring you both something warm and yummy."

"You're an angel, Mrs. P," said James.

"Pshaw," said Sissy. "Now, go."

"Yes, ma'am."

Annie slipped her arm through the crook of James's elbow, and he squeezed her closer to his side, hopefully trapping her there. She felt perfect right next to him. *I give it all to you, Lord.*

"Hello," said Sam. "Got your truck put away okay?"

"Yes, sir. Thank you. I appreciate the gesture."

"Don't be silly. Just makes sense. Have a seat. I have a feeling Sissy will be right behind you with cider and a sweet treat."

"So, what's on the agenda for this evening?" said James.

"You may be sorry you asked that before we're done," said Sissy, coming into the great room with a tray. James couldn't help but notice that her walk and grip seemed much improved from the last time he'd seen her.

Sissy lowered the tray onto the large round table in front of the loveseat without a hiccup then made her way to the sofa, while Sam remained in the comfort of his very large recliner.

"Where are Josh and Mack?" said James, after a careful sip of cider.

"Cheerfully dragging boxes down from the attic," said Sissy with a mischievous smirk. "Not their favorite part of Christmas planning day."

"Point me in that direction and I'll help," said James, setting the still-warm mug on a coaster.

"Sounds good to me," said Josh, entering the room with a large box marked *Christmas—main tree.* "Just follow me. There's a lot to haul down and then we have to distribute it from room to room. Mom goes a little nuts with the decorating, every year."

"Hey, don't knock it," said Sissy. "Christmas is special, and I intend to honor the Savior's birth in the best way I can."

"And we all agree with that philosophy. Don't we, Josh?" said Sam, with a raised brow and a no-nonsense look in his eye.

James came close to laughing out loud at that but did not think it prudent. He didn't want to get on the bad side of either one of Annie's very large brothers, or her dad.

"Yes, sir," said Josh, obviously trying not to growl.

"Then you best get on with it," said Sam.

"Yes, sir."

"I'm right behind you," said James, impressed with the respect evident in Josh's tone. Even if it had been a bit grudging, he'd still managed to show respect for his father.

"Thanks."

Three hours later, the Christmas boxes had been distributed to the proper rooms and the tree had been assembled. Everyone had agreed that it would be too difficult for Annie and Sissy to participate in going to a tree farm to cut down a real tree, considering their present infirmities. Sissy had agreed to settle for pine-scented candles.

"It's fine," she said. "Having us all together is what really matters."

"Right-o," said Sam, as he planted a kiss to his wife's temple.

Annie poked an elbow into James's side, and he jumped.

"What?" he said, curious as to why she found it necessary to hurt him.

"Aren't they the sweetest?" she whispered in his ear, as he inclined his head toward her.

"You bet," he said, slipping a hand down the side of her face then letting it rest on her shoulder. "Just the marriage I'd like to have one day."

Annie's eyes got wide, and he grinned at her. "You know, when the time is right."

James straightened and cleared his throat. If he wasn't careful, he would be proposing on the spot, without any prep work or approval from her father.

He wanted to marry Annie Jo Parker, no doubt, but he didn't want to scare her off. What if she was nowhere near ready for him to pop the question? What if he had misread the signals this whole time? What if she would think him crude and desperate, especially since they had just met in September? He couldn't be one hundred percent sure of what her answer might be. He only knew how much he wanted to marry her.

Help me know what to do, Lord, and when to do it. I want only your best for Annie Jo Parker. I do pray, however, that I fall somewhere in the line of best things for her.

With a fire roaring in the fireplace and a hot meal spread out on the dining room table, the Parker family and James gathered around for a feast that would rival any he had ever experienced, even when his grandmother had been alive. Made him wonder what the actual Christmas meal would be like. Sonya had outdone herself.

"I sure am glad Sonya can follow a recipe," said Josh. "She did good, don't you think, Mom?"

"I must admit, I do," said Sissy, sounding as though she had come to terms with Sonya being in her home, in her kitchen. "Maybe I'll need her a little longer than I thought." The grin on her face sucked all the tension from the room. Knowing Mom had adjusted to this season of domestic aide would help make the holiday enjoyable and relaxing.

Laughter filled the room, and James felt like part of the family. No one treated him like an outsider or talked around him like he wasn't in the room. Each member of the family actively engaged with him, even to the point of a little teasing.

"Hope you're not too sore, city boy," said Josh. "We made you work an awful lot today."

"Josh Parker," huffed Sissy, with a frown.

"It's okay," said James, lifting a hand toward Mrs. Parker. "Makes me feel like part of the family."

"You are part of the family," said Sissy, as though the matter had been settled, long before this enchanted evening.

"Thank you, ma'am. Means a lot to hear you say so."

A moment of quiet reflection was suddenly shattered when a crash rattled the windows and made the men jump to their feet.

"What in the world?" said Sam.

"Sounds like a big tree limb landed on the roof," said Mack, headed for the mud room. "I'll go check it out."

"Take some backup," said Sam.

"Do you mind if I tag along?" said James, joining Mack at the back door. "I'd like to help if I could."

"I won't turn down volunteer help," said Mack.

"Josh?" said Sam.

"I'm going. These two might need someone to help them up out of the snow."

"Very funny," said Mack, shrugging into his coat.

The three men stopped inside the mud room to gear up for the blizzard-like weather waiting for them on the other side of the outer door. Mack held the door in a tight grip until they had all passed through and into the elements. The storm had escalated over the past hour. Maneuvering through it could prove tricky.

CHAPTER THIRTY-FIVE

Take delight in the LORD, and he will give you the
desires of your heart (Psalms 37:4 NIV).

James pulled up the hood on his jacket and the woolen scarf up over his nose and mouth. The north wind blew blinding snow all around them, making it difficult to see.

Following closely behind the brothers, James trusted their judgment on where to go and what to do. Repairing a roof in the middle of a snowstorm would not be fun, but between the three of them, they'd manage. He had to keep telling himself that.

James thought back to his growing up years, yet again. Something he'd been doing on a regular basis since moving back to Lubbock County. Between his dad and Tommy, he and his brothers had been provided a well-rounded education outside the classroom. As a result, James had built up a strong body, parallel with the building up of his brain. He could swing a hammer, lift heavy boards, carry weight on his back, and engineer a complicated security system, with the best of them.

Yet, his confidence had expanded in the few months since he had met the Parker family and witnessed the many facets of running a functioning ranch. Details he had never known about, now flooded his brain.

He realized with some measure of regret that he had spent far too many hours inside a gym, when he could have achieved the same results with hard labor. He'd been enjoying the lessons Bo had volunteered, as well as the camaraderie with the other ranch hands. And now that everything he had owned in Tennessee, especially his beloved racehorses, had been relocated, he'd begun to settle into his new lifestyle. A balance between his official duties as owner and operator of JB Enterprises and his capacity as owner and overseer of JB ranch, had opened his eyes to the benefits of a more balanced and full life. Add the pleasant complication of a relationship with Annie Jo, and James considered himself one of the most blessed among men.

"We're going to get the extension ladder from the barn," hollered Josh, slowing for James to catch up. "We'll need you to hold it in the middle, so the wind doesn't rip it out of our hands. You good with that?"

James gave him a thumbs-up and the three of them headed for the barn. During two prior generations of learning how to manage the challenges winter had to offer, the Parkers had devised a healthy iron framework for the oversized structure, as well as massive doors that provided plenty of room for maneuverability when it came to transporting large implements and trailers in and out. The doors glided smoothly on a heavy-duty track that ran along the entire width of the barn. It helped a great deal that the wind blew from the side of the barn rather than pushing against the front of the doors. Josh pulled in one direction while Mack pulled in the other, until they could slip through the opening.

James stepped inside the barn and waited for the brothers to return to the entrance with the ladder. He glanced around the barn while he waited, noticing that no animals had been housed in here. It had been built strictly for equipment and tack. He wondered then just how many outbuildings the Parkers maintained. Obviously, there were other aspects of their huge operation that he had not seen, which made him all the more determined to learn everything he could about every aspect of ranching life. Still a novice, he made a pact with himself to pay close attention and soak up every ounce of knowledge he could, in as short a time as possible.

Winter wasn't anything to take for granted, up here in the panhandle of Texas. And this year challenged them with especially harsh conditions. James wanted to be ready, be an asset, and not leave everything up to Bo and the ranch hands.

Josh and Mack returned, now wearing tool belts. They shuffled the ladder through the opening then James helped push the door closed. Taking up his position in the middle of the ladder, he used all of his concentration to keep his grip as the wind fought against them.

"Whoa, stop here," cried Mack. Together, the three of them stood the ladder on its end and propped it against the eve of the house. "There's a place to the right where some metal has been torn away from the roof," he hollered. "Help me position the ladder and I'll go up and check it out."

Josh and James walked the ladder to the designated spot then manned each side of it while Mack moved slowly up, one rung at a time, to the roof.

"Hold both sides of the ladder," Josh yelled. "I'm going up."

"Got it," said James, shifting his weight and tightening his grip as Josh started up the ladder.

The wind had changed direction and Mack cried out, reaching for the loosened metal roofing before it tore out of his grasp.

"I'm here, brother," shouted Josh, as he stretched out his arm and grabbed the barn-red sheet, fighting against the wind.

James could barely make out their words or discern their movements through the wall of snow. But he held tight to the ladder, further braced it with a foot on the bottom rung and prayed as hard as he'd ever prayed in his life. He did not want these men to be injured on his watch.

Just when he thought his strength would fail him the ladder shook beneath his hands. Fear shot through him. Had he failed at the one simple task he'd been assigned? Would one or both of Annie's brothers be seriously hurt because he couldn't hold on while two brave souls risked their lives? The assignment had been simple, yes, but not easy. Even though he'd done his best, he could feel the quiver in his muscles.

He increased the intensity of his prayer then dared to look up. Afraid of what he might see, James forced himself to look.

His eyes widened in relief when he realized that Josh was descending the ladder and stood just above his head.

"Thank the good Lord," cried James.

"Mack is coming down too," said Josh, as he stepped to the ground.

"Good," said James. "This wind is about to kick my rear."

Josh chuckled. "No kidding. Weren't no picnic up top, either."

Suddenly, the wind stopped howling and an eerie calm descended around them. James had the distinct impression that this was the eye of the storm, like a tornado, only with snow. God's reprieve, just when they needed to finish this task and get back inside. James squeezed his gloved hands into fists, working warmth and blood into them. *Thank you, God, for keeping these men safe.*

An hour had passed before the three men crowded back into the mud room, covered in snow, and wishing they'd put hand warmers inside their gloves.

"Whew," said Mack, hanging his outer coat on a peg. "I'm glad that's over."

Sam jumped up to meet them when they came through the back door. James followed behind as Josh and Mack removed their sweater hats and shook the moisture out of their hair.

"Feels like my fingers are frozen solid," said Josh.

"Well, get in by the fire, quick," said Sissy, from the kitchen. "I'll be right in with hot drinks and some warm apple pie. What would y'all like to drink?"

"Coffee," said Mack. "Same," said Josh. "Cider," said James. He'd only had a sip out of the previous cup. And he really wanted more of that delectable taste.

"Well, scoot on in there. We added wood to the fire, so you could warm up. Once you're settled, you can give us your report," said Sissy.

"Yes, ma'am," said the three men, in unison. Sissy was still in control. A sweet lady who loved the Lord, loved her family, and expected their allegiance and obedience. She had raised them in the nurture and admonition of the Lord, must like the Bible instructed. She handled them gently, but firmly. And the family respected her methods and loved her unconditionally. The family bond was like a steel trap, lined with velvet.

James did not try to hide the grin that broke the frozen tundra of his face when Annie stepped up close to him, reached up and planted a kiss on his cheek. Right there in front of her entire family. Heat crept up his face, despite the chill from outside.

"I'm so cold I could barely feel your lips," he teased. "But thank you."

Annie took one of his hands between both of hers and started warming it up. "Ah, feels better already," he said.

Tingles ran through his hands as he absorbed the warmth from the fireplace. His fingers began to thaw and the ice in his hair turned to liquid.

"Here's a towel," said Annie Jo.

"Thank you," said James, wrapping it around his head and giving it a good scrub.

"Hey!" said Josh.

"Chill," said Annie Jo, with a chuckle. "I brought one for each of you."

With his hands encircling the warm mug of cider, James scooted a smidge closer to Annie Jo and gave her a wink.

"The damage is not too bad," Mack explained. "No snow can get in the house. Mr. Archer did a fine job when he put that extra heavy layer of wood and tarp down before he screwed on the metal roof. Looks like just a corner got peeled back when a limb broke off that big oak tree at the far corner of the house. I managed to shove it to the ground but won't be doing anything more with it until the sun comes up and the wind dies down. Then I'll call the insurance company to assess the damage. If it's not any worse than I think, we'll be fine until they send someone out. Nevertheless, I'll climb back up there during daylight hours and see what I can see."

Sam sat back in his lounger and listened to his oldest son, all grown up and handling a minor crisis. Alone. Mack had come a long way since his teenage years, when he'd felt overwhelmed by all he'd have to learn in order to run the family ranch. But steadily along, he had taken Sam's lessons to heart, had followed his dad's advice, and graduated with a master's degree in ranch management. He could now stand on his own two feet and carry on an intelligent conversation with a pushy salesman or the local vet.

Pride swelled his chest out a little, until Sam caught himself. Pride was the wrong way to look at Mack's maturity. Sam knew better than to take credit. Being impressed with Mack was one thing. Patting himself on the back, another thing altogether. *Sorry, Lord. I got a little carried away. I am so impressed with how you have worked in Mack's life, so that he is now a man in right standing with you, and with other men. Thank you for showing him the path that would keep him on the straight and narrow, and that he listened.*

I see your hand at work in Josh and Annie, as well. I'm trusting them to you, here, in this phase where they make decisions without my input. For now, and into the future, when they are each ready to settle down and make a home of their own, raise a family, and become the heads of their own households. Carry them close to your heart and teach them not to lean on their own understanding.

Sam had kept his eyes open as he prayed so he could catch the interactions of this close-knit family. As the prayer ended, voices became clear in his conscious mind.

He made eye contact with his wife just as she said, "We are blessed for sure. I talked to Meredith over at the Anderson place and she says half the barn caved in over there. They're scrambling for a place to put everything and get their animals to safety."

"Meredith?" said Josh. "Who's Meredith?"

"The lady Jake hired from the Aboveboard Maid Service. She has really fulfilled a need for them. From what I hear, she has even managed to win over Austin. He eats her cooking and has been talking to her, since he's been confined to the ranch. She said mostly she just listens, which seems to be working. She said he has calmed down a great deal over the past week. I choose to believe there is still hope for him."

James made no comment. As angry as he'd been with Austin, he did not wish ill on him or his family. If this Meredith lady could fill a void in Austin's life, perhaps she could get through to him, when no one else had managed to crack the body armor he'd been wearing since the loss of his mother. Since before that, from what Annie Jo had said. Meredith might even be able to persuade Austin to voluntarily enter a rehab facility. *I will continue to pray for his spiritual, emotional, and physical healing, Lord. He appears to be the one sheep among the one hundred who needs to be rescued. Thank you for sending someone to the Anderson ranch, someone evidently gentle and patient. Someone Austin can trust with his innermost emotional pain. Someone who seems to have accepted him where he is at this point in his life, without judgment or unreasonable expectations.*

"I'm glad she's there for him," said Annie, even as she squeezed James's hand. He glanced down at her and noticed a hesitancy in her gaze, like she wondered if that comment might upset him.

"I am too," said James. "I don't know of anyone who hasn't needed extra support, for some reason or another. I admit, I have spent a lot of time on my knees, seeking forgiveness. I think I'm nearly there.

"And I can only imagine how I might have reacted if I had lost my mom, then you, Annie. It would be a lot to overcome. No matter his motives, the loss is still keen for him. I get it, and I'll be praying for his full recovery."

"Thank you," said Annie and Sissy, at the same time.

"He was a good kid once," said Sissy.

The sadness and sincerity in her tone brought Austin right into the room with them. For the first time since he'd been seeing Annie Jo, James realized how deep the root of Austin Anderson went in this family. They had once considered him one of them. A big part of their future. James's subconscious mind let doubt creep in. If Austin straightened up, James feared he could lose Annie Jo.

Annie squeezed his hand, calming him with the small gesture. The gesture reminded him of every moment they had spent together over the past few months. Every moment of joy, every second of heartbreak, every hour of victory, every glance, smile, and knee-weakening kiss.

He grinned, looking into those large, expressive green eyes that had first captured his attention. And just like that, he was able to push Austin firmly into the past, from whence he'd come. He knew, without question, that he could trust God with his future. A future with Annie Jo Parker.

"Yes, he was," said Josh, in response to Sissy's comment. "Do you think we should see if they need our help tomorrow?"

"I have no qualms about any of you helping the Andersons," said Sam. "I was thinking about offering my services if Jake clears it with Austin. He may not be comfortable with any of us showing up over there. Might not be wise to poke the bear."

Josh huffed out a breath. "He can just get comfortable in the same shoes he got uncomfortable in. I'm going over there in the morning, see how bad things are."

Of all the friends James imagined Austin might have, he would not put Josh Parker on that list. One, he was several years older than Austin, so probably didn't attend high school with him. And two, they seemed so different in their core values.

But if Josh's going to help the Andersons further facilitated Austin's recovery, James was all for it. If Austin got well, the threat of violence would go away, the threat of kidnapping Annie would go away, the threat of destruction would go away.

Yeah, Josh, go, see if you can help. I'd even come with you, if I weren't certain that my presence would launch another territorial war.

***

December 20

Over the next five days God worked one miracle after another.

The sun warmed his face as James stood outside the barn and absorbed its amazing rays. For days, the sky had been gray or white, depending on whether clouds hid all evidence of the sun or snow blocked both the clouds and the sun. The glorious light made him almost giddy.

James let himself twirl around like a kid who had just escaped to the playground for recess. A deep-throated chuckle suddenly made him aware of his actions.

"Sun feels good, doesn't it?" said Bo.

James laughed at himself. Embarrassed, but happy at the same time. "Certainly does. I was beginning to think spring would arrive before we saw the sun again."

"Not all winters are this wet," said Bo. "It usually gets really cold up here, but some winters are so dry, we wish it would snow, simply for the moisture, and to kill a few bugs."

"Can't even imagine that scenario at this moment," James said with a shrug. He stepped closer to Bo, patted his gloved hands together and settled his hat farther down on his forehead as a stiff breeze rushed between them. A reminder that, even in the glare of the sun, winter would be with them, for a while yet.

Gratitude was the order of the day. Bo, dedicated foreman, manifested the larger-than-life picture Barry had painted of him. A strong leader, whose men respected him, trusted him, and obeyed his commands, no questions asked.

"What are you up to today, Boss?"

"Can you keep a secret?"

CHAPTER THIRTY-SIX

No temptation has seized you except what is common to man. And God is faithful; he will not let you be tempted beyond what you can bear. But when you are tempted, he will also provide a way out so that you can stand up under it. (1 Corinthians 10:13 NIV).

The secret had been eating a hole through him. He thought if he didn't get it out, he would disintegrate from the breaking down of his epidermis. Christmas was fast approaching, and he really wanted the question of his future with Annie Jo settled before the New Year. He had spent hours on his knees, listening for the powerful whisper from his heavenly Father, for confirmation that Annie Jo Parker had come into his life for a reason, a lifelong reason. He wanted to claim her as his own, complete with a ring. He wanted her to walk down the street with him as "his girl." Wanted everyone who knew them to be aware that they were serious about one another. Plus, if she accepted his ring, he could stop wondering if she felt the pull of matrimony, as strongly as did he. If she displayed the engagement ring, people would automatically know that she loved him, that he loved her, that they loved each other.

"I suppose I could keep a secret," said Bo. "If I knew it would not cause harm if the truth came out. If you're not involved in something illegal. If."

"Hold it, hold it," said James, stopping Bo, mid-sentence. He didn't want to give his foreman the wrong impression. They worked well together, and he wanted to keep it that way. "It's nothing sinister, I assure you. It's just that I bought this engagement ring, even though I haven't spoken to Mr. Parker yet, or to Annie Jo, for that matter. I plan to propose on Christmas

Eve, but I wanted to say that out loud to someone else, so I could convince myself it's real."

Bo slapped James on the back and laughed out loud. "Good for you, man! I say go for it. I've seen you two together on several occasions and if I know anything about relationships, I'd say y'all have what it takes to make it."

"What does it take?" said James, even though he thought he knew the answer. Bo Mattis was probably ten or so years older than James. Maybe he had learned something along the way that would serve well in his relationship with Annie Jo. He wanted to do this right, wanted her to know how much he treasured her as a person and as a lifelong mate.

"You probably know better than I do," said Bo, with a shrug. "I've been a bachelor my whole life. I buried my head in books so I could bury my arms in mud up to my elbows or pull a calf in the middle of the night. I've slept on straw as many nights as I've slept in a bed. I've been content with how God has used me. Heck, I'm middle aged, already. Don't expect I'll be meeting a woman who would want this kind of life, so I'll keep on just like I'm goin' till God calls me home. I'm good with that."

James shoved cold fingers deep into his coat pockets and let Bo talk. He'd said more in the past few minutes than James had heard him utter since the day they'd met. Made him feel good that Bo would share with him. Be a friend. It meant things were settling between them, in a good way. Bo was strong and had a lot more years to give.

"But I remember a few things my dad tried to teach me. I'd like to think I'd treat a lady the way my dad treated my mom. He said a lady should be treated like a lady, more than a lady, like a princess. And I remember Mom saying Dad treated her like a queen, so I guess he got that one right." Bo shook his head as mirth twinkled in his eyes.

James had yet to see Bo so open, bordering on spiritual. It felt good to know he came from a firm foundation, from a family that had strong morals. Part of that could have been presumption, but he'd worked with Bo for several months now and realized there was really something to the declaration that one Christian spirit can discern another. In this simple conversation, James felt Christ there, with them.

"That one will be easy with Annie Jo. She's amazing." James fell quiet long enough to make a silent vow before God that he would lean on him, trust him to teach James how to love Annie Jo the way Christ loved the church and gave himself for her.

"If you say so," said Bo, with a little tease in his tone.

"Yeah," said James. "Amazing. So, what else did your father say?"

Bo took a moment to think about the question. James waited, eager for any tidbit of information that might make a world of difference when it came to nurturing his relationship with Annie Jo. This one, he wanted to get right.

"Never marry outside the faith. Take your family to church, lead them to the saving knowledge of Jesus Christ, and walk the talk. If your family can't count on you for the truth, the devil can convince them of just about anything."

And there it was, further confirmation of Bo's Christian heritage. James felt the truth of his foreman's words settle in his spirit. If he missed on this point, it wouldn't matter how well he treated his wife and children, the house they built would not stand.

He'd been aware, even as a child, just how serious his dad had taken his duty to tell his kids the truth about Jesus. Every night before bed they gathered in the den for family devotions. His dad would read from the New Living Translation then discuss the meaning of the words. A fact emerged in his memory that hadn't registered before this moment. It hit him like a force so powerful it was almost physical.

"Your father was right," James said, suddenly filled with awe. "I gave my life to Christ during a family devotional. I remember it so clearly now." He swiped at a tear that slid down his face. "I was baptized the Sunday before my father passed away."

A long silence hung between them, before Bo abruptly changed the subject. "I was about to ride fence, check on things. Wanna come along?"

Guess Bo was ready to get on with his day.

But James wasn't sorry he'd shared his secret with his friend. Their conversation had been a sobering reminder that he already had the answers he needed. Love your wife the way Christ loved the church, in a self-sacrificing way. And a three-prong marriage is the only marriage that can stand up against the wiles of the devil, against temptation and frustration and the stress of raising children.

With God at the helm, the husband can trust the way the wheel turns, and his wife can trust where her husband leads.

"Definitely," said James. "It would be a shame to waste such a rare day."

It was cold. The snow had not even begun to melt. But the ride did James a world of good. Even when the cold air moved through his lungs, making it difficult to breathe. The view made up for any discomfort he might have to endure. He continued to discover new and amazing things about *his* ranch. Special touches that made the ranch a mystical place. Apparently, Barry had done his research. Even in the dead of winter, a harsh one at that, plants that stayed green all year poked through the snow in unexpected places. The roads that led to the outbuildings and to every pond or separate fenced pasture had been paved and cleared with buckets and buckets of de-ice spread by conscientious men who did their jobs well.

James and Bo rode fence for about two hours and found nothing untoward. Praise the Lord! His nose and toes had begun to feel stiff and icy cold.

"Ready to head back?" said Bo, as if he sensed James's discomfort.

Their time together that morning had begun a bond that James would carry close to his heart, far into the future. An easy camaraderie that could be defined as solid friendship. The specific term had not been necessary, as an understanding bound them.

Bo would be free to do what Bo did best.

James had done his research. The duties of a ranch manager had been defined online as: *supervise the production and care of livestock and other farm animals. They are in charge of overseeing the raising and birthing of all livestock.* But Bo performed outside the confines of defined responsibility, and James recognized Bo's skillset. The ranch hands trusted their foreman with an admirable allegiance. James respected that connection. God had blessed him, not only with the ranch of his dreams, but with a reliable crew and an admirable foreman.

"I could stand another cup of coffee," said James. "Join me?"

"Thanks, but I got chores need doin'," said Bo, in a matter-of-fact tone. Back to the stoic Bo James had come to know.

And that was the end of the conversation. James had experienced an amazing morning with Bo, with Mother Nature, and his favorite horse. Didn't get to be much better than that. If he had Annie Jo waiting for him back at the house, the picture would be wholly amazing. That one element would complete the puzzle, every corner piece, and all the pieces in the middle.

James Baldwin owned the ranch of his dreams. *Miracle Number One.*

Shrugging deeper into his duster, James started walking toward the barn, only vaguely aware that Bo had dismounted and walked alongside him. Although the sun had come out the temperature still hovered below freezing. He shivered as he moved along, still stuck in his head.

All these years since his father's death, and until this moment James had considered Thanksgiving the saddest time of the year. The week his dad had passed away, without warning. Home in the morning then forever gone from their lives.

A spark of hope started a fire in his soul in this flash of revelation. During that same season of loss, James had been given the greatest gift. God had surrounded him with his love and light—more than enough to see him through the darkest valley he could remember.

They reached the barn where Braveheart awaited. James reached for the handle but stopped when Bo clapped a hand on his shoulder. "I got it, Boss," he said, his voice soft and low, almost reverent. He seemed to understand that James would need some time to process their conversation.

Bo slid the barn door back for James to slip through then waited until the lights came on before he slipped away.

With slow but deliberate steps, James lumbered toward Braveheart's stall. He would have to thank Bo later. For their talk. For his father's wisdom. And for the fact that Bo had sense enough to leave James with his thoughts.

***

"James! James!" cried Annie Jo through the phone line. She sounded excited, more than alarmed. "Can you come over? We have big news!"

"On my way," he said, without hesitation. Whatever the reason, he had an opportunity to see Annie Jo, and wasn't about to miss that chance. "I need to change clothes first. Bo and I have been out riding fence. Do y'all still have coffee or cider available? It's still super cold out."

"You bet. And Mama made apple fritters this mornin'."

"Yum, be there as soon as possible."

The drive to Annie's parents' home had James's brain racing from point A to point B, searching for what kind of news Annie Jo might have that would include him. A newborn calf, maybe? A new horse? Something about her mother's physical condition? He didn't know, and speculation wouldn't give him any answers. The driveway seemed longer than usual what with the snow coverage and the thin layer of ice that challenged the chains on his tires. But he made it without incident, parked in front of the Parker's home then walked as fast as he could up to the door. He raised his hand to knock, but it swung open before his knuckles made contact with the wood.

"James! Get in here. Hurry," said Annie.

James chuckled and followed Annie into the warmth of the great room. After such a long time on horseback, in the cold, it felt like a hug with a down comforter.

"Sure feels good in here," he said, rubbing his hands together.

"Everything okay at your place?" said Sam, from the comfort of his lounge chair.

"Couldn't be better, thanks. Things have been quiet. Fence looks good. If you don't have to be out in the weather too long, the landscape is breathtaking."

"Now," said Annie, "I'll get you some cider and a fritter then we can talk, okay?"

"Perfect," said James. Annie made her way into the kitchen, while James stretched his fingers out in front of the fireplace.

This was a special day, the day he planned to ask Sam for his daughter's hand in marriage. No matter what other news the family had to share. The second step in the plan to make Annie Jo his wife. He had accomplished the first at the jewelry store over a week ago.

Once he had Mr. Parker's blessing, James intended to call his own family and give them a heads-up. He wanted full disclosure, so when the secret came out, the people he cared about most would not be blindsided. But his family had met Annie Jo, had eaten with her, laughed with her, and welcomed her into his mother's home. They had seen them together and his brothers had teased him about finding his one true love, which pretty much told him they approved.

His family would understand and give him whatever support he needed. Just like they had done for Matt, Brooke, Paul, and Kim. So, he was the last one to find romance, real romance, the lasting kind of romance. Not a big deal. The important thing being, he had found it, at last. He loved Annie Jo and believed she loved him back. Prayed she did, anyway.

"Okay, what is going on?" he said, brushing crumbs off his mouth with the holiday paper napkin that had been tucked next to the festive plate that held a warm, delicious apple fritter.

"Meredith called this morning," said Sissy, without preamble.

"Meredith?" said James.

"Remember?" said Annie. "Meredith works for Jake Anderson. She came from the Aboveboard Maid Service."

"Oh yeah, I remember, now. Sorry. Please go on."

"Anyway," said Sissy, "Austin agreed to check into a rehab facility, just this morning. Isn't that great? I've been so worried about him."

So, Austin had agreed to go into rehab, after all. Excellent. James could see how much the Andersons meant to the Parkers. Hopefully, their relationship could be restored. Hopefully, Austin would find his way back to a normal life, sober and grounded. A lot could be revealed over the next 28 days. His heart went out to the guy, and he determined, yet again, to pray for him, every single one of those 28 days. *Kill 'em with kindness* raced through his mind, a wicked thought he chose not to dwell on. Best to not go there.

"That is good news," he said, finding with a jolt of surprise that he meant the words. Perhaps he had fully forgiven Austin of his misdeeds. He didn't wish the guy bodily harm, necessarily, or eternal damnation, for certain. He just didn't want Austin anywhere near Annie Jo. "I hope he finds what he is looking for."

"We all do," said Sam, a solemn look on his face that screamed a history of concern for a kid he had loved like a son.

The room fell quiet. James could only imagine what the individual thoughts of these family members might be. He no longer doubted where Annie Jo stood, a huge relief. Her relationship with Austin would never again expand beyond the boundaries of friendship, if indeed friendship ever again showed up on her radar.

Josh had been the quickest to forgive him but had also taken a strong stand to protect his little sister from any further abuse. Nothing between the Anderson family and the Parker family would ever quite fit the same way as before. The picture on the box had become distorted, misshapen, with some broad gaps and missing border pieces. Disturbing.

Mack didn't say much, one way or the other, but James got the distinct impression that he would not back down from a fight, if it came to that. Every man in the room would stand up for Annie Jo. Without question.

Sam obviously sympathized with Jake, who just wanted his son to be well and whole again.

And then there was Sissy, a born nurturer who also had considered Austin as another son, especially after his mother passed away. Her heart ached for the man he had become, as if Josh or Mack had lost their way. No matter what Austin's future decisions, he would always have a place in Sissy's heart. Even though he had broken it beyond a full recovery.

James could live with all of that. Didn't have anything to do with him, anyway. He had carved his own place into this family and relished that security.

As if she had heard his thoughts, Sissy said, "Can you stay for dinner?" That same nurturing gift extended toward him.

James sighed with yet a deeper level of contentment. Today was shaping up to be glorious. *Thank you, Father. I just can't thank you enough.*

"I'd be honored," he said aloud. "I still haven't gotten around to calling Aboveboard Maid Service, so a good meal from a good cook would make my day. My week, even."

"You've been single all this time, I'm surprised you didn't learn your way around a kitchen," said Annie, shoving his shoulder.

"Ha ha," he said. "I could manage if I wanted to. As it is, I have kept many a local restaurant in business. And I'll have you know they are all happy with my singleness."

The moment of humor passed, and James settled back into the comfort of the loveseat, warm, accepted, and beyond content. Blessed. He absorbed the feeling into the center of his being.

Austin Anderson would be checking himself into rehab. *Miracle Number Two.*

CHAPTER THIRTY-SEVEN

And hope does not put us to shame, because God's love has been poured out into our hearts through the Holy Spirit, who has been given to us. (Romans 5:5 NIV).

Dinner filled the empty spot in James's stomach to the point he almost felt sleepy. But he did not want to go home, just yet. He had one more goal to accomplish that day. He just needed a few minutes alone with Sam. What could he say to get that done?

Then it came to him that he had something Sam wanted. He'd been hinting at it, for days. It could be the perfect ruse to get Sam out of the house, and away from Annie Jo.

"Say, Sam," said James, pushing his empty dessert plate toward the center of the table. "Could you come out to the barn with me for a few minutes? I may have a lead on that matter we discussed the other day."

"What matter?" said Annie, making eye contact, obviously expecting to be let in on the secret.

Not today, sweetheart.

"No way," said James, grinning and waggling his brows. Christmas, a magical time of year. "It's Christmas, and you don't get to know everything."

For sure, this was one secret he would keep close to his vest. He *had* to speak to Sam alone. James had a huge secret. And Sam had a surprise for Sissy. So, this could work.

"Oh, man, now you've really got my curiosity going. I may have to follow you out there."

"Don't you try it, young lady," said Sissy, her tone firm. "You know how I feel about Christmas secrets. Breaking one is appalling. Shaking packages is bad enough, but I forbid any sneaking around. You understand?"

"Yes, ma'am. I was just teasing James. I well remember the consequences of peaking underneath the gift wrapping. I certainly won't do that again."

James's chest rumbled with laughter. He could relate. His mother still had a hard and fast rule about Christmas presents—to the point that the packages were numbered—no names in sight. She kept a corresponding list, matching gifts with recipients, under lock and key, not to be revealed until Christmas morning.

James's parents had instilled in all of them a principal that encouraged them to give, without expecting anything in return. His earliest memories found the family filling and decorating baskets for a list of people obtained through the church. Families down on their luck who didn't expect to celebrate with either a tree or gifts placed beneath it. Their local body of believers worked together, giving sacrificially so a dozen or more families could experience the holiday with joy. The expressions on their faces had stuck with James through the years, and he'd managed to find others less fortunate and pay it forward. Every year. As though his mother could watch him from across the miles. He had witnessed that same generous spirit in the Parker family when they'd decided, on Christmas planning day, which needy family they would bless with an anonymous monetary gift. Their anonymous gift through Heifer International further established his early impression of their magnanimous spirit.

It warmed his heart. Just one more confirmation that he was moving in the right direction.

James followed Sam to the barn, his right hand fisted around the little black velvet box in his jacket pocket. Was he crazy? He was about to ask for this man's daughter's hand in marriage. A girl. No. A lady, he had known only a few months. A captivating woman who had captured his heart with a single glance. A lady with large green eyes and long, flowing, dark auburn hair, who rode like the wind and took his breath away. God had placed her in his path with great care, precision, and perfect timing. He hadn't been searching for a romantic interest, didn't think he even wanted one. Annie Jo Parker had upset the apple cart and shattered every ill-conceived notion about romance that James had conjured up through the years—without even trying.

He was ready. His heart was ready. Eager and anticipatory of a fabulous future with Annie Jo Parker.

But would her dad think it too soon? Would he tell James to go home and give his family some time alone so they could talk the subject to death?

James shook the doubts out of his head. *Just do what you came to do, JB. Leave the rest up to God. He knows better than you do, what is about to take place. Let him have control. After all, Mr. Parker is a reasonable man, who knows what it means to have a tight-knit family. A family he would sacrifice his own life to save. A family that supported each other when the going got tough. Who stood for justice, but let God fight the battles.*

Approaching the barn door, they slid the doors open enough to slip through then closed them immediately. Compared with the out-of-doors, being in the barn was a total relief. Out of the cold wind, James's fingers would have a chance to thaw.

He released the little black box and stretched his fingers, grinning in anticipation. A measure of hope swirled through him. Thankfully, he had followed through with his promise to Sam the day before, and really did have news about the horses. *As always, Lord, your timing is perfect. Thank you for reminding me to make that call yesterday.*

"So, what news do you have for me?" said Sam, his eyes wide, his grin infectious. "Are there two horses available?"

"They are almost identical," said James, a satisfied smile splitting his face. "Gleaming black, one with a white star, the other a lightning bolt, down the front of their noses. Otherwise, they match perfectly. One for you, and one for Sissy. I think you'll be pleased."

What could be better than giving good news to one's future father-in-law in the very hour you come to ask for his daughter's hand? They settled on two bales of hay and talked at length about racehorses and trainers and facilities, and just about everything that James had ever learned on the subject.

He began to feel antsy, like time was running short, and someone from the house would be calling them in at any moment. He searched his mind for a decent segue, cleared his throat then finally said, "Speaking of perfect finds, Sam, I asked you out here for more than a discussion about horseflesh and the merits of owning a racehorse."

"Yeah?" said Sam. "What's that?"

Curiosity filled his eyes, but James could tell that Sam hadn't guessed what else James wanted to say. James was shocked that Sam couldn't see the question emblazoned across his forehead. Wasn't it obvious? Anyway, the time had finally come. James believed with everything in him that he and Annie Jo were meant to be together. He believed with all his heart that God had led him to a quaint little shop he otherwise would never have entered, guided his words and actions—actions that would endear him to Annie Jo Parker, until they met again. Actions that were made of promise, fidelity, and a future together. He prayed, even now, that the business with Austin, the history the Parker family had with him, would not color Sam's opinion of James and his ability to love and care for Annie Jo. One relationship had nothing to do with the other. Absolutely nothing.

"I would like your blessing, Sam. I plan to ask Annie to be my wife. And I want to ask her on Christmas Eve."

No fanfare, no begging, just straight out, the way a big, strong cowboy lived his life, and built relationships that lasted a lifetime. Sam Parker was a good man, a fine husband and father, a man James would be proud to emulate.

James held his breath while he waited for Sam to speak.

"Why the rush?" Sam said, at last, just when James was about to pull his hair out.

"I'm 35, sir, doesn't feel like a rush to me. But I realize you must be referring to the length of time Annie Jo and I have known each other. Well, that is an unexplained phenomenon. Lightning struck the first time I saw her. I was drawn to her like a magnet. When I looked into her eyes for the first time, peace came over me. A peace like I have never known. In fact, I didn't think I would ever allow myself to marry, afraid of hurting someone, or someone hurting me. But that notion dissolved on the very first day I was blessed to be in Annie Jo's company. And everything she has done, and said, since that time, has accumulated and filled my heart with so much love, I can't imagine living my life without her. And meeting her family has further solidified that plan for me. A family who loves God and lives out their faith, inspires hope. A family so much like the home I was raised in. Exactly like the family I want for Annie Jo and me."

Sam snapped a piece of straw and began to chew on it. He closed his eyes, and James noticed his lips moving, as if talking with himself, or to God. He sat very still beside this large, kind, powerful yet humble man, and let him work out what he needed to work out.

A few minutes later, Sam stood and walked over to the barn door. James sucked in a breath, confused, afraid Mr. Parker was done with him and had chosen to drop the subject altogether and go back to the house without giving him an answer. When Sam took hold of the handle on the barn door, James hopped up and jogged over beside him.

"Sir?" he questioned.

"You have my blessing, Son. Just promise me one thing."

"Anything." His heart was pounding now. He'd meant what he said. He would do anything the big man asked of him, as panic threatened to cut off the air supply to his lungs.

"Please consider waiting six months, before exchanging vows. I would appreciate your consideration of the suggestion, and it would give you two some time to get to know one another. Six months is not that long, in the grand scheme of things. Heck, knowing Sissy, it will take that long to plan the thing."

Whew. Sam had not asked the impossible. Had not refused his request. A measure of reservation had passed through his eyes; James hadn't missed that. But the resolve that had followed Sam's prayer had jumping beans dancing in James's gut. This moment could have gone completely pear-shaped and not at all in his favor.

"She's my baby girl," said Sam, one hand on the handle of the barn door and one on James's shoulder. "My *only* girl. If you hurt her, it will not go well with you."

"Yes, sir," said James, filled with respect and gratitude for this godly man. "I understand. You have my solemn word."

"Good to hear," said Sam, beginning to slide the door open.

"But sir, if it's all the same to you, I'll leave the timing up to Annie Jo and Sissy. My family will be happy to work around what works best for y'all. I really do thank you, Sam. You scared me there for a minute."

Sam chuckled. "You should be scared, Son. Marriage isn't all play and honeymoon."

"Yes, sir. I'd be grateful for any advice you have on the subject."

Sam paused then and turned to face James again, his face stoic and serious. "Follow the Good Book and you can't go wrong. Sometimes, it's all a man has to draw from."

James had Sam's blessing.

Miracle Number Three.

***

December 21

James glanced at his watch. Nine o'clock, on the dot. So, where was the girl from the Aboveboard Maid Service? He didn't tolerate tardiness in his business life and would prefer it did not upset his personal life, either. But the house was beginning to show signs of needing a woman's expertise in cleaning, especially a professional who would know how to manage the challenges of a house this large, and its intimidating number of bathrooms.

Even though James lived in the mansion alone, he still would like the rooms to remain ready for company or entertaining. Case in point, the gentleman James had purchased Sam and Sissy's racehorses from would be his guest the following day. The owner had opted to ride up with the horses to ensure their safe and timely arrival. Thankfully, the snow had not returned since the day before, and hope remained for clear skies today and the following day, as well. Which would make for a much safer trip for Mr. Wells and the driver who would be pulling the horse trailer.

James paced across the living room and back then moved to the kitchen to pour himself a second cup of coffee, determined to give the prospective employee another half hour in case she had lost her way to the ranch. If she didn't show, he'd call the service and cancel his request. He refused to put up with incompetence, no matter how well Meredith and Sonya had worked out for the Andersons and Parkers.

The gate buzzed just as James set his mug in the sink. Finally. He raced toward the control panel, punched the intercom button, and asked for a name.

"Lucinda, from Aboveboard Maid Service."

James tried to make eye contact. But he couldn't tell much from the small screen that displayed her features, half in shadow inside the small sedan. No horns seemed to be growing out of her head, so he buzzed her in. There was only one way to find out about her—face to face.

"Park at the bottom of the steps, for now. I'll show you to the garage once we determine if you will be staying."

He clicked off then, not waiting for a reply. He did not intend to hire someone who promised to be tardy every day. She would need to pass a trust test before he considered her a candidate. He would watch her closely today, looking for any obvious sign that she had little or no work ethic. Pay attention to her answers and trust his gut. Any indication that she was lazy or, heaven forbid, flirtations, and she'd be gone before she knew what hit her.

And Aboveboard would be getting a serious letter from his attorney.

James opened the front door then watched Lucinda come up the drive, make the curve, and park at the bottom of the steps, just as he had instructed. The maid service did not require their representatives to wear a traditional maid's uniform, like he'd seen depicted in countless movies of the old South, but they were required to wear a nametag and a bracelet with the company logo etched into them. His first observation was that Lucinda indeed had a nametag, resembling what he had seen online, pinned to her conservative, high necked sweater. And some sort of ID bracelet on her left wrist. She wore no other sign of jewelry and very little makeup. Her bright red hair, streaked with broad strokes of garish white, did not flatter her pale skin, dotted with fat freckles. It appeared to be long, encased in a braid that hung over her right shoulder. He supposed she might be considered reasonably pretty, but he did not need pretty to clean his house. He needed punctual and efficient.

"Good morning," he said, forcing joviality into his tone. "Did you have a hard time finding the place?"

"A little. Sorry I'm late. I turned right when I should have turned left and had to make a U-turn. Sorry, it won't happen again."

Good, not late as a matter of habit, hopefully. Ranches could be difficult to find on long stretches of country roads, he'd give her that. He would soon know the truth, anyway, for he had not requested a live-in maid service. No way. Probably three days a week would suit his needs. It wasn't like he was a pig. But the house did encompass a lot of square footage, so he decided to ask about her availability, once the tour and interview were out of the way. The square footage alone could scare her off.

"Come inside. I have coffee, if you'd like to warm up, and the fireplace is going."

"Coffee sounds great," she said, offering him a fleeting glance. Another good sign. She wasn't flirting with him. He certainly would not abide such behavior. Now that he had Mr. Parker's blessing, he was practically engaged, and didn't need any complications or misunderstandings to muck it up.

"The kitchen is this way," he said, ready to get on with it. He led the way. Once she settled at the breakfast bar, he said, "I'll get us some coffee and we can chat at the table then start the tour from there."

"Okay," she said, showing very little emotion, her eyes straight ahead, rather than ogling him while he worked.

So far, so good.

James led the way, pulled two fresh mugs out of the cabinet, and poured coffee in both. "How do you take your coffee?"

"Oh, just black, please."

"Easy enough. I know how to do that, for sure. I drink it black, as well. Unless it's a well-made cappuccino."

Once James and Lucinda settled at the kitchen island, he asked her simple questions about where she came from, where she lived now, how long she had been doing this kind of work, and if she enjoyed it. Basic information.

"Well, let me show you the house then we can talk specifics," he said, in conclusion, satisfied with her responses. He wouldn't have the real answers he needed until she had spent a day on the job. He may not want to do the work himself, but he knew what results he would require.

"Okay," Lucinda said again. For a fleeting moment, he wondered if she had a vocabulary that extended beyond a mere sentence or two. But then, he didn't really care. Conversation would be kept to a minimum. Just business. He didn't plan to be rude to the lady. But unless they ran out of cleaning supplies, interaction would be minimal.

"Here, I'll take your cup," he said.

"Thank you."

It took a solid hour for the walk-through and the few questions Lucinda asked about James's preferences then they wound up back where they had started, at the kitchen island.

"So, what do you think?" he said.

"It's a big house."

"Right. Are you interested in helping me keep it clean, maybe provide an occasional evening meal or lend a hand when I entertain? Which, I confess, happens very little. I do, however, have a business associate coming for a short stay tomorrow afternoon, and I'd like for the place to be fresh, for him. Do you think you could manage a once-over if I gave you today and tomorrow to get it done? I know it's short notice, but I just recently found out he was coming."

"Oh, it's no problem," said Lucinda, sounding sincere. "It just needs a little spit and polish, so to speak. Just point me to the supply closet and I'll get started right away."

"Let's talk schedule first, please. I don't need or want anyone to live here full time, or work here full time, for that matter. I was thinking three or four days a week. You'd have weekends off, unless something came up. Maybe nine to five, Monday, Wednesday, and Thursday? That way, you'd have a three-day weekend, every week."

CHAPTER THIRTY-EIGHT

Then, after desire has conceived, it gives birth to sin; and sin, when it is full-grown, gives birth to death. (James 1:10 NIV).

Lucinda chewed on her lip and stared down at her interwoven fingers. "I really need to make a full-time wage," she said, her face crumpled in thought. "I'm the sole support for my mother. She's disabled and can't work. I'm sorry, I was hoping this would work out and I could serve in this magnificent house."

She moved like she was going to stand. James hurriedly ran a scenario through his mind, then snapped his fingers. "I've got it. How about part-time work and full-time pay? It works within my budget, no problem. You can make what you need to make, and I can retain the privacy I consider sacred. I have a stressful job, so time alone to regroup is essential to my well-being. I hope you understand."

James fell silent then, waiting for Lucinda to consider his offer. Since she had already agreed that she could manage the housework, maybe she would accept his proposal, get on with the chores for today and tomorrow, and all would be in place for Mr. Wells's visit tomorrow afternoon.

It only took a moment for Lucinda to decide that she would be happy to work part-time for full-time pay. Of course, who wouldn't, thought James. He had made her a generous offer, in line with the financial arrangements he had agreed upon with Aboveboard. And if she did a good job, he would keep her on.

***

December 22

James had been pleased with Lucinda's work ethic. She was a top-to-bottom kind of housekeeper, which was exactly how his mother used to train any new person who came inside their home after Maggie passed away. Thorough, spotless, and quiet. Yes, this could work well.

A few minutes past five the following afternoon, not long after Lucinda had left for the day, Mr. Wells's driver buzzed at the front gate. James opened it with the remote device then called Mr. Parker. Sam wanted to be present when the horses arrived, so he could meet the previous owner and the new trainer, while Sissy was safe at home and none the wiser.

Christmas would be special in a new way for the Parker family. Sam and Sissy would embark on a new adventure, horseracing. And hopefully, God willing, and if James's dreams came true, Annie Jo would get herself engaged. To him.

"Welcome," said James, trotting down the wide steps of the porch, again grateful for the lapse in snowy weather. "Mr. Wells, it's good to see you again," he said, his arm outstretched.

"Quite a nice place you've got here," said Wells, releasing James's hand and looking over the expanse in front of James's home.

"Thank you. And I don't believe I've met your traveling companion."

"Come on up here, Sid," said Wells.

"Yes, both of you, come inside where it's warm. The trailer will be fine right where it is, until Mr. Parker arrives."

The three of them went inside. James gave them a choice between hot apple cider (which he had learned to make with Mrs. Parker's guidance) or coffee, set out some of the muffins he had begged from Sissy that morning then indicated they make their way into the great room, where a roaring fire greeted them.

"Uneventful trip, I hope," said James, finally able to shake the nerves that had plagued him since Wells had informed him that the journey from Kentucky had begun.

"Nice weather, for this far north," said Sid. "Sid Michaels," said the man, stretching out his hand toward James.

"Nice to meet you. Thank you for coming this far. I know that kind of travel can wear a man out, especially hauling such precious cargo."

"I won't lie," he said, with a shake of his head. "I'm glad it's over."

James could identify. If something had happened to the two horses he had purchased on Sam's behalf. He shoved that notion right out of his head. He just wouldn't think about that. Nothing had happened to them. They were here, safe and sound.

Just then, the gate speaker came to life and James hopped up to man the control panel, inside the front closet.

"Hey, James, it's Sam."

"Come on in, Sam. We're in the great room. We'll wait for you before we go out to the barn."

"Thanks."

The back door opened, and Bo came inside. He looked around the room then made eye contact with James. "Sorry to bother you, Boss, but could you come outside for a minute?"

His eyes wide with surprise, James looked between his two guests. "Excuse me, Pete. I need to deal with this. Would you let Sam in the front door in case I'm not back by the time he gets here?"

"Certainly," said Wells, lifting his mug in salute. "Do what you need to do."

"Be right back," said James, hoping he meant it. He didn't know what to expect when he walked outside with Bo, but he knew his foreman could handle most any challenge on the ranch. If Bo needed him outside, he needed to go.

"What's going on?" said James, meeting Bo at the entrance to the mud room.

"Let's have this conversation in the barn, sir. Won't take long. I know you have people waiting for you."

"It's fine, they know stuff happens on a ranch."

Once inside the barn, James looked around but didn't see anything out of the ordinary. They were in the livestock barn rather than the equipment barn, so he wondered if one of the animals had fallen ill. He didn't hear any untoward moaning or groaning, so it must not be that. Bo wouldn't call him out here for a lightbulb issue or a busted gate, so what exactly was this?

Then all six ranch hands appeared in front of him. Stoic, unsmiling, bordering on unfriendly. What was going on?

"I'm waiting," he said, his patience wearing thin. If something troublesome had happened on his ranch, he needed to know about it. "What's the problem?"

"We'd like Bo to speak for us," said Buck.

James turned toward Bo. "Well, what is it?"

Bo cleared his throat. James noticed then that his foreman squirmed under his scrutiny. Totally out of character. Highly unusual for the confident, straightforward foreman.

"Look," said James. "I expect the truth here. I can't do anything to help if you don't tell me what's happened."

"It's that girl you hired on," Bo blurted, swiping a hand across his forehead like it was ninety degrees inside the chilly enclosure.

"What about her?" James's skin began to itch. What could Lucinda possibly have to do with these men? His gut began to curdle the cappuccino he had enjoyed only moments ago.

Bo cleared his throat again, shifted his feet, then stood in front of James and spilled the disturbing truth.

"She flashed her, uh, front, out the bathroom window at two of the guys while they were walking between barns."

"She what?" cried James, his heart pounding. That hot drink crept its way up into his throat. He just might hurl all over the nearest person. Swallowing down the acrid taste, he managed to ask, "Did I hear you right?"

"Don't make me say it again, Boss. Sheesh."

Lucinda? She seemed so mild mannered, mousy even. Quiet, worked steadily while she was under his roof. Had put together some delicious sandwiches for them at lunch and made mango lemonade just like Annie Jo's mother made almost daily.

Lucinda had seemed to fit his needs so well he could scarcely believe what he was hearing. But he wouldn't put up with such rash behavior, such little regard for moral integrity, not for a second. *Lucinda?*

Bo held his hat in his hands, his shoulders slumped. But he held his head high, and his eyes trained on James. He didn't look away, which James appreciated. No matter how it looked, or sounded, Bo was telling the truth. James had to face that fact.

"Sorry to spring this on you while you have guests, but the guys just told me, and I thought you'd want to know, especially if you plan on having her come out again."

James steadied himself, mindful of the river of sweat that trickled down his back and slicked his palms. He did *not* need this complication in his life. Just when Austin had calmed down, he had Sam's blessing to ask for Annie Jo's hand in marriage, and the surprise racehorses had arrived, without incident. But then, life didn't stay on a smooth grid for long, now did it? One challenge after another.

"Did anything else happen that I need to know?" said James, discouraged but determined to deal with one lousy housekeeper.

Bo had been proven loyal for a lot of years. Barry had trusted him with the entire ranch. James had to give him credit. He would defend his men and take care of business. Unpleasant as it might be.

He braced himself, ready to hear what they had to say. It sounded crazy, what little he knew of Lucinda. But you can't always tell a book by its cover. He had learned that lesson through years and years of being in business. "Did she interact with any of you in any other way?" he pushed. "Not that what she did isn't cause for dismissal, it is. Trust me on that. I just need to know if I'm missing anything else."

He had spent weeks alone in the house, putting off hiring a maid, and the first rattle out of the box, he gets deceived. Why would Lucinda start something that she had to know she couldn't finish? And had she pulled similar disgusting antics at other places where she had worked? He thought Aboveboard did extensive background checks to avoid such shenanigans.

Buck looked down at his feet, dragging the toe of his boot across the packed dirt floor of the barn. This didn't look good, not good at all.

"Speak up," said Bo, nudging Buck with his elbow. "Go ahead. Get 'er done."

"Yes, sir." Buck finally said, glancing up at Bo. He then turned his attention to James and managed to look him in the eye, which James appreciated. And he needed something he could appreciate, since his guts were roiling, and he had to hold back the urge to vomit. Buck's next words made him for sure want to puke.

"I had a roll in the hay with her yesterday afternoon," he spat. "When you went next door to see Miss Annie."

James groaned out loud, pushed out a frustrated breath then propped himself up against the fender of a tractor. His knees had begun to shake, and he didn't trust his own legs to hold him steady. "You've got to be kidding me."

"'Tweren't my fault," said Buck, his voice cracking like a pre-teen. "She came sashaying out here with her shirt unbuttoned and pushed me up against the stall door then into the stall, practically knocked me down and into the hay."

James rubbed a hand down his face. "That's difficult for me to hear. Did you?"

"No, sir!" Buck all but shouted. "I came up out of that hay quick. I wasn't about to let her bamboozle me then get fired on top of the humiliation. I might be dumb, but I ain't stupid." His hands went up beside his head, as if in surrender. "'Sides, I know it wouldn't be right. I didn't touch her, Mr. B. I swear."

Bo stepped forward. "For what it's worth, I believe him."

"She's a tart," said Buck. "Plain and simple."

How could this be happening? James trusted the crew and their foreman, and he didn't know much at all about Lucinda. She may have put up an innocent front for him, but apparently, she could not be trusted. If she could be devious and manipulative with his ranch hands, there was no telling what else she might be capable of. He needed to make sure she never set foot on his property again.

"I'll take care of it," said James. "She won't be back. You can trust me on that."

"Thank you for believing me," said Buck.

"Of course, I do," said James. "For now, just get back to work. If I need you, I'll find you. I would, however, like to have a meeting tomorrow morning around nine, so we can go over the holiday schedule, make sure we are all on the same page, and know what each other has planned. Sound good?" There, he had changed the subject. He couldn't let these men see on his face what was happening internally. He needed them to trust him, to know he would back them. The truth sounded outrageous, but he would get to the bottom of it, be firm with the agency, and make sure they knew exactly what kind of woman they had sent to his home. Yuck.

"Yes, Boss," they all said in unison.

"Fine. I'll see you all then, unless something unexpected comes up. Thanks for being honest with me. It'll be fine. I'll take care of it. By the way, you know that the two horses Mr. Parker purchased are being delivered today, right?"

Bo said, "Yes, sir."

"They will be in the race barn with my horses until Mr. Parker comes for them on Christmas Eve. Would you mind keeping an extra eye out, just in case? I'd hate for anything to happen to them, on our watch."

"Don't worry," said Bo, seating his hat back in place and straightening his shoulders. "Won't be any trouble we can't handle."

"Thank you. Well, see you in the morning," said James, as he turned to leave, satisfied that Bo would keep his word—and command of his now-shaken crew.

The old familiar pinch in his heart returned with a vengeance. Women. Nothing but trouble.

But he'd been wrong about that, hadn't he? God had dropped an angel right in front of him, which blew his lifelong theory out of the water. He was in love with a champion. A beautiful, kind, compassionate, God-fearing woman. One rotten specimen could not undo the miracle of true love. Getting the deceptive creature off his ranch, permanently, was imperative. Before she caused any further trouble.

James stomped back toward the house, stewing over the news. It sounded preposterous. But he had no reason to doubt his men. And he didn't know *anything* about Lucinda Powers. *I'll get to the bottom of this whole thing, though, somehow.*

The story of Joseph in the Bible rushed through his head. Potiphar's wife set her mind to have Joseph, since he was well-built and handsome. She tried to coax Joseph to come to bed with her. "How then could I do such a wicked thing and sin against God?" (Genesis 39:9[b] NIV) Joseph had protested. She tried more than once to persuade him, but Joseph stood his ground. She proceeded to throw a fit, convinced her husband that Joseph had tried to have his way with her, and he ended up in prison. Joseph had done nothing wrong but got thrown in the king's prison, on the sole word of the Pharoah's wife.

The memory of that Bible story sent shivers up James's back, enhanced by the snow-covered lane and twenty-degree weather. *No way is anything remotely like that happening on this ranch.*

In a flash of memory, James heard his brother Paul's voice: "Reject every kind of evil." He had heard the words in one of Paul's sermons a couple weeks before he met Annie Jo, but the Lord brought it to mind now, when he needed to be reminded of it the most.

Pushing the matter to the side, so he could deal with it later, James entered the back door. He had guests. Despite the mischievous deeds of Lucinda Powers, he felt a tiny bit of gratitude that she had prepared dinner well enough that he would just have to warm up a few dishes.

What mattered most was that Mr. Wells had safely arrived with Sam's horses, and that Sam would be able to present his wife with a treasured gift on Christmas Eve.

The Lucinda Powers matter would be dealt with, forthwith.

James led Sam, Pete, and Sid into the race barn, where he switched on the light, grateful they came on and that the climate control unit seemed to be functioning properly. He didn't need anything else to go wrong, not tonight, anyway. He had prayed for days for the uneventful delivery of Sam's horses, and could now breathe a little easier. Switching his focus from deplorable women to champion racehorses helped settle his stomach and clear his head. He may not be able to converse intelligently regarding the majority of the female population. But he could fill a big fat journal with equine facts and figures.

The prizewinners James had purchased for Sam and Sissy had proven to be exceptional contenders in their field. Pete had only been willing to part with them because of an unexpected medical diagnosis which brought on his imminent retirement. James's trainer had heard about their availability through his network of trainers, and James had latched onto the opportunity the moment he'd learned about it. His heart went out to the guy who would be parting with such valuable, magnificent thoroughbreds. But his spirits soared at the thought of presenting them to Sam. Not even Lucinda could mess that up.

James observed Sam closely as the horses were escorted from the trailer to the barn. A low whistle escaped the man's lips and James glowed with satisfaction. It would appear he had done well, much better than when he had chosen a maid.

And instantly, there was the image of her in his mind again, exposing herself to strangers. He growled, "In the name of Jesus, get out of my head. Spirit of Lust, be gone. You have no power here."

When he opened his eyes, Sam was staring at him. He stepped closer to whisper in James's ear, "What did you just say?"

"I was whispering a prayer," said James, his savoir faire completely obliterated. "I'll tell you all about it, once we have a moment alone."

"Yes, I think you'd better," said Sam, with a glare. "Don't mess with my daughter, James Baldwin. I won't stand for it."

James's eyes got big. Sam remained calm on the outside, still whispering, but the threat was plain. If Sam had heard James's prayer, he couldn't blame him for being suspicious. Annie had been through quite enough at the hands of Austin Anderson, no way would Sam put up with another idiot, who might be toying with his daughter's affections. Oh, boy, this could be bad, very bad.

"It's just a misunderstanding, Sam. I swear. There's a perfectly logical explanation."

"Uh huh," said Sam. "There'd better be."

*Do not be anxious about anything, but in every situation,
by prayer and petition, with thanksgiving, present
your requests to God* (Philippians 4:6 NIV).

James had less than two days to straighten out the mess with Lucinda, convince Sam that he could be trusted, and get a ring on Annie Jo's finger, so his dream had any chance of materializing by Christmas Eve.

He had a couple things going for him. One, he considered himself an honorable man, who tried to do the right thing. He just had to get through to Sam that he had not experienced Lucinda's advancements. Unfortunately for the distraught man, her target had been Buck. James had merely been praying for the spirit of lust to be gone from his *ranch*, gone from Buck's head. Just gone.

Another thing James had going for him was that Austin was nowhere near the ranch. He would not be released from rehab for nearly a month, so he could show up unannounced and not interfere with James's plan to propose. But then, he was messing this up all by himself, without any help from Austin.

But he couldn't even begin to accomplish any of that until after Pete and Sid left the ranch. This delicate subject could not be discussed in front of house guests. It would be hard enough to talk to Sam alone, without anyone close enough to overhear their conversation.

"Good morning," said Pete, as he entered the kitchen, smiling and looking rested.

"Sleep well?" James forced his head to stay in the moment, even though it felt like ants crawled along his skin and into his scalp. He had to concentrate not to scratch where it itched.

"You bet," said Pete. "Sid will be right down. We need to get on the road as soon as possible. I noticed on the weather channel last night that another huge snowstorm is headed this way. I'd like to be long gone before it hits."

"Smart thinking," said James, lowering his coffee mug to the breakfast bar. "By the way, my housekeeper left a casserole that I warmed up. In case you want some sustenance before facing another long trip."

He was fine. Perfectly fine. He could talk about his housekeeper like a normal, rational human being. And he could wait to talk to Sam until these good men enjoyed a homecooked meal. It was the least he could do.

"Sounds great. Got coffee?"

"Just tell me how you like it."

Amazingly, his voice came out smooth, with no sign of the turmoil that plagued his innards.

Sid came down the stairs then, dragging one suitcase behind him and lugging a large duffle bag on his back.

"Need some help?" called Pete.

"I got it. Do I smell coffee?"

"And a breakfast casserole. Come on in when you're ready, and we'll get fueled up before we leave."

"Speaking of that, I'll need a service station for the truck pretty quick."

"There's one on the first corner you come to, on your way to the Interstate," said James, as he set two mugs of hot coffee on the kitchen island. "Won't be out of your way at all."

"Great. I'm sure we'll be able to find it."

James set out three plates and put the steaming hot casserole and a plate of pop biscuits in the center of the island. Pop biscuits had been his grandmother's term for biscuits that came in a roll you had to "pop" on the edge of the counter to open them. She always said they weren't "real" biscuits. "Real" biscuits were made from scratch. The thought of his grandmother made James smile as he reached for a hot biscuit and the butter dish.

"Oh, I almost forgot. I have honey or blackberry jam."

"Both," said Sid, with a wide grin. "This spread looks like something my mother would make. I appreciate the gesture, James. Been a long time since Mama made us breakfast."

James caught the glisten of moisture in Sid's eye and looked away. A man's memories of his mother were private and did not need an audience.

A half hour later, James waved goodbye to Pete and Sid from the porch then waited until the men had climbed inside the truck before glancing at his watch. He did not need them to know that he was ready for them to be gone. But he was. Beyond anxious. Distraught. He had much to do.

The chore of dealing with Lucinda weighed heavy on his heart. And then there was the matter of Sam Parker, a man he admired, a man he trusted. And he needed Sam to trust the man who wanted to marry his daughter. Ugh.

How had Lucinda fooled the agency and found her way into his house? The Aboveboard agency that didn't make mistakes or send out less than respectable people to perform routine cleaning tasks fort unsuspecting employers. The agency that had earned the reputation that matched their name.

Well, they were about to be challenged.

The agency kept office hours on Saturday until noon, so it wasn't like he needed to rush into anything—but the urgency of the matter compelled him to make the call, as soon as the agency opened for business. Eight o'clock. It was now seven. He had an hour to talk to his ranch hands again, and make sure he had all the ammunition he would need when he called Aboveboard. The name tasted bitter on his tongue. One of their recommended domestic engineers had turned out to be a bad seed.

James waved one last time as his guests pulled away. The instant the gate closed behind them he raced inside to get his hat, duster, and scarf. The weather report must have been spot-on, as the wind had already shifted from the north, and the air turned icy, in the few minutes he'd been outside.

James made his way out to the barn in search of Bo and the other ranch hands. He found the barn empty, which was no big surprise. The long list of morning chores could keep them away for a while. But he needed to talk to them, now. So, he jogged over to the four-wheeled mule, climbed aboard, and headed out, in search of at least Buck or Bo.

He didn't have to look far. Buck and Bo were working together in the corral just south of the barn. James pulled up next to the fence and got out of the vehicle. He gestured for them to join him.

"Hey guys," he said, as the two men approached the fence.

"Boss," they said, in unison.

"Pete and Sid are gone. I was about to call the agency that recommended Lucinda, but I wanted to make sure I understand exactly what happened out here. I don't want to accuse someone of something without having all the facts. Is there anything, anything at all, that you need to add to the events you told me about yesterday?"

Bo looked at Buck and Buck looked at Bo. Something passed between them that made James's skin crawl. Was it guilt, or fear, or frustration? He couldn't be sure. But if something untoward was happening on his ranch, he needed to know about it. Even if it meant losing a hand. They could find a replacement. But he had to be able to trust every single person in his employ. Every. Single. One.

"What am I missing?" said James, his voice tight, his look stern. He had shifted into full-on leadership mode. A role he knew well. "I need you to be honest with me. Like I keep saying, I can't help if I don't know all the facts. Don't be afraid, we can handle it together."

Something else must have happened. He held his breath while Buck cleared his throat.

"Spill it," said Bo. "Or I will."

"Do I need to call a meeting?" said James, the hair on the back of his neck prickling against his collar.

"No," said Bo. "We just need to find Rafe Hollister."

James let his eyebrows rise above the rim of his hat. "Rafe Hollister? What's he got to do with anything?"

"I think he gave the gate code to Lucinda," Buck said in a rush.

The gate code! That's the worst possible thing that could have happened. With the gate code, Lucinda could come back with reinforcements and steal everything of value he owned. With the gate code, any number of disastrous things could happen. None of them pleasant.

"Bo, please bring Rafe to the house. I'll meet you there. I need to get on top of this, at once. I'll call the security guys then call the agency. I really wish you had told me yesterday." He stormed off, not waiting for any further explanation.

"Yes, sir," said Bo.

"What can I do?" said Buck.

"Get back to work," barked Bo.

James heard the response behind his back, but didn't acknowledge it, except for a backhanded wave and a nod. He was too steamed to risk a misplaced accusation or harsh word.

Bo might be miffed at him, but James would deal with that later, if necessary. Headed toward the house, he pulled out his phone.

A niggling in his spirit made him pause before he pressed a single button.

James didn't make any other comment, just spun back toward the mule then took off for the house, pulling his phone out as he went. What a mess.

A couple of scriptures from Proverbs slipped through his head: *Folly is an unruly woman; she is simple and knows nothing* (Proverbs 9:13 NIV). *The way of fools seems right to them, but the wise listen to advice* (Proverbs 12: 15 NIV).

"I need your guidance here, Lord. Please help me know what to do, what to say. If Rafe is repentant and wants to stay on, help me know how to handle it. And for sure, help me know what to say to Sam. I don't know how things got to be so crazy, but keep me firm in your ways, Lord. Bring to mind the words you would have me say. Don't let me mess this up."

"Hello!" James hollered into the phone, as he pulled up to the back porch. "I hate to bother you on a Saturday, but security has been breached. One of the hands gave out the gate code to a random woman, a stranger, really. Anyway, I need someone out here ASAP to check everything, not just the gate. New codes. The whole nine yards. I can't afford to have this woman on the grounds, so please hurry."

James disconnected the call, raced up the back steps, hung his hat, duster, and scarf in the mud room, and tugged off his wet boots, then punched in the number for Aboveboard.

Just as he settled at the table and a lady answered on the other end of the line, Bo came through the back door with Rafe in tow. James gestured for them to have a seat. He placed his hand over the phone and said, "There's coffee, if y'all would like some. I'll just be a minute."

"Yes. Yes, ma'am," said James, returning to the conversation with the agency. "This is James Baldwin. I need to report an incident with the lady you sent out to work at my ranch."

James relayed the events, just as they had been told to him, watching Rafe closely, as he spoke. Relief rushed through him when he noticed that Rafe had tears in his eyes. He only glanced at James, though, before focusing on the mug in front of him. James tried to recall how long Rafe had been working on the ranch. Ten years? Bo had informed him of the background of each man, but he couldn't be certain of every detail about each one of them. *But I will. I need to memorize everything about them, so I can trust that what I think I know, to be true.*

If Rafe had been misled by an unseemly woman, he could forgive him. If he repented and figured out that what he had done could not be repeated, James could forgive that, as well.

"Are you sure?" said James, his ears finally registering what the lady at the agency had said. "Well, I guess you would know. Has Mary reported in?" Pause. "Please do." Pause. "Yes, thank you. I'm sorry, too."

James disconnected the call and placed the phone on the kitchen island, face down. He did not want to be distracted for the next several minutes, while they hashed through the details of the two short days Lucinda Powers had been in his employ.

"What's going on, Boss?" said Bo. "Who's Mary?"

"I'm stunned. The agency never heard of Lucinda Powers. Someone named Mary Pickens was supposed to report for duty here on Thursday morning. They haven't heard from her since she left their office. Something fishy is going on, and I need to find out what it is. Do you have any idea who Lucinda really is, Rafe? Besides that, I need to know what made you think it was okay for you to give her the code to my gate, of all things."

James was so upset he didn't know how much more he could take before the cork blew out the top of his head.

Rafe looked up then. Moisture shimmered in his eyes. "I'm sorry, Boss. She seduced me so thoroughly, I couldn't resist her. I ain't never dealt with a woman like that. Not even in a bar, late at night. She thrilled me and scared me at the same time. I'll do anything to make it up to you, sir."

Rafe glanced at Bo, as if asking for guidance. James followed his gaze.

"I'm trusting you to help me out here, Bo. You know these men better than I do. You handle them on a daily basis. I'll go along with whatever you suggest. Long as you realize I am thoroughly disappointed."

"Really?" said Bo, his eyes wide with surprise.

"I can't presume to know what would help in this situation, Bo. They're your men. I trust you."

"You sound like Mr. B," said Bo, with a slight grin.

"I hope that's a good thing," said James. He needed his association with Bo to be solid.

"He's a good man to emulate. Anyway, Rafe has been with me for almost ten years. We had a talk on the way to the house, and I believe he is genuinely sorry for letting that insane woman get under his skin."

"I appreciate that," said James. "And I can understand how it could happen. I don't know what to do, however, to ensure it doesn't ever happen again."

James moved his eyes to look at Rafe, gripping the coffee mug with both hands. "It can't ever happen again, Rafe. I need to know I can trust you as much as I trust Bo. This ranch is your home, and I'd appreciate it if you gave it the same consideration you would, if you owned it. Do I make myself clear?"

"Oh, yes, sir," said Rafe. "I'd quit women altogether, before I let anything like this happen again."

"Whoa, buddy, don't condemn yourself so thoroughly. But there does have to be some restitution, don't you agree?"

James wouldn't expect any man to give up women completely. He might, however, suggest strongly that they kept up such relations outside his property line.

"What do you think that should be?" said Bo, looking Rafe in the eye.

James did a double take. Bo was asking Rafe what his punishment should be? He never would have thought of that tactic.

Rafe rubbed his calloused hand over the short beard that covered half his face, his eyes squinting. He thought for a full minute before he spoke. "Well, I need to go see my little sister on Christmas day, since this will be our first Christmas without Mom. But other than that, I think I deserve a kind of house arrest. For at least a month. And I'll handle feeding and watering, morning and evening, during that time. I'll write everything down, too, so you'll know exactly where I am and what I'm doing."

James had to admit, maybe the tactic was a good one. The punishment seemed to fit the "crime." But he held his tongue, waiting to see what Bo thought.

"If Boss agrees, I can live with that," said Bo, cutting his eyes toward James.

James held up two hands in surrender. "I'm good. But if you give out my gate code again, you're out of here."

"Yes, sir. I swear, it won't happen again."

With that settled, Rafe and Bo went back to work, leaving James to stew in his own juices.

He stood and stretched, rolling his neck to help loosen the kinks that had formed knots in his shoulders. It had been a stressful morning already, and it was far from over. He still had to deal with the security issues then contact Sam and hope the man would see him. Keeping on Sam's good side was essential. Without his approval, he may as well pack up and move back to Tennessee. A groan escaped as James considered a life without Annie Jo Parker. Unacceptable.

Dropping his head into his hands, he raised a desperate prayer to his heavenly Father. "Lord, hear my cry and answer my prayer. Give me wisdom and insight, discernment, and guidance. I need you, Lord, for I cannot manage any of this on my own."

It was eleven o'clock in the morning before the security team left the ranch and the newly coded gate closed behind them. James heaved a sigh of relief, confident once again that his estate remained relatively safe.

Bo could handle the ranch hands. He had to go see Sam, and soon. His hopefully father-in-law-to-be would be coming in for lunch in half an hour, just like he did every day. And James wanted to be there to greet him.

He needed this misunderstanding straightened out, sure. But he also needed to know what they should do about the matter of Lucinda Powers and the missing Mary Pickens. Everything was a mess. A total mess.

James sent Bo a text to tell him where he'd be, in case they needed anything, then remote started his truck, brushed his teeth, checked his appearance in the bathroom mirror, adjusted his hat, just right, slipped a thick woolen scarf around his neck and shrugged into a fresh, dry duster.

He was going to see his girl and wanted to look his best. It had been two days since he had even talked to her and could only guess what Sam had told her. The thought hurt his brain to even think about. He had to get things right between him and Sam. Until then, he would be no good to anyone.

"Oh," said Sissy when she opened the door. "I'm a little surprised to see you here."

"No doubt," said James, stuffing his hands in his pockets. "I really need to talk to Sam. Is he here?"

"Should be, any minute now," said Sissy. "Come on in, if you dare." The look of disdain on her face made him want to throw up. Even when Austin was acting the fool, he hadn't seen Sissy this disgruntled.

"Look, I don't know what Sam told you, but it's all a big misunderstanding. I can explain. If he'll give me a chance."

The back door opened, and Sam walked in, hat in hand. "James," he said, his face void of expression.

"Can we talk, sir? Please. I can explain everything."

He probably sounded like he was begging. And maybe he was. And if that's what it took, he would gladly do it. He hadn't done anything wrong. And he couldn't stand by and let a misunderstanding ruin his chance with Annie Jo.

"I hope so. Join us for lunch. We can talk while we are all at the table."

"All of us?" James swallowed hard and his stomach roiled, yet again. He couldn't be sure that he would make it through this day with his cookies still on the inside of his gut. It wasn't looking good. And add lunch on top of that? He reached out a hand to steady himself against the doorjamb while he removed his boots. Sweat popped out on his forehead. He removed his hat and swiped his forearm across it.

"I'd suggest you not try to keep any secrets from Annie Jo. She won't stand for it. A lot like her mother, in that regard."

James couldn't be sure, but he thought he heard a hint of humor in that statement. A good sign. Maybe he would come out of this meeting with no broken bones, after all. Maybe.

At that moment, Annie Jo clunked down the stairs. Her eyes went wide when she saw him, and her gaze darted away, straight to Dad.

"It's okay," said Sam. "He came to explain. Let's sit down and have lunch. I'm sure we can figure this all out."

"Hopefully, without bloodshed," James mumbled.

CHAPTER FORTY

*Be joyful in hope, patient in affliction, faithful
in prayer* (Romans 12:12 NIV).

Annie Jo chuckled at that, and James's hope soared through the roof. She couldn't really judge him until she knew the truth, right? *Please let her see the truth, Lord.*

Once Sam said grace over the meal, silence hovered over the small group, while they each passed bowl after bowl around the table. James felt crawly things up and down his spine, even though he felt sure he had not picked up any critters on the drive over.

The uncomfortable feeling stemmed from the glances he could feel stabbing at him. He would have to convince the entire Parker family that he had done nothing to be ashamed of, nothing that could be used against him, or that might tempt Sam to renege on the blessing he had granted James, when he'd asked for Annie Jo's hand in marriage.

James stared at his plate, unable to bring himself to even try to eat. He was sure every morsel would end up back on his plate, but in a less-than-appealing form. His belly growled but he ignored it.

"May I speak?" he finally said, looking right at Sam. He kept his hands in his lap, fingers crossed on both hands, like that would help. It wouldn't. He knew that. But he didn't uncross them, just added a continual loop of prayer to the gesture. His whole life hung in the balance here.

"I wish you would," said Annie, before Sam could swallow the bite of food in his mouth and answer the question.

James turned his head to meet her eyes. And he didn't look away. No matter how this turned out, he had to make sure she knew his heart.

"Where should I start?" he wondered, aloud.

"I'd say, start from the beginning," said Sam. "All we really know is the prayer I overheard you whisper in the barn the other night. 'In the name of Jesus, get out of my head,' I believe you said. 'Spirit of Lust, be gone. You have no power here.'"

James groaned at the memory, but still did not take his eyes off Annie Jo. Much to her credit, she held his gaze. When she raised an eyebrow at him, James decided he'd best get on with the explanation.

He closed his eyes for half a second then said, "Let me see. Okay, here's a good beginning. You might remember that I called the Aboveboard agency, so I could get some help keeping my house decent."

A few grunts around the table. Sissy said, "Yes, I remember. We only have good things to say about the agency, as does Jake Anderson."

"Yes, ma'am," said James, glancing her way. But his eyes went right back to Annie Jo.

"I found out this morning that the person they sent to interview with me, is missing."

Sissy and Annie Jo sucked in a breath.

"I know, it sounds unbelievable. But you'll believe it better, once I tell you this next part."

No one spoke, so James rushed ahead. He wanted this out in the open as much as he wanted it behind him. The fact that it had happened at all made him sweat, in the dead of winter, with snow on the ground.

"Anyway, Thursday morning, a lady named Lucinda Powers showed up an hour later than the agency had scheduled the interview. She said she made a wrong turn somewhere, and that's why she was late. I had no reason to doubt her. She was wearing the bracelet with the agency insignia and what looked like a proper nametag.

"She seemed very shy and quiet. I offered her a cup of coffee then we toured the house. Mr. Wells, a friend of mine, was coming out the next day and I wanted the house to look fresh."

He ran a hand through his hair and pushed out a breath. His lungs were on fire. Telling the story brought it back to life and reminded him of the turmoil he and his men had endured for the past two days. Made him sick at heart.

"Good grief, this is so ridiculous, I can hardly believe it myself. Please trust me when I say, Lucinda did nothing to make me suspect her of anything. Nothing. I swear. I hate this.

"Anyway," he started again. "After the tour we talked about Mr. Wells's visit, about the hours she might be willing to work, and if she could get the house ready, prepare a dinner in advance, and maybe a breakfast casserole, then she could have the weekend off. She agreed."

James could feel the river running down his back. His only hope of getting through this story was the acceptance and trust he saw in Annie's eyes. He took a deep breath before continuing with the distasteful part of the story.

"Sam can testify that right after he came through my gate, I was summoned by Bo to come with him to the barn."

"That's right," said Sam. "I remember. Wells opened the door when I got to the house. We sat around visiting and sipping coffee while we waited for James to return."

"Thank you," said James, with a nod in Sam's direction. "So, I get out to the barn, and I could tell something was up. The men were all there, staring down in the dirt, avoiding eye contact. Long story short, Bo said that Lucinda had exposed herself out the bathroom window while Buck and Rafe were innocently walking down the road behind the house. She was inside, supposedly cleaning."

James ran a hand down his face and blew out a breath. He closed his eyes against yet another ungodly image. After two beats, he refocused on Annie Jo. She had to believe him, to trust him, to still love him.

"I had to believe what they said. I don't know this Lucinda person from Eve. So, I promised them I would investigate it. But with circumstances being what they were, I didn't get a chance to call the agency until this morning."

"What about the prayer," said Josh, sounding accusatory. "Sounds like she exposed herself to you, too."

"No!" James almost shouted. "But the devil kept sticking a picture of how that might have looked, inside my head. And since he can't hear my thoughts, I was growling at him and the spirit of lust to get off my ranch, out of my head, out of Buck's head. Period. And that's all there was to it.

I promise. I promise," he repeated, staring hard at Annie Jo. "You have to believe me. I would never."

Annie Jo jumped up and ran around the table to where James was sitting. She wrapped her arms around his neck and kissed him soundly on the cheek. "I believe you, James. Really."

"Wow. Thank you, Jesus. I've been sweating bullets for two days."

"There's more to the story though, isn't there?" said Sissy, with a frown.

James gave her a questioning look.

"What did the agency say?"

"Oh, that. Yeah. I think we should get the sheriff involved. Mary Pickens didn't report in or return to the agency. We need to figure out what happened to her. And who this Lucinda person really is, and how she finagled her way onto my ranch. I'm a little afraid for Mary. Someone needs to get the truth out of Lucinda."

***

December 24

The phone rang, jarring James fully awake. He glanced at the digital clock beside his bed. Three in the morning. Yikes!

He grabbed at the phone but dropped it on the plush rug beside his bed. With a grunt he lowered himself to the rug and grabbed it up, just before the call went to voicemail.

Without looking at caller ID, he barked into it, "What."

"James, we need you!" cried Annie Jo, tears in her voice.

His heart sank. What now?

"Please come as soon as you can. And bring help."

The line went dead. James jumped into action, his mind roaring to life. Annie Jo's family needed help. What in the world? On the heels of a few very challenging weeks, Satan had fired yet another arrow from his endless quiver.

Shoving his legs into yesterday's jeans, James slipped into a black long-sleeve t-shirt then pulled on his black work boots. He dashed through the bedroom door then headed down the hall to the stairway, dialing Bo as he went. It took a few seconds for him to answer, and he sounded as groggy as James felt.

"Trouble next door," he growled, full of anger without even knowing the source. "I need you and three of your finest to hightail it over there. Be prepared for trouble. I have no idea what is going on, yet."

"On it, Boss," said Bo, suddenly sounding awake. "We'll meet you over there."

James mumbled prayers all the way to the mud room, where he donned his lamb-lined duster, weathered hat, and warmest scarf. A continual prayer crossed his lips as he remotely started his pickup, ran out to the garage, hopped inside the rumbling vehicle, and headed toward the gate.

"I don't know what's happening, Lord," he prayed aloud. "But show us what to do. Expose the culprit, keep everyone safe."

His prayer from that point would be unintelligible to the human ear, but he believed with all his heart that God would get the message, completely clear and unjumbled, by the time it reached his heavenly throne.

James sped up the Parker's driveway faster than normal and with an eye out for anything out of place, out of the ordinary, or out of control. To his right, about halfway up the drive, he witnessed a bright flame of fire coming up from one of the outbuildings, beyond the equipment barn. Far enough away from the house that they could probably get it out before it reached the barnyard. But still too close for comfort. What if the wind suddenly changed direction? Or a spark jumped to the next building. Or the volunteer fire department ran into trouble along the way. Anything could happen. A lot of it, bad.

He called Annie Jo.

"James, where are you?"

"I'm here, headed toward the fire. Are the volunteers on their way?"

"Yes, but I'm afraid, James. Someone came onto the ranch and deliberately set the fire. We think it might have been Austin because Mr. Anderson called two hours ago and said Austin left the rehab facility. Someone from there had called him to warn him that Austin left under his own initiative. But Jake has no idea where he went."

James held back a word his grandmother would not appreciate, took in a slow breath to gather his wits about him then said, "They'll catch him and stop this madness, Annie Jo. Please hold onto that, and don't stop praying. Everything okay at the house?"

"Yes, we're fine."

But then James heard a scream come through the line. Sissy.

"What's happening?" he shouted, his skin covered in a thin layer of moisture that had nothing to do with the weather.

"Austin is in the house," whispered Annie. "He hasn't seen me yet, but he has mother trapped in the kitchen."

"On my way," said James, his heart pounding. "Stay out of sight. I'm coming."

Much as he hated to lose the connection with Annie, he had to get reinforcements ready. He called Bo. "Send two of the men to help with the fire. But I need you to head straight to the back entrance of the homestead. Austin is inside and has Mrs. Parker cornered. Are you armed?"

"Yes, Boss. Right behind you. I can see your truck from here."

"I'll come get you then," said James, to shave a few seconds off getting to Annie Jo, with help. "Send the other two out to the fire."

"I'll hop out and send them on up the road."

"Be right there."

James backed up next to Bo, who grabbed for the door as James swung it open from inside. Killing the headlights, James rolled slowly up to the darkest side of the house.

"We need to be smart about this," said James. "It sounds like Austin is out of control. While I'm calling Sheriff Nelson, go around to the back of the house. I'll distract Austin from the front."

Bo hopped out of the pickup and made his way around the side of the house. James called Sheriff Nelson, but Nelson was already close to the ranch. Someone else must have called him. Annie probably did. She wouldn't just sit on her thumbs while Austin broke into her house and held her mother hostage.

As James approached the front door, he called Sam.

Shouts and a loud roar hung in the background.

"He's in the house, Sam," hissed James.

"He's lost his mind," said Sam. "I'm headed that way. Two minutes, tops."

James disconnected, stuck his phone in his inside pocket then snuck up to the front door. He lifted on tiptoe and peeked through the upper panes. He could see Austin and Mrs. P from his vantage point. She seemed okay, so far. "Thank you, Lord."

But just as James whispered the prayer, he heard Austin shout, "Get out here AJ, or I'll kill her!"

James did *not* want Annie Jo between the door and a loaded gun. It was time to act, before someone got hurt. Before someone got dead.

If they could get their hands on Austin, they could stop this madness, and keep the two Parker ladies safe. A big if, since Austin was already using Sissy as a human shield. He was still a blustering, fuming coward.

Simultaneously, James slammed the front door open, Bo slammed the back door open, and Sheriff Nelson crashed inside, behind James.

"Hold it right there, Austin!" said Sheriff Nelson, pointing his weapon at Austin's chest, his finger hovering over the trigger. "You don't want to make this any worse than it already is."

"Stay back or I'll kill her. I just want AJ!" he shouted, flailing that gun around like it was a toy.

James had witnessed this act before. Things could go sideways in a hurry. "Over my dead body," he growled. He took a step toward the angry man. If Austin kept his eye on James, he would be distracted from harming Mrs. P.

"I'm happy to oblige," said Austin, raising the gun and firing at James, without hesitation.

Pain seared a hole through James's shoulder, but it didn't slow him down. He took a giant step forward and Austin fired again. The shot went wild. Sissy had shoved Austin's arm straight up in the air, just as he pulled the trigger. Probably saved James's life in the process.

Bless her brave heart. She immediately jumped out of harm's way and ran all the way down the hall to the master bedroom, where she slammed and locked the door. *You go, girl.*

James sighed with relief when he heard the sounds from down the hall. At least one of the Parker women was safe. Now he had to ensure that Annie Jo escaped harm, as well.

Then, with no further word of warning, a deafening noise filled the space as gunfire rained down on Austin. Bullets hailed from three different directions, killing him instantly.

A lady James hadn't noticed before, started screaming. She stumbled to Austin's dead body and rested his head on her lap, crying and screaming that he couldn't be dead. He couldn't be dead.

"You've killed him!" she screamed, wailing at whoever would listen, followed by a string of expletives.

When the hysterical lady came into view, James froze where he stood. *Lucinda Powers.*

Annie emerged from the small storage room beneath the stairway. She stopped, mid-stride, and stared at the scene before her. Her hand came up over her mouth. The move muffled a cry of despair, as her eyes searched the room then landed on him. James raced across the space.

"I'm so sorry, sweetheart," he said, gathering her into his arms. She was openly crying now. Thankfully, she let him hold her, as she soaked his shirt with her tears. He couldn't be sure if the gunfire, her mother being in danger, or her ex-boyfriend lying dead on the floor had triggered the hysteria. Regardless, he would be there for her, in any capacity she needed.

Once the gunshots stopped, Mrs. Parker emerged from the hall. Sam ran to her, sweeping her up into his arms, and shielding her from the deadly sight on their kitchen floor.

Sheriff Nelson approached Austin's body, shoved his weapon into his shoulder holster then pulled Lucinda to her feet. Forcing her hands behind her back, he cuffed them together.

"Calm down, Miss. It's over. You're coming with me."

Sheriff Nelson made eye contact with Sam. "I'll get forensics and the coroner out here as soon as possible. Do you have someplace to stay tonight?"

"They can stay with me," said James, pulling Annie in close, unwilling to let even a sliver of light get between them.

"Thank you," said Sam, with a nod.

"Thank you," said Sissy, clinging to her husband.

"Thank you," said Annie Jo, leaning back to look at him.

Her eyes went wide. She gasped, gingerly placing a hand on his upper arm. "James, you're bleeding."

CHAPTER FORTY-ONE

*Can any one of you by worrying add a single hour
to your life?* (Matthew 6:27 NIV).

"I'm okay," he said, not sure if that was the truth. Now that the matter had come up, he was beginning to feel woozy. What? Then he remembered. Austin had shot him.

"Don't just stand there," cried Sissy. "Someone call for an ambulance, while I gather up some towels. We need to keep pressure on the wound to slow the bleeding." A crisis had hit, and her motherly instincts kicked in.

With Annie Jo's assistance, James made it to the sofa. "I think I'd better sit down."

Sissy went back up the hall for towels. His blood loss must be more significant than he thought. He felt dizzy and let his head fall back against the sofa cushion.

He could hear sounds in the room. Voices. But he couldn't make out the words. His brain grew fuzzy. His head went limp. "Mom!" shouted Annie Jo. The last words he heard before everything went black.

A half hour later, James woke up, feeling sluggish, but fully aware of his surroundings.

"Oh, James," said Annie Jo. "You're okay."

He cut his eyes toward the wide, bloody bandage on his arm. Managing a grin, he said, "Yeah. All things considered, I'm okay."

"Ha, ha," she said, smacking him on the thigh. "If you hadn't already been shot, I'd punch you in the arm."

"Sorry. I couldn't resist." He squeezed her hand and said, "I am wounded though, you know. By the way, you're a sight to behold. The most perfect face I've ever seen. Ever. And I'm not saying that just because I blacked out."

His diatribe was interrupted when Jake burst through the back door, covered in black soot. He'd been a good neighbor, helping put out the fire his own son had likely started.

Wild-eyed, he searched the room, his eyes landing on the prostrate form of his son, covered in blood, unmoving. Tears spilled unchecked down his face. He gawked at the reality before him then slowly bent on one knee, and gently closed the lifeless eyes of his only child.

James watched in wonder as Sam joined his friend at Austin's side. Kneeling beside him, he wrapped an arm around Jake's back, lifting him to his feet. Jake turned and collapsed in Sam's embrace. Sam held his friend as he wept for the greatest loss of his life.

James imagined that burying his wife would be at the top of Jake's list. But now he would also have to bury the last in the Anderson line. No one would follow in Jake's footsteps, inherit the ranch, or have little ones to carry on the Anderson name.

It was a tough scene to watch.

Sirens broke through Jake's sobs.

Sam excused himself, settling Jake next to his son then rushed to the front door. When he swung it open, reality struck him like a blow. His mouth hung open at the scene in front of him.

An ambulance squealed to a halt in front of his house, simultaneous with the lurch of a van marked Lubbock County Coroner. A licensed physician doubled as the forensic medical examiner.

The tasks would be two-fold: The ambulance would take James to the hospital to have a bullet removed. And the coroner's van would take Austin to the morgue.

Flashing lights and sirens warred with the serenity of a snow-covered landscape, the peace of a winter night, and the silent gentleness of fresh, fat flakes that settled on his shoulders.

He relished in the few seconds of peace that descended on him before the EMTs came to life and the coroner dragged his large bag out of the side door of the van.

Chaos broke out.

A slew of men and two women invaded his home.

The circumstances remained tragic. The memories would last a lifetime. And his friend's future would be forever altered.

A nightmare on every front.

Sam held the door open for the EMTs and their portable gurney, directing them to James, slumped on the couch. Then the coroner to the kitchen.

***

James cracked an eye open as the anxiety of yesterday slipped away.

Annie Jo slept nearby on a small cot in the hospital room. Watching her sleep left him breathless with wonder. So innocent and precious.

She seemed to hear his thoughts, opened her eyes, and offered him a crooked grin. He could have gazed at her sleeping form for hours on end— but those intoxicating green eyes were worth waking up to.

He just needed her close by—day and night—to experience the full impact of having her in his life.

"Hey, gorgeous."

"Hey, handsome."

She sat up then, unwound that long braid, and shook out her hair. James swallowed hard.

"You're killin' me here," he said.

She stood then, reaching for inanimate objects to steady herself, then finally reached the hospital bed, where James was still hooked to some sort of IV.

Before another word was spoken, Annie leaned forward and kissed him full on the mouth.

It would have taken a third world war to divert his attention.

When she pulled away, sucking air like a lifeline, he had to laugh.

"Best kiss ever, my love."

Annie struggled to pull herself up, but eventually managed to settle on the edge of the bed. James scooted over, so she had plenty of room to sit. Scooting to the end of the bed, she dragged her cast up to rest on the bed next to him.

"There. That's better. I can see your whole face and still be able to touch you."

Her broad smile dwarfed to a pinched look and tears sprang to her eyes.

"You okay?" he said, resting his hand on her ankle.

"I was so scared," she confessed. "I thought I was going to lose you."

"Oh, Babe. I'm sorry you had to see all that come down."

She lowered her head and the tears that pooled on the sheet made him angry at Austin all over again.

"Annie Jo," he said. "Look at me."

A few more seconds passed before she raised her tear-streaked face.

"See?" he said. "I'm fine." He partially lifted the sling on his left arm, and grinned. "Mostly."

She giggled and he wished they were already married. Wished no one had been killed or injured. Wished he could erase all of Annie's bad memories.

But God has a purpose for allowing bad things to happen to good people. If we had no need of faith, we'd be less likely to practice said faith. Less likely to admit we need God and his wisdom to maneuver our way through the difficulties of life.

"How is your family holding up?" he said.

"They made themselves at home in your house," she said, smiling. "Thanks for that, by the way."

"Bo and the guys will guard them with their lives. There's plenty of food in the kitchen, and it's close to home, so Sam can make sure Mack and Josh get their chores done."

He was teasing. Trying to lighten her mood.

"Have you heard anyone say when I can get out of here and go home?"

"The doctor will make that determination when he makes his rounds this morning."

"Oh really? Then I hope he agrees with my assessment, because I intend to be home in time for lunch today."

Annie Jo slapped him on the leg. "You'll do exactly what the doctor recommends, smarty pants."

"Says who?"

"Says me."

The door swung open while they were still laughing.

"Sounds like you're in good spirits this morning," said Dr. Miller. "That's always a good sign."

"Oh," squeaked Annie. "I'm sorry. Let me just."

The doctor waved a hand in her direction. "No, no. You're fine. I just stopped by to check on my patient. You're not in the way. So, how are you feeling? How high is your pain level?"

James wriggled a little higher up on the pillow, testing the pain when he moved.

"Well, let me see. I slept through the night, except when a nurse came in to check on me. The pain is tolerable. Maybe a six? And I'd feel better if I could heal in my own home. Think that could be arranged?"

Dr. Miller studied the chart in his hands, made his way around the bed, and examined James's bandage. "I'll send someone in to change that bandage and take your vitals, one more time."

He cleared his throat, lowered his voice, and said, "Mr. Baldwin."

That sounded ominous. Did the doctor have bad news? James didn't know what to expect but he made eye contact with Dr. Miller, aware of the tightening pressure of Annie's hand on his leg.

He raised a brow at the doctor but didn't speak. Didn't trust his voice to come out normal.

"You're going to be pretty sore for several weeks, so I'm sending you home with a prescription pain reliever and an antibiotic to ward off infection. I expect you to take every last dose of the antibiotic, even if your arm feels good before you run out. Take the pain meds when necessary, but don't overdo it. The dressing on your wound should be changed twice a day. Do you have someone who can help with that?"

James cocked his head and smiled at Annie Jo.

"Yes, I'll do it," she said. "Or Mom, or Josh. Someone. Not to worry."

"Josh?" said James with a frown. "I was hoping."

She swatted his leg again. "I was kidding. I'll take care of you, personally. I'll even learn to make Mom's chicken noodle soup."

"Good. Now that all that's covered, I'll check you out of here. Once you've had breakfast, your bandage has been changed, and we have a record of your latest vital signs, I'll sign your discharge papers. Should be ready to go in a couple hours."

"Thank you, Dr. Miller."

"You're welcome. Take care of yourself."

He nodded in Annie's direction then left the room.

"Good news," said Annie Jo, smiling so sweetly he wanted to crush her to his chest and never let go.

"Great news. You know anyone who might be willing to give me a ride home?"

*****

Christmas Eve and Christmas day passed, with little or no acknowledgment.

The day after Christmas, the Parkers joined Mr. Anderson at church for a quick memorial service. Crowds of people came out for the occasion. Sam had mixed feelings about that. He couldn't be sure whether they were curious about Austin's death or actually came in remembrance of his bull-riding fame. Either way, it was crowded in the room, stifling hot.

He sat in his dutiful place as a pallbearer, Jake on the row behind him, seated with Meredith, who kept a tight grip on his hand. Jake had been an only child, whose cousins lived far away in Idaho, or some such place. Sam wasn't clear on that part. He just knew that without Meredith, his friend would be totally alone on the day he had to bury his son.

The rumors had been true. The domestic help Jake had hired had become his companion. Sam wouldn't dare judge Jake for allowing another woman into his life. No way. His wife had been gone three years now, and Austin had been pushing Jake away, for much longer than that.

Jake was a lonely man with only memories to keep him company.

He simply hadn't admitted directly to Sam that Meredith had found her way into his heart. Made sense, though, if the reports they'd heard were true. Meredith had, after all, been the one person who had been able to get past Austin's wall of resentment and anger. It had taken gentle persuasion on her part. A steady dose of acceptance that had gotten Austin's attention. Her influence had been instrumental in convincing him to check into a local rehabilitation center.

Another oddity. What had changed that made Austin leave the program before it really got started? Lucinda? They might not ever know the whole truth of Austin's tragic end. What mattered most was helping Jake cope, get back on his feet, and learn to live a new life.

A young man, who had once been driven to be the best, perform the best, and marry his childhood sweetheart, had made a hard left turn somewhere along the way. A wide path that led to destruction, had veered Austin away from his original goals. Farther and farther away from the people who longed to love him.

His strong young body now lay at the front of the room, encased in a closed casket.

As the video of his life flitted across the screen, sniffles broke the silence. As a child, Austin had been a clown, playful, and a jokester. In elementary school, he'd been a daredevil who wanted to climb the highest, run the farthest, and ride his bicycle the fastest.

The choices he made in high school had drastically changed him: his attitude soured, which were reflected in the dour looks that flashed before the small audience. The next pictures taken of the family no longer included Janice.

Sam heard Jake moan behind him. The sound of a wounded animal— the sound made him cringe. His friend's agonizing pain could only be imagined. Bowing his head, he began to pray earnestly for Jake to feel God's holy presence, for him to accept the comfort afforded by Holy Spirit. Prayed for him to have the strength and courage to put one foot in front of the other. To keep walking in faith. And allow his friends to *be* his friends.

Help us be all he needs us to be, Lord.

Following the meal, James invited Annie's family, Jake, and Meredith to his house, a neutral place that didn't reek of memories of Austin, especially the kitchen where he had died. Miraculously, the group agreed to the impromptu invitation.

James held the door open for Jake. They made eye contact. James offered a slight nod, but neither of them spoke. He wanted to say something encouraging but nothing came to mind. What could he say? This broken man's son had blamed James for much of his troubles. Annie Jo had chosen James's affections, and rejected Austin. James and Austin had not exchanged even two civil words between them.

When Jake looked at James, did he blame him for Austin's death?

James didn't know how the man felt about him, so he kept his mouth shut and prayed that one day a bridge could be built between them, as their paths would likely cross many times in the future.

James wasn't going anywhere, and Sam would obviously embrace his lifelong friend. James's interaction with Jake would be inevitable.

The bridge couldn't be constructed in one day. But James determined in his heart to be cordial and respectful to this grieving father.

Next to Mr. Anderson, Meredith made her way into the house. "Thank you for having us," she said, a sincere sorrow shimmering in the unshed tears that lingered in her eyes.

"The least I could do. I am so sorry for your loss."

He said it like Meredith had been Austin's mother. Not the case, but she had become a rock for Mr. Anderson and had been the one to encourage Austin to enter the rehab facility, voluntarily. She deserved their respect.

Sissy had told him that Meredith had been a Godsend for Jake. She stood by his side, supported Austin with kindness, and had quickly become a big part of Jake's life. James didn't know if a romantic element came with the devotion, but he thought their relationship could certainly turn that way. Didn't matter today, though. It was too soon after Austin's death to expect either one of them to have courtship on their minds.

The reminder brought a painful reality to the forefront. He had not proposed to Annie Jo on Christmas Eve. And Sam had not presented the racehorses to his wife on Christmas Eve.

Their lives had been tossed into a grinder-mixer, and could not, by definition, come out whole on the other side. Nothing would ever quite be the same again. They would find a new normal, a way to accept their new reality. And move on.

***

December 27

"I'm going to the sheriff's office to make a statement," said Sam. "Wanna come with?"

James jumped to his feet, cringing at the jolt to his arm. "Yes, sir."

He had been at the Parker ranch all morning, helping clean up after the fire as best he could with his left arm in a sling. Regardless, he wanted to be close to Annie Jo, in case she needed emotional support. Or maybe because he needed her support. The Parker family had welcomed his help and James was happy to give it.

He had left his own ranch in Bo's care and given Terri some extra time off with pay, until January tenth. A nice little bonus of time and a month's pay. She had earned both. With all the turmoil surrounding the Parker ranch, he had been out of the office more than in, and she had conducted herself with an efficiency and professionalism he had come to admire, appreciate, and depend on.

He had handled every mini crisis that demanded his attention then declared to his employees and constituents that he would be unavailable, except for dire emergencies, for the following two weeks.

His focus would necessarily be on the Parker family. On Annie Jo.

CHAPTER FORTY-TWO

*But those who hope in the LORD will renew their strength.
They will soar on wings like eagles; they will run and not grow
weary, they will walk and not be faint* (Isaiah 40: 31 NIV).

Sam and James climbed down out of the pickup in synchronized steps and approached the entrance to the sheriff's office at the same time. "After you, sir," said James, gesturing for Sam to pass through the door ahead of him. He followed Sam to Sheriff Nelson's private office.

"Good morning, gentlemen," said Nelson, looking up when Sam stopped in the doorway.

"Sheriff," said Sam. "You were expecting me, right?"

"Yes, yes. Come in. I was just finishing up a report." He dropped the pen onto the desktop calendar and settled back in his creaky office chair. It groaned with the full weight of the sheriff on its back.

James acknowledged the sheriff's greeting with a nod.

"Have a seat," said Nelson, a hand indicating the two metal chairs opposite his desk.

"Do you have news?" said Sam, getting down to business straight away.

James sighed with relief. He'd been hoping he wouldn't have to sit through a half hour of local gossip before someone brought up the obvious reason for this meeting.

"I think I've puzzled it out," said Nelson, scooting closer to the desk and interlacing his fingers atop the paper calendar. "Gettin' that girl to talk was like pulling hens' teeth. She is seething over Austin's death."

James noted the twitch in Sam's jaw and the steely glint in his eye. No one was *happy* about Austin's death, but it had hurt some, more than others.

Hopefully, getting the full story from Sheriff Nelson would give Sam and his family a measure of closure.

"Does Jake know?"

"Everything," said Nelson. "He gave me permission to share the story with you, considering all the trouble." He cleared his throat, clearly uncomfortable.

James wondered just how complicated this thing with Austin, and apparently Lucinda, had become. Mr. Anderson and the Parkers had never seen Austin with Lucinda. Her presence at the Parker ranch the night of the shooting had been a complete surprise. He had to wonder if her behavior at his own house, had been Austin's plan from the start. She had secured the code to the front gate, and it wasn't much of a stretch to believe Austin would do anything for that information.

Even so, it seemed ludicrous that the two of them believed they could get away with such a ploy for very long. Lucinda could have been planning to rob him of every valuable in the house, disgrace him by luring him into an affair—or even take his life. If she hadn't been so careless, she might have accomplished a surprise attack and killed him in his own home.

Stop it, JB. She can't do anything to hurt anyone. Not anymore. And she has no business inside your head. She's caused enough anxiety, already.

Maybe Austin and Lucinda each labored under some sort of mental imbalance. James didn't know about Lucinda, but Austin had clearly killed more brain cells than could be counted. Add the stress of losing everything he had counted on for a profitable future, and Austin could have snapped. Lost control of his own mind, his own reflexes, lashing out at anyone who got between him and Annie Jo.

Austin's irrational behavior had led to his own death. And Lucinda, who had sacrificed a normal life to be with a man who was wholly obsessed by another woman, would likely face a stint in prison.

The weight of guilt pressed down on him, hurling accusations at him in his mind. If he hadn't moved back. If he hadn't met Annie Jo. If he hadn't refused to back down. If, if, if.

And what would have become of Annie Jo, if Austin had been allowed to have his way with her?

The thought sent a shiver up James's spine that would have brought him to his knees, if not for the chair that supported him. Only horror could have become of Austin getting his hands on Annie Jo. Hadn't he proven that already?

James squeezed his eyes tight to block out the pictures in his mind.

No. He would never be sorry he had come between Austin and Annie Jo. Never be sorry he pursued her affections. Never be sorry he'd fallen in love.

Austin had to be stopped. God had made sure all the pieces had been placed on the board, in their exact right spots, at the exact right time. He orchestrated the moves, in accordance with his foreknowledge—and protected the innocent.

The enormity of God's majesty, mercy, and justice suddenly washed over him. All he could do was silently praise his heavenly Savior for being a good, good Father.

He swiped at a tear as he heard Sam say, "Go on."

It took a few seconds to regain his composure, before James glanced at Sam.

The steely look from before had dissolved into resignation. The truth would not be easy to hear. But neither would he back away from it. Cowardice was not his way. He faced life as it came, trusting in God to guide and protect him and the ones he loved. This challenge would be no different.

Sheriff Nelson cleared his throat, yet again, rocked back in his chair, and focused on Sam.

"It's okay," said Sam, his voice steady and strong. "I'm ready to hear it."

James's admiration for the man grew another measurable amount. He wanted to be just like this man, he had learned to love and emulate. As a rancher, as a father, a husband. As a godly man. He wished, now, that he'd had more time with his own father, yet grateful for his stepfather, at the same time.

God had blessed him with godly examples his entire life. Funny that he hadn't caught on, before now, just how blessed he'd been. *Thank you, Lord, for watching over me, even when I didn't appreciate it.*

Sheriff Nelson looked between James and Sam, glanced down at his notes then launched into a rendition of Austin Anderson and Lucinda Powers that boggled the mind.

"From what Lucinda tells me, she met Austin at the rehab facility. He had been there one day and had already decided he did not intend to stay."

Lucinda Powers sat across a small table from Sheriff Nelson, her hands cuffed and attached to a ring in the center of the table. She glared at him, mad and defiant. "I want a lawyer," she said.

"Fine," said Sheriff Nelson. "Who should I call?"

"I can't hire one," she groused. "Now that Austin is dead, I can't get my hands on any money."

"Public defender, then."

"Whatever."

Sheriff Nelson went to the door and instructed Dave to put in a call for a public defender then returned to the table. He sat there, staring at Lucinda, waiting. Five full minutes passed before she started to squirm. Nelson just stared at her.

"You have no right to hold me here," she said.

"Sure, I do," said Nelson. "You were apprehended at the scene of a crime, in cahoots with Austin Anderson. I can hold you for a while, without even charging you. But you will be charged, young lady. Count on it."

"Charged with what? I ain't done nothin' wrong."

"That's not what I heard."

"Heard from who?"

"We could start with James Baldwin. He contends that you are guilty of indecent exposure, conning one of his hands into giving you the gate code for his ranch, impersonating a representative of the Aboveboard Maid Service. Which, by the way, reminds me. Where is Mary Pickens?"

Lucinda squirmed in her seat, no longer able to maintain eye contact with Nelson. A moment later, she glared at him and said, "You ain't got no proof of nothin'."

"On the contrary," said Nelson. "The ranch hands at JB ranch have been very forthcoming about your indiscretions while in their company. One has confessed that he gave you the gate code under extreme duress."

Lucinda started laughing then, loud and maniacal. "Funny," she said. "That old dude was a ball of mush by the time I finished with him. He'd have done anything I said."

"Ah, so you admit it."

Her eyes went wide, and Lucinda cursed.
"Tell me the rest of the story," Nelson urged.

"She told me the rest of the story," said Nelson, shaking his head.

"And?" said Sam, his hands gripping the padded arms of the uncomfortable gray chair.

Sheriff Nelson inhaled, loud and long, then hissed the breath out through his teeth, rolled the pen between his hands then dropped it. He steepled his fingers and stared at them while he talked, as if looking at Sam directly would beak his concentration. His heavy eyebrows met in the middle, as if a hairy caterpillar had decided to nap between his eyes.

James tried not to think about that. It would only make him laugh—and this was no laughing matter.

"The plan was always for Austin to possess your ranch and keep Annie Jo under his control. Of course, he didn't tell the Annie Jo part to Lucinda, she was convinced Austin loved her.

"Anyway, Lucinda kidnapped Mary Pickens after she left the agency, headed for your place, James."

Lucinda's first day at the ranch ran through James's mind. She had been an hour late, claiming she had made a wrong turn. The wrong turn she made, however, led to a kidnapping charge. Two lives, ruined. Austin was dead, and Lucinda was facing a yet-to-be-determined length of stay behind bars.

"Where is Mary now?" he said, hoping she too hadn't been killed in the course of this nightmare. The thought of a murderess making herself at home in his house made his stomach lurch. He managed to keep his breakfast down, however, forcing his attention away from his gut, to focus on the sheriff.

"After an hour of questioning Lucinda, she finally gave us the location. We found Mary locked up in an abandoned service station, three blocks from the maid service office."

"Was she injured?" James held his breath, not knowing what to expect.

"Not bad. Hungry and dehydrated. They treated her for a head injury, replenished her fluids, kept her for observation a few days then released her from the hospital this morning."

"That's odd," said James, confusion showing on his pinched expression. "How did they even know about Mary?"

"Jake and Meredith visited Austin on family day at the rehab facility. Meredith says they talked about everyday stuff, you know, to avoid talking about where they were and why Austin couldn't go home with them. Anyway, the subject came up about how Meredith and Jake met, and she let it slip that yet another one of her friends from the agency had been hired by James Baldwin."

James let a groan slip through his throat and out his mouth. He let his head drop onto his hand, while the arm of the chair supported him. Otherwise, he would have slid out onto the floor. Another reason for guilt to assault him. Made him wonder, though, why the impostor had used her own name to gain access to his home. Why not just take Mary's nametag? It didn't make sense. Nevertheless, she had fooled him completely. That fact alone made his gut churn.

"James," said Sam, a hand wrapped around his wrist. "Listen to me."

James raised his head and turned to face Sam. Thunder pounded in his brain and his stomach roiled, but he managed to hold Sam's gaze.

"You listening?"

"Yes, sir." James pushed the words out, forcing himself to focus.

"See that you do. None of this is your fault. You get that?"

"Feels like I'm the catalyst that started this whole mess." The ifs started repeating in his head, making sweat break out on his forehead. He ignored it.

Sam shook his head and squeezed James's arm.

"None of us can take full credit, son. Austin started down a wrong path, years before you moved back here. We all watched it happening, like a train wreck in slow motion.

"A myriad of bad choices, combined with alcohol, the loss of his mother, estrangement from his father, and Annie Jo's rejection were more than Austin's weak character could handle.

"It's tragic. But none of us could have kept that train from derailing. Push passed the what-ifs and give yourself permission to accept God's grace. He knew what was coming, son, and he grieves right along with us."

Wow. So much had been said in just a few paragraphs.

Thankful for Sam's vote of confidence and obvious wisdom, James gave a slight nod, blinked back tears, and simply said, "Yes, sir. Thank you, sir."

James sat there stunned, until Sam patted his arm then turned his attention back to the sheriff.

"Excuse the interruption, Nelson. You were saying?"

And just like that, the topic switched back to Lucinda.

"Meredith said she realized her mistake the minute she said it. A look came into Austin's eye at the mention of your name, James. But it was too late, she couldn't take back the words. For what it's worth, she feels terrible, like she launched this whole mess into orbit by telling Austin about Mary. I'm convinced it was totally innocent, by the way."

An innocent, sweet lady, trying to help Austin, made one slip of the tongue, and Austin's warped brain shifted into overdrive. The distortion had taken root back in high school, when Austin started following a crowd that walked a dangerous path. James could accept that now. And the longer Austin indulged, the deeper entrenched he became, the more delusional, reckless, and volatile.

He picked Annie Jo as a springboard for his insanity. If he couldn't have her, a girl he didn't know how to love, only possess and control, no one would. He wanted the girl and everything her family owned. He wanted to be part of their family. After his mother died, Austin took a nose-dive, lured by deceit and greed, controlled by alcohol and lust. A sad tale that ended badly.

"What happens next?" said Sam.

"Well, Lucinda will, of course, be charged with kidnapping and assault, and face charges as an accessory to arson and attempted murder."

James flinched at the word murder. It could easily have been him dead on the floor in the Parker's front room. The sling that held his arm in place served as a constant reminder of that fateful night. The night that eliminated a Christmas holiday celebration for two innocent families. The night that had resulted in death and destruction. A cold, windy night filled with swirling snow, harsh words, and flames that licked the walls of a barn that couldn't stand up under the heat. A night that forever changed the lives of the Parkers and Mr. Anderson. A gloomy night none of them would ever forget. The pain might dull somewhat, over time, but the memory would be forever with them.

"You have the right to add to those charges, James. What do you want to do?"

It only took James a moment to make up his mind.

"I think what happened at my place doesn't compare even a little bit. She committed crimes against morality but didn't steal anything. I will check with Buck and Rafe, see if they want to file any charges, since she involved them in her treachery. But I won't be charging Lucinda with anything. She has created a big enough, hot enough cauldron for herself. No need to add another log to that fire."

James and Sam left Sheriff Nelson's office with a more extensive picture of how things had gone down, how Austin had managed to ensnare Lucinda into his plot, use her, and deceive her. Although she joined forces with a criminal, she claimed she acted out of pure motives, out of love for Austin. She would have 'done anything for him'.

It seemed far-fetched that a girl would blindly follow a man into such turbulent waters. In the name of love. Waters so dark and stormy, she couldn't possibly see what lay beyond that first step. A historical reference of such a relationship would be Bonnie and Clyde. In the name of "love" they stuck together. Robbed and murdered together, then died a horrendous death. Together.

The mood in the pickup remained solemn on the ride back to the ranch.

"You're welcome to stay for lunch," said Sam, as he parked in front of the house.

"I won't be in the way? I know you need some time to process all of this. To talk to Sissy…and Annie." He frowned at that. Annie would have to hear all the bad news. Would likely insist on it.

"I'm okay," said Sam, twisting his hands around the steering wheel. "It's Jake I'm worried about. And I believe it would help Annie Jo, if you're here when she hears all the gory details."

"Thank you," said James, with a sigh. He didn't want to be anywhere else, when Annie got the whole story. He wanted to be there for her if she fell apart. If she got her heart broken all over again. Just wanted to be with her, period. "I'd love to stay for lunch."

When Sam and James entered the house, they heard voices coming from the kitchen. James glanced up at Sam, his eyes full of questions.

"Sounds like Jake," said Sam.

They moved together into the kitchen, where they found Jake, Meredith, Sissy, Annie Jo, Josh, and Mack. Sissy was busy making sandwiches, a large platter of them. Annie Jo had propped herself against the kitchen counter and was stirring what James recognized as Mrs. P's famous mango lemonade. That stuff was good, no matter what time of year it might be.

Bowls of three different kinds of chips stood in a line down the center of the long island. A stack of paper plates waited at one corner, and glasses filled with ice waited in the opposite corner.

Meredith and Jake held hands beneath the edge of the island.

Jake turned to face Sam when he and James entered the room.

"Hello, my friend," said Jake, standing to greet him. "I hope you don't mind if we join you for lunch. Sissy called, and we couldn't say no."

The two men locked eyes and James witnessed an entire, silent conversation pass between them. A slide show of emotions passed over their faces, until the exchange settled into resolution and acceptance.

"Mind?" said Sam, offering his friend a side hug. "You should know you're welcome here, anytime. You too, Miss Meredith."

Meredith smiled in answer, and the stress of the morning melted away.

CHAPTER FORTY-THREE

*Now to him who is able to do immeasurably more than all we
ask or imagine, according to his power that is at work within us,
to him be glory in the church and in Christ Jesus throughout all
generations, for ever and ever! Amen* (Ephesians 3:20-21 NIV).

Sam stepped away and joined Sissy, planting a kiss on her cheek. He gave
her a wink, and James felt that stirring in his gut again, a longing that
could only be calmed by the solidifying of his relationship with Annie Jo.
He wanted a ring on her finger. He wanted her to be his wife, in every sense
of the word. He wanted her to be standing in *their* kitchen, and he wanted
the freedom to kiss her. To wink at her, openly. Without being threatened
by two large, overly protective older brothers.

An extra jolt of joy rushed through him when he considered that this
moment of reconciliation for two hurting families had materialized in the
very kitchen where Austin had died. God could bring hope to the hopeless,
joy to the downtrodden, and flood a dark world with light.

We just have to accept the possibility, believe in miracles, and have
faith that God really could take what Satan meant for evil and turn it for
good.

"Can I see you in the mud room for a minute, Annie?" he whispered
in her ear, praying she would respond with enthusiasm.

The trauma was over. The danger, past. Healing had begun with Jake
and Meredith sharing a meal with the Parker family. It was time. He could
feel it in his gut.

"Everything okay?" she said, a flicker of fear shining in her eyes.

"Everything is fine, my love," yet grimacing that she thought of danger first—a direct result of back-to-back traumatic incidents. Broke his heart.

The worst was behind them. For now. He needed to remind her of that fact. Not that he was so naïve to think they would live a stress-free, fairy tale life. Real life came with challenges. No matter how hard a person tried to avoid it.

But today, for the next hour, at least, they could accept rainbows, joy, and peace, as a gift from the Savior.

A perfect launch pad to start their future together.

"Please?" he pleaded.

She needn't be afraid. He was about to propose marriage. No more bad news. Nothing to be afraid of.

"Of course," she said, setting her hand in the crook of his arm, with an open smile.

He blew out a breath, his palms beginning to sweat. He started praying, earnestly.

Annie retrieved her crutches then shifted her focus to him, which made his heart soar. She didn't send a worried look toward her mother, father, or brothers. She didn't excuse herself or offer any explanation. She just smiled at him with a look of curiosity and followed him out to the mud room.

Once the door closed behind them, she started to ask a question. Her mouth opened, she had already taken that deep breath before one plunges in to ask a question. But James placed a single finger lightly against her lips and said, "Me first, please. I'll tell you anything you want to know, but I have to get this out before I explode."

Annie Jo giggled and answered with a nod.

"Thank you."

James lowered to one knee and began a speech he had neither written nor rehearsed. Simply, unequivocally, offered Annie Jo his heart.

"I've loved you from the moment I saw you in that novelty shop, heard your hypnotic voice, and looked into your fabulous green eyes. I wanted to run my hands through that glorious hair, and I could barely stop myself from taking you into my arms and kissing you, without apology or regret. You were so beautiful I could hardly breathe.

"You mean everything to me, Annie. Would you make me the happiest cowboy on the face of the earth and say you'll marry me?"

James startled when Annie plopped down on the bench behind her, which put her at eye level.

She leaned forward, pulled his head toward her, and kissed him with a fervor that circumstances had kept at bay, for days. She kissed him with a passion that matched his own. He didn't want it to ever end.

"I love you, James," she said, resting her forehead on his.

"I'm glad. Now, please answer the question."

The giggle that made James's heart race escaped her lips. He froze, hoping that meant what he thought it meant.

"Yes, James, I'll marry you."

He kissed her again, long and slow, his hands grasping wads of her hair, then running down her back, then sandwiching her face. Tears of joy filled his eyes. Man, how he loved this woman.

Reluctantly, he pulled back then reached inside his coat pocket for the little black velvet box that had been burning a hole in his chest, snuggled in a pocket close to his heart, since the day he had purchased it. He snapped it open and held it toward her.

"Oh," she squeaked. "It's the most glorious ring I've ever seen."

James slipped the ring on her finger just as the door opened behind them.

"What is going on?"

Sam. Alarm filled his voice. Then he stopped and said, "Oh, I see. Sissy, you might want to see this," he called over his shoulder.

Sam's remark brought the entire crowd to the door, with Sissy in the lead.

"What is it?" she said, curiosity plain on her face. "Oh, I see." She looked straight at Annie Jo and said, "You okay with this?"

"Mom," said Annie, drawing her name out like it contained three syllables.

"Well, are you?"

James and Annie stood together and turned toward Sissy.

"Yes, ma'am. I love James, and you know it."

"Good. Now, let's eat. There's a lot to get ready for. A lot to celebrate. Come on, now. Don't dawdle."

She clapped her hands twice then spun on her heel, expecting everyone to follow suit. Which, naturally, they did.

Engaged. The word moved through Annie like a song.

"Can you believe it?" she said, sitting close to James on the porch swing, after supper that night. "We're officially engaged."

She stared down at the ring and a song filled her soul. For a moment, the sadness lifted. For a moment, mercifully, she forgot the turmoil and tragedy caused by Austin and Lucinda. For a moment, she was simply a princess in love with her Prince Charming. Nothing bad even existed. Nothing harmful could get to them in the space of this euphoria.

"I believe it," said James. "I hadn't planned on a mud room proposal, but I'll take it. You said yes, nothing could be better than that."

"If you didn't plan for a mud room proposal, what did you plan?"

Snuggling close to his side, Annie relished in the warmth he exuded. Embraced the love that surrounded them.

"Once I managed to get your father's blessing, I had planned to ask you in front of the Christmas tree, on Christmas Eve."

Another plan thwarted by Austin. December 24th had turned dark and deadly. A white Christmas had been smudged with soot. Blood had stained the floor of the Parker's kitchen. And no one opened a single gift.

"I'm so sorry," said Annie, her voice dropping to a mere whisper, as the memories from that dreadful night engulfed her.

"You're sorry? None of what happened on Christmas Eve was your doing. Don't be sorry. Please. There is no room for guilt, not where you are concerned." He shifted closer to his fiancée and slipped his arm across her shoulders. "Your father said something to me at the sheriff's office that helped with my own guilt."

"Yeah?" she tried to sound hopeful, an attempt to buoy herself up, as well as this incredible man she had pledged her life to love and cherish.

"Yeah. I was blaming myself for being the trigger that set Austin off on a rampage. Sam stopped me, said Austin had set his own course, and the bad choices, the alcohol, and the relationship issues with you, his dad, and losing his mother, were more than Austin's weak character could handle. None of us could have slowed his momentum, no matter how hard we tried. It was simply too late. He had passed the point of no return."

He pressed a kiss to her temple, and Annie wanted to soak in every encouraging word. To believe they had done all they could do. If his own family couldn't reach him, why did she think an estranged friend, or her new beau could crack that thick skull of his.

"Sam said that none of us could have kept that train from derailing. Not one of us. He said, 'Push past the what-ifs'. And I love this next part. 'And give yourself permission to accept God's grace. He knew what was coming, and he grieves right along with us.'"

They sat in silence for several minutes, giving one another the time to take Sam's sage advice to heart.

"I'm glad the ordeal is behind us," James finally said, his voice soft, but hopeful. "I'm sure next Christmas will be tons better. We can't let this one color all the Christmases to come. Think about it. Your family has been spared, Mr. Anderson has a companion to help guide him toward healing, and we have a fresh start to look forward to."

Annie snuggled still closer, absorbing the blessings, embracing her current reality.

"It's getting colder," she said, with a shiver she couldn't hold back.

She didn't want to see him go, but she really was cold, and it was getting late. They weren't married yet. And sitting outside in the cold half the night would just be stupid.

"Yeah. I guess we'd better go in. I should get home soon, anyway. I've hardly been there at all for the past two days. I should at least check in. Although, I feel sure Bo would have let me know of any emergency." Then he snapped his fingers. "Wait, I have a great idea. Come on, let's go talk to Sam for a minute."

"What's going on?"

James sounded excited. Maybe they could be together a little while longer, after all.

"Sh. I'm not going to tell you. Remember what your mother said about Christmas secrets. You'll just have to wait and see. I can't believe I didn't think of it before."

She could feel the excitement emanating off him. Curiosity pushed her to her feet. She managed to balance on the crutches that had been her constant companion for many long, torturous weeks. She was sick of them.

"You'll be glad to be rid of those things, won't you?"

"Ugh. So glad. My armpits are beginning to chafe."

"It won't be long now, sweetheart." He stood back to give her plenty of room. When he slipped his arm around her back to guide her through the doorway, the same thrill she received at every touch zipped through her like a bolt of lightning.

When James stepped inside the Parker home, with the love of his life at his side, a wave of nostalgia washed over him. A feeling of coming home. That "full circle" tingle he'd experienced the day he purchased his ranch.

For years, he hadn't let himself think of Ransom Canyon, or even Lubbock County, as home. He'd lost so much here, all those years ago. His father, their home, a closeness with Paul that had taken months and months to repair.

He'd planted himself in Nashville, never to return.

Tears momentarily blurred his vision. He squeezed Annie's hand and she squeezed back. At long last, his past and future collided, one settling in the background where it belonged, while the other loomed large and promising before him.

The feeling came at him so strong, he had to suck in a breath of air to get his lungs to function. "Will you excuse me, Annie Jo? I need to make a quick call."

"You okay?"

"Never better. I'll be right back," he whispered in her ear. With a gentle kiss on her cheek, he circled back out to the porch swing.

"Hello?" his mother said.

Just the sound of her voice sent tears rushing down his cheeks. Perhaps his brush with death had stirred up the need to be close to his family in a way he had not experienced since, well, for a very long time.

"Mom, it's me," he said, not bothering to fight the release of emotion.

Catherine Baldwin-Churchwell gushed in his ears, exclaiming how sorry she was about the events that had happened over the Christmas holidays.

She and Tommy had come out to the ranch to see him after the shooting and dropped off a few of the gifts from the family. Everyone else had gone skiing, and she and Tommy were headed out to Vail to meet them. 'We'll miss you,' she'd said. 'Please keep us apprised of how things go, here.' She had rested a hand lightly on his bandaged shoulder, let herself cry over him, and begged him to be careful. 'I wouldn't go at all, if you didn't have such fine neighbors, who care for you a great deal.' He had reassured her that there was nothing she could do, that wasn't already being done. Plenty of people were available to assist with the cleanup. He'd be fine.

And he hadn't seen any of them, since. But they would all be home by tomorrow night, and plans had been put in place for the family to get together, catch up, exchange a few gifts that had been set aside, until James could be with them. He'd been happy for them. Really.

Before Annie Jo, he had missed more ski trips than he'd made. More Thanksgiving dinners than he'd care to count. Rolling through life, alone, buried deep in work, had been his choice.

A fresh wave of emotion barreled through him—a mixture of immense joy, tempered with a sprinkling of regret for all the missed opportunities to grow closer to his family.

Hard lessons, the love, forgiveness, and acceptance of his Lord and Savior, coupled with his eye-opening experience with romantic love had changed everything. Shattered his stubborn will. Opened his eyes and his heart.

"Yes, ma'am," he said, slouched comfortably on the porch swing, happy to be alive. Blessed to be in love. Gifted with a family that hadn't given up on him. Hadn't stopped loving him and praying for him. "I'm doing fine, Mom. Better than fine. Super. The cleanup is over. We'll have the remodel finished in a couple days, and Austin's accomplice has been arrested and charged. I just needed to hear your voice, tell you I love you."

"Oh, sweetheart," said his mother, her voice wobbly. "I love you, too. I can't tell you how much it means to me that you are finally home."

There was that word again: Home.

"I have a surprise," he said, buoying up, pushing past the heaviness, embracing the miracle of true love. "Annie Jo and I are engaged!"

That set his mother off on a long, excited chant about how pleased she was that he had found someone to love, someone so lovely and sweet. Everyone had fallen in love with Annie Jo at Thanksgiving, and now she would be a permanent part of their family. A miracle he hadn't dreamt possible, just a few short months ago.

"I'd like to bring her to the party Saturday night. Think that would be okay?"

Of course, it would be better than 'okay.' His mother was thrilled with the news. "Bring her whole family. You know they'll be more than welcome. And there's never a shortage of food."

And so, it was set. Celebrating Christmas had been delayed—not canceled.

James ended the conversation feeling more alive than he had in weeks. Months. Years, maybe. So many burdens had been lifted, he thought he might float off the swing, if he didn't hold on. He smiled big, closed his eyes for a moment to thank the good Lord for so many blessings then popped them back open when he heard the front door creak.

"You okay?" said Annie, leaning on those reliable, yet cumbersome crutches. "I was beginning to worry."

"I'm fantastic," he said, grinning, still in awe that this precious lady had said yes. "I was just checking in with Mom. All is well."

"Good. You ready to reveal the secret? Curiosity is eating me alive."

James chuckled, stood, stretched, then joined Annie by the door. "You bet."

James and Annie Jo entered the kitchen just as Sissy yelped.

"Sam Parker, get hold of yourself." But there was no malice in her tone. Rather, she looked flushed and happy. Each passing day she had become stronger, recovering physically from the mild stroke, with grace and diligence. Didn't mean she was giving up her housekeeper, though. She and Sonya had learned to work together, and managed to form a friendly bond, in the process. Sonya had worked as hard as anyone to erase every trace of the tragedy that had marred the kitchen floor. The family had taken a vote and the construction crew had set to work on December 27. The flooring in the kitchen and dining area had been replaced with treated, distressed wood of medium oak. The walls had been painted a pale yellow, and the sliding glass door replaced with double pane French doors that opened out onto an enclosed redwood deck. With the help of the hands from JB ranch, the Parker brothers, and James, the finishing touches would be completed just in time for the Christmas celebration at the Baldwin estate.

Things were falling into place.

"Ahem," said Annie, with a giggle.

Annie Jo squeezed his arm, and brough his head back to the present moment. Sissy was chastising Sam for his shameless flirting.

"See, I told you to watch yourself," Sissy was saying, as she lightly slapped her husband on the chest. "There are people lurking about."

"Lurking?" said Annie Jo, with a raised brow.

James released a chuckle he couldn't hold back. Being in love with your wife, and showing it, after forty years of marriage, fit his idea of a perfect union. He loved that about his future in-laws.

"She's kidding," said Sam, hugging his wife from behind, his chin resting on top of her head. "She just gets flustered when I romance her before the sun goes down and people are still up walking around. Makes her nervous."

"Oh, you," said Sissy, her hands resting on his, at her waistline, no longer struggling to get away from him.

"Don't let us get in the way," said James, soaking up the love that permeated the room. "But if I may change the subject. I was just thinking, Sam, now that my Christmas Eve wish has come true, maybe it's time yours did, too. What do you think?"

James widened his smile when Sam's eyes lit up, as though he had forgotten the Christmas Eve surprise he'd planned, not so many days ago. But when the light dawned, it shone brighter by the second. His whole face lit up with joy. He hugged his wife a little tighter, planted a kiss on her temple, and whispered something in her ear.

"I'll get my coat," she said, instantly compliant.

"Where are we going?" said Annie Jo, with a raised brow.

"Not far," said James, offering nothing more than a wink. "You'll be safe with me."

"Safe?"

Fear found its way into her eyes again, and James wanted to punch himself.

CHAPTER FORTY-FOUR

*You will eat the fruit of your labor; blessings and
prosperity will be yours* (Psalm 128:1 NIV).

With a calm voice, James said, "I just meant you don't need to worry about anything." He placed his hands on her shoulders. "Do you trust me?"

"You know I do," she said, just above a whisper, the concern melting off her face, her eyes beginning to clear.

"Good. Then please get wrapped up in your warm coat and boots, and all will be revealed, in due time. I promise. Nothing to be concerned about."

"Are we going in a vehicle or walking somewhere?" she said, hobbling on those eternal crutches, toward the mud room.

"Vehicle," he said, answering her departing back. "Like I would expect you to walk."

She was scheduled to get her cast off the next day, and he certainly did not want to do anything to jeopardize that coming to fruition.

Coming back from the mud room, she beamed at him from across the room. He winked, and she blushed, just like her mother had done a few moments ago, at the amorous affection of her faithful husband. He was truly blessed, into such an amazing family. To be marrying this intoxicating, yet innocent woman.

While Annie Jo and Sissy put away the last of the folded dish towels and cloth napkins, James joined Sam the mud room. H shrugged into his duster, settled his hat on his head, tucked a scarf around his neck then pulled on his black now-worn black boots.

"I was talking to my mother earlier," he said. "Since Christmas didn't happen for us this year, the family is getting together Saturday evening for a meal. Nothing fancy, no gifts necessary. She invited your family to join us. What do you think?"

Sam paused, one sleeve on, one sleeve off then looked at James.

"It has been a rough Christmas, that's for sure. I'm pleased that your mother wants to include us. I assume she knows about the engagement."

"She does now. And she adores Annie."

Sam's brows drew together. James remained quiet, giving the big man an opportunity to complete whatever thoughts were going through his head. He'd seen this tendency to pause before he spoke, on more than one occasion.

And suddenly, James remembered his father doing the same thing. It was a bittersweet memory, as were all the memories he had of his father. He had died so young, and they had missed out on a lot of good years. James didn't claim to understand what God allowed. Or what he prevented for that matter. But he had learned to accept some things on faith alone. While we walk this earth, we will never be capable of understanding all the ways of a just and loving God. Humans who love the Lord live by faith, not by sight. If they could *see* and *understand* all things, they wouldn't need faith.

"Would I be asking too much if I invited Jake and Meredith?"

Ah. No small wonder he had to think on that request.

The words rushed out of Sam like he was afraid it might be the wrong thing to say, but at the same time knew it was the only right thing to say. James could hear the doubt in the question and realized this compassionate, sensitive cowboy was hurting for his best friend. Maybe inviting them to the festivities would help Jake get past another hurdle—rejection because of his son's choices. If Jake felt welcome in the Baldwin home, he would have another avenue to expand his circle of friends. Sam understood that. James could honor the man's integrity and loyalty. And be glad to do it. He knew his family well enough to know that Jake and Meredith would be welcomed with open arms. No judgment. No questions.

James remembered Sam saying that Jake had dropped out of church for a while, but that, with Meredith's help, he'd been regular in attendance, for weeks now. Sundays and Wednesdays. He would likely carry loss with him, for the rest of his days. But he could also know peace, in the midst of trial.

That kind of power can only be found in the presence, grace, and mercy of God Almighty.

"I'm sure Jake and Meredith would be welcome," James said, without hesitation. He patted Sam's shoulder and met his gaze, straight on. "Feel free to invite them. I'll tell Mother to set two more places. Entertaining is like, her favorite thing. She'll be thrilled."

Tears filled the big man's eyes, as he gripped James's forearm. It took a second or two for him to recover enough to speak. "Thank you, son." He pulled in along breath then let it out, slow and easy. "I don't know how to thank you."

"No need."

Annie Jo laughed with delight when she realized James had turned up the driveway to his own ranch. What was he up to? She found, however, that it didn't matter, she was just happy to be with him, to be free of the dark cloud that had hung over them for months. It might be December 27th, but Christmas had finally arrived for the Parker family. She determined to enjoy every moment given them. Their recent brush with death, watching in horror as her childhood friend shot the man she loved. Then seeing Austin crumple to the floor, as he succumbed to the bullet wounds that took his life.

Austin shot James, but James had left the retaliation to the law. Between Sheriff Nelson, Bo Mattis and a third party yet to be identified (most every cowboy on the ranch carried a pistol—and every man not fighting the fire had come running for the homestead), Austin was taken down. It was over. Lucinda Powers had been locked away, and they had nothing more to fear.

It would take time, but the pain would eventually lessen. One day, she might even look back on the good memories she had shared with her childhood friend. And smile.

One day.

But those memories had no place here, tonight.

The adrenaline began to flow faster when they turned toward James's racehorse barn. Tingles made her shiver, like wild horses ran up and down her spine, scrambling to get free of a sturdy corral. Her father had wanted to branch out into racing horses, for years now. Had he taken the plunge?

Reaching across the console, she squeezed James's arm. Tears of joy filled her eyes and all she could do was stare at him. Words failed her. He smiled back, a wide, happy smile that made her heart race.

"Oh, James, what have you done?"

"Just a favor for a friend," he said, as he parked in front of the racehorse barn.

All four of them came together in front of the pickup. Bo appeared, seemingly out of nowhere. "Everything's ready, Boss."

"Thanks, Bo, I appreciate it."

"My pleasure. Well, I'll get back to the boys. They've started a penny ante poker game. They're all bad, so I hate to miss a chance to make a dollar, which is about all the biggest pot will be." He chuckled, gave James a mock salute, nodded toward Mr. and Mrs. Parker and Annie Jo, then strode off toward the barn at the opposite end of the lane.

"He's a good man," said Sam.

"Priceless," said James. "I'm very blessed he decided to stay on."

"I'm dyin' here," said Annie Jo, tugging on his arm.

Chuckling, he started forward. "Yes, ma'am. Right this way."

He opened the barn door, led them inside then turned on the light. Sam hurried forward, looking over every stall, until he spotted the Christmas treasures.

"Come over here, Sis," he said. "I have a surprise for you."

Sissy glanced up at James, but he just shrugged his shoulders. "He's waiting, ma'am."

Sissy stepped away from them and Annie Jo squirmed at James's side. "Hold on there, little filly. This is your dad's business. Let's step outside and give them a moment alone."

"But I want to see," she said, squirming.

"You will," said James, as he nudged her out the door. "Give your dad his moment in the sun."

***

December 30

The Parkers opted to take the Suburban to the Baldwin Estate, so the entire family could ride together. James and Annie Jo volunteered to sit in the way-way back, so her brothers would have room to stretch their legs. Of course, that was why—it had nothing to do with snuggling.

The gesture had been possible since Annie Jo's cast had come off two days earlier. Her leg was still weak and pale, but her bone had healed properly. The doctor did not expect any complications.

But if asked, James would have to admit they'd volunteered for the furthest back seat for other reasons as well. The seat in the way-way back was smaller, and not as wide, so he and Annie Jo would necessarily be forced to sit closer together. She squiggled up next to him and his heart pounded beneath his shirt. He had promised Annie Jo's father at least a six-month engagement. He was beginning to regret that decision. And he'd only been engaged for a few days.

"It's right up here on the left," he said, as his mother's home came into view.

Sam whistled from behind the wheel, as did Josh from the middle seat. Mack twisted around to stare at him.

"What?"

"Nothing. Just didn't expect this," he said, gesturing toward the mansion. "How big is it, anyway?"

"Three floors above ground and one below," said Annie Jo. "It's magnificent. You'll have to get James to give you a tour."

Sam stopped in front of the house and behind what James knew to be Kim and Christian's Lexus SUV. Matt had parked his silver Denali in front of Kim, and Paul had parked across the street. He glanced behind them, pleased that Jake and Meredith had agreed to follow them in. He watched while Jake gave Meredith a hand down out of the pickup.

"Let's go in," he said. "Pretty sure they're not going to come out here."

"Right," said Sam. "Stay put, Sissy, I'll come around and get your door."

"You certainly will," said Sissy, with a grin.

Josh ducked out, followed by Mack, who folded down the seat in front of them, so James and Annie Jo could disembark. Sam and the boys came around to the back of the Suburban. No way was Sissy Parker coming to a dinner and Christmas bash without her contribution of food and gifts. She had set James down and made him tell her all about his siblings, their wives, their children, his mother, his stepfather, and even the housekeeper. Maybe especially the housekeeper, now that she appreciated the treasure a housekeeper could be. Sissy made sure there was a special gift for each one of them. And she made two kinds of cobbler, cherry and blackberry. Sonya had been invited as well but had opted to take the chance to spend some time with her own parents. She would be back to work on January 2nd.

When James stepped up onto the sidewalk he breathed in the deep, cold fragrance of fresh air, appreciating, for the first time, the splendor of a white Christmas. He stood there in front of the house for a long moment, smiling like an idiot. Home base. The roots of his beginning.

A flood of memories washed over him, like he hadn't experienced since he'd returned to Lubbock County. Truth be told, he had made a point to avoid memories of his childhood. It had been many years since he had let anything in, except the hurt and grief. He knew now, that was a dumb way to live. A man is made of everything that had come before—the good, the bad, the ugly, and the glorious.

James Bartholomew Baldwin, at last saw himself as a combination of them all. He had struggled with being the runt of the litter, with being the only single sibling, the only disappointment to his parents. But he'd channeled all his disappointments, insecurities, and five-foot-ten-inch frame, into making something of himself. He'd used the brain God had blessed him with. He'd used his love of numbers and the power of compound interest to secure a place in the business world, through the fascinating field of security and technology.

And all his efforts had brought him full circle, back to where he'd started, back to his roots, back to the very sidewalk and yard that he had taken for granted as a child. Right into the arms of the most splendiferous woman in the world. *Thank you, Jesus.*

A gentle hand on his arm brought him back to the present. Annie Jo's sweet voice tickled his ears. "You okay, James?"

He grinned down at her. "Yeah, just feeling sentimental."

She squeezed his arm. "Let's go inside, it's a little chilly out here."

"Okay, folks, right this way," he said, waving his arm in a forward motion like a Sargent leading his troops. "Welcome to the Baldwin estate."

The door opened before they reached it and Catherine rushed out onto the porch. "Come in, come in," she said. "It's too cold to be hanging out in the snow."

James played the role of doorman and held it open while everyone piled inside, his face beaming.

The smell of turkey and dressing and all the trimmings floated out to greet them. Once Meredith and Jake had made it inside, James pulled the door closed behind him, his heart full. His eyes misty.

Merry Christmas.

As he turned toward the great room, Angelica (Angel) wrapped herself around his leg. "Uncle James! Uncle James!" she cried, her adorable squeaky voice broadening his smile. "One of my favorite uncles."

Ah, yes, ever the diplomat. Angel owned the hearts of everyone who knew her. Kim and Christian had adopted her at age three, after her parents had been murdered. The Lord had sent her into their lives through a miracle. And since then, Angel had lived up to her name. A little angel.

"Hey, sweetheart, it's good to see you." His heart filled with joy that ran down his face in rivers.

"Good to see you, too," said Angel. "Don't cry, Uncle James. It's *finally* Christmas."

"You're right," he said, wiping the moisture from his face. "It *is* finally Christmas."

Taking her hand, he said, "Come with me. I'd like you to meet some special people."

"Okay, but why don't you come over to the Christmas tree, so you can introduce everyone at the same time." That was Angel. A bold, courageous planner, who planned and executed the best means to get a job done, expediently, and encouraged others to help along the way—with charm and charisma.

"That's a great idea," said James, as he followed the little darling across the room.

Angel stood next to him while he made introductions. "And I have a special announcement—in case someone here doesn't already know. Annie Jo and I are engaged!"

Hoots and hollers filled the space all the way to the second story landing. The Baldwins had waited decades for James to find a girl who could break the spell he had cast over himself.

And now, not only had he moved back to Lubbock County, but had found a good girl to settle down with. A good girl from a good family. A girl who loved the Lord, first.

A fuss was made over Annie Jo's ring before the entire group broke up into couples. They filled the large dining table plus two smaller tables, one especially for children.

Angel led the way for the children then proceeded to make sure every child got every type of food they wanted, even though she was not the oldest.

Once plates had been scraped, rinsed, and loaded into two commercial size dishwashers, a vote was taken to wait until after gifts had been opened to bring out dessert. Then everyone crowded into the great room with a group of children seated on the lower steps of the stairway.

Angel volunteered to help hand out presents and accepted one gift after another as Kim handed them off to her. She made her way around the room, handing out presents, and smiling her captivating smile, until there were no more packages left under or on the tree.

The gifts were then opened in groups of families. The last to open theirs were Jake and Meredith. Tears filled both their eyes once they realized that every member of the Baldwin-Churchwell family had remembered them when they shopped.

"Thank you," said Jake, tears filling his eyes, as he pulled out a long cashmere scarf that would more than likely warm him for the rest of his life. Next to him, Meredith sucked in a breath as she lifted out a lamb-lined poncho made of wool, in a vibrant red that complimented her near-black hair. "I'm speechless," she said.

Slowly, a round of applause began. It went around the room, with everyone standing to their feet.

When the room quieted, Catherine approached the couple. "I'm sorry if we put you on the spot. That was not our intent. But James told us that you lost your son not long ago, and we wanted to express our condolences. We couldn't think of a better way to help you than to let you know you are not alone. We are all children of God, Mr. Anderson, Meredith. I can only imagine the pain you must be dealing with. So, please, if there is ever anything any of us can do, please don't hesitate to ask."

Meredith jumped up and flung her arms around Catherine's neck. She did not hold back the tears, just let them flow, as if Austin had been her own son, and God had sent an angel to help her deal with his death.

When Meredith pulled away, Jake was at her side, also weeping. "I can't tell you how much this means to us. I don't know what James has told you, but my son was not kind to him."

"I don't need to know," said Catherine. "And James didn't tell me anything, beyond the fact that you had lost your only child. It breaks my heart."

"Thank you." His limbs trembled and his lips quivered, but he seemed to receive their gracious invitation and gifts with genuine appreciation.

James beamed with pride for love of his family. A Christmas miracle had happened right before his eyes. It didn't matter to his mother what kind of man Austin had been. She just knew a father had lost his child.

James knew his mother well, and it was obvious to him that she had called a family meeting to plan this entire evening. They had more than likely shopped with great care for a special gift for this hurting couple. Every time Mr. Anderson wrapped that scarf around his neck or Meredith lipped that poncho over her head, they would be reminded of Austin, of this night, when his loss had been acknowledged. And James had a feeling that the memories they pulled up of Austin would only be the best memories they had of him, from childhood to his adult years, when he still had a mother who loved him, he'd been part of an amazing family, and a celebrated bull rider. It certainly would not be the trouble Austin had caused, or the lives he had put in danger, or the alcohol consumption, reckless driving, or stubborn willfulness that had cost his life.

And after tonight, hopefully Jake and Meredith would never feel alone, or lonely, again.

Christmas Eve – One Year Later

That is why a man leaves his father and mother and is united to his wife, and they become one flesh (Genesis 2:24 NIV).

James Baldwin stood in front of a full-length mirror, fastening the initialed cufflinks that had been a gift from his stepfather. His heart swelled with love for the kind, compassionate man who had loved James's mother since his high school days—yet married a girl in college who found herself with child and no one to turn to.

Not long thereafter, James's mother married Tommy's brother-in-law. Sadly, Tommy's wife died in childbirth, and her mother bribed a judge to get custody of her granddaughter then proceeded to tell her that her father had died. Which later turned out to be true—only not the father she knew. Tommy had not been her biological father, but had claimed her as his own, before she'd been born.

A short while after Bradley Baldwin died of a brain aneurysm, Tommy came across Catherine in the grocery store back home in Nashville, shopping for Thanksgiving dinner. The flame that had burned in his heart for years and years and years burst into a full-blown fire that could fill a king-sized fireplace. He then waited more years while Catherine kept a promise to herself, not to marry until her children had grown. She kept that promise, but as soon as Kim graduated high school, Tommy proposed then married Catherine Baldwin.

Like a complicated, intricately woven symphony, they came together at just the right time, aligning two lives that had been on parallel roads for decades.

James looked at Tommy inside the mirror just behind him, over his left shoulder. "Thanks for always being there for us," he said. "It took me awhile to realize what you must have gone through, loving, and waiting for, my mother. I have only been waiting for Annie Jo a little over a year, and I could barely handle that little bit of time."

"Wasn't easy," said Tommy. "But well worth the wait. Your mother is an amazing woman. And I was privileged to love her all those years. She let me into her life. Waiting for the marriage, I admit, was double tough."

True. Catherine had been strong, determined to protect her children, and fierce when it came to acquiring the family estate, which had been left to her in her husband's will, a will that Bradley's mother had paid an attorney to keep secret. Didn't work. One of the junior partners of the firm tracked her down by following her career as a concert pianist, informed her of the truth, and promised to come to her aid, when she challenged the probate proceedings that had been finagled by Bradley's mother.

With the same degree of tenacity, Tommy had befriended Bradley's father, who helped him secretly visit his daughter. It became a long, complicated ordeal, but eventually Tommy's daughter learned the truth about her mother, her biological father, and her grandmother. An ugly truth. However, Holy Spirit convicted Grandmother Baldwin of her wicked ways and she accepted Jesus as her Lord and Savior. The family estate had been restored and family relations repaired.

The power of God called down by prayer can move mountains.

Plenty of mountains had been moved. Love had blossomed in the desert. Streams of living water flowed over salt-beds and transformed them into gardens.

James Bartholomew Baldwin, the youngest son and brother to four siblings, would stand before Pastor Mason today and wed Annie Jo Parker. The final chapter of 106 Arrowhead Drive has been written.

The wedding planner rapped on the door where Annie Jo had spent the past three hours with her mother, James's mother, Meredith, Brooke,

Jessica and Kim. The five-minute warning. This was it. She would soon be Mrs. James Baldwin.

The Lord had blessed Lubbock County with yet another white Christmas. Annie stood at the window, patiently waiting for the signal, and gazed down at the lawn that stretched out in front of the Baldwin estate. Catherine had graciously offered her home, and she and James had agreed to exchange wedding vows here. Annie Jo would walk down the same staircase Catherine had glided down when she married Tommy. James would be waiting for her in front of the very hearth where Tommy had waited for Catherine. It was all very magical and romantic.

The entire ground floor of the mansion had been converted into a winter wonderland for the occasion. White carpeting hugged the stairs then ran across the great room, right up to the altar, as if the blanket of white that covered the lawn had been brought inside. Three potted, white-flocked Christmas trees, decorated with tiny twinkling lights and gold ornaments, formed a line situated diagonally from each end of the massive fireplace. Paul, Christian, Matt, Josh and Alessandro would stand beside James on one side, while Bethany, Brooke, Kim, Jessica and Jo would stand next to Annie Jo, on the other. Mack had volunteered to serve as usher. And adorable little Angel would walk the short aisle as a very mature flower girl, scattering deep-red rose petals along the way.

The ten-foot family Christmas tree had been decorated in Catherine's traditional white and gold ornaments and skirted with a golden tree skirt that spanned ten feet in diameter. In lieu of a traditional wedding reception, the evening would be filled with food and fellowship for the Parkers, the Andersons, the Baldwins, and the Churchwells. Innumerable packages covered the space beneath the tree in anticipation of the festivities to follow the ceremony.

Annie Jo turned at the sound of the five-minute warning. Her mother was there to reassure her. "Meredith and I will go find our seats. Take care coming down the staircase, please."

"Yes, ma'am," said Annie Jo, automatically.

"We'll stop her fall, if she trips," said Bethany, with a giggle.

"And I'll be there to grab the train," said Sonya, who would follow Annie Jo down the staircase.

"Good, then I'll leave my daughter in your capable hands. We'll have a seat for you once you have delivered Annie Jo safely to the bottom of the stairs, Sonya."

"Thank you, ma'am. I'll see you down there."

Paul and Jo came together at the top of the stairs, descending together slowly, as a member of the Lubbock Symphony Orchestra played softly on the organ. Once the couple reached the mid-point of the stairs, Brooke and Alessandro, then Matt and Jessica. Right behind them, Kim and Christian, followed by Bethany and Josh.

Once Bethany and Josh set foot on the floor of the great room, Sam and Annie Jo began their descent.

"You look beautiful," said Sam, as moisture clouded his vision. "All grown up, but too young to be getting married. You know it's killing me to do this, right?"

Tears filled his eyes and Annie Jo frowned up at him. "I'm older than you and Mom were, Dad. And don't you dare make me cry."

"Yes, ma'am," said Sam, not at all remorseful, and unashamed to cry. "But I sure am going to miss you."

"Ha," said Annie Jo, nudging him with her elbow. "I'll be two doors down."

"Uh-huh. Not the same thing. At all."

"He is wonderful though, isn't he?" she said, squeezing his arm.

"If you're happy, I'm happy," said Sam, trying to sound tough. If he didn't, he sure enough would collapse.

When they reached the bottom of the stairs, the music swelled, louder and bolder. Sam led his daughter, his youngest, his only girl, to her soon-to-be husband. The music quieted when Sam and Annie stopped in front of James.

"Who gives this woman to be married to this man?"

"Her mother and I," said Sam, with a catch in his voice. He kissed Annie Jo's temple then placed her hand in James's outstretched one.

"I love you, Daddy," she whispered, before stepping away from her father, to join James, in front of Pastor Mason.

James had confessed that he was too nervous to write his own vows, and Annie Jo had said she would be happy for them to use traditional ones. She would be just as married, wouldn't she?

"Oh yes," James had whispered in her ear, on the porch swing of her parents' home, following Thanksgiving dinner the month before. "Just as married. I hope you realize I have been a very patient man."

Annie Jo had giggled and snuggled closer to her fiancé. "By January first, you'll be well-versed in being my husband."

"I'm pretty sure it will take a lifetime to accomplish such a feat," he'd said, then pressed a kiss to her temple and drew her close to his side.

"I want to play a game," Annie Jo *Baldwin* announced, between dinner and gifts.

Every child in the room got excited and started clapping and hollering. But Annie raised her hands and said, "Calm down, it's not that kind of game."

Where shrills of delight had bounced off the walls, groans followed.

"I think there are some new games in the playroom that will suit all of your ages," said Catherine, with a double clap. "I planned ahead you see. I figured getting you to remain calm all the way through a wedding *and* dinner would be pushing it. Anyway, run on up there and play with whatever suits your fancy. When we're through with Aunt Annie's grownup game I'll come get you and we can open gifts. Sound like fun?"

"Yes, Gran," said every parent in the room.

In unison, the children echoed, "Yes, Gran."

And like a small herd of cattle, they raced up two flights of stairs to the top floor of the house.

"Now," said Catherine. "What sort of game did you have in mind, Annie Jo?"

Annie had to clear her throat a couple times before words would come out of it. Catherine had referred to her as "Aunt Annie." The realization seemed wonderful but strange at the same time. She had never been anyone's aunt before, having two bachelor brothers. And suddenly, she'd become an aunt to four adorable children who could charm the socks off just about anyone who knew them.

"Well," she said, dragging out the word, stretching the vowel to its maximum length.

"Is it a difficult game?" said Sissy.

"No, but I think it is very important to the future of my marriage." She had spent the better part of the past year finding out how James's siblings had met and married their spouses.

Matt met Jessica at Catherine and Tommy's wedding. Jessica had been Kim's best friend when she'd come to Texas to attend Texas Tech University, a college she chose based on two things: she had earned a full scholarship; and her grandmother on her father's side lived in Lubbock.

Jessica became an adventurous reporter, then put herself in the middle of the Vice President's daughter running away, which caused a stir with her love interest, Matt Baldwin. She survived the ordeal, pledged her life to be Matt's bride, and had ultimately slowed down her career, once she became a mother. Soon afterward, she found an avenue for the adventures she had pursued during her career as a reporter: a successful author of international spy novels. Matt Baldwin remained an airline pilot for Southwest Airlines.

Brooke, the heart surgeon, had been educated in Rome, Italy, where she fell in love with, and eventually married, Alessandro Romani. Annie hadn't mentioned it to anyone, but Brooke's story had been her favorite. She could only fantasize about such a grand adventure, and falling for a handsome, wealthy, foreign dignitary with a mesmerizing accent. Just thinking about it made her swoon a little.

She would not, however, have traded her own romantic story for anyone else's. No way. She was thoroughly in love, thoroughly content.

Paul and Josephine (affectionately known as Jo) met at a Christian youth camp where they had both volunteered as counselors, their first summer out of high school. Together, they came against all sorts of odds, overcame the challenges of two near-death experiences (one each) at the vicious scheming of an old high school classmate of his, faced the horrific details of Jo's childhood, the attack on her person, and the presumption by a doctor that Jo should never have children. They beat the odds, trusted God, stayed married, and had a son.

Then there were Kim and Christian Devereaux. A catastrophic blizzard hit Lubbock County and three lives were impacted, changed, and fused together over the course of seven enlightening, life-altering, inspiring, and scary days. Kim Baldwin discovered that it was okay to be the woman she had grown up to be. And more than okay to fall all the way in love with her best friend, Christian Devereaux. They rescued three-year-old Angel Cane and her teacup Yorkie from the backseat of a car left abandoned in the storm. Angel's parents had been brutally murdered, yet God had sheltered her and protected her with the presence of angels. Angels only she could see, when she'd been abandoned, and even while she'd been kidnapped, and again at her parents' memorial service. Today, their family also consists of a baby brother, whom Angel doted over like he was one of her dolls.

Annie Jo had also memorized Catherine and Tommy's love story. Each family represented in the room had survived seemingly unsurmountable odds and built lasting relationships and close-knit families. She wanted that kind of marriage, a marriage that would withstand the challenges and atrocities that come at believers when they least expect it. A marriage that would rival even the union of her own parents. A marriage that had a godly foundation and roots that went on forever.

"You think this game will affect the future of our marriage?" said James, curious beyond words. "Now, I'm intrigued."

"Okay," said Catherine. "I'm game."

Then, for the next hour, each couple gave a similar testimony. Faith, honesty, forgiveness. Cling to God and each other. A three-ply cord is difficult to break. Seek help when you need it, and don't be afraid to admit it. Listen to Lord-led teaching. Be strong in the Lord, look at yourself in a spiritual mirror, and ask God what needs to be changed in you. Especially when you wish God would "fix" your mate. Let him take care of your husband's or wife's shortcomings. Pray for them, earnestly. Love them, unconditionally. Focus on the good, and brag on them. Tell your man how much you appreciate him. Never assume he knows it. Tell your wife how much you love her. Never assume she knows it. Communicate, communicate, communicate.

And never believe the lie that marriage is a 50-50 proposition. You best go into it believing, and reconciled to the fact, that a good, lasting marriage takes 100 percent give—on both sides.

Annie Jo Baldwin maintained a tight squeeze on her husband's hand. "We can do this," she heard him whisper in her ear.

She turned her head to look him in the eye. "You have already demonstrated what kind of man you are, James. I'm not afraid. Not really. But I wanted to hear from other successful couples, just how it's done."

"Great. I'm not afraid, either. In fact, let's get the kids down here and open some presents. I'm ready for a honeymoon."

He hugged her, planted a kiss on her cheek, and whispered, "I love you," in her ear.

"Oh, you," she said, with a giggle. "I'm looking forward to the rest of our lives, way beyond the honeymoon."

Catherine spoke from across the room, "Take it from one who knows, honeymoons don't have to end."

"Amen," said Tommy, and Matt and Jessica, Paul and Jo, Kim and Christian, Sam and Sissy, and Brooke and Alessandro, in unison.

James caught a glimpse of Jake Anderson when he took the opportunity to whisper his own private message to his girlfriend. Which title, by now, had been well established.

Meredith blushed, something James had not witnessed, since they'd met. She seemed strong and courageous, bold, and stable. All good qualities. And blushing looked good on her.

Heal their hearts, Lord. Help them find a way to carry on, without Austin. And help us remember to be there for them.

✳✳✳

When the plane touched down in Hawaii, Annie Jo Baldwin had to hold back a squeal. They had left a snowy Texas only nine hours ago and would need an entirely different wardrobe, now that they had reached this luscious, tropical island. Inside the terminal they were met by exotic women who draped leis over their heads, smiled big, and welcomed them to the islands. They held hands as they made their way to the luggage carousel. Just like newlyweds should.

Annie Jo felt like a tiny speck in the universe, so small, yet so blessed and cherished.

Her family had been on vacations while she was growing up, but never long distances from home, and certainly never to Hawaii. There seemed to be too much work to do that held them to the ranch. Too many practice hours on Glory's back. She hadn't considered it a hardship at the time, it was just life. And she loved her family, her barrel-racing, even the work. And the silliness that could be her brothers' claim to fame. They had plenty of belt buckles and trophies of their own, but always managed to add spice and humor to most any situation. They worked at keeping their baby sister in the limelight, proud of her skills as a champion barrel racer.

She had been blessed with good people for a family, blessed with good friends, and now blessed with a godly man who loved the Lord, and treated her like a queen. What better place than Hawaii to celebrate their union? Pretty close to heaven on earth, if she had to guess.

The luggage carousel made a long, slow, oblong trail in front of them. She watched carefully to make sure they didn't miss their bags. "There's mine," she said, pointing to the shiny copper finish of her favorite rolling bag. James reached for it, easily lifting it off the revolving floor. "Oh, and there's yours," she said, as soon as her luggage had settled firmly next to her.

James chuckled then grabbed his own dark leather upright that could double as a duffle bag. An ingenious invention that had served him well, for the past five or more years.

"It felt strange packing summer clothing in December," said Annie Jo.

Taking the handle of her luggage, she headed toward the exit. Then together they shoved through the revolving door, happily squeezed together…like newlyweds.

When they stepped out into the afternoon sun, a broad-shouldered Hawaiian man with a toothy grin stood holding a sign that read James and Annie Baldwin. He stood beside a long, shimmering, opal-colored, stretch limousine.

"Is that for us?" whispered Annie Jo, her eyes wide.

"Pretty sure," said James, pulling her close. "Come on, there's lots to see and do while we're here."

"I've never been inside a limousine," she said, still in whisper mode, still staring. She felt like a country bumpkin, much like she'd felt the first time she entered the house at 106 Arrowhead Drive.

"Well, it's just like any other car, except you don't have to steer it."

"Very funny." She nudged him with her elbow, thankful he hadn't made light of her inexperience.

"You ready?"

"So ready," she said.

Raising up on tiptoe, she shared a kiss with her husband, right there on the sidewalk. She could get used to this treatment. In no time.

She realized, deep in her heart, "this treatment" wasn't the means of her happiness. Simply being Mrs. James Bartholomew Baldwin would go a long way toward that end.

A Scripture from a long-ago Sunday school lesson came to mind as Annie Jo rode along, next to her sweetheart, in the back of the stretch limousine. The reminder brought a smile to her face. *Though you have not seen him, you love him; and even though you do not see him now, you believe in him and are filled with an inexpressible and glorious joy.*

"You okay, sweetheart?" said James, encircling her with both arms.

"Better than I ever dreamed possible. Thanks again, for coming home, James."

"Lubbock County is great," he said. "But *you* are home."

THE END

Dear Reader:

A word from my heart…

Caring and Sharing

God has been gracious to me, allowing me to open my heart to you. But I want you to know that I have not been gifted as a teacher; that's my husband's department. My spiritual gift (every time I take the test) is very strong as encourager. Even in that, my studies are not "aimed" at you. God convicts me, even spanks me, as He reveals life lessons for me to share with you.

Some lessons come about because we mess up, repent, pray, and listen for God to teach us, directly. To repent doesn't just mean you are sorry. It means to turn away from (go the other direction, change your mind). Change what you're doing and get away from the temptation to do what you just ran away from.

Then some lessons come straight out of the Bible. Lessons we don't have to experiment with to learn. Look for those lessons in Proverbs or read the Ten Commandments. If we're thinking at all, we do <u>not</u> want to learn the hazards of adultery—from experience; or murder; or stealing. The hard lessons seem to be "easy" to avoid. But are they? Really? The door doesn't have to open very far for Satan to stick his big toe in. I know, of my own personal knowledge, of one case in particular:

One Wednesday night, a sweet Christian lady came to choir practice. The man seated behind her commented that her perfume smelled great. One simple compliment. But the evil one used that seemingly innocent gesture to get his toe in the door. It led to an adulterous affair, two divorces, and a church split. For you see, the sweet Christian lady happened to be married to the music director.

It's easy to point fingers at people who have fallen in ways that we have not. That kind of judgment, however, is also dangerous. Matthew 7:1-2 reads, in the words of Jesus: *"Do not judge, or you too will be judged. For in the same way you judge others, you will be judged, and with the measure you use, it will be measured to you."* Yikes! This might be an area in which it would behoove us to tread lightly!

Proverbs 5:21-22 says: *My son, do not let wisdom and understanding out of your sight, preserve sound judgment and discretion. They will be life for you, an ornament to grace your neck. Then you will go on your way in safety, and your foot will not stumble.*

So, how do we do that? Do not let wisdom and understanding out of our sight. In Psalm 111:10, we read: *The fear of the LORD is the beginning of wisdom; all who follow his precepts have good understanding.*

Proverbs 2:6—*For the LORD gives wisdom, and from his mouth come knowledge and understanding.*

So again, wisdom and understanding come from the LORD and from His mouth come knowledge and understanding.

How many ways can we keep wisdom and understanding in our sight? One of the most prevalent ways to keep the LORD's words in our sight is through the written Word, i.e., read the Bible. And when we pray, we might try waiting around long enough to hear what God wants to say to us *before* we rush into our day or fall asleep at night.

We can keep the word of God close by listening to godly preachers (and not just on Sunday morning). We can read anointed writings in devotionals and God-inspired books. Even an inspirational novel can be packed with notable life lessons. And I believe we can also keep the words of God close to us through Christian music.

In the 1980's, the original group *Newsong* sang these words: *"I don't wanna hear another song about the world; 'cause the world never did nothin' for me."*

Finally, in James 1:5, we are told *exactly* what to do: *If any of you lacks wisdom, he should ask God, who gives generously to all without finding fault, and it will be given him.*

Guard your hearts, my friends. Lean not on your own understanding, but in all your ways acknowledge Him, and He shall direct your paths. Learn from Him, become more and more like Him, so others will want what you have. For in the end, that's what it's all about: how many souls we can lead to salvation.

Whether you plant a seed, water the seed someone else planted, or are blessed to see your efforts come to fruition, caring and sharing are ways that others may have an opportunity to *see* Jesus, learn to *love* Jesus, *follow* Jesus, and *be* Jesus to the world.

Kathy Highley